I'll See You in Paris

ALSO BY MICHELLE GABLE

A Paris Apartment

I'll See You in Paris

MICHELLE GABLE

THOMAS DUNNE BOOKS   ST. MARTIN'S PRESS   ☙   NEW YORK

THOMAS DUNNE BOOKS.
An imprint of St. Martin's Press.

I'LL SEE YOU IN PARIS. Copyright © 2016 by Michelle Gable.
All rights reserved. Printed in the United States of America. For information, address St. Martin's Press, 175 Fifth Avenue, New York, N.Y. 10010.

www.thomasdunnebooks.com
www.stmartins.com

Designed by Anna Gorovoy

The Library of Congress Cataloging-in-Publication Data is available upon request.

ISBN 978-1-250-07063-0 (hardcover)
ISBN 978-1-250-10313-0 (international, sold outside the U.S., subject to rights availability)
ISBN 978-1-4668-8096-2 (e-edition)

Our books may be purchased in bulk for promotional, educational, or business use. Please contact your local bookseller or the Macmillan Corporate and Premium Sales Department at (800) 221-7945, extension 5442, or by e-mail at MacmillanSpecialMarkets@macmillan.com.

First Edition: February 2016

10   9   8   7   6   5   4   3   2   1

For my mom,
Laura Gable,
the best there is.
And for great mothers everywhere.

I'll See
You in
Paris

One

"Maybe she'll surprise us," Eric said.

They walked along the path toward the barn, Annie's sandals crunching against the gravel. It was eighty degrees, unusually warm for that time of year, an Indian summer. The sun was bright, the hillsides green and flashing. The leaves had not yet begun to change.

"Surprise us?" Annie said, her stomach wobbly. Somewhere in the distance a horse whinnied. "Uh, no. My mom doesn't surprise anyone."

"Come on, have a little faith. It happens all the time. You think you know someone and suddenly . . ." He snapped his fingers and turned. "Just like that. Boom. A complete one-eighty."

As he spun around, Annie laughed.

"Laurel Haley doesn't make one-eighties," she said. "Her entire life's been a strictly measured line going in one direction."

Except for a slight detour, she hastened to add. The detour being Annie.

"But she loves you," Eric said, taking her hand. "And I know she'll be as excited as we are. I can feel it."

Annie smiled, his relentless optimism enchanting her every time. He was unflagging with it, dedicated to perpetual sunniness like he was working it out in boot camp. She couldn't decide if this was a very useful or extremely dangerous attitude for someone about to board a Marine Expeditionary Unit bound for the Middle East.

"Maybe you're right," she said, succumbing to his Eric-ness yet again.

It wasn't impossible. Laurel claimed Annie's happiness was her number one priority. She was happy with Eric. Perhaps this really was enough.

They paused by the stable's entrance. Annie inhaled deeply as a gaggle of tween girls loped past, all lanky and athletic and at the start of beautiful but not quite grown into their breeches or boots.

"Okay," she said. "Here we go."

She took a few cautious steps forward and then peered into one of the stalls where she saw Laurel tacking a horse.

"Beautiful job today, Sophie," Laurel said as a mother and daughter scooted by. "I'm out of town for the next two weeks. Margaret will be doing the lessons for me."

The young girl waved, and then grinned at Annie as she passed. Sophie was one of the twenty or so children Laurel taught for free. Medically challenged girls, those not expected to live long or those not expected to live well. Even when Laurel worked full-time at the gleaming law firm downtown, she always made time for these girls.

"Oh, hi, Annie!" Laurel said as she buckled the mare's bridle. "Eric. I didn't know you guys were here."

"Was that your last student?" Annie asked, feeling Eric's presence solid behind her. "Are you busy?"

"Nope, not busy at all." Laurel tightened the strap. "Just finished a lesson and headed out for a ride. So, what's up?"

She gripped the reins in her right hand, face playing at a twitchy smile. Laurel always knew when Annie was up to no good, when she was hiding something or stretching the truth in some important way. This savvy baffled Annie given her mom lived in the narrowest possible world, comprised of work and Annie and the horses. Laurel quit her job a year ago so now it was down to Annie and the farm. How was it she understood so much?

"The two of you have something to tell me," Laurel said, breaking the ice because no one else would. "Might as well fess up. I think your nervous energy is about to spook the horses."

"Ma'am, I wanted to get your permission," Eric started, his voice strong and assured.

Annie winced, waiting for Laurel to drop a big fat cloud over them. Her mom was kind, generous, at times outright funny. But Laurel could sniff out a bad idea from a mile away and was never afraid to complain about the smell.

"I'm sorry I didn't ask you first," Eric went on. "But, well, there's not a lot of time before my deployment. And y'all have your trip to England. Everything's happened so fast. But I'm asking now."

Oh God, Annie thought, heart sprinting. *Maybe this is a mistake.* But it was already too late.

"May I marry your daughter?" he asked.

After that: silence. Even the horse seemed uncomfortable, sheepishly kicking at the hay.

"Ma'am . . . ?"

"Are you truly asking me?" Laurel said at last. "Or are you telling me?"

"Mom!"

"It's okay, Annie," Eric said and rubbed her arm. "We've ambushed her. Give your mama the chance to adjust."

"I'm weirdly not that shocked," Laurel said with a careful laugh. "Somehow I knew this was coming."

"I love her, Ms. Haley. I swear to you before God and country that I will treat your daughter better than any prince she's ever dreamed."

"My daughter was never one for princes," Laurel said. "Annie's not that kind of girl."

"Mom, can you chill out for a second?"

"*Chill out?* Annabelle, honestly."

"Ma'am, I love Annie," Eric said, his Alabama accent at maximum strength.

Though Annie's insides puddled at the sound of it, she knew her mom was skeptical of anything resembling romance. Futures were best made in barns and investment accounts, not in "I love yous" from handsome young marines.

"I'll make this world a better place for her," he added.

"Oh, Eric," Laurel said, and chuckled again. "There are so many things I could say right now."

"How about 'okay'?" Annie grumbled. "That'd be a good start."

As much as she wanted her mother's approval, and held out the feeblest hope she'd receive it, Annie understood what Laurel saw. The whole thing smacked of desperation, of *what the hell am I going to do with my life now?* Screw it. I'll just marry the next guy I meet.

Standing in that barn was a mother, and before her was an unemployed recent college graduate. Beside the graduate was a man—if you could call him that— a twenty-one-year-old marine about to board a float destined for Afghanistan.

This marine was suggesting marriage, to the jobless daughter no less, who'd been dating a different boy only a few months before. By the time Eric returned from deployment, they will have been apart longer than they were together . . . times seven.

All that and Annie had met him at a dive bar. She was sucking down the last dregs of a bad house wine while listening to her best friend, Summer, lament that working in a senator's office wasn't so much public service as coffee service. Starbucks runs in exchange for a paycheck and health care sounded like a re-spectable gig to the incomeless Annie but Summer disagreed.

"I'd rather be unemployed," Summer insisted.

"And have your mother buy your birth control pills?" Annie asked.

"Admittedly that would be awkward. But it's just so damned boring. I want to be doing more."

"Don't we all," Annie said, and took a final gulp of wine.

Without warning, a man rose to his feet.

He was a large boy really, screamingly clean-cut and soldierly, a marine as it turned out. A round of drinks on him, he announced, to celebrate his upcoming deployment and to thank them, the citizens, for supporting their efforts. Annie's first thought was, *Thank God, because I can't afford another drink.*

Her second was: *Wow, that guy is hot. Too bad he likes guns.*

Amid backslaps and handshakes, the brown-eyed, black-haired puppy dog of a man then gave an impassioned speech about fidelity and freedom and the U.S. of A. It was a week after 9/11 and so the response was deafening. By the end of it, every person in the bar stood, looped arms with a neighbor, and belted out the only song that mattered.

And I'd gladly stand up next to you and defend her still today.
'Cause there ain't no doubt I love this land God bless the U.S.A.

"Jesus Christ," Summer said when the excitement dissipated. "Why do I suddenly feel like joining the navy?"

At once Annie was changed.

At once she was done with aloof Virginia boys and their swoopy hair, those lame belts embroidered with smiling whales. She wanted a hero, a man with a little spirit, a guy who could raise a room to sing.

Perhaps it was the result of too much Edwardian fiction in college and the hours spent soaking in whimsy. Or maybe he was that valiant. Either way, with 9/11 the entire world changed, in major ways and in minor ones, all the way down to, it seemed, Annie's taste in men.

There was no decent way to explain this to Laurel, of course. Military or not, you simply didn't marry someone you met last month. Annie wanted her mom to be excited but understood why Laurel couldn't find it in herself to even pretend. A tiny part of her wondered if Laurel was right. She was about most things.

"Don't pressure your mother," Eric said, reaching once again for her hand. "Ma'am, any questions you have about my family or my character, I'm pleased to answer."

"Eric," Laurel said and sighed. "It's nothing against you personally. In the three seconds I've known you, you seem like a very nice boy. But you're young, you've only just met. On top of that you're going off to war."

"Geez, Mom, don't be so dramatic. This isn't 1940."

"A war's a war."

"She's right," Eric said.

Annie blinked. *A war's a war.* He was going off to fight, wasn't he? Did she even appreciate what it meant to be a marine? Had the people in the bar comprehended what they were singing about?

"At least tell me you're waiting," Laurel said. "That you'll get married when he's done with his tour. All his tours. When the war is over and there are no more deployments."

"Yes, of course," he said, though they'd agreed to no specific timing.

And done? Eric would never be done. This was his career. He was in it for the long haul, one deployment tacked onto the next, a long trip with only breaks and no end.

"Okay," Laurel said and exhaled loudly. She closed her eyes. "Good. Wise move." After several moments, she opened them back up. "Well, let's see the ring. There is a ring, yes?"

"Of course there's a ring!" Annie chirped.

She extended a jittery, unsure hand in her mom's direction to display the faintest chip of a diamond of a ring. A tenth of a carat? A twentieth? Even the gold band was so delicate it nearly disappeared. Good thing Annie had petite hands.

"It's beautiful," Laurel said, sounding genuine and almost comforted by the modest piece of jewelry. Eric Sawyer wasn't some spoiled kid supported by his parents. The same could not be said for Annie.

"Again, ma'am, I'm sorry I didn't ask you first. I'm a traditional man. I should've followed the appropriate etiquette."

"In case you haven't noticed," Annie said. "We're not exactly a traditional family."

There was no father to ask, is what she meant. A traditional path would've involved the dad. Who would walk Annie down the aisle anyway? Her mother? A pair of geldings?

"Okay." Eric flushed, the pink high on his cheeks. "All right."

"Well, congratulations, you two," Laurel said as she led the horse out of its stall. "Sorry to dash but I want to get a ride in before dark. Eric, please join us for dinner, if you can."

"Yes, absolutely," he said, stumbling over his words. "Thank you. I'd be honored."

When Laurel was out of the building, on her horse and galloping into meadow, Annie turned to face Eric for the first time since they walked into the barn.

"That went okay?" he said timidly.

"It did," she answered with a nod. "Maybe even better than expected."

Yet she felt unsettled.

Even with Laurel's tacit approval, something wasn't right. Annie should've been filled with love right then, toward her fiancé and her mom who was, if not excited, at least gracious. But despite these things going for her, going for them, there remained a hole, a slow leak of something Annie couldn't quite explain.

Two

Two o'clock in the morning.

Annie's luggage was packed. She'd double-checked her passport and plane ticket. Not one but two weepy e-mails were flying through the Ethernet toward Eric. Everything was ready to go but her brain refused to rest. If she didn't get rid of the collywobbles, she'd never get to sleep.

A letter, Annie thought. She should write one last letter to her fiancé, and do it the old-fashioned way, with paper and a pen. Her mom sounded so retro. *He's going off to war.* As the soldier's best girl, she needed to play the part and writing letters seemed romantic anyhow.

When she crept downstairs an hour later, stamped envelope in hand, Annie discovered she was not the only one awake. She paused at the threshold of Laurel's office, hesitating before she spoke.

There her mom stood, behind her desk, fully dressed with the lights blaring around her. On the desk was a box. On her face, a scowl. Already the scene was disorienting.

"Mom, what's going on?"

"Oh geez! Annie!" Laurel whopped her chest. "You scared the crap out of me."

"Sorry! Can I come in?"

"Yes, of course. So you're having trouble sleeping?"

"Apparently."

Annie walked cautiously into the room. Everything continued to feel muddled.

"I can't sleep either," Laurel said as she hugged a tattered blue book to her chest. She was wide-awake but did not seem altogether in the room. "I never can before a flight. It's infuriating. So, I assume you're all packed?"

"I am. Mom? Are you okay?"

"I hope you brought warm clothes," she said absently. "England can be dreary this time of year."

Laurel set down the book.

"Any time of year," she added.

With that same blank look, Laurel started wrapping her hair in a knot at the base of her neck. For twenty years she'd sported a low, tight blond chignon. The tucked-in woman, the ice-queen attorney. Laurel was probably the very paragon of understated law-firm style back in the day, but Annie had to think it'd grown tired after twenty years. She imagined new associates mocking her, placing bets on when she'd finally find a new look.

Then Laurel sold her share of the partnership and the chignon came down. Her hair was surprisingly long and curly and wild. But now, on the other side of the desk, Laurel was trying to wrap it back up again. Old habits died hard, it seemed.

"Mom . . . are you . . ."

"I enjoyed having Eric for dinner," Laurel said, and let her hair go free again. "He's a nice young man."

"Thanks, I, uh . . . yes. He is nice."

Nice. For an English lit grad she really should do better than "nice." It was a half-assed compliment for the so-called man of her dreams. Laurel was polite enough not to call her on it.

"Sorry the house is in such rough shape," her mom said. "I forget sometimes how badly it needs to be fixed up."

"Eric doesn't care about that kind of thing. And it's not so bad. I think he was a little impressed, even."

Their home *was* impressive—from the road. Or when squinting at a great distance. It was large and white and grand, but shabby at its core, the inside comprised mostly of knotty wood and must. Billed as a "fixer" when Laurel bought it fifteen years before, there'd never been any plans for fixing.

But Laurel and Annie loved the house, even if neighbors, friends, and college boyfriends questioned its value, market or otherwise. Didn't they know what they had out there? Everyone from inside the Beltway wanted a horse farm in Middleburg, more so given that plane-sized hole now in the Pentagon. With even the slightest effort, Goose Creek Hill could be a gold mine. The whole deal would have to be renovated stud to stud first, of course, but the place had potential.

"I do love our rambling shack," Laurel said, frowning at the desk and the old blue book on top of it. "Even if it costs a gazillion dollars to heat."

"Mom, you seem kind of preoccupied. Is everything okay?"

She braced herself for the answer. Because while Laurel had been perfectly pleasant to Eric, it was clear she did not approve.

"I'm fine." Laurel lowered herself onto the green leather chair. She rubbed both eyes with the backs of her wrists. "Just anxious about our trip. Oh, Annabelle . . ."

"Mom. Please."

"So you'll go through with it?" She looked up. "This marriage?"

"That's why I said yes when he asked me. You think I'm making a bad decision."

"I do. But you're in love," Laurel said, not unkindly.

"I am. And just to put it out there, I'm not knocked up or anything."

Laurel laughed and then more seriously added, "Have you even been together long enough to get pregnant and also realize it?"

Annie bristled, but it was a fair statement.

"I'm glad you're happy," Laurel said. "And Eric is a charismatic young man. A sweet Southern military boy who loves his mama—every parent's dream."

"So what's the problem, then? You said it yourself. I'm happy. He's a great guy. What more do you want?"

"God, if it were only that easy," Laurel muttered. "It's not that I want any one specific thing for you. I just don't want my baby girl to choose the wrong guy, even if it's for the right reasons."

"You can't name one bad thing about him," Annie said, her voice getting high. "How can you call him the 'wrong guy'?"

And what experience did Laurel have with right or wrong men anyway? As far as Annie knew, her mother hadn't entertained a single significant relationship in the last twenty years. Work, horses, Annie. Annie, horses, work. No room for frivolity. No room for falling in love.

"You think I don't know what I'm talking about," Laurel noted. "That I'm some doddering old lady who can't recognize a good love story when she sees one. But, believe me, I have *some* experience in matters of the heart."

"Who was he?" Annie blurted.

Laurel jolted.

"Excuse me?" she said.

They never had this conversation. They danced around it. They flirted with its edges. But mother and daughter did a hero's job of ignoring the subject of *him*.

The two women lived a mostly sweet life at their ramshackle farm, enjoying their good fortune and pretty views. Who *he* was didn't matter. It had no bearing on their lives. Or so Annie had told herself, out loud and in her mind, ever since she was a little girl. Laurel said early and often the man wasn't worth knowing, and so Annie took her mother's word for it.

Until now.

"My father," she said, as if it needed clarification. "I want to know the details."

"The details aren't important," Laurel insisted, as she had a dozen times before. "He was someone I thought I knew. And he didn't want any kind of life with us. What else do you need?"

"A name would be nice."

"His last name was Haley."

"Yeah, I gathered," she said. "So why does it say 'unknown' on my birth certificate? You two were married. We both share his name. He is known."

"I don't understand why you suddenly care so much about a man who was incapable of caring about us."

"I'm getting married. And I don't even have the words to tell my fiancé where I came from, who I am."

"The man who got me pregnant is *not* who you are," Laurel said, gritting her teeth.

Heat rose to her face, for perhaps the third or fourth time in Annie's life. No matter how many beer cans under the porch, or escaped horses galloping through town, Laurel maintained an aggravatingly neutral demeanor at all times. Annie wished she'd lose her shit every once in a while, but Laurel was too rational for anything like that.

"He's a little bit who I am," Annie said, testing her. "Don't you think it's important—"

"Your father was a dangerous person," Laurel said, her jaw tense as she spoke. "He fought battles for which he didn't have the weapons and so I took us out of the crossfire. Don't get me wrong, I don't blame him entirely."

"Of course you don't."

"But he was unknown to me in the end, which is why your birth certificate says what it does. There's also the legal side."

"There always is." Annie rolled her eyes. "Counselor."

"Hey. It's important. I didn't want anyone trying to . . . stake a claim. That's not the right phrase but I can't think of a better way to put it."

"So was he incapable of caring? Or you wouldn't let him?"

"That's not fair."

"I agree," Annie said. "It's not. So, is he still alive?"

"No."

She expected some hesitation, a pause for half a beat. But Laurel spat out the word so sharply and with such bite Annie almost felt a sting.

"All right," Annie said, feeling off balance. "I guess that's that. What about his family? Don't I have, like, grandparents somewhere? Aunts or uncles?"

"I don't know. Maybe. They wanted nothing to do with us. Why should I waste a single second worrying about them? For Pete's sake, Annie, after twenty-two years now I'm not enough for you?"

"It's not like that at all."

"It's exactly like that." Laurel sighed and picked up the old book again. "We leave in a few hours and I have a lot to sort through before then. Maybe we can—I don't know—talk more when we're there. Banbury is . . . it's hard to explain. It's a different place."

That Laurel didn't have a way to finish the sentence bothered Annie because nothing about the trip made sense. The party line was that Laurel had to shore up a land deal in Oxfordshire. Family business, she claimed. But what kind of business could this possibly be?

As far as Annie knew, their family tree was mostly barren, woefully branchless.

She didn't have siblings, and neither did her mom. Laurel's parents and grandparents were deceased. There was an uncle-type in Chicago, some third or fourth cousins in San Diego, plus a sprinkling of others throughout the country. All of them were Christmas-card cordial, but if she'd met them, Annie didn't remember.

Yet there was another tree, somewhere. Her dad's. Maybe it was as meager as theirs. On the other hand, perhaps it was a redwood, or whatever the British considered a significantly gargantuan tree.

"Does this trip have anything to do with him?" Annie asked. "The family land? Was my father British?"

"Uh, no." Laurel chuckled without smiling. "The man who gave me you has nothing to do with Banbury."

"Earlier today I told Eric that you're more predictable than the sunrise. But maybe I was wrong. So many things don't make sense. My father. This English home, which you've owned for decades but are only selling now."

"It's my retirement, sweetheart."

Laurel sighed again and threw the blue book into a box. Annie leaned toward it and tried to make out the faded gold words on its cover. There was something familiar about the book, and her mother's demeanor while holding it. It was curious as Laurel was never much of a reader outside legal tomes. This, despite a very crowded bookshelf behind her.

"Okay," Annie said. "I get that it's your retirement but where did the property come from? Specifically? Who gave it to you?"

"A distant relative, someone without any direct heirs. Might as well have picked my name out of a hat. I've had the home a long, long time." Laurel smiled. "Almost as long as I've had you. Though of course you're far more valuable. And the property is not so chatty."

"Why are you selling it now?" Annie asked, still suspicious. "If you've had it for so long?"

"I wasn't being flip when I said it's my retirement. That's always been the plan, and in the last few months the land around it has come up for sale, making my property more valuable. Most people can't retire before age fifty. I'd still be working if I didn't have this in my back pocket."

"So that's it? The mysterious house is nothing more than an investment?"

A funny look wiggled across Laurel's face.

"Yes," she said. "Something like that. Listen, Annie-bear, we need to get to bed or we'll be dragging in the morning. Let's talk more on the flight. Or once we are in Banbury. We'll have plenty of heart-to-hearts, about property, marriages, whatever you want."

Laurel looked at once tired, weary, and well beyond her age. For a moment Annie regretted pushing so hard.

"Mom, I'm sorry. It's just with everything . . ."

"Nothing to be sorry about. Good night," Laurel said, and rubbed a hand over Annie's head. "I'm headed upstairs. See you in the morning. I love you."

With a final sad smile, Laurel slipped out the door. Annie listened as her mother's footsteps retreated.

Once the floorboards groaned and squeaked overhead, Annie scrambled over to the cardboard box. Inside were several bound sets of paper, legal documents mostly. On top of them sat the book, that ancient blue book. It niggled at her as she lifted it from the box.

"*The Missing Duchess,*" she read. "By J. Casper Augustine Seton."

Annie fanned the pages beneath her nose. They were old and yellow, mustier than Goose Creek Hill itself. She let out a cough and flicked open a page.

They said you weren't anyone until Giovanni Boldini painted you. But of all the famed women he rendered, the princesses and countesses and heiresses, the Duchess of Marlborough was deemed the most enchanting.

"Annie?" her mom called from the top of the stairs.

She jumped, fumbling and bobbling the book before ultimately saving it from a union with the floor.

"Are you coming upstairs?" Laurel asked. "Please turn out the lights."

"Yes! I'm coming!"

Annie took one last glance at the foiled lettering on the cover. Then she slid the book into the back of her sweatpants and shut off the light.

Three

The Duchess of Marlborough was born Gladys Deacon on 7 February 1881 at the Hotel Brighton in Paris. She was the eldest, and most beautiful, of four exceptionally lovely girls.

The Deacons were a stormy, storied crew. Gladys's tortured, moonstruck father descended from the Boston Parkers, a family with more money than sense. Like any senseless gentry, the money soon matched their level of cunning. Which is to say, not much.

—J. Casper Augustine Seton,
The Missing Duchess: A Biography

The innkeeper was almost cartoon-grade British with her ruddy complexion and flat, uneven teeth.

"We're known for our cakes!" she sang. "You have to try our cakes!"

Her name was Nicola. Annie couldn't make out if she was closer in age to Laurel or to herself, one of those people who seemed young and old at the same time.

"There's a bakery down on Parsons Street," she said, fluffing pillows as Laurel and Annie filed in behind her. "Theirs are scrumptious but you can't go wrong anywhere round here. Do you find this room suitable? I can move you, we're not too busy. This is my favorite, though. It gets the best light. Plus they don't make this pattern of bedspread anymore. It's one of a kind!"

"The room is perfect," Laurel said, and set her bags on the bed. Nicola promptly moved them to the suitcase stand. "A complete delight."

Their room was all English countryside with its whitewashed wood floors, sloped ceilings, and matching wrought-iron twin beds. Annie could tell that Laurel wasn't thrilled with the size of the beds but loved the room on sight.

The town was charming too, if not lacking a central square and featuring, according to Nicola, a "right mishmash of shops running higgledy-piggledy to and fro." Annie saw through a dormer window what appeared to be the town's focal point: the Banbury Cross, a tall stone spire erupting out of the middle of a roundabout.

"I knew you'd find it top-notch!" Nicola said. "I'll let you two settle in. Ring if you need anything. I'm at the front desk all day and night. Alrighty then. Cheerio!"

Nicola spun around and jostled downstairs. Annie and Laurel smiled weakly at each other.

It was the first time they'd been truly alone since their clash in Laurel's office. Was it resolved? Would they talk more? Get to the bottom of this father business? Or would they instead resume their usual ways? Annie wondered if she even cared. Right then the only feelings she could muster were of being tired and missing Eric. Seven months of not seeing him. How was she going to last?

"So here we are," Laurel said. "And it's raining. Of course."

She began sorting through her handbag.

"I know we just arrived, but I have to leave in a few minutes," Laurel went on. "A meeting with a solicitor. You're welcome to join me, or you can hang out here. I can't imagine my meeting will be of any interest whatsoever."

Annie sighed, surprised her mother had an obligation so soon. This "vacation" was starting out on a real high.

"Maybe I'll go with you," Annie said, and slumped down onto the bed, physically exhausted though she'd spent most of the last twenty-four hours on her duff. "The weather's for crap plus it's not like I have anything else to do."

"As your counsel, I advise against it."

Laurel lifted the clothes from her suitcase, then refolded them and placed them into drawers. She lined her toiletries in the washroom, the little bottles standing at attention like soldiers. Annie wished her mom would leave her luggage momentarily unpacked, enjoy the change of scenery for at least a minute or two. But with Laurel there was always something to be done.

"I can't find the converter," Laurel said, as Annie leaned back onto her elbows with an extra large sigh. "Did you grab it? I need to charge my phone."

"Should be in my carry-on."

"That's right. I saw you put it in there."

As Laurel reached toward the bag, Annie remembered what she'd stashed inside. She sprang from the bed.

"Wait!" Annie yelped. It was the fastest she'd moved all week.

"Good grief, Annie, you almost knocked me over."

"I'll get it. Here."

She handed her mom the power converter as Laurel's battered copy of *The Missing Duchess* shifted down into the bottom of Annie's backpack.

"Okay . . ." Laurel said, one eyebrow raised. "Thanks."

Would she be mad about the book? It was hard to guess, but on the train from Heathrow, Annie asked about it. Laurel's response was puzzling, mostly because it wasn't a response at all.

"What book?" she'd asked.

Their relationship wasn't perfect but usually Laurel treated Annie with truthfulness and respect, nameless fathers notwithstanding. This was a woman who, when asked by her kindergartner whether storks had to carry twins one at a time, treated the child to a full rundown of the vagaries of procreation. Laurel never shielded her daughter from anything, even when Annie preferred to stay in the dark.

Of course, there was the question of her father so Laurel was known to skim the tough parts of a story.

"*What book?*" Annie parroted as they bumped through the countryside. "That book. The book book. From . . . home."

"I'm pretty sure we have more than one book," Laurel said. "We could open a used bookstore with what you've brought home in the last month."

"No, this is your book. The blue one. It's old."

"I have a lot of old books in my office."

"You were holding it last night?" Annie tried.

"Hmm." Laurel shrugged. "Probably picked it up along the way, like most things in that ancient house."

Annie nodded but wasn't buying it. There was something about that book.

In twenty years she could scarcely remember Laurel reading anything other than legal briefs, the *Wall Street Journal*, or guides to management effectiveness passed on by a boss. Laurel had a collection of first editions lining her library walls but she'd never taken one out, as far as Annie knew. Moodily clutching books about duchesses was Annie's style, not her mom's.

The book felt familiar though, more so by the hour. Distracted by days and miles and the ache of missing Eric, Annie closed her eyes and tried to pull up the memories. They jammed somewhere behind her eyes.

"I was thinking," she said as Laurel bustled around their room, bumping into desks and lamps, unaccustomed to the tight Banbury space. "I'll stay here until you get back. I feel like . . . reading."

"Good plan. There's a fireplace down in the library. Might be just the spot to crack open a book and have some tea."

"Or be force-fed Banbury cakes," Annie added with a smirk.

"Nicola is indeed inexplicably jazzed about currants and puff pastries." Laurel picked up her phone. "Well, that was helpful. Not charged at all. Do you mind if I leave it here? I don't want to strand you but it's about to die."

"If there are any emergencies I can figure out what to do. Nicola seems conscientious. She won't let me die in a fire or get coerced into any cults."

"That's reassuring."

"So, go! Scat!" Annie said, wiggling her fingers, suddenly itchy to be alone. "Be gone with you!"

Laurel gave her a worried smile, as if she were hesitant to leave her daughter, twenty-two and engaged to a man she hardly knew. They were in a new town and Annie might find herself lost in more ways than one. Alas, Laurel had stuff to do and Taking Care of Business was her greatest skill.

After reapplying a new coat of lipstick, Revlon Tickled Pink, in production since 1983, Laurel grabbed her handbag and scooted out into the hallway. The door had not even clicked when Annie shot across the room and rescued *The Missing Duchess* from the bottom of her bag.

"What book, my ass," she mumbled, lifting the cover.

She turned to the first chapter and began to read.

In human relationships she offered nothing but an offensive arbitrariness, pursuing people in a flattering and ensnaring fashion, only so as to be able to break off with them noisily when the fancy struck her.—Art historian Bernard Berenson, on the Duchess of Marlborough

"Sounds delightful." Annie snorted. She read the first sentence.

I arrived to Banbury on a Tuesday.

"Banbury?" Annie blurted, astonished.

She glanced out the window at the Banbury Cross. Sentence number one and already she was getting somewhere. Or, rather, she was there already.

It was cold and wet, she read on, *as Banbury preferred to be.*

After checking into an inn of middling regard, I stopped by a pub, figuring it was the exact kind of place where news gathered. I ordered a Watneys Red Barrel and set to work.

Four

A background for the uninitiated.

By age ten Gladys Deacon had lived in four different countries.

At eleven she was placed in the custody of a convicted murderer. She was kidnapped at twelve.

At sixteen she debuted in London where she met her future husband, who was already married.

By twenty-one she was living independently in Paris, in an apartment she owned alone.

In 1906, at the age of twenty-five, Gladys cemented her friendship with Marcel Proust, which led to friendships with the most eminent writers of the era: Hardy, Wharton, Waugh. And of course Henry James.

Then there were the men, her incalculable lovers, too many to list as the index to a book should never be longer than the story itself. It suffices to say that by the time she married, Gladys had run through a roster of bachelors, eligible and otherwise. She dated the Duke of Norfolk, Roffredo Caetani, the Duke of Camastra, poet Robert Trevelyan, French politician Aristide Briand, General Joffre, and Lord Francis Pelham-Clinton-Hope.

owner of the Hope diamond. Unfortunately forty-five carats was not suffi-cient diamond weight when the suitor also had a wonky leg.

For a time Gladys Deacon was engaged to the Crown Prince of Prussia, a tall, blond, shy sally of a man. The arrangement fell apart be-cause she was not a princess and did not like being reminded of it. A shame, that. Their marriage would've created a German-American alli-ance and, they say, prevented the First World War.

—J. Casper Augustine Seton,
The Missing Duchess: A Biography

They'd been in Banbury for three days.

The land deal was already rocky, the terms changing by the hour. Laurel attended one meeting after another. Annie considered tagging along as there were only so many quaint streets to meander, a limited number of townsfolk to chat up. The limestone cottages were cute, yes, but there were so damned many of them.

"Castles," Laurel said. "There are some beautiful castles nearby. Plus, London! We have to do London. I promise we'll act like proper tourists soon. I even brought a fanny pack and a list of ways to embarrass you."

Castles were fine, fanny packs or not. London would be exciting. But at that point Annie would've settled for a few meals that weren't rushed, one conversa-tion that didn't involve rumination on negotiating tactics. Her mother promised sightseeing. She promised bonding and "plenty of time for heart-to-hearts." Laurel's heart didn't seem to be in it. Her mother had never felt so far away.

"Could we get married on the farm?" Annie tried over breakfast one morn-ing. "We'll keep it low-key, of course. A real bootstrap kind of affair."

Best to broach prickly topics with talk of budgets, she decided. Laurel wouldn't be able to resist such levelheadedness and thrift.

"You never have to ask to use the farm," Laurel said. "It's as much yours as it is mine. In any case let's not worry about that now. When we go to London, what plays do you want to see?"

"We'll keep it small. The wedding. Close friends, family. Not that we have much of either."

Annie had been awake most of the night, trying to figure out how she'd track down her father's side of the family to invite them to the wedding. Maybe she'd get Oprah involved, though illegitimate horse farm girls were not so sad a tale.

"Annabelle, what's that face?"

She mentally cursed Eric and his sweet-talking, married-three-decades parents. She had met them once, at a semidisastrous meal in Georgetown. Over a plate of fried calamari, they asked what her daddy did. Annie admitted she didn't know and the whisky pounding ensued. At the time she hadn't even known he was dead.

"Are you all right?" Laurel asked.

"Oh, um. Yes. I'm fine."

"Well, what's your answer?"

"Answer? About what?"

"The shows you want to see! Are you sure everything's okay? You don't seem yourself."

Funny. Laurel didn't seem herself, either.

"Annie?"

"Yes, yes." She shook her head. "Everything's good. Whatever. We can see whatever. Just, uh, don't make me see *Les Miz* again."

She liked *Les Miz*, but what did it matter? Annie had very little faith the trip to London would happen at all.

Five

"Hello!" Annie stood in the doorway, searching for a host. She caught the bartender's eye. "Table for one?"

"Sit wherever you'd like."

He gestured to the room.

"Thanks!"

She grinned her big, toothy American smile and took a booth by the back, even as she contemplated whether she really wanted to stay. The outing was Nicola's brainchild as the innkeeper had grown weary of watching "forlorn tourists sit by the fire gnawing on biscuits and old straws."

According to Nicola, the George & Dragon was the best pub in town. It was also the only pub in town and "filled with a bunch of old goats most days of the week," but they had palatable food and plenty of pints for desolate American travelers. It would do for the likes of her.

Once seated, Annie glanced around. The pub's diners did indeed include a distribution of grizzly souls, plus a family trying to control their toddler son to no success. Annie ordered tea plus a bacon and brie with cranberry. She told the waiter to take his time.

As the man walked away, Annie reached into her bag and pulled out the book. She turned to the spot where she'd left off earlier that morning when she stole a few pages while Laurel showered. It was marked with a photograph of Eric, which she pressed against her chest before reading on.

What happened to the duchess? What happened to the woman who dated kings and princes and statesmen? In 1934, the duchess left her castle as well as society and the very foundation of her existence. Or, as friends and family would tell it, Gladys Deacon vanished into the pink horizon.

"Pardon me," said a voice.

A man appeared beside her. Annie had noticed him when she first walked in. Most of the pub's customers were short, molelike, with Rudolph the Reindeer noses and exaggerated, furry ears. But this guy was tall, tanned, and had a thick mass of wavy white hair. He looked like an aging film star, the other patrons his background players.

"That book," he said, without introduction. "Where'd you get it?"

"Oh." She paused. "A local bookstore?"

The words were out of Annie's mouth before she could question why she said them. What was it about *The Missing Duchess* that made people want to lie?

"Trudy's place?" he asked. "She had a copy?"

"Yeah. Sure. I guess."

She glanced away, hoping he wouldn't think to verify her story with this Trudy person. The man continued to stand there and so Annie returned her eyes to the page.

As reports would go, the duchess left Blenheim Palace at dawn, taking her innumerable belongings as well as her title. All her possessions, loaded onto lorries, destination unknown.

People inquired after her, and how could they not? Gladys Deacon's visage was so superior, her looks so fabled, John Singer Sargent refused to paint her portrait for fear of not possessing the talent to properly capture her beauty.

"The duchess." The man tapped her book. "She used to live in this town. As the legend goes."

"So I've gathered," Annie replied without looking up. "Though I haven't made much progress. No spoilers please."

"Is it good? The book?"

"Like I said, early innings, but it's okay so far. The author tends to digress though."

"Well, the guy was a hack. Only thing he ever published."

"The book is swell," she said, vigorously keeping her gaze down. "I was kidding."

Go away, you old geezer, she thought, though did not mean it. Truth be told, it was nice to have company, to hear another person's voice.

"Why'd it catch your eye?" he asked. "At Trudy's?"

Annie studied the cover. It was blue, textured, and plain, the original jacket long since gone. Why *would* it catch her eye? It'd not stand out in a library of two.

"I was, uh, already apprised of the Duchess of Marlborough," she said. "Seemed like an interesting subject. I hadn't run into the book before."

"I think there are approximately three people on planet earth who've run into the book before."

"So she wasn't a hot topic in town?"

"Oh, she was a 'hot topic,' all right. Imagine a woman, a rumored duchess, with spooky blue eyes who ran round Banbury helter-skelter, shooting guns and shouting obscenities. People bolted in the opposite direction whenever they saw her."

"Sounds like a reasonable reaction, given the firearms."

"Well, you do have to pay attention to the crazy ones." He tapped his forehead. "Either they're dangerous or the exact kind of people you want to know."

"Why would you want to know them?" Annie asked, finding herself amused. She slipped Eric's photo back between the pages and closed the book.

"Because, young lady," he said. "The dens of the mad often hold the greatest riches."

"Um, okay."

She laughed nervously. Though he was charming and older-man handsome, Annie couldn't help but wonder which den of madness this guy might've crawled out from.

"The woman denied it, however," he told her. "Said she wasn't a duchess. Called herself Mrs. Spencer."

"When I'm ninety years old, if people want to confuse me for a duchess, I won't stop them. Heck, I might even insist upon it. Hello, sirs! The Duchess of Middleburg calling. Where's my tea?"

The man removed his glasses, dropped them into his pocket, and sat down across from her.

"I'm sure you'll have no shortage of men willing to bring you tea," he said. "Mind if I join you?"

"I think you already have. So. You seem to be one of the regulars." She motioned toward the other white-hairs in the pub. "How long have you lived here?"

"In other words, I am fairly advanced in years. Was I one of the wary towns-folk?"

"You said it, not me." She smiled. "So, did you know her? The supposed duchess? Were you two friends?"

"Friends?" He grimaced. "Gawd blimey. How old do you think I am? She was born a hundred and twenty years ago. No. Lord no. We weren't friends."

"I wasn't trying to offend—"

"Trying and doing are two different things. No, young lass, I've not seen one hundred and twenty summers just yet. But I was here when that cut-rate author came to Banbury to write his stupid book of nonsense. My name's Gus."

He extended a hand.

"Annabelle," she said. "But I also go by Annie."

"And I also go by the Earl of Winton."

She laughed at the joke but Gus's face remained stern.

"Something funny about that?" he asked.

"Well, yes. No. I mean . . . the Duchess of Marlborough and now the Earl of Winton?" she said. "I didn't realize there was such a stronghold of peers in this village. Does Burke's know about this?"

Gus cracked a smile.

"Yes, of course they do," he said. "That's the very point of their existence. How are you familiar with Burke's? You are an American."

"Sometimes we read books," she said. "Or hear about things that happen outside of the United States. Shocking, but true."

"I find you suspicious," he said.

"*I'm* suspicious? I was sitting here reading quietly, minding my own business, when you walked up. If anyone's suspicious it's strange men in pubs at one o'clock in the afternoon."

"Touché. What I meant was, I thought Americans were staying home right now. Avoiding air travel. Waving flags. Setting off fireworks."

"Not all Americans," she said, prickling.

Eric was in the middle of an ocean right then, floating at no discernible place. The fireworks he might soon set off she could not contemplate.

"I'm sorry," Gus said, and gently touched her hands. "I'm not trying to poke fun. This has been a grievous tragedy. For the entire world."

"No. It's not that." Annie shook her head. Well, it was that. But also more. "It's fine. Not fine, exactly. I don't like thinking about it."

"Understood. I'm sorry. I have atrocious social skills. They're pitifully out of practice living in this 'derelict hamlet,'" he said, using the duchess's own words and offering a sly grin. "And what hamlet are you from, my new American friend? Do I detect a Southern accent?"

"Yes and no," she said, amazed to find herself smiling.

Whoever this Gus was, this Earl of Winton, he had a certain salty appeal.

"I'm from Virginia," she said. "Which is Southern to anyone who doesn't live in the South." For a wistful moment she thought of her Alabama boy. "Do you get many of my compatriots around here?"

"Oh, we've had a few. We used to get all kinds before the coffee-processing facility closed a few years back. So why *are* you here? Visiting someone?"

"For work," she said, then blushed. It was—what?—the second lie she'd told him? The third?

"Working bloody hard, I gather. Reading all day in a pub. Sounds like my kind of job. Is your company hiring any dashing, slightly older Brits these days?"

"Very funny. I'm . . . I'm a scholar actually."

Again she cringed. Lie number three? This one was not as egregious. A scholar was the most recent thing she had been. Plus last week she'd perused a few grad school catalogs. A scholar she could be again.

"I'm getting my master's," she continued, rolling out the lies with a startling smoothness. "Concentrating in Victorian and Edwardian British literature."

These fabrications were not completely off base, Annie assured herself. British literature had been her concentration in undergrad, which of course explained the lack of employment to anyone who asked.

"Ah," Gus said. "So you're here on an academic tour."

"Something along those lines. Research, mostly. For my thesis."

Annie could almost believe that it was true. In Oxfordshire, with Laurel, she hoped to prove something. Of course "who's my daddy" would impress nary an English department, or even an old guy in a pub.

"Poking around used bookstores in a 'derelict hamlet' seemed like a decent start," she added.

Did it? So many lies, Annie couldn't even keep how she felt about them straight.

"Well, do you have something there?" Gus asked. "For your thesis?"

"I don't know. Maybe?"

"Most people didn't believe him, you know," Gus said. "The author."

"Believe him about what?"

"About her title. About her love for the duke and their doomed romance. His thesis was never really proved, which was probably the prime reason his book was such a spectacular bomb."

He said this almost happily, with a notable spark of Schadenfreude. Gus was glad for this man's failure.

"Do you know him?" Annie pointed to the name on the cover. "Seton?"

"I did. We all did. Alas, the man who wrote that book is long since gone."

"Oh." She frowned.

"Chin up! Nothing morbid. Unfortunately for the poor bastard. He simply . . . moved on."

"Moved on to where?"

"Not through the pearly gates, if that's what you're imagining," Gus said. "No, the old fellow went to Paris in 1973 and in Paris he remains."

"So you do know him?"

"That man is unknowable." Gus glowered. "We were acquainted at one time but he's now hazy in my mind. He first came here, to Banbury, from London in . . . let's see . . ." He squinched his eyes. "Around Christmas 1972. Have you reached the part where the duchess despises Christmas?"

"I haven't."

"Yes. Christmas 1972. Seton wasn't too well received, by the duchess or anyone else. Can't fault them for it. He was the exact kind of arsehole you'd expect." Gus gave a little grunt. "Young. Spoiled. Thinking he had tremendous literary talent. His parents were tired of his unfulfilled ambitions. They wanted him to get a real job. This book was his last attempt at a career. Not sure the poor bastard ever succeeded at a single damned thing he tried."

"So you guys were the best of pals, I gather."

Gus scowled.

"No. 'Pal' is not the word I'd use."

"I was only kidding . . ."

"You have the book," Gus said. "Which means you have one side of a very multisided tale. I can help, if you want the full story."

The full story Annie wanted was of her mother, but she felt intrigued. Though Gus was probably nothing more than a blathering drunkard, Annie had an afternoon to kill. To spend it gabbing about duchesses with the so-called Earl of Winton wasn't too bad of a prospect. Maybe there was a bit of a researcher in her yet.

"You know what, Gus?" she said. "I'd love to hear the whole story. If you have time. I am suddenly awash in it myself."

"Brilliant!" His face lit up. "Ned!" He signaled to the bartender. "Another cider! What are you having?"

"Just tea."

"Two pints," he said. "Well, Annie, the first thing you must know is the author came to town thinking he had the inside track on the missing duchess. Everyone else thought she was dead. But when the fellow arrived at the duchess's home someone else was already there. Her name was Pru. And wouldn't you know it? She was an American, like all good interlopers tend to be."

Six

Gus began his story in Newport, nearly a decade before Annie was born.

Picture an old woman, he said, sitting in an ornate, drafty home beside the sea. Before her is a young girl. The girl is beautiful, all light and gossamer. Though she is luminous, she is also unsteady, glinting like a candle's flame.

"So you've come for the job," the old lady said.

"Yes," answered the young woman, who went by Pru. "I found it in the paper."

She was nineteen years old, a bookish girl who left university after only one year to get married. In April she learned there would be no marriage and so Pru had spent the prior six months addled, confused, bumping around as if lost in a pinball machine. But in her purse was the newspaper ad that might finally help her land.

> **WHITE COLLAR GIRL NEEDED.** Oxfordshire, England. Personal assistant req'd for cultured older woman living alone. 400 dollars per month and free board. No exp necessary. Only a love of literature and the English countryside.

The girl matched the admittedly slim requirements. She had the right experience, which was none, and did love books. Though she'd never been to England, Pru recognized this post as the answer, the precise action she needed to take. It was time to go away, to travel far. The Atlantic Ocean was the distance she ached for.

"I can give you references," Pru said when the woman didn't respond. "I'm a literature fiend and I'm close with the—"

"How old are you? Twenty if you're a day."

The woman was the niece of the would-be charge, but seemed far too old to call anyone aunt. Regardless, she'd evidently drawn the short end of the family stick and was responsible for dickering with the old bat in England. Best to foist caretaking duties onto a stranger for some nominal fee. What was money for if not for that?

"I'm nineteen," Pru said. "And I'm very independent."

"I'm sure you are." The woman sniffed. "But don't you have better prospects? By which I mean any other prospects at all?"

"I'm college-educated," she said. A stretch, to be sure, but not a lie. "And I was engaged to be married."

"You were engaged?" the woman said with a wheezing giggle. "A broken engagement. Well, well, well, you'd fit in with my aunt quite well."

"Not broken," Pru said. "He died."

The words stunned even her. Pru usually didn't have to say them herself. There was always someone else around to relay the ghastly tale.

"He died?" the woman gasped.

"He died," she returned with a nod.

He died, he died, he died.

Pru repeated the words in her head. Even now they didn't feel right though she'd been there when Charlie's remains returned home. She'd watched as they installed the box of him into the family mausoleum.

"So the answer is no," Pru said. "I have not a single prospect."

She shivered and wrapped a shawl tight around her shoulders. Pru was slight, a slip of a girl. On top of that the grand Newport home was cavernous and cold. The windows were open, baroque curtains drooping around them like heavy eyelids.

"Oh my. He passed? Was it in Vietnam?" The woman made a face as Pru nodded. "He died in Vietnam. Lord have mercy. He's one of those."

"One of what?" she asked. "A soldier? A brave man?"

Pru feigned ignorance but understood what this woman saw, what most of the nation believed.

The war had long since worn out its welcome. Citizens were dying at an alarming clip. Those who survived were judged as baby-killers or nancy boys. What the bloody hell had they been up to anyhow? They should've won the blessed thing by now. The lads were nothing like their fathers, who had previously saved the world.

In Pru's mind, Charlie was a hero. But he was also an idiot. His parents expended tremendous effort to backdate a fictitious sporting injury and Charlie declined to accept it. It did not sit well with him, the lying. But the lie would've saved his life.

"Bloodthirsty heathens," the woman muttered under her breath.

"He died in April," Pru said, eyes watering. "During the Easter Offensive. They found his body somewhere near Kon Tum. His name was Charlie."

"Isn't that the nickname for the Viet Cong?"

"It is."

"Ha! The irony."

Pru sucked back a thick swallow of tears.

"A damned shame," the woman said. "All of it."

"I agree entirely."

"And now you need a job. A way to support yourself."

Pru nodded again, tears shimmering on her lashes. She'd stupidly hoped Charlie's family might help, perhaps provide a job at their dry-goods conglomerate. Pru could type memos. She could warm someone else's coffee.

Alas, she reminded them of Charlie, which reminded them that he chose his death. They couldn't forgive him. And they couldn't forgive her for not convincing him to stay.

So, yes, she needed to support herself. But more than that, she had to recover from all she'd lost.

"Why not return to school?" the woman asked. "Finish your studies?"

"My family no longer has the means," she said simply.

Her parents died when she was young, the money for her studies frittered away by the relatives who raised her. Pru received a scholarship, but when she left because of Charlie the administration made it clear: she was giving it up for good.

"No longer has the means," the woman echoed with a remote chuckle. "Well, isn't that how most good stories begin?"

And so she hired Pru on the spot.

The woman didn't ask for references, or for her to verify the "love of litera-ture and the English countryside." Pru chalked it up to her appearance, to those clear green eyes and wide-moon face. Charlie used to say she was heavenly, ethereal. It was a touch flowery, but Pru knew her daintiness and quiet demeanor were often confused for a certain grace.

After the proper documents were secured, an attaché escorted her overseas. He was a butler of some sort and seemed equal parts annoyed and tickled by the adventure. All throughout the plane ride and in the hired hack to Banbury, Pru deliberated his purpose. It was 1972 and young women traveled unattended. As far as she could tell, his only business in England was to deposit her on the doorstep of an estate called the Grange.

"You didn't have to come with me," Pru said as they made the final leg of their journey. "I realize it's a bit late to say so, but I could've traveled on my own."

"This is for your own safety. The mistress of the manor is quite a force."

"So chivalrous," she mumbled. "And I don't find sweet old ladies particu-larly intimidating."

Suddenly the car sputtered to a stop in front of a stone house.

This? No, this could not be the place. The manor. The so-called estate.

Pru had been in the Newport home, Graycliffe. It was on the beach, fifty rooms they'd said, and so opulent it outshone its commendably palatial neigh-bors. But this "Grange" looked downright uninhabitable, leaning so far to the left that, well, God help town residents if there ever was a mudslide.

The home didn't even have a proper roof. It might've been thatch-style once, but was now splintered and disintegrating. More windows were broken than were intact and reams of chicken wire encased the property. All around assem-blages of livestock pecked and snouted at the dirt.

"Is this . . . ?" she began.

A man burst through the front door. He was reedy and ancient, sporting a wide straw hat, soiled trousers, and no shirt. He waved madly at his visitors.

"Get away!" the person yelled. Pru quickly ascertained he wasn't waving but brandishing a revolver. "Get away or I'll shoot you between the eyes! I've done it before!"

"I thought she lived alone?" Pru said, heart pounding.

Then she realized. This wasn't a man. The screaming, ranting figure was a woman.

"Oh my God."

"Ah yes," the attaché said with a sneaky smile. "We have arrived. Welcome to the Grange."

Seven

Over the years, rumors placed the Duchess in London and Rome and Paris. A few spotted her at the Hotel Splendide in Cannes. Renowned priest Abbé Mugnier reported she was not traveling but instead holed up in a dilapidated estate in Chacombe-at-Banbury, an Oxfordshire hamlet.

According to reports, the priest visited his old friend once a year, on Christmas Day. If he tried more often, Gladys shooed him away with warning shots or a vicious pack of snapping geese. Sometimes she leaned out a window and dumped a bucket of water on his head.

The world was skeptical of Mugnier's reports from the Grange but the doubting always struck this writer as bizarre. Here was a religious man, a fellow known as *"le confesseur des duchesses,"* the confessor of duchesses. Surely he would know of which he spoke. When I tracked down his fifty-seven *cahiers de moleskine* at the Diocèse de Paris, I found the proof I sought.

—J. Casper Augustine Seton,
The Missing Duchess: A Biography

"It wasn't the most auspicious welcome," Gus said, draining the last of his cider. "To be greeted by century-old nude breasts. And a gun."

Annie tried not to blush.

Half of her wanted to chastise this dirty old man for mentioning boobs while the other half was sniggling like a thirteen-year-old boy. She felt at times old-fashioned and hopelessly juvenile, as if she could've been born in 1879 or 1979. Maybe that's what happened when you grew up on a farm and were raised by someone like Laurel, who was about as nonworldly as a person could get. It was a marvel Eric found anything in common with her at all.

"Have I offended you?" Gus asked. "My apologies. I can be a real duffer. Comes with age. Though I don't know what my excuse was before."

As he fidgeted, Annie thought she could hear his bones creak.

"Not offended!" she chirped. "And frankly I'd be more put off by the gun. So that was her, I presume? The duchess? No offense, but how scary could she have been? She was, what, ninety years old by the time Pru answered the newspaper ad?"

"Ninety-one. Alas, my dear, we have not established the identity of the screaming harpy. It was the woman *rumored* to be the duchess, but whether she actually *was* the duchess remains to be seen."

"What do you mean, 'remains to be seen'? You've read the book, right?"

"Yes. It's been a while, but I've read it."

"Look, I know we're playing this coy game. No spoilers and all that. But let's be honest, we already know it's the duchess."

She turned the book to face Gus.

"Read this part," she said and ran her finger below the words. "'Amongst the writings found.' Start there."

Amongst the writings found in Abbé Mugnier's journals were detailed descriptions of his visits to the Grange. In his diaries he also had a receipt from the Royal Oak, a pub not far from the Grange itself.

Oddly, few believed the claims of l'abbé, when he was alive and especially after he died. The man was probably a pettifogger, they decided, mooching off the privileged and prestigious as he did.

Plus, what would the Duchess of Marlborough, this most illustrious creature, want with the hovel he described? She once lived at Blenheim for Christ's sake, where her blue eyes were painted on the portico ceilings and winged sphinxes with her face marked garden paths.

At Blenheim she entertained the likes of King George and Queen Mary if you're one for royalty, Douglas Fairbanks and Mary Pickford if you're partial to film. How could Gladys Deacon leave this grandeur to live alone? Her only guest an aged priest, her only companions a cavalcade of forever-breeding spaniels?

Annie clapped the book shut.

"Basically this . . . priest to the stars," she said, "confirmed the duchess lived at the Grange. And the author agreed. Where's the big mystery?"

"Well, if you can't trust a writer, then whom can you?" Gus said, a sparkle playing at the corners of his gray eyes. "Writers are never fib-tellers or fabricators of any sort."

"You're really going to string this out for me, aren't you?" Annie said, smiling in return.

"What do these paragraphs tell us?" he asked. "An old man claimed to see her, once a year, on Christmas. Odd date, given the duchess hated the holiday. And the author?" He snorted. "Well, here's a piece of advice, something you should've learned at primary school. Don't believe everything you read."

"That's the damned truth," she grumbled. "So the woman at the Grange. She was crazy? Demented? Violent? All of the above?"

"All, some, or none of the above," Gus said. "Depending on who you'd ask. Walking around naked and wielding firearms does not typically lead to a reputation for sanity. On the other hand, some thought it was a ruse, that she pretended to be crazy in order to keep people away."

"Like with the angry geese."

"Yes. Or the powerful weed killer she used to spray 'fuck you' in her front lawn."

"Not for nothing, but this woman, if she was 'the duchess.'" Annie rolled her eyes and held up air quotes.

"Let's call her Mrs. Spencer. She would've preferred it."

"Works for me. Well, this Mrs. Spencer was a real piece of work. Maybe even, how do I put this elegantly?"

"A bit of a bitch?" he said with a wink. "You're going to have to get that blushing under control if you plan to sit around pubs with the likes of me. But you are correct. Mrs. Spencer and the duchess were both described using a host of unflattering terms, such as sociopathic, ruinous, and out for blood. Of course Pru, our American assistant, knew none of this."

"You have to feel for the old broad," Annie said. "The woman was alone for decades. That'd make anyone nutty. Why'd the family wait so long to hire someone?"

"Mrs. Spencer didn't want anyone else to live at the Grange. Her niece Edith tried to intervene dozens of times over the years, a promise to her mother that she'd look after Auntie. But just as the old woman shooed away priests with gunshots and cold water, she used decidedly less pleasant tactics with people not of the cloth."

" 'Fuck you' in the lawn," Annie guessed.

"Precisely. Bows and poisoned arrows, too. Unfortunately, over time, Mrs. Spencer's behavior grew more erratic. Perhaps she was becoming increasingly senile, or suffering from lack of attention. Whatever the case, third-party complaints about her increased. Phone calls were placed overseas. The family could no longer ignore the situation."

"Something had to be done," Annie said. "Still. It's pretty remarkable that she was living independently at ninety-plus years."

"If she truly was independent," Gus said. "Because of course there was Tom."

"Tom? Who the heck is Tom?" She opened the book and flicked through some pages. "I don't see any Tom in here. I thought she lived alone?"

"Maybe. Maybe not. Tomasz was a displaced Polish man. He'd been with Mrs. Spencer since 1951 or so the story went. A handyman, she claimed. The only loyal man in her entire wretched life."

"So what happened to him?"

"No one knew. Was he alive? Dead? Had he even existed in the first place? Because though townspeople had heard his name, took for granted rumors of his existence, no one reported seeing him after 1955, though he'd lived at the Grange some twenty years by the time Pru showed up."

"Did anyone recall meeting him? Ever?"

"A few people," Gus said with a shrug. "In the early fifties. After that, nothing, although Mrs. Spencer referred to him often. To would-be visitors she'd screech 'Watch out! Tom will get you!' Or 'Don't go near the barn! Tom is in there!' Tom was almost always 'in the barn.' A queer place for the handyman of a falling-down estate."

"Why didn't anyone check?" she asked. "Sneak a look?"

Gus tossed his head back and laughed, deep and low and from his gut. She felt her face redden and burn.

"It seems a simple enough solution," she sniffed. "I don't know why you find it so hilarious."

"Sure. Simple enough if you don't mind a bullet to the arse."

"But it's a big property, right? Why wouldn't someone prowl around? See what was up?"

"A brilliant idea. That is, aside from the aforementioned bullets, the barbed wire, a herd of wild boars, a few poisoned spears, as well as about a dozen other hazards. Other than that, a winning plot!"

"I get it, the estate was impenetrable."

"Mostly. Plus everyone was anxious about what state he'd be in, this Tom, in the barn for twenty years or more."

"What did they imagine?" she asked. "A dead body? A live, withered one chained to a wall?"

"Yes and yes."

"I assume Pru didn't know about him. Or any of the other threats."

"No, she did not," Gus said. "It's why Edith Junior settled on the diaphanous young American. She'd tried to hire a half-dozen staid British-governess types but they all sussed out the situation and declined the post. The family was lucky, really. Pru had no experience but was the exact right person for the job."

Eight

"Hello, Mrs. Spencer," the attaché said. "This is your new companion, Miss Valentine."

"Valentine. What a name."

"Perchance you might put on a shirt. Display a little polish."

"What the hell do I need with polish at my age, Reginald?" The old woman slipped the revolver into an ankle holster and hitched up her trousers. "Or a companion for that matter?"

"My name is Murray. As I've told you countless times."

"Hello there, I'm . . ."

Pru went to shake Mrs. Spencer's hand but the woman yanked all appendages out of reach, contorting her face as if Pru might be riddled with disease.

"Your manners are immaculate, Mrs. Spencer. It's always so nice to be reminded."

The attaché, named Murray as it turned out, sighed and placed his briefcase on the hall table atop a pile of clipped-out newspaper articles. There were more articles spread across the floor—hundreds, thousands perhaps. As wind gusted through the broken windows, the papers fluttered like leaves.

"Regarding your new companion, m'dear," Murray said. "There've been myriad complaints from the locals plus a well-placed call from the head of the county. Everyone's concerned about your welfare. Plus no one's keen on witnessing accidental gun deployments."

"There's nothing accidental about my shot."

Pru would've snickered if she hadn't been so stupefied by the woman and her house.

"So I need to be 'dealt with,' you're telling me," Mrs. Spencer said.

"Precisely. As such, your options are admission to the local sanitarium or the company of a lovely young woman with impeccable references. Ergo, our Miss Valentine."

Pru flashed him a look, eyebrows punched up into her hairline.

Impeccable references? Admittedly, she dropped some big names during the interview, but as far as she understood, no references were verified. If the aunt had checked, it's unlikely Pru would've gotten the job.

"She knows the Kellogg family," Murray went on. "Are you familiar with the dry goods people?"

The woman, this Mrs. Spencer, removed her straw hat and dropped it on Murray's briefcase. She shook out her hair, which was fine, translucent, and hung halfway down her back.

"The dry goods people," Mrs. Spencer said. "Is that right?"

Her eyes were an arresting and startling shade of blue, like glaciers. When they met gazes, Pru felt a sting of cold across her chest. How would she ever get warm in a place like that?

"That's them," Pru said, her mouth dry.

Was it possible that Charlie's family had uttered a single nice comment about her, or even a neutral one? She couldn't picture them recommending her. Then again, they probably just wanted Pru out of the country.

She'd done nothing wrong per se but what kind of woman couldn't keep her man at home? They were Berkeley students, for Christ's sake. University of hippies and draft dodgers, a school filled with nonpatriots. At the very least, she could've gotten "accidentally" knocked up and guilted their golden boy into remaining stateside.

"The Kellogg family adores our Miss Valentine," Murray said, and lightly tapped Pru on the shoulder. "Go on. Tell her."

"I, uh, have known them for about two years—"

"Save your breath," Mrs. Spencer said. "As if I give a shit about the Kelloggs. Come. Follow me. The both of you."

Pru gave a muted smile as they made their way deeper into the home. Who gave a shit, indeed. Well, she gave one. But she didn't want to.

The Grange was imposing from the outside, not due to size but because it carried a palpable moodiness, as though it produced its own dark weather. But once inside, the home grew more foreboding and expansive with every step. As Pru moved along, the ceilings rose above her, walls jumped out of her grasp.

"Try to keep up!" Mrs. Spencer bellowed.

The woman quickened her pace, just for fun, just so Pru and Murray would have to jog.

"Crap!" Pru yelped as she tripped over a hole in the parquet floor. She leaped to avoid falling into a second one. "What the hell?"

"Excuse her language," Murray said. "Americans. You know."

"No excusing necessary. I'm pleased Edith Junior would dare hire someone possessing even the slightest hint of moxie."

Pru felt grateful for the compliment as "moxie" was not a word usually ascribed to her. Maybe this wasn't the worst possible situation after all.

"And speaking of manners," Mrs. Spencer rambled on. "You could've provided some warning that you were bringing a nonresident alien to live in my house. That's some how-do-you-do. Perhaps she's a thief. Or a murderess."

"You're the one with a handgun, Mrs. Spencer."

"I don't know why my niece pays you a single red cent. Honestly, Ferguson."

"Murray. The name's Murray."

"Hold on," Pru said, her voice hoarse from lack of use, not to mention the clouds of dust swirling in the air. "You didn't know I was coming?"

"Lord no." Mrs. Spencer sniggered. "You're unknown to me before today, which is probably for the best. Had I recognized Perry from the road I would've shot you both on sight."

"Thank heavens for lucky breaks, then," Murray said.

Pru turned to him. "Mrs. Spencer didn't know about me? You didn't tell her?"

"Believe me, we tried." He exhaled loudly. "Mrs. Spencer, Edith rang you umpteen times. You were fully aware of the situation but chose not to listen, per usual."

They stepped into the kitchen and for Pru almost onto some chickens. She blinked. The place was a scene. Trash. Broken furniture. Upended appliances. Enough animals to start a petting zoo.

Pru would soon come to learn that nothing in the room was used for its intended purpose. The stove provided the home's heat, the multiple refrigerators were for storage, and the furniture sheltered Mrs. Spencer's crop of amorous spaniels. These dogs were the reason for the holes in the floor, too. Mrs. Spencer cut them so the pups could clump together beneath the floorboards, burrowing like small woodland creatures.

"I don't know why Edith thinks I need assistance," Mrs. Spencer said as chickens clacked by her feet. "As if she knows what I need at all. The woman's exactly like her mother, who'd just as soon see me dead as properly looked after."

"Edith cares about you," Murray insisted. "She's loved you for a lifetime and only wants to ensure you're healthy and happy. Also, the entire population of Banbury is terrified."

"That's hardly my problem. They're silly. And bored."

"People are moving out of Chacombe because of you," Murray said. "Local estate agents are in a frenzy. You are single-handedly depressing home prices."

"I think declining property values have more to do with the floating pound than an old lady in the countryside. Though I s'pose I can't expect the village rubes to comprehend basic economics. Anyhow, I don't much care what they say. They've been wagging tongues about me for decades. Not an ounce of it is true."

"The gossip about the revolver," Murray said and pointed to her ankle holster. "Seems reasonably accurate."

"As if that isn't their favorite thing about me! The Shooting Duchess!" Mrs. Spencer lit a cigarette, a Woodbine. "What a story for them to tell." She looked at Pru. "Lest you believe the townsfolk sane, they think I'm the long-lost Duchess of Marlborough."

"A duchess?" Pru said, trying not to smile. "Really?"

"A load of horseshit." Mrs. Spencer blew a stream of smoke over her shoulder and into Murray's face. "What would a duchess be doing in this derelict hamlet, I ask you? Especially a duchess of that caliber. The ol' D of M was the most beautiful creature to ever exist. The press called her 'the embodiment of sunshine.'"

"A bit of an exaggeration, don't you think?" Murray asked.

"I'm merely repeating conventional wisdom," Mrs. Spencer said with a little shrug. "So, based on the not-so-trustworthy accounts of a bunch of hayseeds, you've brought some pretty young thing to look after me?"

"I have."

"And what if I reject this proposition?"

"Regrettably, that's not an option," Murray said. "If you wish to continue living in your home, Miss Valentine is your choice. Otherwise I have a bed reserved for you in the O'Connell Ward at St. Andrew's Hospital."

"St. Andrew's!"

"You see? Miss Valentine is not such a bad alternative."

Stomach lurching, Pru considered how she might be a suitable replacement for a mental institution. It was funny how quickly a perfectly decent option could morph into a horrifically bad idea. When was the next flight to Boston? she wondered.

"As I've said, Mickey, I've lived alone for decades without incident."

"Not without incident, m'love. And you've done wondrously. Alas, you are over ninety years old. Don't you want help around here? It would be nice to have some company at least."

Mrs. Spencer sighed, her blue eyes fixed on a windowpane. She seemed to be relenting, or plotting. There was something very purposeful in the way she chose to humor Murray. It was quietly frightening.

"I'm not alone," she said, and turned in his direction. "Have you forgotten Tom? He's in the barn."

"Yes. Tom. In the barn."

"Tom!" Pru yipped. The ad mentioned only one person to look after. "Who's Tom?"

Murray leaned in. Pru felt his breath hot on her neck.

"Some groundsman, allegedly," he said. "Yet the landscaping is garbage. Presumably, this Tom is a figment of Mrs. Spencer's highly acrobatic imagination."

"I can hear you, you know."

Murray pulled back.

"Until I see evidence to the contrary, what else am I to believe?" he asked, then looked again toward Pru. "Allegedly 'Tom' lives in a barn but no one's seen him in a quarter of a century. He's a Pole, by the by, a displaced person from the war. Mrs. Spencer spent far too much time with Germans in her younger years, I suspect. And now she has her very own Polish indentured servant. Dreams do come true in the end."

"That's quite enough. Lord Almighty. You pay Hitler one compliment and no one ever lets you forget it. I stand by my statement."

"She lauded Hitler," Murray said in a stage whisper.

"All I said was that he accomplished a lot!"

"That's one way to put it."

"When you think how hard it is to create a rising in a small village, well, he had the whole world up in arms. He was larger than Churchill. Churchill couldn't have done that!"

"You and Adolf Hitler, birds of a feather. You both create risings in small villages to great success."

Mrs. Spencer rolled her eyes, then grabbed a black cloak from a broken-down chair. Pru had been so hypnotized by the woman's eyes and her back-and-forth with Murray, she'd nearly forgotten about Mrs. Spencer's bare chest.

"So you insist upon staying," she said and looked at Pru.

"I'm not sure if 'insist' is the word . . ."

"She does," Murray said. "She insists. We all do."

"Fine. Off with you, henchman to the awful Edith Junior. Miss Valentine, come with me. I'll show you to your rooms."

Nine

Pru's eyes sprang open.

It was early morning. The room was dead dark except for a single candle glowing above her head. Behind the flame was a pair of crystalline blue eyes. Behind the eyes, a face like rumpled tissue.

Pru scooted up onto her elbows.

"Mrs. Spencer?"

She was disoriented, out of breath, but not nearly as terrified as she should've been. Was she really so heartbroken, so numbed and paralyzed that she couldn't muster a prudent level of panic?

"So you're still with me," Mrs. Spencer noted, holding the light close to Pru's face.

"Yes, ma'am."

"I half expected you to flee in the middle of the night."

"I've been hired to do a job, Mrs. Spencer. I plan to do it and do it well."

Plus Murray had left that evening, her only opportunity for escape probably sitting in a lounge at Heathrow, if not somewhere over the Atlantic. Not that it mattered, or that she'd even go with him if given a second chance. The Grange was a pit but there was nothing left for Pru back in the States.

"Look to the right," Mrs. Spencer barked.

"Excuse me?"

"Turn your head to the right. Do it!" She clonked Pru in the skull with the brass candleholder. "Now!"

"Sure thing," she said, one eye fixed on the flame.

What this seemingly demented woman might do behind a partially turned back Pru couldn't begin to guess.

"I gotta be honest," Charlie wrote in a letter not received until after his death. "Out here it's hard to tell the good from the bad. They all look the same."

Damn if that wasn't true about most things.

"My goodness," Mrs. Spencer said.

Pru felt the heat of the flame alongside her cheek.

"You have the perfect Hellenic profile. It's exquisite. You are a lucky girl."

"Oh. Thank you?"

"You remind me of myself."

Mrs. Spencer snuffed out the candle and reached over to flick on the bedside lamp. The woman smelled a little sweet, like baby powder, but also sour. Pru scrunched her nose though the scent wasn't altogether unpleasant.

"What time is it?" Pru asked. "Maybe we should talk in the morning?"

"Don't be such a pansy." Mrs. Spencer dropped onto the bed with a small bounce. "It's well after four o'clock. We rise early at the Grange. Bixby! Diamond!" She whistled through her teeth. "Up here! Up with Mama!"

First came the sound of nails clacking on the hardwood floors and then the zip of two tawny-coated spaniels into the bed. The dogs spent several seconds scrabbling and yapping about the yellowed lace coverlet before ultimately settling against Mrs. Spencer's thigh.

"The animals are permitted on the furniture, I take it?"

"This is their home, more than yours," Mrs. Spencer said. "Speaking of my home, why are you in it?"

"I thought Murray explained everything? Your family placed an advertisement for a personal assistant . . ."

"No. I mean, why are you here? With me? And not doing some grander thing? Child, I'm asking if all of your talents have been brought out of you."

"Ha! Well, that's the question, isn't it?"

"Yes. It is the question. So I'm waiting for an answer. Do they not teach the particulars of holding a basic conversation over in America?"

"No, they do. It's just . . . it's not something I've been asked before. So yeah. Sure. My talents have been brought out of me. Not that I had many to start."

"Well, what are they?" Mrs. Spencer asked. "These talents. I'm positively dying to know."

"Er, well, I'm a voracious reader."

"That's truly more of a hobby. An honorable one, mind you! But a hobby all the same."

"I'm fairly competent in writing essays."

"Lord Almighty. You are in rough shape, aren't you? Vastly insecure."

"I wouldn't say 'vastly.'"

"I can smell it a mile away. But you're smart. I can smell that, too. I myself am a certified genius, despite being raised by a mother who was beautiful but not so sharp. I was a miracle. Differential calculus was too low for me!"

"Well, class is in session," Pru said, trying for a joke. "Maybe you can teach me a thing or two. I'm horrible with numbers. I guess I prefer things that are made up."

"Why are you here?" Mrs. Spencer asked again. "Why? You should be attending university instead of living with an ancient dame in the countryside. Education is everything. It smooths a life."

"I did attend college. In California. I was a literature major, for a while."

"Yes, and then?"

"Then . . . I left."

Pru was in no mood to recount her backstory, or to deflect the uncomfortable combination of pity and disgust she was bound to receive. Her fiancé was dead, which was a tragedy, but surely he'd obliterated more lives than one. It wasn't even a fair trade.

"So your leaving was about a fellow," Mrs. Spencer said with a cluck. "A little advice, Miss Valentine. Never let a man dictate your life."

"That's not exactly what happened."

"I didn't get married until I was forty years old—by *choice*. I had my own apartment, in Paris no less, when I was half that. An independent woman, at the turn of the century. You beatnik, hippie feminists think you're sailing uncharted waters but I've done it all before. Even the drugs."

"I'm hardly a beatnik or hippie."

Pru thought of her friends back at Berkeley with their protests and marches and flowerized names. Debbie who was Petal and Linda who was Daisy and every last one of them who so quickly turned on Charlie, and on Pru, when he didn't fight his draft.

"As a group, they'd be offended you thought I was one of them," she added.

"So, what was it, then?" Mrs. Spencer asked. "Your face is as sad as a gala without guests. I'm sensing a broken engagement?"

"More or less."

"For Christ's sake. Don't mope around because of a silly betrothal gone awry. If you haven't racked up a few, you're doing something wrong. The minimum ratio is five engagements for every one marriage. The bare minimum! Mine is much higher, as you'd expect."

Mrs. Spencer looked toward the ceiling and chuckled through her nose.

"Ten to one?" she said. "Fifteen? No matter. You don't get married for the first time at age forty without *promising* to marry a string of fellows along the way."

"What's the point, then? Of accepting proposals you don't intend to follow through with?"

"Why, you're dumb as a post!" Mrs. Spencer said in a tone that was hard to read.

"That settles that, then."

"Oh, calm down. I say it with kindness. Silly girl, engagements are about the celebration and pomp. The good bits without the trouble that comes later. As soon as the wedding is over, so's the party. Salt mines and skimpy meals the rest of your days."

She lifted the covers and scooted in beside her. Pru inched to the far side of the bed.

"You mentioned you love to read," Mrs. Spencer said.

"Yes," Pru replied, eyes closed as she willed the woman back to her own quarters. "I was a literature major. It's one of the reasons I came to work here. They told me you love books, particularly those by British authors, which was my concentration."

At least it would've been, had she gotten that far.

"Edith Junior said that? About my passion for literature? Well, well, well. She got that bit right."

"Mmm." Pru's thoughts blurred.

God, she was tired. So tired. She couldn't remember the last time she felt truly awake.

"Thomas Hardy." Mrs. Spencer nudged her in the side. Pru reopened her eyes. "Do you like Hardy?"

"Yes, of course. *Tess of the d'Urbervilles. Far from the Madding Crowd.* 'And at home by the fire, whenever you look up there I shall be—and whenever I look up, there will be you.'"

A shudder ran through Pru's chest.

"Oh good Lord," Mrs. Spencer said. "Don't get maudlin on me."

"That's a quote from *Far from the Madding Crowd*," Pru said as tears pooled in her eyes.

"Of course I know what book it's from! Hardy was a friend of mine. Please. Your crying. I can't take it."

"'I shall do one thing in this life—one thing certain—this is, love you, and long for you, and—'"

"'Keep wanting you till I die,'" Mrs. Spencer finished. "Yes. We know."

She made a gagging sound as Pru let the tears run down her cheeks.

"Stop it!" Mrs. Spencer ordered. "Stop it right now! You must put the boy out of your head. It's not worth the agony. You didn't want to marry him in the first place."

"Yes. I did. With every part of me."

"Very well, then. Hang on to your romantic Hardy quotes but I have a few myself. 'People go on marrying because they can't resist natural forces, although many of them may know perfectly well that they are possibly buying a month's pleasure with a life's discomfort.'"

"We would've been different," Pru whispered, her voice thin as a strand of hair.

"Knock it off, Miss Valentine. I can't tolerate the mewling. What about Proust?" Mrs. Spencer said, her words fast and sharp like a poke in the ribs. "Do you like Proust?"

"Excuse me?"

"Proust. Marcel Proust. What are your thoughts on him, O erudite literary major?"

"To be honest, I haven't studied much Proust," Pru said, sniffling.

"YOU HAVEN'T STUDIED MUCH PROUST?"

"I mean, I have. Some. But he's not really my thing. I like Hardy. Wharton. Evelyn Waugh. Henry James."

"I knew all of them. Personally. And they have nothing on Marcel. You have no opinion on the man? Not a single thought? And you consider yourself well read?"

"Naturally, I admire *À la recherche*. A new way to approach the novel, its own genre and whatnot. So, he's decent. But, in general, Proust not my bag."

"*Not your bag?* Marcel and I are closer than siblings. I won't mention you said that."

"Isn't he dead?"

"For a time he was my dearest friend," Mrs. Spencer said, her voice slowing, her body falling more heavily into the bed. "Any reader should appreciate what Proust meant to the literary world. He made us cognizant of the importance of memory when reading a book, how pivotal the setting and circumstance. So whatever sentimental notions Edith's advertisement conjured, whatever visions you had of moping about the Cotswolds, book in hand, were planted first by Proust."

"You seem to have led a fascinating life, Mrs. Spencer." Pru pulled the blanket up to her chin to ward off the chill. "I look forward to getting to know you better."

"It's too late for anyone to know me. Oh, Marcel! I miss him so! He and I, we brightened the salons of Paris! The Ritz conservatory. All up and down the Rue du Faubourg-Saint-Honoré. Hardy. You love Hardy? Here's your next literature essay, Miss Valentine, a use for your sole talent. Why not explore the French versus English spirit as shown in prose? With Hardy as testament on the latter?"

"Okay, I'll take it under advisement."

"I had the most heated discussion with Lily de Clermont-Tonnerre on the very topic one night at Thérèse's salon. Comtesse Thérèse Murat's salon, if you must know."

"Sure, Comtesse Murat," Pru said with a yawn.

"Cocteau was there, too. Got his bloomers in a right knot over it, that poor drug-addled maniac. Such splendid times! Of course Mother hated these exploits of mine. She thought all the flitting about salons hurt my ability to make a proper match. But as I told her, 'I go there for the conversation, not the mating.'"

Pru chuckled sleepily.

"I've lived in the most glorious places," Mrs. Spencer went on. "My prior home was every centimeter as monumental as Versailles. But oh, Miss Valentine, you should've seen Paris."

Pru's mind began to hum as Mrs. Spencer spoke on, recounting the parties and salons and debates with Europe's brightest literary minds, its shiniest artistic talents.

Before long Pru nodded off to the woman's dulcet voice, her head filled with images of the Parisian streets at midnight, its gaslamps hanging in arcades, dancing the people home.

Ten

To understand the future Duchess of Marlborough, one must first understand her past.

Gladys's mother was Florence Baldwin Deacon, a renowned femme fatale from a celebrated New England family. She wasn't particularly intelligent but had the compensating attributes of extraordinary beauty and unmatched sophistication. Gladys's father was bright-minded but cold and austere. He met his death at age fifty-seven, after contracting pneumonia in a mental hospital.

Florence Baldwin's father, Gladys's grandfather, was Rear Admiral Charles Baldwin, a man wealthy beyond description. He was so celebrated that five hundred marines escorted the coffin at his funeral. William Waldorf Astor was a pallbearer.

The duchess's other grandfather was a real scrapper, coming up in American society through various bootstrap enterprises, including a whale boating business. Alas, his greatest accomplishment was marrying Sarahann Parker, a descendant of the breathtakingly wealthy Boston Parkers, a family that produced an unending line of adulterers and adultered-upon, all of them gorgeous and sad.

No Baldwin or Parker was ever happy, despite the money and gilt and their salacious sexual appetites. Gladys's mother chased the ever-elusive joy for a while until she landed bang in the center of a worldwide scandal. One lover, one baby, and one international incident that changed the course of their lives, especially the life of her eldest, the beautiful, tempestuous Gladys.

—J. Casper Augustine Seton,
The Missing Duchess: A Biography

Annie crept through the hotel room door, backpack socked against her chest, book hidden safely in the bottom.

"Where have you been?" Laurel asked from the corner. She sat in a chintz chair, a stack of papers in her lap. "I was almost starting to get worried."

"Oh," Annie said, heart thumping like she'd just come home from a field kegger or sneaking out to meet a much older boyfriend. "I didn't realize you were waiting. Or that you'd be back already. You haven't been around, so . . ."

"Mmm." Laurel bobbed her head in agreement, or in acceptance, as she thumbed through the papers in her lap, sticky notes jutting out from all sides. "I apologize. I'm sure you've been bored. This isn't exactly the trip I envisioned, either."

"Deal not going well?"

"That's one way to put it. They're playing hardball. Who 'they' are, the buyers, or the owners of the adjacent parcels, or the lawyers, I can't decide. Everyone was desperate to get this done a month ago and suddenly nothing's right."

"I'm sorry," Annie said, and lowered onto the bed. "What a gigantic pain in the ass."

"It's how these things go, I suppose. I've spent more than a few years as a corporate attorney and though my expertise isn't exactly in U.K.-based land transactions, I'm not falling for any of their tricks."

"You get 'em, Mom."

Laurel straightened the stack of papers and tossed them onto the desk beside her.

"So what have you been doing all day?"

"Not much," Annie said. "Wandering around Banbury. Having tea. The usual."

"Specifics, girl. I want specifics. Where'd you go? What'd you see?"

"Banbury Cross. A few English gardens. Some bakeries. Endless limestone."

Annie yanked a rubber band off her wrist and pulled back her thick, wavy, jumbled mess of a hairdo. Though the sky was clear when she stepped into the pub, it was drizzling by the time she left. On the short walk home, the dampness exploded her hair to three times its usual size.

"Yikes," Annie said, accidentally catching a glimpse in the mirror. Once again, she envied her mom's horses and their slick, shiny, never-frizzy manes.

"Did you eat anything?" Laurel asked. "Please tell me you had more than the so-called biscuits Nicola lays out each day."

"Yes, as a matter of fact. I went to this pub? The George and Dragon?"

"Right. I think I've seen it. Nice place?"

"It was okay. Mostly I drank tea and read. Had a few bites of a sandwich."

"Was it good?"

"The sandwich?"

"No," Laurel said. "The book."

"Oh." She paused. "It's funny. It's a book you have, I think. The one about the missing duchess? I mentioned it the other day?"

Laurel stared at her blankly.

"I found it locally," Annie continued. If the lie was good enough for Gus, it was good enough for Laurel. "I happened upon a used bookstore owned by a woman named Trudy and recognized it from your library."

"How odd."

"Mom, have you been here before?"

"Annie . . ."

"No offense, but you're not a big reader. Yet you have this book. And it's about a woman who lived in Banbury. Now we're in Banbury and it turns out you own a piece of land in this very spot. But I'd never heard about any of this until now."

"I've been here," her mother said and stood. She looked not at Annie but over the top of her head, toward the cross. "I came through Banbury years ago. Decades."

"Why didn't you tell me?"

"There's nothing to tell, really. During college I did the, um, backpacking-through-Europe thing."

"You," Annie said, amused. "You, who wouldn't let me join Girl Scouts because of the camping requirement? You went backpacking? Voluntarily?"

"I know. It was a bit of an ill-fated trip." Laurel shook her head. "In multiple ways. I came to Oxfordshire because . . . well, because I had the vague notion of some people I should see here, folks who might be family."

"The people associated with the land you're trying to sell?"

"Yes. Exactly."

"Did you track them down?"

"Not really. The trip was a waste. I never found what I wanted, which is how most poorly planned odysseys end up. I left here feeling pretty dejected."

"Well, at least you got some free property out of it."

"Yes. At least there's that."

"Is that when you bought the book?" Annie asked. "*The Missing Duchess?* When you visited Banbury?"

"I don't remember exactly." Laurel's eyes flittered away. "Probably, though. The duchess was big talk in this town, her own tourist attraction, though she'd died by the time I came through."

"So you remember the book."

"Yes. No. I mean. It's not . . . it's hard to explain, Annie."

"You lied to me."

"I didn't lie. It's hard to explain."

"Yeah, you mentioned that. I thought lawyers never found anything hard to explain."

"I was a different person then. Seeing the book." Laurel bit down on her lip, then exhaled. "It's not about the book. It's about the memories the book brings up."

"Proust," Annie said.

"Excuse me?"

"Proust talked about the importance of memory when reading, the effect of setting and circumstance."

"Did he? Well, you would know," Laurel said with a smile. "I guess that's why I paid the big bucks for your schooling."

"Yes, so I can have knowledge of dead writers. A very useful life skill. It is so very perplexing that I don't have a job."

Annie didn't mention that the knowledge came not from her spendy education but from chatting with a stranger in a bar.

"How have I never heard of you backpacking through Europe?" she said. "I *mean* . . . what? I can't imagine you doing anything that free-spirited. Mostly you're all business, all the time."

"I did go to college in the seventies," Laurel said. "We were all a little looser in those days. Or we tried."

"But you graduated from an all-girls school with insane academic standards," Annie pointed out. "How many 'loose' people could there have been at Wellesley? Or at Georgetown Law?"

"There were a few. And many more who were trying to be free spirits but didn't necessarily pull it off. Ah, tales of misspent youth. Before you get married, make sure you have a few tales of your own."

"I still don't get it," Annie said, her mother's story nagging at her. "I'm sorry. I'm not trying to beat a dead horse but—"

"You know I hate that expression."

"How come you haven't brought this up before?" Annie asked. "How did you not mention it on the plane ride to London, or during dinner last night, or even over coffee this morning? You're a nostalgic person. You get teary-eyed about horses and summer interns. Then there's this book, which stirs up all kinds of bittersweet memories. I say this with all due respect, but what the hell, Mom?"

Laurel inhaled deeply, as if to speak, then held her breath there, locked safely behind her chest. For the first time Annie saw not a rigid, rule-abiding horsewoman but instead a person with a past.

"Was he with you?" Annie asked, the answer suddenly so obvious. "When you came through Banbury with your friends? Was he backpacking, too?"

"Who?" Her mom blinked.

"My father. Who else?"

"No. God no. He was nowhere near my life then."

"Then what is it?" Annie stood. "What happened?"

"Annie, if you ever decide to have children—"

"Of course I'll have children!" she snapped. "Eric is dying to become a father!"

Laurel frowned.

"Not now or anything," Annie added hastily. "But, Mom, we're doing it. We're getting married. You're not going to talk me out of it."

"I understand that," Laurel said with a nod. "Listen, sweetheart. Teaching your children to be their own people, to exist outside of you, is tough. You want them to avoid repeating your past mistakes but you're also wary of forcing them to repeat the good stuff, too. That comes with a whole set of expectations that doesn't work for anyone."

"Which is why you didn't mind that I majored in English, instead of finance like you."

"Something along those lines."

Unlike her daughter, Laurel never would've graduated college without a legitimate career path. Not that fake researcher wasn't growing on Annie. But when she first declared her major some two or three years ago, it was a half-assed rebellion, a test, which Laurel readily passed. Her mom put up exactly no fight.

"Annabelle, I'm having a very hard time with your engagement," Laurel said, chin and voice trembling. "Eric is a lovely person but when I look at what you're missing . . ."

Annie thought of Mrs. Spencer, a woman who had had her own apartment in Paris at age twenty, over a hundred years ago. She tried to picture her mom at twenty but it felt like trying to read a book in the dark.

"Maybe I'm not missing anything," Annie said, to her mom and to herself.

"Maybe not. Listen, I'm not a perfect parent. Even now I'm trying to figure things out. I want you to be independent. I want you to see the world and experience the awesome. But I also want to save you from the pain. These desires, mostly they conflict."

Annie wondered if her mother regretted it.

If Laurel regretted putting every ounce of everything into her daughter and her job. See the world? Experience the awesome? Perhaps Laurel had done these things before becoming a mom, but twenty years was a long time to hold the same pattern.

"I love you," Annie said, for lack of anything better.

It was all she had left. Annie was hungry. And exhausted. And not sure where to go from there, their two minds unlikely to meet. Annie was having a hard time seeing her mother right then. She didn't even know where to look.

"You're a great mom," she said.

This, if nothing else, was true.

"Oh. Thanks," Laurel mumbled. "I try."

"Seriously. The best. All my high school friends thought so."

"Good Lord," Laurel said with a laugh. "The endorsement of teenagers usually means you're the opposite of a great mom."

"Don't worry, you were adequately strict. But nice. Normal. And people like horses."

"The horses have saved the day more than once."

Laurel walked toward the closet. She reached down to grab a pair of flats, which were lined up beside the rest of her shoes. Above them hung a row of carefully pressed slacks. Meanwhile, Annie's clothes sat in a towering mound atop her suitcase.

"I have to go into London tomorrow," Laurel said. "Only for the day. We'll do a real sightseeing trip when this is all over, but do you want to join me? You can explore while I have another soul-sucking powwow. Other lawyers. Ugh. So, whaddya say?"

"Um, I don't know," Annie replied, surprised to be thinking of Gus, and of the duchess. "Ya know I'll pass. Hang out here."

"I thought you'd seen the sum total of Banbury proper?"

"Yeah. But." Annie shrugged. "I don't feel like schlepping around London alone. I'd rather go together, when we have more time."

"Okay. But I'll miss you." Laurel said this distantly, her face not on Annie but turned toward the window, and the Banbury Cross outside. "Should we get something to eat? I'm famished. What about that place you mentioned earlier?" She flipped back around. "Do they serve dinner?"

"No!" she snapped. "No. I mean, they serve dinner but I ate there for lunch. Let's try something else. Didn't Nicola mention a nice restaurant in a neighboring town?"

"She probably did, though I tune out ninety percent of what she says." Laurel tilted her head toward the door. "Shall we?"

"Sure, but can we stop by the lobby first? I want to shoot Eric a quick e-mail. Tell him about my day."

"You poor thing. Thanks to my endless meetings, that's going to be the dullest e-mail between two lovebirds since the dawn of time. Or the dawn of e-mail.

'Dear Eric, today I did nothing while my mother committed various acts of child neglect.' "

"Actually," Annie said with a smile. "The day wasn't so bad."

With that, Annie grabbed her bag, taking with her not only a wallet, but *The Missing Duchess*, visions of Mrs. Spencer, and the feeling of words left unsaid.

Eleven

Subject: **Earl of MEU**
From: eric.sawyer@usmc.mil
Date: Oct 30, 2001 11:32
To: anniehaley79@aol.com

The Earl of Winton?

If that doesn't sound like a sack of crap, I don't know what does. Be careful, Annie. You're a trusting girl. Too sweet for your own good. That's how you ended up with me, I'm pretty sure.

I'm sorry things are off with your mom. Maybe she really doesn't remember the book? It might be hard for a big-brained reader like you to grasp but sometimes books are just a bunch of papers between two thicker pieces of paper. You should probably dump me on the spot for that kind of talk. Good thing I'm not there in person. That's probably blasphemy in the eyes of Annabelle Jane Haley.

But of course I'm not with you. I'm here, on an MEU. Traveling fifth-class to Kandahar, which I can't picture even though I've *seen* pictures and videos. It still feels like fiction to me, a place described in a book. I don't know what to expect when we get there. It's a brave new world, even for those of us who are trying to fix it.

I love you, Annie. Be safe.

Eric

Twelve

In Paris, Gladys's mother met her match with famed homme fatal Émile François Abeille. Abeille was a relatively plain figure made dashing by his family's Suez Canal–acquired wealth. Also he had a deep voice. A very deep voice. An associate who knew him said it "went all the way down to his goolies." The yacht and access to Paris's most private clubs topped off his charms.

Florence and Abeille met because of a past-due bill, which was generally the only type of bill Florence Deacon bothered to have. When Abeille heard the married—but "open"—beauty had rung up quite the tab at Doucet's, the most fashionable atelier of the day, Abeille telegrammed Mrs. Deacon with a message.

If the lovely Florence was willing to meet at his private apartment, he'd gladly pay off the debt, plus any that might follow. It was a very fair trade from Mrs. Deacon's view. Her daughters were starting to come up in age. If she were to be the mother of a duchess or a princess, she would have to dress the part.

A casual observer might think, why, this woman sounds like a prosti-tute. And, if you want to get to the nuts of it (so to speak), that's exactly

what she was. A prostitute with a short, highly discriminating client list. It
was a job that paid exceedingly well.

—J. Casper Augustine Seton,
The Missing Duchess: A Biography

"Nicola?"

"Oh! Crumbs!"

The woman fluttered a hand against her neck as she reluctantly ripped her
eyes away from an episode of *Coronation Street,* which was playing on a small
television behind the front desk.

"You scared the bejeezus out of me," Nicola said, fixing an engine-red curl
that had gone rogue near her cheek. "Oh dear! Look at you. Alone again. Why'd
your mother bring you all this way if she was going to strand you so repeatedly?"

"It's fine," Annie said. "I don't mind being alone. I wanted to ask you about
this book I found . . ."

"You know, I can accompany you on some sightseeing adventures, if you'd
like!"

"No, that's okay. I don't want to take you away from the inn."

"Not a problem. My cousin is staying with us. A real do-nothing if you ask
me." Nicola rolled her eyes. "He can sit at the desk for a spell while you and
I paint the town."

"Really, it's fine," Annie said again. "Listen, I came across this biography."
She passed the book to Nicola.

"Have you read it?" Annie asked.

"Where'd you get this? Trudy's place?"

"Yes. Trudy's. Where else?"

Gus. Her mother. Now Nicola. If any of these people decided to ask Trudy
about her number one customer, she'd be in a hell of a tight spot.

"Ahh, Trudy," Nicola said. "We've known each other since we were girls."

"Yeah, she's a peach."

As Nicola squinted at the cover, Annie realized the book seemed more beat-
up than it had the day before. The blue was grayer, the pages more yellowed.

She snatched it back.

"Have you heard of it?" Annie asked. "Or the woman it's about?"

"Honey, if you don't let me see the book, I can't answer."

"Sorry. It's just fragile. Old."

"Aren't we all?" Nicola said. "Come now, show me the thing. Who's it about, did you say?"

She passed it back.

"*The Missing Duchess . . .*" Nicola read, showing little-to-no recognition whatsoever.

"She lived here," Annie said, cringing as Nicola's fingers made teeny grease spots on the linen. "Or so the story goes."

Was it possible the woman hadn't been the town terror or its most noteworthy citizen? Annie half expected Nicola to react like Gus, identifying the book on sight.

"The Duchess of Marlborough disappeared from her palace in the thirties," Annie said. "And was found in Banbury forty years later. Does any of this ring a bell?"

"Well, everyone knows Blenheim Palace and its celebrated Marlboroughs."

"Then you must know of the duchess?" Annie pressed. "Her real name was Gladys Deacon but she called herself Mrs. Spencer? Passed away in her nineties. Probably around 1978 or 1979?"

Nicola looped a strand of hair around her pinkie, mouth twisted in contemplation.

"I was under the impression the duchess was well-known in Banbury," Annie said. "Is that not true?"

"Could be. I grew up in Banbury but I didn't really live here, if you catch my meaning."

"Um, not exactly."

"Mum sent me off to school as soon as one would take me. She had many brilliant qualities, but mothering wasn't one of them. While I was growing up, Banbury was my 'home' but I was only ever here for school holidays."

"So you don't remember Mrs. Spencer?"

"Hmm. It's somewhat familiar. Although 'Spencers,' ya know."

"She ran naked through town?" Annie tried next. "And lived at the Grange?"

"The Grange?" Nicola made a face. "Oh God, that horrific bodge? What a place. I wish whoever owns it would do something with the property instead of letting it go to rot."

"So you *do* know the place?"

"You bet. My best girlfriend lives next door. She loves to josh about 'accidentally' setting the home on fire. Pat's just the type to do it, too, if she could avoid incinerating her own home in the process."

Nicola handed the book back.

"I have some recollection of the woman who lived there," she went on. "I was a wee thing when she was alive, and mostly away at school. But I do recall that the local schoolboys would sneak onto the property, carrying back enough ghost stories to fill a book. It's funny, now that I think about it, I always had the sense she was more legend than woman."

"I don't think you're alone in that."

"So, what's your interest?"

"Oh. Well." Annie paused. "She's a captivating figure. Obviously. Given she was the subject of ghost stories and folklore. And I'm an English major so reading about the writers she consorted with is pretty juicy. On top of that I'm, uh, working on a little research project . . ."

"A research project?" Nicola balked. "Your mum said you were unemployed. Out of university and with nothing to do vocationally."

"Did she now?"

In what manner did "Mum" drop that piece of knowledge? Was it said as a complaint? A matter of some unavoidable fact?

"Oh, golly, Annie, I didn't aim to upset you."

"Don't apologize, please. It's true. It's no vacation for me."

"She was perfectly lovely when she said so!" Nicola insisted. "Not bitter a'tall! Listen here, young lady. Whatever feelings a mum has toward her children are rooted in the feelings she has about herself."

"Gotcha," Annie said with a sharp nod. She was suddenly very anxious to get outside.

"No judgment here, m'dear. You're young. Faff about however you please. It's a young woman's privilege and there's plenty of time ahead for the serious bits. Your mum is a little overemployed if you ask me. Lord Almighty." Nicola shook her head, the curls moving in concert. "We're all so bloody damaged, aren't we?"

Annie nodded, mystified. Here was a woman with infinitely more depth than the innkeeper who greeted them, the one stewing in floral patterns for fifteen minutes straight. They were all so bloody damaged, indeed.

"Tell me about this project," Nicola said. "What do you plan to use for your research? Other than a ratty old book?"

"You said your friend lives next door to the Grange?"

"Patricia. That's her."

"I'd love to see the property," Annie said. "Learn a few ghost stories for myself. Do you have the address?"

"Sure. It's . . ." The woman thought about this. "Four Banbury Road. It's privately owned, by what purveyor of bad taste and poor neighborly manners I cannot guess, but privately held it is. It may be abandoned but you can't trample through willy-nilly. I don't s'pect you wish to be jailed for trespassing in a foreign country."

"No! I don't!" Annie barked out a laugh. "I only plan to check it out from the road."

Already Annie knew she'd try to get inside. As long as she didn't disturb anything, or take anything, the arresting authorities couldn't get too perturbed. If caught, she'd chalk it up to being a clumsy tourist, affect a foreign accent or feign a loose grasp on English if necessary. Annie knew a little Spanish, and some French.

"Well, if you stop past, pop by Patricia's afterward. She'd be chuffed to host you!"

"Will do. Thanks, Nicola."

"Care for a bike? You can walk but biking is always more fun! There are biking tourist groups these days, did ya know? Personally I don't fancy all that spandex, but they bring the business."

"Fantastic idea," Annie said. "I'd love to borrow one. Maybe I'll take a ride through the Cotswolds afterward. No spandex though, promise."

"A ride shouldn't be so bloody lonely, though." Nicola frowned.

"You're sweet to worry, but I'm an only child. Being alone is my gig and this is temporary. My mom isn't usually like this. She's retired, actually."

"Ha!" Nicola huffed. "Retired? Coulda fooled me. Anyhoo. Annie, I'm pleased to lend you a bike. Come with me, I'll show you where we keep them."

Thirteen

THE GRANGE
CHACOMBE-AT-BANBURY, OXFORDSHIRE, ENGLAND
NOVEMBER 2001

And what of the husband, of Gladys's father?

Edward Deacon knew all too well of his wife's flexible marital standards, likewise her flexible legs and other body parts. And he was fully apprised of the manner in which these parts interacted with Abeille's.

But Florence swept off his concerns, forever reminding her husband of his lack of culture and sophistication. Parisian flirtations were common, expected even! The only people who clucked about it were the help.

—J. Casper Augustine Seton,
The Missing Duchess: A Biography

Annie pedaled up Banbury Road into Chacombe Parish, eyes fixed on the horizon.

Somewhere past the huddled limestone cottages sat the Grange. She pictured a towering, crumbling manse, a building stooped and keening. It would lord over everything beside it, casting a long and crooked shadow across town.

But before Annie stumbled upon any decayed manors, the road split, right there in the middle of a bunch of very unimposing homes. Middleton Road went right, the Ring veered to the left. Banbury Road had ended.

"What the hell?"

She stopped her bike on a triangular patch of grass and examined the sign again. One car puttered past, and then another. In the distance she heard the squabble of birds.

"Banbury Road?" she said, taking a few laps around the sign. "Where did you go?"

The bird chirping intensified and soon Annie realized these were not geese but a flock of middle-aged women walking hurriedly in her direction.

"Excuse me!" she called to the fast-walkers. Annie jogged toward them, wheeling her bike alongside. "Pardon! Sorry to bother you!"

They didn't slow, not a hitch in their pace.

"If I could have just a minute of your time!"

The women halted in unison. They each raised a left brow, the seamless choreography of a tight-knit and determined group.

"Hi!" Annie said brightly. "I'm a researcher. From out of town. Do you know where I might find the Grange?"

The women stared vacantly.

"The Grange?" Annie repeated, squinting in the sun. "At number four, Banbury Road. Next door to 'Patricia'?"

It was possible one of them knew her. It was possible one of them *was* her. Perhaps Annie could name-drop bookstore Trudy next.

"You passed it already," a woman told her.

"Yes, I know I passed the road. That's the problem, I can't figure out how to pick it back up again."

"No," another said. "You passed the Grange. A few lengths back."

"What?" Annie turned toward the path from which she'd come. "That can't be right."

They were in Chacombe proper. The George & Dragon was within a few blocks' distance. The buildings around her all looked the same: limestone, each one rolling into the next as naturally as the grass and trees and boxwood surrounding them. There wasn't a haunted house in sight.

"I'm trying to find the *Grange*," Annie said, enunciating. Maybe they had trouble with the accent Gus accused her of having. "The estate where the Duchess of Marlborough once lived? Mrs. Spencer?"

"That's the spot," one confirmed, pointing. "Four Banbury Road. You can see the front gate from here."

They spun around and continued on their speedy way.

Winded, and with a stitch in her side, Annie checked the address she'd written down. Four Banbury Road, just as the women said. Why hadn't Gus told her the Grange was only a few blocks from the pub?

"What a pain in the ass he is," she groused, and leaned her bike against a tree.

Hands on hips, she studied the building at 4 Banbury Road, along with the ones beside it. Annie understood why everyone had been in Mrs. Spencer's business. Her neighbors had had no choice. They probably saw her crawling into bed with Pru.

Annie hadn't imagined the Grange to be in the thick of things. The property itself was sprawling, but the main home was not the ever-growing behemoth Pru saw when she first walked through its halls. Even Goose Creek Hill was bigger.

Well, this shouldn't take long, Annie thought.

Stepping gingerly toward the front gate, she could almost feel Mrs. Spencer—and Pru—on the other side of it. Annie shook her head. It'd been thirty years. Those people were long gone.

At the gate she paused. There was a note tacked onto it, dated a few days before.

Application for Grade II building: House. Early 18th century. Coursed limestone and ironstone rubble, missing roof, brick stacks, two stories plus attic, three bays. Main doorway in second bay from right and has wood lintel and plank door. Four-light window to right has wood lintel, wood mullions, and iron casement. Similar three-light window to left. Doorway in second bay from left has wood lintel and four-panel door, part glazed. Two-light window to left with wood lintel, wood mullions, and iron casement. Similar window on first floor. Left gable end is coped with kneelers.

Annie slipped it into her pocket. So much for her promise not to touch anything.

With a deep breath, she nudged the gate. It creaked open. Annie glanced around for prying neighbors, or another crop of speed-walkers. She wouldn't have to contend with whizzing bullets or screaming harpies but Annie was trespassing. She was committing a crime.

With not another soul in sight, Annie ventured farther onto the property, crunching across thick blankets of rebellious roses and weeds. She stepped over cement statues and upended lawn furniture as she made her way to the north side of the home, and a partially hidden door. It didn't face the street, but Annie remained at the mercy of any Chacombe busybodies nonetheless.

Peering over her shoulder, Annie turned the knob. So this was it. She was going inside.

The door stuck.

She tried again, jiggling and pulling. Despite the effort—and the cursing—the door remained firmly locked. So did the next one, and all of the doors after that. It was a lot of security for a home with so many broken windows.

"Good grief," Annie muttered, clearing the glass from a nearby dormer with her backpack, speed-walkers be damned. *"New study finds majoring in literature may result in nefarious behavior."*

Annie tossed her bag over the casement and hoisted herself into the frame. Her years spent as a cut-rate gymnast were finally paying off. Laurel would be proud that all those participant ribbons could so nicely lead to a life of crime.

Holding her breath, Annie pushed aside the heavy black drapes which, according to the book, the duchess doused in oil four times per year. No surprise there, Annie thought. They smelled of something old and faraway.

"Yuck." She coughed, and then covered her mouth.

Once all the way inside, Annie rested on the sill and assessed the room. Below her were scattered papers, a few books, and what appeared to be a collection of rib cages from small animals. No one could really die in the haunted house from some old book, right?

As her stomach seesawed, Annie jumped down.

She was in a dining room, judging from the long oak table that dominated the space. The chairs were gone. On the walls, rectangles marked the places artwork once hung. Annie treaded down the hallway. As she walked up the stairs, the wood made not a clonking sound but something squishier, like moss. Annie caught her breath at the top step, grateful that her mom wouldn't have to suffer the stigma of a death-by-burgling obituary.

"All right, Grange," she said. "Whatcha got for me?"

In the first bedroom, Annie found a bare mattress on the floor, beside it a collapsed bed frame filled with books. Hardy. Proust. Wharton. She was reaching toward one of the Hardys, *Tess of the d'Urbervilles,* when her hand brushed against something cold.

Annie leaped back. It was a revolver.

Choking and wheezing, she sprinted into the neighboring bedroom. Annie lived in hunt country but she'd never touched a gun.

"It's just an old piece of metal," she told herself, heart punching the inside of her chest. "It's not like it can go off on its own."

Or maybe it could. What did Annie know about firearms? What did she know about old lady ghosts who liked to shoot them while alive?

"Good grief, get a hold of yourself," she said. "Ghost stories. Nothing more."

Annie looped around the room four times in an effort to calm herself down.

"Annie," she said. "Don't be such a wuss."

Inhaling, she surveyed the room. In it sat another bed, its frame intact. Beside the bed was a desk. On the desk, a typewriter. Annie craned her neck to more closely scrutinize the walls. Yep, those were bullet holes.

Aside from its one-inch frosting of dust, not to mention a healthy mountain of black soot accumulated in the fireplace, the room was relatively neat. A bed. A desk. A few pieces of paper. Annie's dorm rooms were far worse. Where was all the clutter Gus promised? The old lady hoarding? This was starting to look like a waste of a misdemeanor.

Sighing, Annie crouched to inspect beneath the bed. That's where the good stuff usually was. Even she had had incriminating evidence under hers back in the day. A roommate's skirt borrowed without asking. A mostly empty vodka bottle. A pack of cigarettes, only one used.

"What, no guns?" Annie said. "Mrs. Spencer. I'm disappointed."

Aside from dirt and grime and dead spiders, all that was under there was scattered paper, typewritten from the looks of it. With a gnash of her teeth, Annie stretched as far under the bed as she could muster and made contact with a few sheets. After dragging them out, she sat back on her heels, her knees gray from the dust.

"Transcripts?" she said, her eyes scanning the page.

The author's notes? An interview? Annie flicked through the pages.

Surely you'd encountered the duke at some point.

You met at Blenheim, you said?

Come, Mrs. Spencer. Please sit back down.

She didn't know if the pages had value or if they'd matter to anyone still alive. But ace researcher that she was, Annie did understand one thing. She was looking at the very start of the story, the place where *The Missing Duchess* began.

Fourteen

WS: You tell me you're not the duchess.

GD: Because I'm not.

WS: But you ran in celebrated circles. Surely you'd encountered the duke at some point.

GD: Of course I met the duke.

WS: Because you were married to him.

GD: I'm sorry you think a lady must marry every man she meets.

WS: But his family reported, multiple times, that his missing wife is here, at the Grange. Mugnier the priest made similar statements.

GD: Yes, yes, I can see why a priest who died thirty years ago would know who lives in Oxfordshire today. Tell me, Seton, how long do you plan to go round and round like this? I've told you. I never loved the Duke of Marlborough.

WS: But you were married to him.

GD: We had no kind of marriage.

WS: But you knew him.

GD: Didn't I just say that? Yes, of course I knew him! I have a crumb of social standing, for the love of Christ.

WS: How did you meet?

GD: The duke? Blenheim, I suppose. It's hard to recall. It was his wife Coon who brought me round. She was my closest girl.

WS: Note to manuscript. Coon is Consuelo Vanderbilt, the prior Duchess of Marlborough.

GD: Note to manuscript. This author is a tosser. Who needs to be reminded of Coon?

WS: Okay, then. Tell me about your friendship with Consuelo. How did you meet?

GD: Actually, now that I think about it, I met her through the duke, instead of the other way around. Yes. That's right. I encountered him at a London soiree when I was sixteen. Coon wasn't there. She

was recuperating from the birth of their first child.
Wretched child, that.

WS: Your future stepson?

GD: You'll never hear me claiming that wanker as
part of my family. Anyhow, old Marlborough thought
his wife and I would get along famously. He took me
to Blenheim to meet her. Coon was in the doldrums
and he wanted me to perk her up.

WS: You were sixteen when this happened?

GD: Yes. Why do I feel like I'm repeating myself?

WS: Very well. So the year was 1897.

GD: Yes. Wait! No! No. That's just silly. It couldn't
have been 1897 as I would've only been two years old!
[Laughs] A mere toddler!

WS: But instead you were sixteen?

GD: Yes. As I've mentioned. Repeatedly.

WS: Well, you've just implied you were born in 1895,
and 1895 plus sixteen is 1911.

GD: Oh, the writer is good with numbers, is
he?

WS: By 1911, the duke and duchess had been separated
four years. She wasn't recuperating from childbirth
and in fact she'd already moved out of Blenheim and
was living on her own.

GD: Well, perhaps I was younger. Maybe the year was . . . 1909? I would've been—

WS: Fourteen. By your math. But I saw your name in the guest registries at the palace, written in 1901.

GD: Ever hear of a transposition error? Sakes alive, do you fancy yourself a bloody mathematician or a writer? The year is not the point. The point is that Coon and Sunny—

WS: Note to manuscript. Sunny—

GD: Was the Duke of Marlborough. Earl of Sunderland. Ergo, Sunny. Jesus. Are you going to do this for our entire interview?

WS: I just might.

Fifteen

GD: She was beautiful, Coon was. Dark, exotic. She had these slightly slanting eyes.

WS: Note to manuscript. Mrs. Spencer is pushing at the corners of her eyelids, as if to demonstrate the slant. Now she's rolling her eyes.

GD: [Snort] Coon had a touch of the Japanese about her.

WS: In contrast to your fair skin and those wide, haunting blue peepers of yours.

GD: Well, I wouldn't call them haunting. But yes. The contrast made us stand out when jaunting about Paris. Italy and Germany, too.

WS: It must've been startling; the differences Sunny saw when he watched the two of you together.

GD: Forget Sunny. We enchanted half of Europe with our differences. Black and white. Dark and light. Though, of course, we were both beautiful. I can say that now that I'm as old as Methuselah.

WS: You're still beautiful, Mrs. Spencer.

GD: Full of bollocks, but I appreciate the favor of your compliment. In any event, our personalities were as different as our visages. She was so shy, sweet Coon. Most didn't know she was also hard of hearing. Her reputation for being snobbish was mostly due to this.

WS: "A black swan aloof in soundless waters."

GD: Yes, that was my Coon. Poor thing, so depressed in that cumbersome palace. I tried to buoy her. Brighten her marriage, that home, her life. It was all so utterly, heartbreakingly without an ounce of cheer.

WS: Reports have you cheering multiple members of the home.

GD: Well, I tried. Hold on. Surely you're not referring to Sunny?

WS: Why would I be referring to the duke?

GD: Let me tell you. I was a WELCOME distraction to Sunny and Coon.

WS: Note to manuscript. Mrs. Spencer smacked the table when she said the word "welcome."

GD: That table won't be the only thing smacked if you don't knock it off.

WS: Mrs. Spencer, please continue.

GD: I can't! I've completely lost my mind!

WS: Most would agree.

GD: Not my mind! My train of thought! You have me so befuddled. You're a wretched conversationalist, you know that?

WS: My conversational skills are probably why I've become a writer. Come, Mrs. Spencer. Please sit back down. That's better. Now. Please tell me why you were a welcome [Clap] distraction at Blenheim.

GD: Because the poor girl didn't want to marry the man in the first place. Then he installed her in that god-awful monstrosity of an alleged home.

WS: Most find Blenheim unmatched in beauty and grandeur in the United Kingdom. Even the world, if not for Versailles. The royal family envies the palace. It's better than anything they've got.

GD: I don't give a damn about the royal family and their shit tastes. They've never had to live there. And they should count themselves lucky. Otherwise they'd be even more miserable than they already are.

WS: But the stately rooms? The gardens? The grottos?

GD: The palace was oppressive. Coon had a

predilection for melancholy and that home sucked every ray of sunshine from the tender girl's soul. She cried every night. She prayed for God to turn her into a vestal virgin.

WS: Vestal virgin?

GD: A woman freed of the social obligation to marry and bear children. Of course she was far too late for that.

WS: Sounds like Coon had a glum personality.

GD: She wasn't a zippy sort, no. But let me tell you, when the Marlboroughs separated and she moved to London, Coon flourished as a single hostess.

WS: And after she made her move, you swooped in and made yours.

GD: I've haven't swooped a day in my life.

WS: When Coon left Sunny, and was finally happy, you were free to pursue your best friend's husband, free to consummate the simmering attraction you'd felt for a decade.

GD: Attraction. Ha. Give me some credit.

WS: Your stepson reported that you behaved shamelessly toward Sunny, even when he was married to your Coon.

GD: You mean Henry? He's about as reliable as a drunk. Did I flirt with Sunny? Yes. At times. Just as

I flirted with five to eleven other men in a given
evening. There's nothing wrong with a little
Parisian flirtation, as my mother always said.

WS: Parisian flirtation usually refers to sex. Note
to manuscript. Mrs. Spencer's face has reddened.

GD: Listen here, you tosser. In those years, Coon
meant everything to me. Could you imagine? If I'd
been in love with my best friend's husband?

WS: Yes. I can imagine. "She had no tolerance for
scenes which were not of her own making."

GD: ARE YOU QUOTING EDITH WHARTON AT ME?

WS: Ah. The woman has a sharp ear for literature.

GD: Edith was my friend. And she would be outraged,
a hack like you vomiting up her sublime words.

WS: So you're angrier at my quoting of Edith Wharton
than with the implication you stole your best
friend's husband?

GD: For God's sake, yes! Because the implication is
so ridiculous. Coon was my best friend.

WS: But it happens, Mrs. Spencer. It happens all
the time.

GD: Stealing someone's husband is an awfully big
responsibility. If a woman chooses that path, she'd
better be damned sure the man is worth the effort. And
lest there be any doubt, most men are decidedly not.

Sixteen

Gladys's mother was pregnant with her fourth and final daughter, Dorothy, when her marriage took its final hit.

The pregnancy itself was a source of contention, as Edward Deacon suspected the baby wasn't his. Not an unreasonable fear given the hours his wife spent in Abeille's company, and the time Edward saw the two of them exiting a lingerie shop together. And who was the first person to lay eyes on baby Dorothy after she was born? Abeille himself. Edward was inflamed.

"All French women receive these platonic visits from their men friends while they are lying-in," Florence claimed, always quick to chalk up bad behavior to Parisian sensibilities.

His wife wasn't French and so Edward remained unswayed by the country's customs. Adultery was adultery, especially when one was from the States.

Not that Florence or Abeille were concerned by Edward's fury or his threats. To them he was nothing but a silly, harmless dilettante. They certainly did not consider him the type of man who'd chase his wife's lover about a room and then shoot him three times through a couch.

—J. Casper Augustine Seton.
The Missing Duchess: A Biography

Annie found Gus in the same corner booth, sipping his same type of cider. How many years had he done this for? she wondered.

"Hello," she said and tapped his shoulder. "I hoped I'd find you here."

"This is a refreshing development," Gus said, removing his glasses. He folded up the paper in front of him and went to stand.

"No, please," she said. "Don't get up."

Annie sat across from him.

"Mind if I join you?"

"I believe you already have," he said with a smile, an echo of her words from the day before. "So, working hard as per usual?"

"Work?" She blinked.

"Your thesis?"

"Oh right." She sagged in her seat. "Yes. Well, I'm kind of stalled out right now."

"Perhaps you should focus on your research," he said with a wry smile. "Instead of whatever you've been getting into today. Your clothes are filthy."

Annie glanced down. It looked like someone had dredged her in dust. Pinching together her fingers, she lifted a string of cobwebs from her jeans.

"I borrowed one of the inn's bikes this morning," she said. "I guess I'm a messy cyclist. Now that you mention it . . ."

"What did I mention?"

"I went past the Grange today on my ride."

In lieu of a response, Gus took a sip of cider.

"You know, the Grange?" Annie said, forehead lifted. "Home to Mrs. Spencer? And to Pru?"

He nodded, lips pinched together, gray eyes holding steady with hers.

"You didn't tell me it was, like, around the corner," she said.

Gus cleared his throat.

"Didn't I?" he said.

"You did not." Annie shifted in her seat. "And, boy, did I get the wrong impression of the place. You made it seem so massive. Hulking."

"Is that right?"

"Yep. But it was pretty much just a regular house. What's up with that? The story. What I saw." Annie held her hands at two different levels. "They don't match up."

"I don't recall ever commenting on its size."

"But what about Pru? When she walked through, she felt like the home was changing and growing around her."

"She did, but in a way that had little to do with verifiable square meters."

"And the inside, it was . . ."

Gus's eyebrows shot up.

"The inside was *what*?"

Annie stopped, then added in a lame mumble: "Probably more cavernous."

"Any other observations?" Gus asked, eyeing her, sizing her up. "About the property? From the road, naturally. Because you have more sense than to trespass."

"You bet! Tons of sense! I'd never do anything like that!"

"That's a relief," he said. "So is this why you tracked me down? To express your disappointment in the home's size and make promises as to your ability to follow laws?"

"Yes. That." Annie pulled the book from her backpack, careful not to let any stolen papers sneak out. "But also *The Missing Duchess*. I need more."

She slid the book toward Gus.

"For example," she said. "How long after Pru came to work for Mrs. Spencer did the author show up? Didn't you say it was around Christmastime?"

"Yep," he said, and drained the last of his cider. "Late December. Ned! Hey, barkeep! How 'bout you bring me two more? One for now, one for the road."

"Sure thing, mate," the man said and sniggered amiably. "One for the road. As if you could ever hold out that long."

Gus turned back toward Annie.

"So," he said. "Is this how it aims to be? The young researcher batters the local fogy with questions, no time for pleasantries and how-do-you-dos?"

"I'm sorry," Annie said with a wince. "My manners are, shall we say, blunted these days. My mom would be appalled. Let's start over. So. How are you this afternoon?"

"I'm adequate." He smirked.

"Nice weather, eh?"

"Not particularly."

"So, uh, what do you do in your free time? Hobbies or anything?"

"You're looking at it."

"What about a wife? Kids?"

Or grandkids, she did not add. Gus was the right age to have them but Annie had sufficiently offended him for one day. No use pointing out that she saw him as old.

"Kids?" he said. "Nah. Not me."

"Oh, I, uh. I'm sorry to hear that."

"Sorry? Why? It's not an affliction, merely a fact. I'm close with my niece. She's damned good enough for me."

"Sounds like you made the right decision, then," Annie said awkwardly.

She was pretty wretched at this pleasantry business, his requested how-do-you-dos.

"No wife, either," Gus said. "And before you ask, I've never been married because I never found the right woman. Simple explanation for a lifetime of questions."

Annie tried to conjure up an artful response.

Sorry, mate.

The game's not over.

In the next life, maybe less booze.

"So, this banter is going well," she said with a rigid smile.

Suddenly Annie wished *she* had a drink in front of her and contemplated flagging down Ned.

"Bloody sad," Gus said.

"Well, I've heard marriage is more trouble than it's worth. Parenthood too. My mom—"

"What? No. Not that. On the telly."

Annie looked at the screen above the bar. On instinct, her stomach clenched.

The feelings never changed, no matter how many times she watched the footage. A second plane into a building. The smoke-crush of the towers to the ground. Mayhem erupting on camera. All the mayhem that could not be seen. Even after a hundred viewings it didn't seem real.

"Jesus," she said, recoiling with the impact.

Here they were, nearly two months out, and the news would not move on, not even in some other country.

"Haven't the faintest why they keep showing it," Gus said.

"I agree." Annie's eyes remained glued to the screen. "It's messed up."

"Did you know anyone?" He pointed toward the television. "Lost that day?'

"Yes," she said. "No one close. But yes."

She had a friend, a sorority sister named Megan, who died in one of the towers. Megan worked a bond-trading desk, whatever that meant, and was engaged to be married. She would always be that. Engaged. Her future lost in the rubble.

Most people who lived on the East Coast knew someone who worked at the World Trade Center, or someone who knew someone. Megan was a few years ahead in school so they weren't close, despite being "sisters." But it was hard not to be sad about her death. And harder still not to feel like a jerk, as though Annie were using Megan for some twisted claim to fame.

"I'm sorry," Gus said. "About your friend. A damned tragedy."

"Thanks. And it was. But like I said, we weren't close."

"Doesn't make it any less awful."

"I guess you're right. It feels weird—unnatural—to think she's not around."

She heard the quiver in her own voice.

"And yet," Gus said. "The deaths carry on."

"It really is sickening how often they replay the footage. Here's hoping a celebrity does something awful ASAP."

"I was referring to the new deaths," Gus said. "The servicemen and women. All those young people now going off to war, and to what end?"

Her face blanched.

"Sorry, Annie, I know he's your president and all," Gus said. "But I'm suspicious. I mean, hell, not too hard to get a nation behind you if everyone's afraid and desperate to believe in something."

Annie covered her mouth with a hand. Desperate. Is that what they were?

Eric was fine. He would be fine. At any rate, he was at that moment safe, on a float, in the middle of the ocean. Annie had nearly convinced herself that it was the *only* place he'd be until they saw each other again.

"The prez had to do something, right?" Gus continued. "Make a show. And people are rallying because revenge is sweet. It's like what Mrs. Spencer said about Hitler. 'Well, he had the whole world up in arms!' "

"I hardly think Bush is Hitler."

"No, no, of course not. I don't mean to get political. I know this is a sensitive topic for you Yanks. Easy to criticize when it's someone else's damned country. Even if we're sticking our necks in it, too. Blimey, Annie, you're downright green. I'm the biggest arse around."

"Don't, uh," Annie sputtered. "It's just, um, unpleasant. Sad. Whatever your politics. Sometimes I don't even know what to think myself."

Gus nodded, took a sip of cider.

" 'The war has not accustomed me to death,' " he said, changing the tenor of his voice.

"Proust?" she said.

"Bingo." He pointed the glass toward her. "Mrs. Spencer's favorite. I adore you bookish girls."

"I'm engaged," she blurted. "To a marine. He's on his way to Afghanistan right now. That's why I got so upset about the war comment."

"Oh Christ," Gus said. "Jesus f'ing Christ. I noticed the band on your finger, and that you twirl it continuously. I should've asked but figured you'd tell me if you wanted me to know. What an arse. What a goddamned arse."

"No. It's okay," she said, although it wasn't. Not exactly. Annie closed her eyes. "I wish he was in a different line of business. An accountant. Going to law school. But this is what he chose. And he was a marine long before we met."

She opened her eyes again and was surprised to find herself taking a sip of Gus's drink.

"The ironic part is that Marines aren't deploying to Afghanistan, as a rule," she said. "He just happened to be going on an MEU, a marine ship, that was already deploying. And now they have the pleasure of being some of the first associated with the war. Oh, excuse me, Operation Enduring Freedom."

"Shite. Wrong place at the wrong time."

"Yep."

Then again, had he not been deploying, they never would've met. Less than one percent of Marines were going out. Inconceivable odds, though her best friend Summer called them the odds of finding true love. Annie and Eric were destined for each other, she insisted. It sounded giddy and perfect on three glasses of pinot noir, but a war was a big price to pay.

"That's some tough stuff," Gus said. "I don't know what to say."

"No one does. And don't feel like you have to. It could be worse."

She thought of the 9/11 families, the spaces now empty in thousands of lives.

"Engaged to a bloke going off to war," he said with a cluck. "Not unlike our Pru."

"God, I hope I'm nothing like Pru. Especially in the fiancé department."

"Blimey, none of this is coming out like I've intended. I didn't mean to imply—"

"Please." Annie slapped at the air. "You haven't said anything untrue. All I can do is assume I'll see him again, that Eric's safe return is the only possible outcome. Everything else is fiction, happening to a bunch of unlucky bastards without faces or names."

"A bloody decent stance to have."

"My mom accuses me of being too romantic, of living in literature and books. But I'm a-okay ignoring the bad stuff and only picturing the ship returning; the thousands of family members waiting near the harbor.

"In my little fantasy, when he returns, the government will give Eric a desk and a phone at the Pentagon. We'll have a couple of kids and they'll grow up knowing their father was a hero once, even though he's transformed into an ordinary dad. Delusions. But they work for me."

"Lovely delusions," Gus said, eyes watering. "All of them."

"Well, I've always favored fiction," she said with a defeated sigh. "To quote Edith Wharton, 'We can't behave like people in novels, though, can we?'" Annie took another sip of his cider. "Though I'd like to wager that we can."

Suddenly Mrs. Spencer's words popped into Annie's head. "ARE YOU QUOTING EDITH WHARTON AT ME?" For a moment she found a smile.

"That's what I like to see," Gus said. "A cheerful Annie."

"And cheerful Annie is who I prefer to be." She shook her head. "Time to change the subject before I turn into a puddled mess. Please, Gus, take me back to the Grange." She pointed toward the book. "Help me forget, for a little while."

"That's a mighty tall order."

"It worked for Pru," Annie said, forcing a brightness she did not feel. "She got over her fiancé, eventually. Right? Otherwise this story is just too sad."

Gus frowned. It was a long while before he spoke again.

"One could say it worked out," he said at last. "I suppose. Depending on the one you asked."

Seventeen

After a week at the Grange, Pru's activities fell into a steady rhythm.

Whatever apprehension she first felt about waking up with a ninety-year-old woman in her bed, to speak nothing of the accompanying milky old-lady smell, she soon got over. Or she ignored for the sake of her ongoing employment. Pru had nowhere else to go.

Though she grew accustomed to the pattern of her days, the nights were another matter. Unexpected bedmates notwithstanding, Pru struggled to sleep, mostly because of the voices. Real or imagined, in her head or in the home, muffled conversations disrupted any hope of peace.

The darkness brought with it the sound of a male, sometimes a woman, and it happened nearly every night. Pru mentioned it once, to Mrs. Spencer's vast hilarity. Perhaps the bed reserved at the O'Connell Ward should go to Pru instead, she guffawed. Although, every once in a while, Mrs. Spencer would ascribe the voices to Tom.

Come dawn, Pru didn't have time to ponder the disturbances on account of the fifty or so spaniels she tended to daily. She fed the dogs, tidied their messes, groomed them, and then mopped up ever more messes due to their very efficient digestive tracks. With no less than twelve bitches and an unending parade of newly born pups, there wasn't a hairless speck of real estate in the whole bloody place.

"Miss Valentine!" Mrs. Spencer would call out. "Reina. Have you seen Reina? No one sets foot off this property until we find Reina."

Better finding Reina than serving midwife to Princess. Pru had seen enough puppy births to know she didn't want to see more of them. Not that she had a choice.

Alas, despite the amount of time she spent with them, Pru couldn't distinguish Reina from Arthur from Bixby from fuck-all. The dogs all looked the same to her, male or female, from this litter or from that.

But Pru played the game. She'd roam the yard aimlessly looking for Reina, with a solemn face of purpose but accomplishing nothing. Mrs. Spencer always found the missing pooch, in the end.

And then there were the cats. All of those cats. Twenty-five? A hundred? They were too bountiful to estimate. The cats were the reason for the unplugged refrigerator, as it turned out. Whenever a feline met its demise, Mrs. Spencer stored it in the icebox to be dealt with later. Of course, later never came.

The work was dull, but constant, Pru's hours mostly packed. When she had a spare moment, Pru meandered into town to grab a bite of something perishable, a treat she couldn't enjoy at home thanks to the cat-in-the-icebox arrangement. For her part, Mrs. Spencer ate minimally, which matched up with her gaunt frame well enough.

Charlie would've been horrified to see his fiancée reduced to such circumstances, but Pru didn't mind all that much. More puppies nipping at her legs meant less time thinking of Charlie, dusty and alone in the family mausoleum. Where did he die first? she often wondered. Was it in his head, or at his heart?

And Mrs. Spencer had a knack for detecting when her employee's mind began to stray. The second she noticed Pru was not fully engaged with the task at hand, Mrs. Spencer dialed up a ribald Parisian tale or yet another reference to the barn man Tom.

"Did I tell you about the time he kidnapped those German POWs for me?" Mrs. Spencer asked one afternoon while they waited for a dog to finish laboring.

"Kidnapped? Why, Mrs. Spencer? Banbury too short on men for you?"

"Very funny, Miss Valentine. No, my apple trees required pruning and Tom is afraid of heights."

"And you desperately needed your trees cut back?" Pru said. "In the middle of a war?"

"It was 1945 thus hardly the middle. Regardless, Tom showed up with two Krauts and they got to it straightaway. The men were knowledgeable, quick, and well behaved. Those are the Germans for you. Oh look! Here comes the first puppy of the litter!"

Mrs. Spencer was not the only individual who liked to raise the topic of Tom. Locals were also keen to discuss the man, though they didn't know what to make of him either.

It was universally agreed upon that Tom had lived among them at one time but fell into a black hole of existence around 1953. One person seemed to recall the German POW story, but couldn't be sure.

"Have you seen him?" they all asked.

"Have you found the body?"

"There must be a body."

"How about bones?"

"A mummified corpse?"

Pru didn't fault them for their macabre assumptions. Who hadn't seen the movie *Psycho*? Possessed by a dead mother, or a dead landscaper, it was all the same. Plus Mrs. Spencer was considered a bit of a psycho herself, given her propensity to tear through town shouting obscenities and threatening peoples' lives.

"You speak to me that way again, Mr. Haverford, and you'd better check for a bomb beneath the hood of your precious lorry!"

"It's Harris, not Haverford. And I'm a missus, not a mister!"

"Car bomb, old man! Beware the car bomb!"

"I don't mean it," Mrs. Spencer would insist later, at home, by the stove. "Some people like to hunt. This is my sport."

After only a few weeks, Pru had several dozen stories like these to tell.

Was she afraid of the old woman? Perhaps. But a month in, Pru had sustained no serious injuries, physical or otherwise. Even the verbal insults did not much sting. The most threatening aspects to life at the Grange were the partially collapsed ceilings and gaping holes in the floors.

"Don't worry, Charlie," Pru would say to the night sky. "Guns? Rumored dead bodies? That's nothing. It'll be rotted wood that does me in."

In the end, Pru decided tales of Tom were nothing more than village scuttle-butt. And the voices she heard were probably the adolescent boys who skulked around the property, using slingshots to hurl pebbles and other projectiles through the windows. Pru herself had been beamed in the head with a turnip.

Plus it was in Mrs. Spencer's very nature to play up rumors of the man. The woman knew full well the townsfolk longed for a gothic tale. Everyone loved a ghost story and so she gave them one. There'd probably never been a Tom at all. It's what Pru told herself anyhow. She had to find some comfort, enough to allow for a little rest.

Eighteen

"I'm going to make Christmas dinner!" Mrs. Spencer announced.

"Hmm," Pru answered, on reflex.

Christmas dinner. It was probably another of the woman's ambitious schemes that never came to fruition. Just like the proposed freight elevator and in-ground swimming pool.

"What do you think, Miss Valentine?"

"Sounds fab," she said.

Pru glanced down and made a face. Puppy gunk. Everywhere.

"Does he really need to be hand-fed?" she asked.

This particular dog was fed via eyedropper three times per day, for no discernible reason other than he was particular, like so many other creatures in that house. Meanwhile they had no shortage of runts and spaniels with eating problems that were left to fend for themselves.

"Miss Valentine? Are you listening?"

Though she wasn't listening, Pru nodded and wiped both hands on her trousers. Already her sartorial standards had fallen into grand disrepair. Not that there was anyone around to notice.

"What do you think, then?" Mrs. Spencer pressed. "A homemade Christmas?"

"Really?" Pru said as the pup nipped at her hand, breaking the skin. "You're serious about it?"

"Of course I'm serious!"

"A dinner seems like a lot of effort."

And unsanitary besides, what with the stove used for foot warming and home heating and the dead cats in the fridge.

"You think I can't cook?" Mrs. Spencer said. "Is that the problem?"

"Heavens no," Pru said, though that was exactly what she thought. "I truly believe you can do anything you set your mind to."

And this was equally true. The woman was old, frail, her mind forever careening into faraway places and long-ago years. Yet through the cobwebbed stories of Proust and Paris and grand literary salons, Mrs. Spencer remained formidable somehow. She was made of strength, a rare metal perhaps, available only to the elite.

"It's the kitchen," Mrs. Spencer guessed. "You think the kitchen is in poor shape."

She couldn't help it: Pru laughed.

"Is something funny, Miss Valentine?"

"Mrs. Spencer, I don't *think* the kitchen is in poor shape. I *know* it is. There's only one working appliance and you use it to warm your toes."

On top of that there were at best three and a half plates plus a dodgy spattering of pots, most of them filthy black. Forks were used for dog grooming, and just that morning Pru had watched Mrs. Spencer scrape calluses from her heels with a silver spatula.

"You think I can't make do?" Mrs. Spencer said with a hip-jut and a humph. "I was in Paris during the Great War. The first German shells hit in 1918 and not a week later I made Easter dinner in my very quaint kitchen. We were under ration!"

"Mrs. Spencer . . ."

There was no way to hear the word "Easter" without Pru's brain tacking "Offensive" on the end of it. A holiday, forever ruined. Of course, for Pru, most things ambled back to Charlie eventually.

"And it wasn't merely the limited ingredients I was dealing with," Mrs. Spencer continued. "When I ventured out for provisions a shell landed thirty yards before me."

"Mrs. Spencer, *please*."

"My skirt was blown straight over my head! I was saved from flying shrapnel, and certain death, by my fur shawl. Miss Valentine, you're so pale. You weren't even there."

"I don't like talking about wars."

She'd not told Mrs. Spencer the details of her so-called broken engagement. While the much-maligned "Edith Junior" was apprised of the situation, the two didn't speak. Or if Edith spoke, Mrs. Spencer didn't listen. For now, Charlie's death was a fact Pru kept for herself. She didn't know how Mrs. Spencer might use the information against her. Pru only sensed that she would.

"You don't like wars? What do you even know of wars? Pretty girl locked safely in a house? Miss Valentine, right before me." Mrs. Spencer tightened her jaw. She aggressively wiped away tears that were not even there. "Right before me four people were blown to atoms. For ten days I was constantly seasick from the memory of the sight."

"Blown to atoms." Pru cringed. "Wonderful. Many thanks for such a detailed description."

"You are so weak-livered! My only point is that in a kitchen much smaller than ours and with bombs exploding around me, I devised a gourmet spread for a group of twelve."

"I'm sure you impressed everyone with your talents," Pru said as the dog hurtled down from her lap and took to relieving himself on a nearby rug. "But we're not in Paris and there's no war. At least not here. We have other options for a holiday feast. Plus you hate Christmas. What did you tell me? It is more . . ."

"More a day of sad recording of changes come than of satisfied banter. But no matter. I'm doing this! We're doing this!"

The old woman sprang to her feet, dogs and eyedroppers flying. Without putting away the supplies or even changing out of her bedclothes, Mrs. Spencer grabbed a pair of boots and her old straw hat, and set out to town in her little black Austin.

"Dare I eat the feast?" Pru griped as she lifted herself from the ground. "Four medium cats, cooked in a red wine reduction sauce. Ouch! Damn it!"

She nearly tripped over a dog.

"So . . . many . . . animals . . .," she said wearily and paused at the window.

Gazing out across the orchard, Pru placed both hands at her back, which ached from hunching over dogs. As she stretched, Pru noted how beautiful the property was that time of day. The sky was flat, the light draping across the frosted vines and branches. It hadn't snowed but they promised it soon would. Moments like these, the Grange was not so bad.

As Pru turned away from the window, something caught her eye: a flash of white. A chill shot through her body. The white was from a man's shirt.

After fumbling about for a pair of moccasins, Pru slipped on her shoes and tramped out across the yard, a coat wrapped tightly around her nightclothes. Pajamas in public were apparently de rigueur at the Grange. *Birds of a feather,* she thought with a smirk.

Suddenly, across the yard, the white flashed a second time.

Only the boy hoodlums, Pru told herself as her heart drummed. But not even she could buy her own lies.

To start, this person was inside the property, undeterred by the stone wall and its blanket of thorns. The figure was also taller and far better dressed than the neighborhood scallywags. Plus it was clearly a man, a grown adult. And he was walking straight toward her, his mouth stretched into a determined scowl.

Nineteen

Because of her mother's transgressions, Gladys's first taste of being the subject of gossips worldwide came at the tender age of eleven. One could speculate that this early introduction to the vagaries of public life made her the woman she became. Dramatic. Attention-seeking. Forever paranoid she was being watched.

—J. Casper Augustine Seton,
The Missing Duchess: A Biography

"So that was Tom, right?" Annie asked. "That Pru saw in the garden?"

"You're under the assumption Tom was a real person, then."

"I don't think Mrs. Spencer was nearly as crazy as she pretended to be. It was all part of her act."

Gus smiled.

"That's a bold theory," he said, rising to his feet. "This early into the story. Well, Miss Annie. As always, it's been a pleasure."

He reached out a hand.

"Where do you think you're going? We're not done!"

"Sorry, my captivating new friend. As engaging as I find your company, I have an appointment to keep."

"An appointment? What appointment? I don't believe you."

"You might find this astounding but old men have obligations too, even ones that do not involve the swapping out of bandages and colostomy bags."

"Sorry, Gus," she said. "But I call BS."

He chuckled and wound a plaid scarf around his neck.

"I'm sure it seems preposterous that another person would voluntarily meet with an old plonker like me," he said. "Truly, what else do I need to accomplish other than to sit in a bar all day getting semipissed?"

"I didn't say that . . ."

"Oh, but it's true! Most of the time. But every once in a great long while I have a specific engagement to keep. You think I can hurtle this gracefully toward the grave on my own? No, there are doctors, dentists, and financial planners involved."

Gus reached out his hand again. This time Annie reluctantly took it, but not before letting out a few grumbles.

"I've enjoyed our conversation," he said. "I do hope to run into you again."

Annie shook his hand, deliberating how she might manufacture another meet-up. She wanted more of his tale, something beyond the pages of transcript she had in her bag.

"Yeah, it's been swell," she muttered. "But before you leave, tell me who Pru saw in the garden."

"You've decided it's Tom. Let's leave it at that. It's probably better than the real story."

"But the real story is what I want!"

"Tell me, Annie. Why do you care so much about the duchess? Or Pru? They're just a bunch of unknowns, most of them dead."

"I told you. I'm a researcher."

The lie was now so thoroughly absorbed Annie might as well have been taking it intravenously. She believed it with every part of her.

"Right," Gus said. "But researching what, exactly?"

"Er, um, literature!"

"Literature," he said with a small grunt. "As in all the literature?" He made a sweeping motion with his hands. "The full canon of written works? That seems like an awfully big theme from which to bite."

"No, no. Ha, ha, ha." God, her forced laughter sounded way too much like a donkey braying. "It's, er, um . . ." She thought of Eric. "War. The effect of war on cultures as revealed through prose."

Annie smiled, feeling mildly pleased with herself. It sounded reasonable. She didn't know much about thesis statements but probably would've accepted the story if someone tried to hawk it to her.

"War through prose, huh?" he said.

"Yup." Annie bobbed her head.

"And how does *The Missing Duchess* fit in?"

"Well, you see, it's an interesting study as it was written at the tail end of the Vietnam War."

"By a Brit. And it wasn't published until several years after the war ended."

"But its protagonist lived through two world wars. Also, the shooting of her mother's lover by her father. Love is war, right?"

"Hmm," Gus said. "Interesting. Very interesting topic. Especially when one considers the background of Pru, who is not in the book but part of the story all the same."

"Yes! Exactly! A happy accident."

"You know, I did wonder if you were making it up, the research bit. I thought perhaps you had another reason for nosing around."

"Ha!" Annie yapped again. "I can see where you might've thought that!"

She laughed some more because what else could she do?

"All right," he said. "I'll tell you who Pru met in the garden. But not now. I really must go. Can you meet me tomorrow?"

"Sure! Yes! Of course! Tomorrow would be perfect."

Gus eyed her warily, his brows cocked and crooked. He'd likely never encountered a literary researcher with such a spastic level of interest.

"Meet me in the morning," he said. "Is eight o'clock too early for you?"

"Too early for a bar?" Annie said and glanced around. "Uh, yeah."

"Give me some credit. I do go other places. Tomorrow we change locations. Eight o'clock. Meet me at the Grange."

Twenty

GD: Of course my father shot Coco.

WS: Why do you say "of course"?

GD: The man was with my mother, when she was four days postpartum, having just birthed a child that was probably the visitor's and not the husband's! Coco was unbothered by Father's anger and so Father had to make a show. He shot Coco right through the couch.

WS: Do you mean "through the crotch"?

GD: Did you not hear me say "couch"?

WS: Is that a euphemism?

GD: No it's not a euphemism! I'd say pecker or nads or twigs and berries if that's what I meant.

WS: Yes, I suppose you would.

GD: It went like this. Coco hid behind the couch. My father shot him, three times. He died. There was a trial.

WS: Of worldwide fame.

GD: I'm not sure about "worldwide" but Henry James wanted to pen a book with Father as the primary character. After the trial, Daddy spent some time in prison. He was released and everyone eventually moved on. Everyone except dear old Dad. He died in a lunatic asylum, driven mad by remembering what he'd done. And as for me, mais en fin je suis la fille de l'assassin. That, dear writer, is how my story goes.

Twenty-one

"Mais en fin je suis la fille de l'assassin."

Was this a stab at humor by Gladys Deacon? Or an excuse for her boorish behavior? One could hardly condemn the woman for her wild capers and socially devastating blunders. Poor thing, it was part of her destiny.

Mais en fin je suis la fille de l'assassin.

But in the end I am the daughter of the murderer.

—J. Casper Augustine Seton,
The Missing Duchess: A Biography

Annie stood near the gate, heaving as sweat trickled down the backs of her thighs. She was hot right then but the running shorts and windbreaker weren't going to cut it if she stopped moving. Her legs and arms were already goose-pimpled from the chill in the air.

Hopping in place, Annie checked her watch. Suddenly a voice shouted her name. Annie looked down Banbury Road and spotted Gus waving from around the bend.

"Over here!" he called. "I've gone round back!"

"I can see that," she said, running toward him. When she reached his side she grabbed a tree to catch her breath.

"Hello," he said, smiling dryly.

"Hi."

"I didn't take you for a casual runner."

"I'm not. I'm a most formal runner."

What Annie was, was somebody in need of a reason to leave the hotel when Laurel wanted to sit around and sip tea. And wasn't that just her luck? The one time Annie had plans her mother did not. Laurel was too confused to question Annie's unexpected spurt of activity. Like Gus, she didn't take Annie for a casual runner, or a runner at all.

"Why are we all the way back here?" Annie asked, sides cramping as she suffered the consequences of her lack of exercise regimen. She really should've visited the college rec center at least once. "Is this a secret entrance or something?"

Without a reply, Gus turned and marched down the alley. Annie followed dutifully, like a puppy, her sneakers rolling over the gravel and rocks.

"You're awfully out of breath," he noted. "For a 'most formal' runner."

"It's the backpack's fault," she said, pointing behind her. "Brought it for, you know, snacks. Water. Provisions."

"Provisions?" Gus cranked his head to look at her. "Where exactly did you jog from?"

"The Banbury Inn?"

"That's not a kilometer away!"

"But it's up a slight incline."

She raised her forearm in a much steeper pitch than the road ever dared be.

"Yes," Gus said. "Slight. *Very* slight. Ah. Here we are."

He paused next to a narrow limestone building the color of toast.

"The rumored former abode of Tom himself," he said.

Annie peered into the windows, which were broken through, just like at the main house. Inside, the cottage was bare save the various spider colonies camped out in the corners of the room.

"Well." She stepped back. "Looks empty."

"Yes. That's what happens when a property changes hands. I'd assume the main house is empty, too."

It was, mostly, and she badly wanted to tell Gus what she'd found. Annie wanted to tell him about the revolver, the manuscript pages, and the books stacked inside a broken bed. And she wanted to ask what happened to the rest of it.

"When did Mrs. Spencer sell it?" Annie asked. "The house?"

"Well, *she* didn't," he told her. "Mrs. Spencer died in the late seventies. The family auctioned off most of her things the year after. They raised a tidy sum. I recall such goodies as a Chaucer manuscript, a 1526 Erasmus, and a book of sexually explicit drawings by D. H. Lawrence."

"*Lady Chatterley's Lover,* indeed."

"The drawings fetched more than the Chaucer. Damned shame, because I wanted to get my hands on them but lacked the requisite funds."

"You ol' perv," Annie said and rolled her eyes. "So who bought the home?"

"A trust owns the building, according to public records. No one's done anything with it, as you can see."

"Her family didn't want it?" she asked.

"S'pose not. Most of them were here, during the auction, to inspect the home and its contents. She had quite a few nieces and nephews."

"Like Edith Junior?"

"She was her niece, yes, but Edith predeceased Mrs. Spencer. Edith Junior had three daughters herself," Gus said. "All of them wealthy as the devil. They probably preferred the money over an old dump of an estate."

Annie nodded, then shivered. The dried-sweat chill was starting to set in.

"So the intruder?" she said, gesturing toward the barn. "Was it Tom? Escaped from his cell? Arms out like zombies? Shackles clanging?"

"Not exactly. But this barn is how the intruder penetrated the property." Gus jiggled the doorknob. "You see, someone left the back door unlocked. As a result, Pru's new compatriot turned this very knob and walked right on through."

Twenty-Two

"What are you doing?" Pru yelled as she clambered across the wintered gardens. "Hey! You there! I see you!"

The figure disappeared.

"Might as well show yourself! Get back here!"

But the man had vanished. Like a ghost.

Pru stopped at the goose pond, its surface just starting to crackle and freeze. Where did he go? Behind a tree? Inside the barn? How did he even get onto the property in the first place? The boy hooligans had been trying for years, to no success.

"Hello?" Pru called out meekly.

She glanced down at her feet and the shabby, crummy slippers that covered them. Above the shoes, her legs were bare and speckled with fleabites. Farther up was the ratty gray nightgown last laundered on some other continent. Pru looked out across the orchard to the old house. The place was making her mad.

She turned to go.

Then: another rustle. Louder. Heavy-footed.

"I know you're there!" she called. Maybe she wasn't crazy after all. Or not in that particular way. "We have guns!"

Pru scrambled toward the noise, tripping over branches and stones.

"I'm not screwing around here," she said. Then mumbled, "As evidenced by the seriousness of my attire."

The right words, as it happened. The would-be sneak thief couldn't resist. He stepped out into the sunshine.

"There's nothing wrong with your attire. Comfort first, I always say. The name's Seton."

He extended a hand.

Pru jumped and promptly backslid down an embankment toward the pond. She grabbed on to a tree branch to save herself from submersion, not to mention death by hypothermia. The pond was partially frozen and, worse, infested with goose excrement.

"Need some help there, miss?"

"How did you get through the gate?" Pru asked, huffing as she hoisted herself back up to safety.

"A little chicken wire never held me back," the man said.

"You broke through the wire?"

"Sure."

Truth was, he'd come through Tom's mythical barn. The girl seemed pleasant enough but the man had seen something in the building. Maybe even something big. So he preferred to keep the information to himself. For now.

"Chicken wire's like an old chum," he added. "Mum used it around my cot to keep me inside."

"Seriously?" Pru's eyes went wide.

"Nah." The man laughed. "Not that I can recall. But it does sound like something she might do. Anyhow. Like I said, the name's Seton. Win Seton."

He extended his hand again as Pru studied his face.

This Win Seton was on the youngish side, though definitely older than Pru. He was tall, his blond hair thick and cropped tightly to his head in a manner that surprised. Pru had grown accustomed to the shaggy mops at Berkeley. Even Charlie's hair hung to his shoulders before he buzzed it off for the army.

Oh dear, Pru thought. *This man must be old-fashioned. Nay, ancient.*

In fact he was thirty-four and so her assumption was correct.

"Ah, the young lady is already softening toward me. I can tell. A relief to not be shot."

"I'm not softening!" she said. "You still haven't explained why you're trespassing!"

"I do apologize. You startled me."

"I startled *you?*"

"I thought the property was empty," he said. "I saw the lady of the manor motor off into town in her little black car. She has a license to drive that thing?"

"She drives it all the time." Pru sniffed.

"Yes, well, I'm quite certain I just saw her mow into a herd of school-children. She was laughing. The children were not. So. You haven't told me your name?"

"You're trespassing on *my* property and you want a name?"

"Your property, is it?" he asked with a squinch.

"Well, I mean, not exactly. But I live here. Did I mention you're a trespasser?"

"Yes, I believe so."

He grinned, blue eyes crinkling at the corners. Win was attractive, but in a lazy sort of way, like he'd never had to work too hard for anything. As though he'd been mollycoddled all his life, which was the general status of things.

"I'll fess up," he said. "I'm a trespasser. But also a writer, which means I'm a danger to no one but myself."

"Okay, Seton," she said. "Mr. Seton. If you're a writer, why do you dress like you're on a hunting safari?"

She pointed to his crisp white shirt and khaki trousers.

"The lady of the manor, as you call her," Pru went on, "positively hates shooting animals for sport. In fact, before large hunts she used to sneak out at dawn and scare the animals from bushes and trees. So if you saw the ducks or foxes and think there's shootable game on this property, think again. Also, it's cold. You'll probably catch pneumonia in that getup."

Win laughed again.

"So sweet of you to be concerned with my health!" he said. "And I am famil-iar with the lady's antihunting sentiment. She used her infinite spaniel collection to flush out the prey, did she not?"

"How did you know . . ."

"She has a million stories," Win said. "A few of them might even be true. And her affinity for tall tales, fair one, is why you find me standing before you."

"Come again?"

"As mentioned, I'm a writer. And I'm here to pen the biography of the woman who lives here."

"Mrs. Spencer's biography?" Pru said, a little baffled. "I must tell you, I don't think she'd be too keen on the idea."

"We're all mates here."

"Not exactly . . ."

"Enough with this 'Spencer' rubbish. Let's call her what she is. Gladys Deacon. The dowager duchess. Lady Marlborough."

"She insists she's not the duchess."

"Oh yes." Win smirked. "I'm sure she does. Now, please kindly show me to the home. Let's wait for your 'Mrs. Spencer' to return. She will not be shocked to see me."

Twenty-three

"Is it your habit to let strange men into the house?"

Mrs. Spencer dragged them into the parlor. She backed Win and Pru up against a cupboard using a chair and what appeared to be some sort of spear.

"Mrs. Spencer, calm down," Pru said.

"Lord Almighty! Americans! No wonder you get yourselves enmeshed in pointless, stupid wars!"

"I thought you were expecting him?"

Pru could feel the man's presence beside her. She moved several paces to the right.

"Mr. Seton told me you knew he was coming," Pru said.

"Yet he had to sneak onto the property while I was out. Does that sound like someone I was expecting? Use your brain!"

The woman had a point.

"But he said . . ." Pru tried.

She felt a tickling by her ear and turned to see a cat peering out from behind a book. Conrad. *The Duel*.

"I don't give a cow's tit what he said!" Mrs. Spencer crowed. She tossed the chair against a wall. "For Christ's sake! Do you even know the first damned thing about him?"

"Well, not exactly . . ."

"He's probably some sort of confidence trickster, wanted throughout the U.K. But you don't care."

"I care, Mrs. Spencer. I do."

"Charmed the pants right off you, no doubt, with those good looks of his. I guess you're headed for betrothal number two. I'll host the party here at the Grange."

"Betrothal? He's a thousand years old!" Pru said. Then she turned to Win: "Sorry, it's just—"

"No apologies necessary." He put up both hands. "A spade's a spade and all that. One thousand years exactly. Lady Marlborough—"

"MRS. SPENCER!"

"First off, let me say that this is a marvelous room," he said, gesturing. "You have an unparalleled collection of books and art."

"Which you want to steal, presumably."

"No! Not in the least. But where's the rest of it?"

"Rest of what?"

"Now, now, don't be coy."

"Oh go fuck yourself."

"Mrs. Spencer!" Pru yelped.

Win made a sound—either a laugh or a choke. Pru could not tell.

"I have no ill intent," he insisted. "Quite the opposite, actually. You see, I'm a writer."

"A writer, huh?" Mrs. Spencer snorted. "Well, that's a dubious pedigree if ever I've heard one. What have you written?"

Win flushed. It was a tough issue for the man, being positively ancient and in his midthirties almost, with not much to show for it. He'd endured the past dozen years or so as one of your standard, ten-a-penny struggling writers. His lack of success was a much-trodden topic among his otherwise successful family.

Oh sure, he had the swagger and the charisma, the faux hunting garb and quick laugh, but deep down he was criminally unconfident, as most failures and/or writers typically were.

"Yes, writer? Go on. Speak. What magical tomes have you penned?"

"Er, um, well. Nothing in the public domain," he finally settled on. "Yet."

Pru felt a momentary gut-pang of pity. Win Seton was a bit of a loser, she decided. Aimless, sad, and hopeless, like a little boy who dropped every ice cream he ever held. She wanted to give him a hug.

"Nothing in the public domain," Mrs. Spencer echoed with yet another snort. "How rather on the nose."

"But I aim to change that by writing your biography."

"My biography? Who cares about some old lady in the countryside? Or is it that you don't want anyone to read your work? You seem to be doing a bang-up job of that already, without my help."

"Lady Marlborough—"

"Mrs. Spencer!"

"The interest in you remains strong," he said. "People still whisper your name at parties and dinners!"

"Oh codswallop!"

"You *must* comprehend your legendary status throughout England and in all of Europe, really. America, too, from what I've gathered."

He looked toward Pru, who shrugged.

"Silly boy. There's not a person outside the gates of this property who gives a whit about me!" Mrs. Spencer said.

"I spent many summers at Blenheim," Win said and cleared his throat, waiting for a reaction.

Poor sod, Pru thought. The bloke was faring worse with each breath.

"At Blenheim," he repeated. "They spoke of you endlessly, decades after you'd left. New people were born. The old ones died. Marital unions formed and broke apart. The circle of life in full effect. Through it all, talk of you."

"I'm not familiar with this Blenheim place."

"It's your family seat. Don't tell me you've forgotten. Is she . . ." He turned to Pru and made a circular motion at the side of his head. *"All there?"*

"I can hear you, Seton."

"She seems perfectly sane to me," Pru said with a sideways smile.

"Right." Win laughed nervously. "Surely you haven't forgotten Blenheim, Mrs. Spencer?"

"Now that you mention it, the name rings a bell. Isn't that where Coon lived? During her first marriage?"

"If by 'Coon' you mean your old pal Consuelo Vanderbilt, your preceding Duchess of Marlborough, then yes."

"I'm not a duchess!"

Blenheim.

Pru's mouth curled in reflection. Blenheim. As she looked between Seton and Mrs. Spencer, it struck her. The name was at once shiny and familiar, like an American penny found on a foreign street. Tidbits gleaned at university were still there, it seemed, despite the shoddy dress and flea-bitten legs.

"You summered at Blenheim?" she asked Win. "Isn't that where Churchill was born?"

"Yes," he said. "The very place."

"Jesus. Here we go again." Mrs. Spencer rolled her eyes. "That old bastard Churchill. He was not a great man. Of course he wasn't. The English just like to create heroes and worship them."

"I think respect for him is fairly worldwide," Pru said. "So you can't pin it on the Brits."

"He just had a certain faculty for making noise. There are people who go through life bashing cymbals. He was one."

"Goodness, Lady Marl—Mrs. Spencer," Win said with a chuckle. "If you were chummy with Sir Churchill then you must have some tales to tell, dowager duchess or not. To be frank, I plan to write the biography at any cost. You might as well have your say."

"I'm confused. Are you writing a book about me or about the Duchess of Marlborough?" Mrs. Spencer asked, one eyebrow cocked.

"Either or. It depends on you."

"Hmph." She crossed her arms.

"And Proust!" Pru chirped. "She was pals with Proust!"

Mrs. Spencer shot her a look.

"What? You told me about your pal Marcel on my first night here. You never mentioned it was a secret."

"Even better," Win said. "Proust. Churchill. Shall we name the others?"

"Thomas Hardy," Pru said, feeling Mrs. Spencer's glare bore into her. "Edith Wharton. J. M. Barrie. D. H. Lawrence. H. G. Wells. E. M. Forster. All the good initialed folks."

"Honestly, Miss Valentine! Do you ever stop?"

"Mrs. Spencer," Win said, outright grinning now.

He was entirely enchanted by Pru. Problem was, he had no capacity to enchant in return. It was not in his genetic makeup. He only hoped to not repel her altogether.

"Surely your story is fabulous," he said. "If nothing else, you're intriguing enough, *lovely* enough, that the good people of Banbury think you're Gladys Deacon. As you must know, she was universally agreed upon as the most intelligent and beautiful woman to ever exist."

"I'm sure she wasn't as spectacular as all that."

"Oh but she was! With that fine-spun, red-gold hair. Her stunning blue eyes. And that magnificent style! The bright colors . . . the fur, the feathers, the beads."

Mrs. Spencer made a puffing sound but then—could that be right?—she reddened. Had Win Seton gotten to her that quickly? He was buttering up the old broad, any goat could tell. Pru found herself impressed.

"Feathers and beads?" Mrs. Spencer said. "Sounds a bit obvious. Like a damned peacock."

"A dazzling peacock."

"They also thought the duchess was nuts," she said. "Did your Blenheim exploits teach you that? The duke's family thought the great, grand Duchess of Marlborough was touched in the head."

"Only because she went missing," Win said. "Nearly forty years and for no discernible reason."

"Her husband was dead. He left her alone, in a prison, with people who despised her. Is that not ample reason for you?"

"A prison? Surely you don't mean Blenheim."

"Of course I mean Blenheim! It's a monolithic beast of a supposed home."

"Lady—Mrs. Spencer—I've been to Blenheim countless times. It's breathtaking. Surely the duchess would've been pleased by the meticulous grounds, the statues of her likeness in the gardens, those blue eyes of hers painted on the portico ceiling."

"What's a little paint and some plaster?" Mrs. Spencer grouched.

"Even if the palace didn't please the duchess, surely she could've absconded to their London home, or her private Paris pied-à-terre. Why would a woman of her stature disappear so completely?"

"You'd have to ask her directly."

"Please, Mrs. Spencer," Win said. "Let me write about you. Allow me to commit your life to the page. We'd have a jolly good time in the process, the two of us." He glanced at Pru. "The three."

"I'm not sure," Mrs. Spencer said, and began to pace. "I'm not sure about any of this."

"You do have fascinating stories," Pru said, jumping in. "The German POWs who cut your trees. The years you spent in Paris. All those broken engagements."

With that, Mrs. Spencer leaned forward and tried to wallop Pru in the head with a newspaper.

"You *would* be interested in broken engagements," Mrs. Spencer harrumphed as Pru ducked out of reach. She turned back to Seton. "Well, writer, if I say yes, I suppose you'd make a gadfly of yourself and set up shop in this very house."

"Please call me Win. And yes, that's the idea. To stay in residence. It would enable me to get closer to the subject."

"Also you probably don't have a quid to your name."

"Think of yourself as a patron to the arts," Win said.

"Oh Lord, that must mean you fancy yourself the art. I don't know." She sighed. "What do you think, Miss Valentine?"

"Uh, what?" Pru said. She did not expect to be called to vote. "Me?"

"Yes, of course you! Good grief, and they say *I'm* touched in the head. What say you, Miss Valentine?"

It was the question, wasn't it?

What exactly *did* Pru think of this unfamiliar man? The sort-of-handsome writer who'd shown up in the brush wearing pressed attire? Clothes that were, it must be said, already sullied by dog hair and slobber.

"I guess it's fine?" she said tepidly.

He didn't seem dangerous. Of course, just because someone wasn't dangerous didn't mean he wasn't trouble.

On the other hand, it'd be nice to have another (human) body in the house. Someone to guard against the specter of Tom and, more important, help clean up after all the damned dogs.

"How do you feel about spaniels?" Pru asked.

"Wonderful creatures. Positively aces."

Pru turned toward Mrs. Spencer.

"Let's do a trial run," she said. "See how it works out."

"A trial run? Miss Valentine, you're barely out of yours."

Mrs. Spencer tried to frown but her resolve was splintering.

"All right," she said at last. "I'll permit this dreggy writer to live with us and pen my memoirs. What a waste of paper."

"Brilliant!" Win said and gave a loud clap. "Who wants to help with my baggage? It's out on the street."

"Before you start hauling all your rubbish into my home, one thing I want to make clear, Mr. Seton."

"Like I said, call me Win."

"I will not call you Win. For one, it's impolite. For two, it reminds me of Winston Churchill and you do not want to be mistaken for him. Mr. Seton, this book will be mine, not yours. I get the final say on what goes into it. Do you understand?"

"That's what I planned all along," he said.

"Also I want a cut. A financial interest."

"A cut?" Win gawped. "That's not how biographies customarily work."

"I don't care about custom!" she said. "I care about what makes me happy. This is your choice. I give you my time and you compensate me as I please."

Win pretended to ruminate on the offer, though everyone in the room knew he'd agree to the terms. Money was not the point of the book. The book was the point. Moreover, he'd made precisely nothing from his authorial endeavors thus far. Mrs. Spencer was welcome to her half of zed.

"Very well, Mrs. Spencer," he said. "I accept your proposal."

Frankly, he didn't have another choice. What was the price of a dream anyway? Win Seton was willing to give up half the money for the whole of this, his last chance to prove his worth.

Twenty-four

THE GRANGE
CHACOMBE-AT-BANBURY, OXFORDSHIRE, ENGLAND
NOVEMBER 2001

Gladys's father was arrested for murder. "Parisian flirtations" aside, you simply couldn't shoot someone through a couch and expect to get away with it.

That is, unless you cried adultery. In those days, murder was an acceptable response to a cheating wife. Had Edward Deacon attested to Florence's dalliance with the now-dead Coco, she would've been the one in the clink. But Mr. Deacon refused to turn her in. Noble or stupid? It was certainly up for debate.

Mrs. Deacon did feel some guilt about the outcome. Immediately after her husband's sentencing, she canceled an engagement with the Princesse de Sagan. Florence didn't care to endure a luncheon less than twenty-four hours after her husband was carted off. She may not have loved him, but Florence Deacon had some semblance of a heart.

Alas, the press did not take kindly to this social misstep. Famed dandy Count Robert de Montesquiou wrote a poem about the event, asking at the end, "Does disaster preclude politeness?"

Evidently, it did not. Florence would not make such a mistake again.

—J. Casper Augustine Seton,
The Missing Duchess: A Biography

"I like this Win character," Annie said. "I'm glad Pru had the good sense to let him stay."

"Ha!" Gus responded with a small arf. "Well, you can join the very short line of people who have ever shared that sentiment. You like him in what manner, exactly?"

"I don't know. He seems funny, affable."

"Yes, he *seems* that way, doesn't he?"

"You're a tough customer," Annie said. "So this marginally affable Win Seton wrote a book called *The Missing Duchess*. In your story he's writing about Mrs. Spencer. So voilà! Your not-really-a-mystery is solved. Mrs. Spencer is the Duchess of Marlborough. The duchess is she."

"The mystery is hardly solved. My dear, you are a pretty thing, smart as a whip, but I feel as though you're not listening with both ears. Win said he'd write the book with or without the woman's assistance. He was exactly the kind of person who, if Mrs. Spencer had become the least bit troublesome, would've written whatever the hell he wanted just to put something on the page. And Mrs. Spencer was always troublesome."

Gus started walking back down the road, away from the Grange. He indicated for Annie to follow.

"Wait," she called. "Maybe we should try to—"

"Go inside?" he finished for her, smiling over his shoulder. "You are persistent. And cruel. Poor old man, one foot in the grave, and you want to get him thrown in the brig?"

"You're not anywhere near the grave, much less one foot in it."

Annie jogged to catch up.

"Sorry, mademoiselle, no trespassing for me today," Gus said. "Let me walk you back to your hotel. The Banbury Inn? Nicola Teepers? Whew. She's a chatty one, isn't she?"

"You don't know the half of it."

Once her pace finally caught with his, Annie wrapped both arms around herself. Her teeth clattered. She could feel winter coming.

"Here." Gus unwound his scarf and passed it her way. "Borrow this. What were you thinking, coming out here in nothing but a pair of skimpy shorts? It's brass monkeys outside."

"I was jogging."

"You were doing nothing of the sort. Heaving, more like."

"Hey!" she said, laughing as she wrapped the scarf around her neck.

Around them the air was damp and chilled. The sun shone overhead but the morning fog settled in the foothills. The cold was so much *colder* in England, so wet and final. It was nice to have something to guard against it. What was she thinking, indeed.

"I wish you were up for some breaking and entering," Annie said, debating whether to tell him how easy it was.

"A tempting offer, but I must pass. This old codger's not nearly nimble enough for such larks. You'll have to find someone younger if you're looking for a coconspirator."

"Maybe I can suss out some of those Banbury hooligans," she said. "The ones who used to torture Mrs. Spencer."

"Those very hooligans are now the doctors, teachers, and councilmen of this great town."

"How disappointing," she said. "Though I guess that's the way life turns out. People grow up. They mature." Annie pretended to look at an invisible watch. "As for me, any minute now. I'm sure my mom is waiting."

"I've been trying very hard to prevent maturation myself," Gus countered.

"Hold on." Annie turned to face him. "Were you one of them? A miscreant-turned-notable?"

"Lord no! Do I look like a town notable to you? What an insult." He gave her a little wink. "I shudder at the thought."

They walked a few more steps in silence, nothing but the sound of the road beneath their feet, the hum of cars in the distance.

"Who do you think controls it?" she asked. "The trust that owns the Grange? Not an old hooligan?"

"Last I heard it was more or less in the hands of developers, like all decent Oxfordshire parcels. Doubtless they'll turn it into miniestates any day now."

"Yeah, I've heard the market's hot around here lately," she said, thinking of her mom.

"Aggravatingly so. Banbury is starting to get hip to Londoners, God forbid. Estate agents are crawling all over the place. Homes that have been in families for centuries are coming onto the market. Everyone's a seller, at a price."

Annie thought of Laurel's own land deal, her mother one of the many selling out to the highest bidder. There was comfortable retirement on one hand, and sullying quaint countrysides on the other. Annie would not mention this to Gus.

"Basic economics, I suppose," she said, feeling morose. "Which is why I've always preferred books. Much to the detriment of my bank account and long-term job prospects, of course."

"I tell you what, Annie, this world would do better to have more like you in it. Practicality is overrated."

"Someone needs to tell my mom."

A few more steps and they stopped in front of the inn. Annie looked up at her room but couldn't make out if anyone was in it.

"Are you traveling alone?" Gus asked. "Or with a companion? I can't recall you mentioning one way or another."

"Oh," she sighed. "Mostly on my own."

Eric would not like this conversation. He would not like it one bit, seeing as how he was convinced the Earl of Winton was either a pervert, a kidnapper, or both.

Sometimes Annie wondered if she'd told Eric on purpose, to make him mad. She promised to marry him but her mother's qualms were beginning to infect her. God, how she loved that big Southern boy. But God, she was dumb to marry so young.

"On your own?" Gus said with a frown.

She started to nod, hearing Eric's voice ("you told him you were *alone*?"). It seemed somehow weird to say she was traveling with her mom, as though Gus might write her off as a bored schoolgirl not worthy of his time.

"I mean, I'm not totally alone," Annie quickly clarified. "I'm meeting some family members along the way. But, you know, mostly it's just me."

This was not so far from the truth.

"Are they expecting you any time soon?" he asked. "I have to be somewhere later this afternoon, but I might have time for another tale about the misanthrope you find so alluring."

"He doesn't sound too misanthropic to me," Annie said. "Seeing as how he helped himself onto the property, then shacked up with two women he'd never met."

"For a crack at the so-called duchess he was willing to manufacture some base level of sociable behavior. Make no mistake, though. Seton's appearance in Banbury was about the book, and the book alone, and he planned to stay at the Grange until he squeezed every last drop from Mrs. Spencer and finally wrote the damned story he'd pined after for so long.

"Trouble was, though Win Seton felt so bloody sure that she was Gladys Deacon, he forgot the most elemental things about the duchess. Namely, that she lived only in half-truths and the best lighting, and, most important of all, the long-lost Duchess of Marlborough never, ever played by the rules."

Twenty-five

At first, Pru thought the writer wasn't permitted to leave his room.

Otherwise, why would he stay up there, day after day, pounding the devil out of his typewriter with a crazed, helter-skelter look in his eyes? Win Seton hardly ate, rarely drank, and was withering by the hour.

"Mrs. Spencer, you have to let him out," Pru implored after nearly a week of suffering his uncomfortable presence. "You can't treat him this way. It's the holidays! Have a little compassion."

"Treat who?" Mrs. Spencer said in her carefully honed pretend naïveté. "And, by the by, Christmas is over. The giving season is *finit*."

"You know exactly who I'm talking about. You've locked the poor writer in his room. Forget the giving season, this is basic human decency."

"Miss Valentine, that's preposterous. Tell me, have you seen any chains? Any locks on his door?"

"Well, no, but I haven't really—"

"I see you go in there," Mrs. Spencer said with a snigger. "Toting food and companionship and Lord knows. Surely you would've noticed signs of bondage. Or is it that you *want* to find signs of bondage?"

"Absolutely not!"

"Did it ever occur to you that he relishes the situation? Maybe reclusiveness is his preferred state. The man *is* a writer."

"Yes, but—"

"He's come to write, not consort with pretty, if not slightly vaporous, young girls. As shocking as you may find it."

True, he was there to write, but Win Seton hadn't made a lick of progress on his book. Oh sure, the constant snap of the keys was fine and dandy but it couldn't have been a biography he was writing. Mrs. Spencer had given the man precisely nothing to work with. Pru sat in on every confab, so knew this as fact. And every evening it went like this.

At seven on the nose, Mrs. Spencer would change into a dramatic silk dressing gown. She'd call Pru into her company and announce: "Time for my interview!"

It didn't matter if Pru was in the middle of a chore, or if there were dogs half fed, half bathed, or half birthed. Mrs. Spencer would run Pru down and drag her upstairs to sit watch. The man was a "likely deviant," Mrs. Spencer claimed, and Pru her chaperone.

"Are you ready to pen my memoirs?" she'd trill and plant herself at the edge of Win's bed, highball in hand.

Her hair, the gown, those diamonds winking in the lamplight, all a far cry from her customary soiled trousers and straw hat. Even the cocktail was wrong. Mrs. Spencer didn't drink, as a rule, and instead preferred laudanum to calm her nerves. Pru didn't understand it at all.

"Start with my profile," she'd say. "What do you think of my profile?"

"Perfect Hellenic proportions," Win responded obediently.

From the outset the writer accepted his role and played it to the hilt. Flatter, flatter, and when all else failed, flatter some more. One could never go wrong when referencing "Hellenic profiles" and so Win did without abandon. It was a commendable perception for a man blessed with rascally schoolboy charm in lieu of intellect.

"Hellenic," Mrs. Spencer said with a happy sigh, every time. "Yes. Thank you for noticing. God has blessed me well."

As Win told it, if Mrs. Spencer *was* the duchess, then God had nothing to do with her legendary silhouette. Gladys Deacon was born with a small kink in her nose, a quirk that vexed her from the start. She also deemed her eyes unacceptably close together and therefore vowed to ameliorate her oh-so-many physical flaws.

To that end, a teenaged Gladys Deacon set off on a worldwide tour to survey the most prized busts and sculptures in creation. She studied each piece, diligently analyzing and recording the distance between eyes and the lengths of the noses. Eventually, she arrived at the ideal proportions and took her data to Paris, where she underwent a series of wax injections to achieve this artlike perfection.

"I've never heard such a thing!" Mrs. Spencer claimed whenever Win brought it up. "Wax injections! Honestly. No, silly writer, I was born with this most original and God-given face."

And so it went between Win and Mrs. Spencer. He prodded. She denied. He wheedled. She demurred. Pru sat watching, wondering what the bloody hell they were all doing there. Everyone was haggling for something, but from very early on the end result was obvious. Not a one of them was going to get what they wanted. Not even Pru.

Twenty-six

"Hello," Pru said, standing sheepishly in the hall.

She had a sack in hand, in it a jumble of foodstuffs she'd acquired in town.

"I thought you'd like something to eat? May I come in?"

Win didn't look up from his typewriter. Instead he made some sort of roll-nod gesture, which Pru took as invitation. With a begrudging smile, she stepped through the doorway.

"Hopefully Mrs. Spencer won't mind me visiting her memoirist unsupervised," Pru said, padding gingerly across the room. "I feel like, I don't know, you're not getting enough food or something. Silly notion, probably. But with the conditions downstairs . . ."

Hands trembling, Pru placed her offering on the desk: a handful of cabbage, two apples, a few links of sausage, and a wedge of Oxford Blue. Already beside him sat a mug of tea and a half-emptied sleeve of biscuits.

"Worried about my eating habits?" Win stopped typing and glanced up with a crooked smile. "I've never felt so loved."

He was handsome for an old bloke who didn't shower much, Pru decided, but then immediately shook her head. There was no use thinking about the man in flattering terms. She didn't want to feel more toward him than she already did. Vague and distant pity was emotion enough.

"I'm not worried about your eating habits," Pru said. "Seeing as how you don't have any." She paused, hand on hip. "Good grief. I really sound like a mother hen, don't I? You're a smidge old for that."

"Right. A *smidge* old. What was your estimate when we met in the garden that day?" he said. "A thousand years or thereabouts?"

"Oh geez . . ."

"I'm only joshing," he said with a droll wink. "Anyhow, I'm all for mother hens. My own mum wasn't interested in any henning so it's a nice change of pace."

"I never really had a mom, either," Pru blurted. "I don't know why I just told you that."

"Not to worry." He put a cigarette between his lips but did not light it. "I never really had one, either."

Win punched out a few more words while Pru stood awkwardly in the middle of the room, emptied bag dangling from her arm.

"Is there something else you need?" he asked from the side of his mouth not working to hold onto the unlit cigarette.

"Uh, er, not really."

Win glanced up.

"So, I'll be going . . ." she said.

"Wait," he said, surprising them both. "Don't leave. Do you . . . do you want to chat?"

Win rolled his eyes at himself. *Fancy a chat?* Blimey, how could a girl resist so compelling an invitation? What a wanker.

"That's okay," Pru said, wisely. "I don't have much time for a chat."

She took five quick strides toward the door but, much to his amazement, turned back around before leaving him altogether.

"I have to ask," she said. "You're not . . . Mrs. Spencer isn't detaining you? Under lock and key? Or guns and poisoned arrows? You are allowed to come and go, yes?"

Win laughed. He was in a sorry state alright. A passerby couldn't ascertain whether he was a prisoner or a free man.

"Believe it or not," he said. "I choose to live and work in these conditions. A testament to my quality of life, it must be stated. But I understand your confusion."

"Okay, but what are you writing?" Pru asked. "I'm sorry if it sounds rude but I can't figure it out."

"What am I writing? The book about the duchess. I thought I made that clear?"

"You did, but I've been here and . . . I've watched. And listened. Does Mrs. Spencer come in here without me sometimes? Is that it?"

"No. Never."

"Then what the *hell*!" Pru said, exasperated, making a "halt" motion with both hands. "I mean, really! You're up here typing like a madman. All day, all night. The incessant, relentless clacking. I've sat through your so-called interviews but she's given you nothing. Nada. Zip. Unless I'm missing something, which is entirely possible."

"No, you're not missing a thing."

Win stood. She could almost hear his knees creaking from disuse.

"Then what is it?" Pru asked. Nay, begged. "What are you doing in here?"

"It's simple," he said. "I'm playing the long game."

"The long game?"

He nodded and then grabbed several sheets of paper from the windowsill.

"My brother would argue that's my life's philosophy," he said, turning the paper over in his hands. "But in this case, it means I'm willing to wait her out. The duchess is famous for her disobliging nature, universally known for conducting business on her own bedlamite terms. To expect anything less would go against natural order. So, for now, I work on the bits I've gathered through my preliminary research. She'll come round on the rest. Eventually."

"Assuming Mrs. Spencer is the duchess," Pru said.

"Oh she is. One hundred percent."

Win tossed the stack of paper onto the bed. Before realizing what she was doing, Pru shuffled over to snatch it.

"Hey now!" he said. "You can't go nicking other peoples' private correspondence."

"Is this your book?" she asked, the pages hot in her hands.

"Well." Win sighed. "Yes. It's the start of it."

```
Lllllllllllllllllllllllllllllllldkfawawetwlcw
Werrejq32rjklwfe
Fuck. This.
```

"A riveting read," Pru muttered.

Fuck this. Truer words had not been spoken.

So this drivel was what he'd been hammering out, early in the morning and well past midnight? It was gibberish. Nonsense. Pru considered that he might not be a writer and instead some homeless bloke on the make, just as Mrs. Spencer had suspected.

"Oh, for Christ's sake," Win said and flicked his (still unlit) cigarette onto the floor. "Keep going. The first page is merely the accidental spill of some writerly frustrations."

"I'll say."

Pru flipped to the next page and was relieved to find genuine, bona fide sentences. Paragraphs, even. She began to read.

They said you weren't anyone until Giovanni Boldini painted you. But of all the famed women he rendered, the princesses and countesses and heiresses, the Duchess of Marlborough was deemed the most enchanting.

The future duchess was born Gladys Deacon in Paris on February 7, 1881, though she would later claim the date was 1883, and later 1885. Lady Marlborough loved to play with her birthdate, ticking it up a year or two for every decade that passed. A fair enough trade, when a person made it close to the century mark.

"Nicely done," Pru said, though didn't wholly mean it.

His prose was sufficient, but the story was not exactly groundbreaking. Whatever "preliminary research" he'd conducted was for shite.

"What else have you got?" she asked and turned another page.

It was blank. She flipped again. Still blank. After thumbing through the rest, Win shirking in the corner, Pru realized this was all he'd written. Two bleeding paragraphs.

"Well," she said. "I see what you mean about the long game."

"The young American said with tangible disdain."

"I'll be in the book? Not sure how I feel about that."

"Look. You said it yourself. She's given me bugger all to go on and you're the liveliest person in this joint, even if you blush if forced to utter more than two words."

"You're some kind of charmer," Pru said with a roll of her eyes. "So what happens if Mrs. Spencer doesn't give you the rest of it? Will you write her story anyway? Make something up? Or will you just leave?"

"No. I won't leave."

Win sighed again and then sat on the edge of his bed.

"This may sound positively bonkers," he said. "To someone like you, so young and with limitless possibilities. But this writer nonsense? It's all I've got."

"Surely not *all*."

"It certainly is. And if I give up on it, then what do I have? Nothing. And to suddenly have nothing, no direction, no future at all, is a terrifying prospect. I can't explain it."

"You don't need to explain it," she said. "I've—"

"You'd simply never understand."

Pru turned away as a blanket of red spilled across her powder-white face. She'd been on the cusp of telling him she knew a thing or two about dim futures, but the miserable bloke made it so damned hard to create a real human connection.

"You want to write her story that badly?" Pru asked, face hot. "That you'd subject yourself to poor ventilation, middling food, and a general lack of hygiene? Not to mention all the damned dogs. You are that committed to telling the duchess's tale?"

"Yes," Seton said, after a great, long while. "It may sound crazy, but apparently I am."

Twenty-seven

They sat in Win's room as snow swirled outside.

The house bent and wailed in the wind, the three of them warmed by the fire, which Mrs. Spencer kindled with letters from "unexceptional lovers."

"Were they unexceptional in social status?" Win wanted to know. "Or in sexual performance?"

Pru blushed, despite the cold. She pulled the bearskin throw farther up onto her shoulders with one hand and held a book to her face with the other. She'd taken to reading during these interviews, to pass the time between Mrs. Spencer's filibusters. No one seemed to mind, or even notice at all.

"Ha!" the old woman barked. "Sex or status. That *is* the question, isn't it?"

"Tell me about the men," Win said. "Unexceptional or otherwise."

"I don't have ample time left on this earth to tell you about the men."

"Fair enough. I'll be specific. Let's begin with the Duke of Marlborough."

"Nice try. But no."

"Why not? Because you can't speak to his sexual prowess? Or you don't want to?"

Mrs. Spencer pretended to take a sip of bourbon. It dribbled onto her purple silk gown.

"All right," he pressed on. "If you won't yield on the duke, surely you can regale us with stories of your prior betrothals, the broken hearts you've left along the way."

"Ah!" Mrs. Spencer's face brightened. "Well, there were quite a number of them. I was very attractive in my youth. As your friend Miss Valentine can attest, if a woman has the beauty, she will also have a history of affiancing. She's already one down."

"Mrs. Spencer!" Pru said, and yanked her gaze from the book.

That night it was H. G. Wells, *The Island of Doctor Moreau*. Dog-Man, Hyena-Swine, and Fox-Bear Witch were appropriately ghoulish for a dark and howling winter's night at the Grange.

But certainly when I told the captain to shut up I had forgotten I was merely a bit of human flotsam, cut off from my resources, and with my fare unpaid . . .

"Oh, Miss Valentine, don't fret! One betrothal at your age is acceptable. It's true you have a ways to go, more's the pity, but it's a valiant start!"

Win's eyebrows lifted straight off his face.

"Well, now," he said. "I've ragged her a bit, joked that I'd include her in my book. But it's beginning to seem like a better idea by the minute."

"That snoozer?" Mrs. Spencer said and affected a yawn. "Miss Valentine is a pretty thing but her life story wouldn't fill a cocktail napkin."

"You two are much too kind," Pru grumbled. "Really."

"Fine then," Win said, an eye still on Pru, who tried to bury herself beneath the bearskin throw. "Let's leave Miss Valentine be and discuss the Crown Prince of Prussia. It's one of my favorite Blenheim stories, told often, as it's where the two of you met. I couldn't walk past the tennis courts without picturing you on them."

"Never played a set in my life."

"Prince William of Prussia," Win continued. "Little Willy they called him. You beat him. In tennis, at a minimum."

Mrs. Spencer snorted.

"Oh, Little Willy," she said. "Little indeed."

"He was tall," Win said, wiggling his mouth to chase away a smirk. "And fair from head to toe. Rumor was Little Willy's ears would turn red in your presence. I feel as though I have the same effect on our Miss Valentine."

Pru glared at him from over the top of her book.

"I only blush when I'm perturbed," she said.

"Perturbed. Riled up. Excited beyond reason. So, Mrs. Spencer, as the story goes, the young prince first saw you at Blenheim, where he witnessed your wicked serve and ultimately fell victim to your punishing forehand. Your beauty and intellect enchanted the man and your athletics paralyzed him. No one had ever beaten him before. And Little Willy liked his beatings."

"You make it sound so libidinous," Mrs. Spencer said, her lips twitching into a smile.

"By week's end," Win said. "Whilst on a drive, you coaxed the confirmation ring right off his finger and declared yourselves engaged. Much to the dismay of the kaiser, as you were never a true princess."

"I don't need a fledgling biographer to tell me that I'm not a princess."

"You'd lured Willy into an engagement though he was, as everyone knew, happy to be caught. He never would've had the balls to do it himself, to upset *Vater*."

"You've got that right," Mrs. Spencer mumbled.

"When political powers on both sides of the Atlantic heard about your engagement, a surge of relief washed across the globe. This would not be a simple marriage but instead an important alliance between Germany and the United States."

"I've had many engagements, Mr. Seton, but I don't recall a single one of them surging anything across the globe. What's an alliance anyway but a verbal agreement among two separate people with opposing interests? Easily formed, quickly broken."

"They say the two of you could've prevented the first war."

"Oh, I hardly think—"

"Mrs. Spencer, admit it. Everyone knows your love might've saved the world."

Twenty-eight

"Their love might've saved the world?" Annie said. "Don't you think that's a tad much?"

"No," Gus said. "Why, is that what you think?"

"Uh, yeah. This author is every bit as dramatic as Mrs. Spencer herself, from the sounds of it."

"Admittedly, he was prone to theatrics about all manner of things. But in this regard he was correct. Even Churchill echoed the comment. And he never would've voluntarily given Gladys that much credit."

"I still don't understand why Mrs. Spencer refused to admit she was the duchess."

Annie uncoiled Gus's scarf and handed it back to him. She shivered in the brisk, sunny air.

"The duchess's reputation wasn't exactly sterling," Gus pointed out.

"I get that, but it's not like Mrs. Spencer was the town's most respected citizen, either. What did she have to lose? I would've been, like, damned straight my beauty was capable of keeping men from war!"

"So you remain convinced that she was the long-lost duchess?"

"Look, it's very cute how you're trying to frame this as a mystery but there is no other conclusion. Take Consuelo Vanderbilt. We know that she was the Duchess of Marlborough."

"We do."

"And we know that she and Gladys were close friends."

"That's correct."

"Mrs. Spencer herself told Win and Pru that she and Coon were the tightest of pals. So there you go. One example of many."

"Surely Consuelo Vanderbilt had more than one friend."

"Perhaps. But probably not another friend that close. Coon was timid and insecure because of her hearing problem. 'A black swan aloof in soundless waters,' et cetera. She needed Gladys Deacon. Their relationship was special."

"An aloof black swan? Where did you hear a thing like that?"

"I can't remember," Annie said, heart beginning to thrum. "Um, probably in the book?"

The words were from the transcript, which was in her backpack, Annie realized too late.

"The writer mentioned it," she blathered on. "I'm pretty sure."

"I don't think it was in the book," Gus said, eyes darkening.

"Whatever. The point is . . ." Annie moved the backpack from her right shoulder to her left. "When triangulating the data, the information lines up. Not only with Coon, but all the other little details."

"Triangulating . . ."

"Yes, you know."

Annie drew a shape in the air that was decidedly not a triangle. A sloppy rhombus, at best.

"Aren't there usually three sides to a triangle?" Gus asked.

"Yes, that's generally how triangles work. But like I said, I hate math. Or whatever shapes are. Geometry? That sounds right."

"So, then, where's your third side?" Gus asked. "The first side is the book. The second is our conversations. What's the third?"

"Uh, I think it's just an expression?" she said, face flaming.

"Tell me, Annie, what is your third source of information?"

"I think you're focusing on the wrong thing here."

"You went into the Grange, didn't you?" he said, and narrowed his gaze.

"After you showed up at the George and Dragon looking dusty and unkempt, asking oddball questions about the property, I knew something was amiss. But I thought, no, this girl is not a criminal. She is a sweet thing, missing her fiancé and getting lost in a book."

"Gus . . ."

Annie closed her eyes and sighed. The wind whipped around her. She could almost imagine herself in the parlor of the Grange, a bearskin throw pulled to her chin, winter streaming through the gaps in the walls and doors.

"Fine," she said. "I'm busted. Yes. I went inside the Grange. Call it—"

"Research? Nice try."

Her eyes popped back open.

"Intellectual curiosity," she said. "I'm a researcher."

"Intruder more like. Or a nuisance."

"Nuisance? Ouch. I'm not that bad."

"A nuisance in the legal sense, as in a public nuisance."

"You've got me!" Annie threw her hands up. "I'm a trespasser. I've committed a crime. Why are you so bent out of shape about it? Do you own the house or something? If so, not to worry, I left everything intact."

Most everything anyway.

"No. I do not own the house," Gus said. "I simply think nosy young 'scholars' should do a better job of ingratiating themselves to locals. By the by, I'm not paying the bond following your inevitable arrest."

"I'm sorry I snuck in there," Annie said, though she wasn't, not particularly. She was only sorry that she'd irritated Gus. "I just wanted to have a look around. I didn't mean any harm."

"So, then, what did you see on this look-around? I hope you reaped some reward for your misadventures."

"Honestly, there wasn't much to see. A few books. Some leftover pieces of furniture. It appears Seton's desk and typewriter are still there."

"Really?" Gus's face, formerly grumbly and squished, perked up. "His typewriter?"

"Someone's typewriter. It's beside a window, in a room at the top of the stairs."

"His typewriter. Huh. That would be something."

"I also found these."

Annie wiggled out of her backpack and started to unzip the top before reconsidering. Gus would confiscate the pages, most likely. Not that he had any greater claim to the manuscript than she did, but at the very least he'd yell at her again.

"Gosh darn it," she said. "Guess I left them in the room."

She zipped it back up.

"You left *what* in the room?"

"Um. I think I came across, er, some transcripts? Interviews between Win and the Duchess?"

"Brilliant. And in which room did you leave these filched pages?"

"Well, mine."

"Blimey, Annie. You nicked them? Add it to your list of civil transgressions."

"Come on, Gus," she said. "Ease up. It's only scrap paper, left there for Lord knows how many years. Why are you such a hard-ass all of a sudden? I thought you were one of the good guys."

"I'm not sure how you ever acquired the notion that I'm good."

"I've never broken a law in my life," Annie said, her voice starting to shake. "Maybe some underaged drinking ones, but not, like, real crimes. Nothing that'd hurt another living soul. Honestly, Gus, I'm a nice person!"

He let her snivel and suffer for many more moments than were necessary, but probably the exact amount of time she deserved. Annie hated herself for being such a snoop. Eric would be appalled.

"Gus, I'm sorry, I don't even know what to say."

"Crumbs, Annie, I shouldn't be so hard on you," he said. "I'd just hate to see you get into any sort of legal mess, traveling 'mostly alone' as you are. Call it fatherly concern, not that I'd know the first thing about it."

"Don't apologize," she said. "I understand."

She didn't know the first thing about fatherly concern, either.

"Oh, I wasn't apologizing," Gus said. "You are most certainly in the wrong. But tell me, what else did you see over at the Grange? Since a crime has already been committed you might as well reveal the results of your felonious behavior."

"Honestly, I was a little disappointed," Annie admitted. "The house was dilapidated, as expected, the grounds around it nothing but weeds and overgrowth. But the inside? You said it was cluttered."

"I said?"

"Well, your story. Plus it was in the biography. And while the place wouldn't win any *Good Housekeeping* awards, I expected a lot more . . . *crap*."

"Crap, is it?" Gus said, letting free a smile. His usual ways were beginning to creep back in. "I'm sure Mrs. Spencer would appreciate the inference."

"Okay, wise guy, according to Win Seton, there *was* literal crap, of the spaniel and cat varieties."

"Touché, young criminal. Touché."

"That's not what I meant, though," she said. "The home was mostly empty. The furniture was gone. The dishes, removed. Artwork was pulled right off the walls."

"I told you they auctioned off the home's contents upon the woman's death. Anything with value would've been sold decades ago."

Annie thought of the papers in her backpack. Were those valueless? She assumed the market for first drafts of minimally read books wasn't exactly the stuff of bidding wars, but the pages meant something to her. For Gus to call them worthless felt like an insult.

"I'd like to see those transcripts," Gus said, reading her mind, or more likely her face, which was never a decent fortress against her innermost thoughts.

"Sure," she said with a nod. "I'll, uh, gather them up."

Suddenly the front door of the inn flung open. It cracked against the far wall. A squall of lavender and curls spiraled in their direction.

"Annie!"

Nicola came tearing down the walkway, her coat flying out behind her.

"Annie! Miss Annie! Your mother's been looking for you! She only just left."

"Mother?" Gus said archly. "I thought you were traveling alone?"

"Mostly!" Annie said. "Mostly alone!"

"Your mum left a message," Nicola said, and jammed a peach-colored slip into Annie's hand. She shot Gus a scrutinizing look.

Annie smiled weakly at both of them as her eyes scanned the page.

A—

Why do I feel like I'm being punished? An early run?
A suspicious tale if ever there was one. I'll be tied up in
meetings all day, but please be ready by six o'clock for dinner.
Love you greatly. —Mom

Annie crumpled up the note and shoved it into her backpack.

"Thanks, Nicola," she said.

"Also, a message has come in, from your intended. I didn't mean to pry but you left your e-mail open. Anyhoo, the computer is available if you'd like to use it."

"Okay. Thanks for letting me know. By the way, do you know my friend . . ."

"Yes, we're acquainted," she said. "How's your brother?"

" 'Bout the same," Gus said. He turned to Annie. "The older brother might have the responsibilities but everyone loves the kid brother more."

"Give him my warmest regards!" Nicola said.

"It would be my pleasure." Gus extended a hand toward Nicola, and then to Annie. "Well, I best be off. Cheers, ladies. And, Annie, please. As appealing a proposition as it might seem, try to keep yourself out of trouble. That smile helps but it's not going to cover up every crime."

Twenty-nine

Subject: **Please be careful**
From: eric.sawyer@usmc.mil
Date: Nov 5, 2001 6:48
To: anniehaley79@aol.com

This old man is a good old charmer . . . too charming if you ask me. The research must be fun and the duchess . . . she's wild. But Annie, don't get yourself into any messes you can't get out of. Of course you can't undo the transcript stealing. So yes, absolutely, read them. I guess "fake researcher" is turning into the real deal. Seems like you're good at it.

So. The war. It's going well so far. We're almost done. Just kidding. We're still on the MEU, making our way toward AFG. I wish we'd get there already. There's a lot of nervous energy on the float, all that damn anticipation.

It must sound strange, that we want to fight. Well, that's not exactly right. It's like this. We've been tasked with something huge, and we're nervous because we want to do our jobs and do them right. It feels important. Monumental. A large load we have to carry alone. The few, the proud, and all that. On the one hand is glory, on the other . . . I can't even think about it.

Plus there's a little something called revenge. Revenge for all of the destruction. No one will say it, but . . . well . . . there it is. Man, we all desperately hope to do some good out there. We want to do right by our nation, and our parents, and all our wonderful Annies back home.

Not that there's anyone like you—sweet, pretty, brilliant. I swear, Annie, sometimes it's like you popped right out of a novel and into my life. It's the famous "too good to be true" except that you're real. And believe me, I've tried to find the chink. So far, no dice. I know you'd point to your living and employment situation, but all that's temporary. A person's job is not who they are.

Well, I'd better go. As anxious as I am to get to the gettin' on, I'll have a lot fewer opportunities to write once we're there. Our distance will be compounded the second I step off this boat. I can't imagine missing you more than I do now.

Stay happy. Stay safe.

All my love,
Eric

Thirty

WS: Tell me about Bernard Berenson.

GD: What does one say about the greatest art historian who ever lived?

WS: The "greatest"? Come now.

GD: Bernard was solely responsible for creating a market for Renaissance paintings. If not for him, there'd be no quote-unquote Old Masters.

WS: There is also the converse. Some say he manipulated the market and drove prices to unreasonable levels.

GD: A person has to earn a living.

WS: Customarily, yes. From what I've read, you and Berenson traveled together extensively.

GD: We did. I often joined him on trips to secure various pieces of art. He trusted my keen insight and objectivity. Assessing art may sound like a quite fanciful occupation but B.B. was under a lot of pressure. His clients were top-of-the-line.

WS: Such as?

GD: Henry Clay Frick. William Randolph Hearst. J. P. Morgan. Andrew Mellon. John D. Rockefeller. To name a few.

WS: That's quite a pedigree.

GD: Well, he was quite a man. B.B. taught me a tremendous amount. About art, of course, but also dedication. He'd travel to monasteries in the farthest outreaches of civilization to examine a single brushstroke.

WS: Astounding.

GD: Not big enough a word.

WS: But the two of you were rather disparate in age.

GD: One year or a hundred between us, does it matter?

WS: And what about Berenson's wife?

GD: Ah, old Mary. A serious woman, and a respected art critic in her own right. She liked to pretend

I was a silly, simple girl. Couldn't tolerate the intellectual competition because she couldn't compete on looks. With me, there was nothing she could feel superior about.

WS: I thought you and Mary were friends. You once asked B.B. to pass along the following message to her. [Sound of papers rustling] "My love in honeyed streams to that sweetest of white mice cooked in gooseberry jam."

GD: We were friends, for a time. But that's what friendships do. They end.

WS: Ah, so cooked in gooseberry jam by and by. Note to manuscript. Mrs. Spencer appears wistful.

GD: Mr. Seton, I have no place in my life for wistful.

WS: But you cared about Berenson deeply, didn't you?

GD: I loved him in ways you could never understand.

WS: Tell me, Mrs. Spencer, if you were so close, how come you stopped speaking in 1920?

GD: I believe he passed. That's the problem I often faced, seeing as how I was so much younger than everyone I consorted with.

WS: That's not true. I meant the first part! Please! Calm down! No need to throw things, Mrs. Spencer. I was referring to the bit about his passing. Berenson died in 1959. Not so long ago but long after you lost touch. Forty years almost.

GD: You sure know how to make a gal feel like roses.

WS: I'm sorry, Mrs. Spencer, I'm only trying to get a story, flesh out your varied cast of characters. So what happened?

GD: What happened? [Deep sigh, then three long beats] Same as always. A series of misunderstandings. My engagement to Lord Brooke, for one, he did not relish. Many rows followed and then a final, damaging crack. We never exchanged another word.

WS: How bleak.

GD: It's the manner of human nature, though, isn't it? Our bonds can't last. Despite our best efforts, the rest of the world always gets in our way.

thirty-one

WS: But you've told us yourself—your father shot your mother's lover. Another thread linking you and the duchess.

GD: Crimes of passion happen often enough. The French wanted to pass a damned law about it! This story [Sound of newspaper thrashing] is not about them.

WS: Reading from the New York Times article. "Deacon's Line of Defense. The Killing of Monsieur Abeille" by Alexandre Dumas.

GD: . . .

WS: Quoting from this same article. "At midnight Deacon goes to the door of his wife's rooms and hears a noise which convinces him that she is not alone. He returns to his own room to get a revolver. At the same time he warns the secretary of the hotel, who goes with him. At Madame's door they wait three minutes. Madame opens the door in her night toilet, holding a candle in her hand. Thinking it is his duty, he enters, despite the resistance of his wife. He discovers a man whom he recognizes as Abeille and fires at him thrice." Thrice. You have mentioned this to me prior. Three times through the couch and whatnot.

GD: A coincidence. Everyone knows there are only three plots in this world.

WS: A rather specific plot, this.

GD: I'm not sure why you want to spend so much time and attention on an assassin.

WS: Are you referring to your father? Or the man from the article?

GD: My father. [Audible sighing] Both. I'm not sure what you want me to say.

WS: It must've been an onerous situation for your family.

GD: I was . . . away at school. Anyhow, in the end, my father only served a year's sentence. And got himself a nice cell besides. All's well.

WS: "Well" is probably not the most accurate word, I'd reckon.

GD: True, he was a tragic figure but even now it comforts me to remember his last words before being carted off. "Take care of the children." Said to his brother.

WS: So his last thoughts were of you.

GD: Yes. My father, for all his problems, did love us. He loved Mum, too.

WS: But he cut her out of his will?

GD. He did. It rankled her something fierce, of course, but at least he left the four of us girls with trusts and income for life.

WS: Even Dorothy? The bastard child?

GD: Please don't speak of my sister that way. She cannot help where she came from. But, yes. Illegitimate. Out of wedlock. Love child. And so on. Dorothy was allotted the same as the rest of us.

WS: How did your mother react to the change in beneficiaries?

GD: The lack of income hurt, certainly. Mum was somehow the richest woman I've ever known whilst also never having a cent to her name. On top of that, as soon as Father was released and the divorce finalized, he earned custody of us.

WS: Many would find it unconscionable that the court released children into the home of a convicted murderer.

GD: Convicted unlawful injurer. Murders aside, as a man, Father was deemed a much better guardian than some wanton sex-obsessed slag, as Mum was no doubt considered.

WS: Your mother must've been gutted.

GD: Thoroughly, yes. But Mummy always found a way around her troubles. And a way to maintain her gilded lifestyle.

WS: When I used the word "gutted," I was referring to the loss of her children.

GD: Oh, that. Well, the custody situation didn't last. She kidnapped us from his home before too long. So everything turned out fine.

WS: Other than for your father, who died in a sanitarium. Note to manuscript. Mrs. Spencer is shrugging, but also tearing up.

GD: My eyes are watering on account of your gamey scent. When exactly was the last time you showered?

WS: You're not the first to ask. Mrs. Spencer, I can understand why it's hard for you to talk about this.

GD: Hard? Not necessarily. While the situation presented a unique set of challenges, one must contemplate whether it was for the best.

WS: If what was for the best? The shooting? Or the kidnapping?

GD: All of it. Every last miserable detail. It resulted in my parents' divorce, for one, which was beneficial to everyone involved.

WS: Including you, who received all that money.

GD: I won't apologize for my father's generosity.

WS: I'm not asking you to.

GD: On top of that, the scandal forced Mother into a different sense of purpose.

WS: How so?

GD: In a blink, her options were limited. She could no longer portray herself as the toast of Paris. Or of Rome. Her time in the limelight ended swiftly and so she focused on finding partners for her daughters instead.

WS: A sacrifice in a way.

GD: Not that she became asexual, mind you. Mother had to pay the bills somehow. But before the "event" she tried to sop up all of the attention, like a spotlight-seeking sponge. After the shooting and the divorce and the kidnapping, she decided to let us shine instead.

WS: Perhaps I wouldn't be sitting here, then, if your father hadn't shot someone.

GD: Hmm. Yes. Perhaps if not for that, you'd be pestering some other woman, mistaking HER for the duchess.

WS: Do you ever miss him, your father? I know you've mourned your mother since the day you learned she'd passed. But what about your dad?

GD: My father left me his name. He left me his money. But mostly he remains a shadowy figure. I know he was a cavalry officer in the Civil War. He was dark and fiercely intelligent. He made quick friends with those he met. But mostly I remember he was a very good shot.

Thirty-Two

Gladys's mother was nothing if not determined.

When Florence decided to focus exclusively on making matches for her girls, she succeeded beyond her wildest dreams. And well into the nightmares of various wives throughout Europe.

Dorothy, the baby of the family and daughter of the slain lover, married a prince and a then a count. At one point she carried the storied name of Radziwill.

Pretty but cantankerous Edith wed a wealthy industrialist. What she lacked in title she made up for in cash, and many times over. The other sisters would be forever jealous of Edith, and her ability to spend without thought.

As we know, Gladys would go on to marry the Duke of Marlborough but not before she smashed through a cadre of notables such as Prince William of Prussia, Hope diamond owner Lord Francis Pelham-Clinton-Hope, the Dukes of Norfolk and of Camastra, General Joffre, Lord Brooke, among untold others.

These relationships may not have lasted but they all contributed to the very essence of Gladys Deacon. When someone complimented her political knowledge at a dinner party, Gladys famously proclaimed, "Of course I'm well informed! I've slept with eleven prime ministers and most kings!"

—J. Casper Augustine Seton,
The Missing Duchess: A Biography

"Please be ready by six o'clock for dinner," said the note from Laurel.

Whatever grain of regret Annie had about the false-jogger story disappeared at around 6:10.

By 6:15, her annoyance turned to anger.

When the clock hit 6:45, Annie wrote off her mother completely. Who was this unreliable woman and what had she done with Laurel Haley? At least Annie had a few "friends" to keep her company, stolen as they were.

Sifting through the pages, Annie thought about Mrs. Spencer and how living with her must've been unnerving in ways that had little to do with yowling outbursts or physical threats. It was the woman's carefully guarded cunning that frightened Annie the most. How had Win ever wrenched a book from her?

With a sigh, Annie pitched the transcripts onto the desk, and then watched as they slid, slow-motion style, straight toward an open bottle of Diet Coke. She screeched when the drink toppled over.

"Shit!" Annie lurched to standing. "Annie! You idiot!"

She swiped the papers from the desk.

"Dammit!"

She blew on them. She shook them. She held them up only to watch helplessly as trails of Diet Coke ran to the floor.

"Annie, you *wanker*," she said, eyes watering.

She was done for. The drink's delicious chemical black magic would obliterate the papers as surely as it was eating away at her insides.

"Dammit all to hell."

Just her luck. The one time she made any sort of coordinated contact between two separate objects ended in disaster. Her youth softball coach would be pleased to know she was not made entirely of striking out.

Annie kicked at the chair in frustration, but missed of course, then peeled the most soda-drenched sheet from the desktop. After pressing it against her shirt, Annie held it up to the light.

That's when she noticed. On the back of the paper was an address, written in pencil, in what appeared to be a woman's hand.

24 Quai de Béthune
144071200

The address of someone in Paris perhaps? And what was the second line? It wasn't a zip code. A phone number, maybe?

Without thinking, Annie picked up the phone and began to dial.

"We're sorry, but your number cannot be reached as dialed. Please try again."

Annie frowned. She remembered from a semester abroad junior year that the correct country code for France was 33. Annie tried again but the congenial-voiced British lady was back. *We're sorry . . .*

With a small huff, she hung up. Probably better not to get through. She'd have a hard time explaining long-distance charges to her mom.

"Quai de Béthune," she said as she paced the room, staring at the address.

It sounded familiar, which was why she guessed Paris, but Annie couldn't exactly place the name. An address along the Seine, most likely, as you needed water to have a quay.

"Quai de Béthune," she repeated and inspected the paper.

It was starting to crumple and dry, a faint brown blotch marring the sheet top to bottom. Annie glanced at the other papers on the desk, most of them equally stained and damp. She'd kick herself but would probably bungle that, too.

"Damn it," she muttered. "Gus is going to kill me."

Suddenly, she heard a click.

Annie lifted her head with a jerk. Across the room, the doorknob jiggled. Her heart jumped.

"Crap!" she yelled, and scurried to collect the transcripts. "Shit! Shit! Shit!"

Most were wet. She could already feel them clumping together.

"Annie?" Laurel said. "Are you in there? Dang it, my key always jams in this lock."

"Yes, yes, coming!"

She looked at the papers now in her hands, and saw no choice but to cram them into her backpack. Annie cringed as the sheets bunched together into soggy globs of pulp.

The door popped open.

"Oh, hi, Mom," Annie said to the rasp of her backpack's zipper.

She chucked it toward the bed, almost pummeling Laurel as she made her way across the room.

"Ugh! I'm so late! Whoops . . . flying backpack."

"Nice of you to show," Annie grumbled.

"I am so sorry," Laurel said.

She paused to catch her breath as Annie gawked, astonished to see her mom looking so wild and unkempt. Laurel's face was shiny, her hair a riot of knots and gnarls. And the suit. It looked like something out of the donation bin at church.

"Mom?"

"I'm sorry, I'm sorry," Laurel said again. "The meeting ran over and traffic was abominable and . . ."

She stopped, then exhaled, appearing to deflate all at once.

"In other words," she said. "All the regular excuses."

"Yeah," Annie answered with a grunt. "Exactly. Your excuses are getting old so feel free to sell them to someone else because I'm no longer in the market."

Annie should've given her mom more leeway, seeing as how her own actions of late weren't exactly beyond reproach. But she couldn't help herself, an alarming trend the past few days.

"Honey, you seem agitated," Laurel noted.

"Of course I'm agitated! You're an hour late and I'm starving!"

It was both of these things, but also more.

Yes, Annie was miffed at her mom and her stomach felt like it was trying to reach through her skin for something to eat. But she was also unfairly irritated with Eric for being so wonderful and then getting on a ship. And she was bugged by Nicola Teepers, proprietress. The woman could've included international dialing instructions beside the phone.

She also resented Gus for spooling out information in dribs and drabs, as slow to the story as Mrs. Spencer was with Win. Hell, Annie was even mad at Mrs. Spencer, a woman dead some twenty years.

But more than all of these people combined, Annie was most furious with herself. The Diet Coke spill. A "job" she loved that was a complete invention. And what kind of person could be mad at Laurel, Gus, Nicola, and Eric in the first place?

What exactly was Annie getting worked up about anyway? How could a book drive her so thoroughly insane, an old tale that was probably more fiction than fact? Of all the people in Gus's story, Annie couldn't believe it was Win that she sympathized with the most. The book, the story, these things were make-or-break for the man. How was it Annie completely understood? Why did she feel the same way?

Thirty-three

THE GEORGE & DRAGON
BANBURY, OXFORDSHIRE, ENGLAND
NOVEMBER 2001

Sometime during her thirteenth year, Gladys learned about the Duke of Marlborough's betrothal to Consuelo Vanderbilt, whom he wed in 1895 in exchange for $2.5 million worth of Beech Creek Railway stock.

"I suppose you have read about the engagement of the Duke of Marlborough," Gladys wrote to a friend. "O dear me if I was only a little older I might catch him yet! But *hélas!* I am too young though mature in the arts of woman's witchcraft and what is the use of one without the other? And I will have to give up all chance to ever get Marlborough."

Sure, she spent a few moments envying Consuelo's good fortune and glittering new existence, but Gladys Deacon was not a woman who stopped at moral or romantic defeat. She vowed to get Marlborough, and in the end, that's exactly what she did.

—J. Casper Augustine Seton,
The Missing Duchess: A Biography

Annie hesitated in the doorway.

She scanned the bar and decided Gus wasn't there. Another strikeout for the hapless Miss Haley. Annie let her shoulders slump and shuffled back toward the sidewalk.

Then came a sharp whistle.

"Annie!" called a voice.

She poked her head back inside.

"Hey, Ned!" she said. "I, uh . . ."

"He's over there." He jerked his thumb toward the corner. "Fading into the woodwork, the old codger. I'm as shocked as you are."

Annie squinted toward the rear of the pub and there sat Gus, in a booth, sipping cider with another man. His companion was a spindly fellow with a mop of curly black hair and a beak of a nose. So Gus knew other people. An unexpected surprise.

"Miss Annie?" Ned said, raising his forehead questioningly. "You can go on. Don't think he'd mind."

"Oh, I don't want to bother them," she said. "I'll catch Gus later! Cheers!"

Annie stepped back, eyes still caught on the mysterious meeting in the corner, when suddenly the corkscrewed man stood. He and Gus traded a mostly forced hug, followed by a series of aggressive back-pats. Wallops, more like. The man belted out a final "good-bye" and strode Annie's way. She froze. He swept past, smiling warmly in her direction.

"Annie!" Gus hollered just as she was about to (inexplicably) follow the strange man. "You've arrived just in time! My schedule's cleared for the day!"

"Oh, um, hi," she mumbled, staggering toward his table. "What's up?"

"Not much is *up*. And how are you this lovely afternoon? I see you remain on the lam from authorities."

"You're hilarious."

Annie thumped her backpack onto the table and slouched down in the booth.

"You all right there, love?" Gus asked.

"Who knows," she said. "So who was that guy? I thought you didn't have any friends."

"Grace Almighty. You're right testy today, aren't you? And that, my dear, was no friend. That was my brother Jamie."

Gus folded up his newspaper, then removed his glasses and set them on the table.

"Brother?" Annie said, blinking. "You have a . . . oh. Right. Nicola mentioned that. You never talk about him. Ever. It's weird."

"What's there to say? There's not much to him." Gus took a sip of cider. "So what is it?"

"What's what?"

"That." He pointed at her with his glass. "Your face. The utter lack of cheer."

"Oh. I don't know." Annie thought about it for a second. "It's hard to say. I feel stuck, I suppose."

"Stuck? In what way?"

In every way, if she was being honest.

Annie was stuck in the duchess's story, for one. And in Win's and Pru's. She was also physically stuck in England, her mom mostly absent and her fiancé on a boat.

On top of that, her very existence was stuck, trapped in the space between childhood and being an adult. Eric was off fighting wars; meanwhile she probably couldn't even lease a car without Laurel's signature.

"Annie?" Gus prodded.

"I'm just so frustrated," she said. "All around and across the board. I'm just . . ."

She couldn't even finish the sentence.

"Ah. So this is about the research project."

"Yes, among other things."

"I'm not surprised," Gus said. "You're an empathetic person. You're probably so deeply mired in the story, you've picked up on Win Seton's disgruntlement."

"That's part of it. But, Gus. Seriously." She tossed up her hands. "You're every bit as bad as Mrs. Spencer!"

"As bad as Mrs. Spencer?" His eyes widened. "I don't know if you've just complimented me or you want me to sod off."

"You left me hanging the other day, outside the inn. A million pieces of the story scattered everywhere. I realize Nicola interrupted us, but you dumped the mess on me, and then you bailed."

"I *bailed*?"

"You're not making this easy. And I have to say, it's not appreciated."

"Annie, every story has a pace," Gus said. "Including Mrs. Spencer's, and Win's. I can't just vomit it all up in one go. As a devotee of literature, you should know this implicitly."

"Well, some stories move too slowly. Sluggish plots are the worst."

Annie unzipped her backpack and pulled out the transcripts.

"Here's what I've been reading," she said. "And yes, they're stolen and, yes, I've spilled Diet Coke on them and, yes, I'm a horrible steward of important documents. And to what end? It seems like most of what Win knew about Mrs. Spencer, the duchess, whoever she was . . . most of what he garnered was from newspaper articles and gossip columns, not from the woman herself."

"Let's see what you have," Gus said, putting his glasses back on.

He did a hero's job of appearing calm, of not seeming like he wanted to throttle Annie. For the first few seconds anyway. But when he turned over the most Diet Coke-laden sheet, his face went white.

"Annie, this n—"

"I know! I know!" she said, and clonked her head on the table. "I'm the worst."

She looked back up.

"Reason number four hundred thirty-seven that I'm so agitated," she said. "I'm a spaz. A klutz. Not to mention the world's most overachieving meddler."

Face locked in an expression Annie could've read (irritation? bewilderment?), Gus handed back the transcripts. He wiped a dribble of sweat from his forehead.

"You're not nearly as bad as all that," he said.

"I beg to differ," Annie said. "So what's next? What happens after this? Help a mess of a girl out."

"What happens after *what*?"

"Did Mrs. Spencer finally crack?" she asked. "Or did Win just grill the poor woman until she keeled over from exhaustion or old age? And let's not forget the wan and waifish Pru Valentine observing from the corner. She must've read like a thousand books by the time Win got his written."

"Well," Gus said, eyes holding steady to the transcripts on the table. "Mrs. Spencer eventually started talking. She did begin to aid Win, albeit in her own marginally helpful way."

"Marginally helpful. Sounds about right. So did she finally cop to being the duchess?"

"Not precisely. She gave Win more to work with, but her usual 'I'm no duchess' rigmarole remained."

"Why'd she even bother, then?" Annie asked. "If she wasn't going to tell the whole story why not keep yammering on about chickens and geese?"

"A fair question and she probably would've done exactly that, absent a little interference from the universe."

"The *universe?*"

"Or God. Fate. What have you. You see, nearly overnight, Mrs. Spencer began to see Pru not as a diaphanous, wide-eyed household employee but a bona fide romantic rival. And no one, especially not an *American,* was going to steal the woman's carefully crafted, century-old show."

Thirty-four

"So I brought you duck," Pru said, setting a plate on Win's desk. "Not our ducks, of course. From the market. Although, who knows where they got them, so perhaps they're ours after all."

She nudged aside a few errant pieces of paper, fully expecting Win to bat her away. He was particular about the kind of mess he liked to have. But instead he sat unmoving, arms hanging limply like wet ropes in his lap.

"What's the damage this time?" she asked. "You're not improving the 'moody writer' cliché, by the way."

"I thought she'd bite the hook," he said in his most pitiable, sad-sack voice. "With Prince Willy dangling helplessly on the end like that, world peace in the balance. I thought this story would finally take flight."

"She gave *some* color," Pru pointed out. "It wasn't a total waste."

"What do you know of it? You were reading a bloody book."

"I can do two things at once. And the Prince Willy conversation happened days ago! Why are you still twisted round the axle about it?"

Win glanced up and with one hand pushed back a chunk of floppy hair. Gone was the precise crew cut, which seemed so hopelessly old-fashioned when Pru first saw him. Even his formerly smooth face was now covered in stubble, partway to a beard. Facial hair: another thing Win Seton could only start and not finish all the way.

"Has it really been days?" he asked. "It feels like hours."

"Times flies when you're having fun. And you are clearly having a blast. Come on, try some duck. You look gaunt. Moping must really take it out of a person."

"It makes no sense," Win said, refusing to listen. "Gladys Deacon was nothing if not showy, full of her own greatness. Preventing a war? How is this not enough to wring the duchess out of Mrs. Spencer?"

"Maybe she truly sees herself as Mrs. Spencer."

Either that or the writer was wrong from the start. It was a theory Pru had been batting around for the last several days.

Thirty-four years old and he'd accomplished little. Win Seton was an authority on exactly nothing and, on top of that, seemed perfectly content to hole up in a room like a naughty child from a Dickens novel. Pru didn't understand how a bloke could seem so aimless and yet so determined at the same time. It made her question everything.

"This is never going to happen, is it?" Seton moaned. "The whole deal will go balls-up and everyone will be right about me. Every last damned person."

"Oh, you'll be fine," Pru said halfheartedly as she arranged the duck. "Mrs. Spencer will come around."

Pru didn't necessarily believe this and in fact understood where Mrs. Spencer was coming from. They were both rather fed up with Win's relentless sulking. You'd think he was the one who lost a fiancé in the war. Or the one pretending to be crazy as a loon.

"I can't go up there again," she announced the next evening as Mrs. Spencer cooked a batch of eggs on the stovetop.

"So don't," Mrs. Spencer answered simply.

"You could fix him, you know."

"Gracious. And how might I accomplish that?"

"If you gave the poor bastard even the slightest drop of information, you could turn this whole thing around."

"A drop of information?" Mrs. Spencer balked. "Have you not been paying attention? Every blasted night I go up there and spill my secrets!"

"The only thing you've spilled is whisky and chewing tobacco," Pru said.

"And thanks to your lack of help, the entire content of his story could fit on a matchbook, and I fear he's irreversibly depressed as a result."

"It's not my fault he's a shitty writer," Mrs. Spencer said as she scraped the eggs into a chipped cobalt bowl.

"It's a game to you, same as threatening townsfolk. Same as your cats with their half-dead and partially strangled mice. Just throw another rodent onto the heap."

"His queries are nonsense." Mrs. Spencer turned a salt shaker over the eggs and shook with zeal. "How am I supposed to answer questions about someone else's life? Now. Go deliver his food."

"I think you should. Then stick around. Do some reminiscing. Give the man an anecdote or two."

"No, thank you."

"I don't know why you derive such enormous pleasure in being so damned fussy!"

Pru swiped a loaf of bread from the counter and stomped off, rolling her eyes as she went.

"Stupid, bananas woman," Pru said, clomping up the stairs. "Stupid, bananas house."

At the top step, she hesitated. Pru looked toward Win's room. Though his light was on, she didn't hear the usual smack-ding of the typewriter or the even squeak of his chair. Seton was a vigorous typist, always putting his full body weight into it as he careened his way down the page.

"Win?" Pru whispered.

Perhaps she'd finally have a spot of luck and he'd be sleeping or showering or passed out in his own filth. They wouldn't have to talk and Pru could leave his plate outside the door in true Dickensian fashion. It was getting awkward, the ongoing dialogue about the book that wasn't happening. Welcome to the family, Win would've said, had she told him how she felt.

"Mr. Seton?" she said.

She prodded the door open. Like everything else in the house, it whined with the slightest tap. As Pru shuffled forward, she noticed Win's desk was empty, save three flies buzzing around an old, dirtied plate.

"Oh thank God." Pru leaned against the doorjamb and exhaled loudly. "Maybe you've finally decided to bathe. Or put an end to your misery."

"No such luck," said a voice.

She whipped around. Win sat on the bed, a bottle of wine lodged between his thighs. Freud would have a field day with that one.

"I . . . uh . . ." she stuttered.

"I'm afraid you've found me alive and kicking. Don't fret, Miss Valentine, you're hardly the first to express such opinion. Come, won't you join me? Misery loves company. Especially in the form of mysterious young companions of the clinically insane."

Thirty-five

"Oh, hello," Pru said, heart knocking against her chest. "I didn't see you there."

"Obviously."

"I'm sorry, I didn't mean . . ."

Win shook his head and waved her off. She strained to keep her eyes at window level or higher, given the man was in his underclothes, the bottle of wine jutting aggressively from between his legs. Pru noted that his thighs were athletic, ropy, and blanketed in blond hair. Then she promptly scolded herself for noting them in the first place.

"I'm the one who should apologize for my indecent state and vulgar behavior," Win said. "You know, you're far too refined to be living here."

"I'm not even close to refined, which is probably why I haven't run screaming for the hills as any sensible person would've by now."

"Perhaps 'refined' isn't the best word. You do have a certain, shall we say . . . 'womanly dignity of a diminutive order.'"

"Womanly dignity of a diminutive order," she repeated.

The description was not his. Pru closed her eyes and at once remembered the smell of the book from which the words came.

"Hardy?" she said, and opened her eyes again. "Am I right?"

"Yep." He nodded, then took a swig of wine. "Said of Bathsheba's maid Liddy in *Far from the Madding Crowd*."

"So I'm the maid?"

"Aren't you?"

"Yes," she said with a sigh. "I suppose that's exactly what I am."

"Aw hell, don't be blue. I'm the resident miserable wretch. You have the dignity, at a minimum."

"You're hardly a wretch," she lied.

"You are the one who suggested I should off myself only moments ago. Good grief, don't look so plucked. You were right." He took another drink of wine. "Someone *should* put me out of my misery."

Win picked up his voice recorder, which had previously been on the bed.

"This bloody device," he said. "Do you know what's on it?"

"Your conversations with Mrs. Spencer?"

"Correct. Otherwise known as nothing. Zed. Sweet Fanny Adams. Here. Let me play a chord."

He pressed a button.

"The geese," Mrs. Spencer said, her voice crackling on the tape. "A family of geese lives at the pond. Every night at six o'clock they take flight, right on cue. Together they make one large circle around Banbury and then return home. I like rituals, don't you, Mr. Seton?"

"Oh yes, Lady Marlborough, nothing grander than geese rituals."

Win clicked another button.

"Why don't we fast-forward to another point in ol' GD's tales," he said over the scribble-scratch of the tape.

"GD?"

"Gladys Deacon. Or God Damn. Take your pick. All right, just tell me when to stop. Any place! Any a'tall!" He lifted his finger. "And release."

"Sometimes I lose count of the chickens," Mrs. Spencer said. "You probably think I let them run amok, without any sort of tracking system. Well, I do let them run amok. Who shouldn't be allowed to do that? Alas, I keep careful inventory. I know their names and where each one is at the close of the day."

"Geese and chickens," Win said and turned off the tape. "Don't forget the swans and speckled guinea fowl. Even an ornithologist would find the recordings insufferable."

He sighed, cocked back an arm, and chucked the recorder. As it crashed against the wall, Pru jumped. She was accustomed to his grousing but did not expect any demonstration of mettle. It was reassuring, in its way. Win had some life in him yet.

"You should be careful," she said, darting over to fetch the device. "I doubt Mrs. Spencer would buy you a new one."

When she bent down, Pru noted the recorder was intact. Despite his (previously) brawny appearance and the backslapping 'allo-mate footballer attitude, the man didn't seem to be much of an athlete. She'd witnessed more damaging tantrums committed by the toddlers who lolled around outside the Banbury crèche.

"No recorder?" Win said. "A tragedy because what on God's green would I do without detailed information on yard chickens? You can keep it, Miss Valentine. I'm not sure what your hobbies are, or if you have any sort of education whatsoever. But surely you can record something of note. Lacking philosophical insight or quadratic formulas to solve, you could sing into it. Warble some Don McLean. You, the Grange's own Miss American Pie."

"I've never met a man so ensnared in his own self-pity. You're like a damned rat that keeps returning to the same trap. And yes, I do have some education 'whatsoever.' I went to Berkeley." Pru raised a fist. "Fight the man. Here."

She thrust the recorder in his direction.

"Take the damned thing," she said. "You'll need it. At some point."

"Will I?" Win sighed again. More deeply this time, as if he wanted to be sure all of the Cotswolds heard. "Sit down."

He patted the spot beside him.

"Why would I do that?" she asked.

"You're done for the day, aren't you?" he said. "The spaniels are washed, clipped, nursed, and neutered . . ."

"If only they were neutered."

"The old lady's about to retire for the night. Come. Join me." He patted the bed a second time. "We're housemates, in this mess together and all that. We might as well be friends."

"You've been quite into the wine, I gather."

"We can toast to my ongoing failure."

With a sigh, Pru plunked down onto the bed.

"I can stay," she said. "For a minute."

She wasn't "done for the day" but Win was more interesting than shoveling dog feces, which was the very best she could say about him.

"Here," he said and passed her the wine. "Bottoms up."

Pru took the bottle and peered into it. Might there be glasses downstairs? Or was she supposed to guzzle straight from the top? Pru wasn't the persnickety type but some stemware would've been nice.

"Where'd you get this?" she asked.

"Brought a few liters with me." He released a silent, though pungent, burp. "My family owns a winery. Welsh Wine. It's for shit and I advise you never to put it near an open flame. But, alas, it is wine. And sometimes that's all you need."

Pru was never a wine drinker. She enjoyed the occasional beer in college, a few tokes on a periodic joint, but that was the extent of it. However, she was now holed up in a haunted house, her only human companions a writer and a lunatic. Wine seemed like a damned logical medicine to take.

"Well, here goes nothing," she said and downed a gulp.

As it slid into her throat, hot and slightly burning, Pru immediately understood his comment about the open flame. Within seconds, her belly loosened. Pru tipped the bottle back again.

Win might've been a little drunk, but he was a lot befuddled. It was a remarkable situation to have a female exactly where he wanted her. In this case, voluntarily entertaining his attempts at conversation.

And Pru was something more than most, different from the ordinary gals he met at university and in not-so-subtle setups arranged around his parents' supper table. All those Imogens and Rosalies and So-and-So Poppleswell-Hawkes, not a one as appealing as Pru.

Oh yes, he'd noticed, she'd be surprised to learn. Though seemingly on a one-way journey to Duchess-ville, Win Seton had developed no small regard for Pru. She was lovely and smart and had a wicked snap of humor beneath all the jitters and nerves. He didn't know her well but the truth was Pru intrigued him from the start. Now that she sat beside him, the big problem was what to do with her, the bigger yet how he might entice her to stay.

Thirty-six

THE GRANGE
CHACOMBE-AT-BANBURY, OXFORDSHIRE, ENGLAND
JANUARY 1973

"So, my fair American," Win said as they passed the wine back and forth between them. "What are you doing here?"

"Delivering your food, same as always. But if you want me to leave . . ."

Pru rose to her feet. Already her legs were warm and weak.

"No," Win said, and pushed her back onto the bed gently.

He did not immediately move his hand from her lap. A chill rippled through Pru's body.

"Stay," he said. "And I didn't mean why are you here, in this room. I meant why are you here? In this old house, with that old lady? Here, have another sip."

"I could ask you the same thing," she replied, increasingly emboldened by the wine, its taste continuing to sting the back of her nose. "As opposed to you, I'm getting paid. Quite handsomely at that."

"Well, your excuse is far superior to mine."

"Not exactly a high hurdle."

"Ouch! I think I have a scar from that hit." He chuckled in return. "You think it's odd, don't you? That I care so much about this old broad?"

"Odd is one word for it."

"I mean, what precisely have I accomplished in the last three weeks?"

"Nothing as far as I can tell," Pru said, and took another drink.

"So much effort. So much unneeded strife! Subjecting myself to drawn-out confabulations, fretting over blank tapes, possibly catching typhoid in this dank and musty home. All in the name of research."

"You said it, not me."

"Don't I know there are hungry children in the world?" he rolled on. "Natural disasters? There are wars, for Christ's sake! In Africa. And the Orient. Thanks to you chirpy Americans, there are entire villages being blown to bits!"

Pru flinched, and then swiped the bottle from his paws.

"Now I see why you're a writer," she said. "You don't have the proper interpersonal skills for a real job."

"You'll get no dispute from me."

Damn, he was blowing it already and didn't even know why. Alas, no surprise there. Mishandling the attentions of this pretty young thing was only a matter of time.

"Listen, I'm not sure what I said to offend—"

"I may live in a dilapidated mansion," Pru said, cutting into his sentence with the bite in her voice. "And I might work for an old woman who likes to shoot at people for recreation. But at least I have the good sense not to spout off about things I'm completely ignorant on."

"I do tend to do that, don't I? Anyhow, I enjoy being the nob. Expertise is overrated and my boggling nature makes people grateful not to be saddled with my very convoluted brain. I'm doing society a favor! Come now, enough with that sour-lemon face. I'm allowed to have an opinion on things. What do you call it in America? Free speech?"

"Yes, free speech, which doesn't necessarily entitle one to act like an ignoramus."

"Jesus H. A bit tetchy about Vietnam, are we?"

Win tipped over the bottle but they'd sucked it dry. He wondered if she wanted him to open another.

"TETCHY!" Pru said. "Do you have any manners at all?"

"What's wrong, never met anyone against the war?" he asked, and discarded the bottle onto the floor. It hit the boards with a clonk, then rolled toward Pru. "You said you went to Berkeley. I hear there are a few protestor-types round there."

"You don't know the first thing about it," Pru said. "So I respectfully request that you button your piehole."

"Damn, I didn't expect such spice—"

"And, since we're speaking of wars," Pru continued, good and fired up now. She kicked at the bottle and watched it roll back toward him. "You're welcome for saving your pale, puddingy countrymen from the Germans."

Win's face dropped. He opened his mouth to speak but nothing came out.

The man was many things, not the least of which was Banbury's resident village idiot, but Win Seton was never intentionally unkind. Yes, he was accidentally cruel at a near-criminal rate, but never on purpose. He hadn't realized he was doing it until he saw how low he'd brought the girl. All the way down to his godforsaken level. And for what? He didn't give a shit about Vietnam, either way.

"Shite on a biscuit," he said and ran both hands over his stubble. "Aw, Miss Valentine, I didn't aim to be such an arse. I was going for waggish. And failing spectacularly as it happens."

"Yeah, you weren't funny at all," Pru said, and crossed her arms.

She studied him for several moments before finally speaking again.

"But I probably overreacted," she admitted. "It's a sensitive topic for me."

"Oh Christ," he said, the truth hitting him with a crack. Of course she was sensitive about Vietnam. *Of course.* "You have some beloved fighting the Charlie over in Nam, don't you?"

Pru bit her lips together, refusing to answer, unwilling to kick about in this game.

"Fuck it all to hell," Win said. "Please forgive me, if you can. I'm a writer. We exaggerate. We make nonsensical statements and see ourselves as cleverer than we could ever hope to be. Here! Let me open this bottle. Let's have another and forget this conversation ever happened."

Within seconds, a cork popped. Before he could blink, Pru grabbed it and took the first swig.

"No, you're right," she told him after a satisfying gulp. "I am 'tetchy' about the subject. There is no beloved in Vietnam, though, sorry to report."

"Really? No grand love blasting away the VC?"

Eyes stinging, Pru shook her head.

"Nope," she said. "None at all."

"Thank Christ! That's a relief. I almost piddled myself. If you haven't noticed, I'm brilliant at putting my foot in my mouth. I bodge everything. Always."

"You didn't 'bodge' this," Pru said. "You simply didn't know."

He reached for the bottle but she pulled it back for one more gulp.

"You want to know something funny?" he said as Pru finally relinquished the wine. "When Mrs. Spencer was talking about betrothals . . . huh." Win looked pensive for a second. "A discussion not involving domesticated birds. Outstanding. At any rate, as Mrs. Spencer sermonized on the importance of racking up fiancés, she gave you this *look*."

"Mrs. Spencer gives me many looks. Eye rolls. Winks. Glowers of spite."

"This was a conspiratorial look," Win said. "It made me wonder if that's why you were here. Figured you'd ditched some poor bloke, a warmonger perhaps, and came to hide out in jolly old England."

"Well, you were wrong," Pru said, head weaving. "No jilted fiancés. No ditched warmongers for miles."

"Damn, I hate to be wrong. Happens far too often."

A junked fiancé in Vietnam? She should be so lucky.

Pru was the one ditched. Either intentionally or by circumstance, she had been cast off by every single person in her life. Charlie. Her parents. Various aunts and second cousins thrice removed. College friends. Even Charlie's parents.

Oh, she was faring adequately at the Grange, caught up in the daily tasks of spaniel-grooming and writer-minding. But sometimes in the thick part of the night, when the owls had flown home and the old house stopped chirring, she would find herself panicked, breathless with just how very alone she was.

If she died at the Grange (gunshot wound, tetanus, name your poison) there'd be no place to send her remains. Murray, Edith Junior, Mrs. Spencer, now Win. These, the four measly souls who knew where Pru was. Only two of them were even on her same continent. Only one would bother hassling with the outcome, likely packaging her up with the cats.

"Put a smile on that mug, Miss Valentine," Win said, discomforted by seeing someone more sullen than he. "Chin up. It'll be okay."

Pru pondered what Win might think if he knew the pictures playing in her mind. Dead cats. Obliterated fiancés. Her body parts boxed and stored away.

"I'm sure one day it will be okay," she said, unconvincingly. "I'm just not there yet. So is there more wine? I feel like this bottle is smaller than the last."

Win thought then that he probably should've kept the bird from the booze. Pru was young and fresh livered, her ability to battle alcohol's dispiriting qualities heretofore untested. He was corrupting the only decent creature in the whole bloody place.

"Oh, Miss Valentine," he said and uncorked a third bottle, healthy livers and bad influences be damned. "You're a beautiful girl. There will be plenty of blokes to eighty-six in your future. Having been on the receiving end of many such exchanges, I know of what I speak."

He inspected the wine before passing it to Pru.

"It's not that I want to—"

"Think we can get Mrs. Spencer to partake in this swill?" he asked, ripping into her train of thought, ramrodding straight into the progress she was beginning to make toward the truth. "It might get her talking."

Pru grunted. Mrs. Spencer. Of course. It always went back to *The Missing Duchess*. There was absolutely nothing else to the man. He was even more pitiful than she first surmised.

"You really are something," she said.

"Thank you."

"That was *not* a compliment."

Pru snatched the bottle from Win's hand and took another sip, the heat of the wine continuing to fill her body and mind.

"I don't get it," she said after a hard swallow. "Why are you so obsessed with her? Mrs. Spencer. Lady Marlborough. Gladys Deacon. Whatever you want to call her. This is the first you've met, right? Technically I've known her longer than you have."

"That's true. But it *feels* as though I've known her forever."

"That makes no sense. Also, it's highly irritating."

"It's like this," he said with a contrived chortle.

Irritating? Was he really that terrible?

"My life's been filled with these fairy tales," Win continued. "Countless stories of the legendary Gladys Deacon. In my head, she's this mythical creature, a chimera-witch hybrid whose powers never waned."

"Plus she was beautiful," Pru added. "So that helps."

"Yes, sure. That's true. As an adolescent, her portraits stirred . . . well, they stirred something inside of me. Or, rather, on the outside if you want to speak medically."

"Oh, God, please stop," Pru said. "No more commentary on the stirring of your appendages. So do you love her?"

"Who? The duchess? God no! She's nearly a hundred years old."

"So she's about your age, give or take."

"It's curious," Win said, grinning, nothing forced about his humor this time. "You have a spirited mouth for someone who appears so perpetually blush-faced and innocent."

Win thrust the bottle into Pru's hands and took to pacing the floor.

"Let's put it this way," he said. "To me she was a myth, a legend."

"Isn't a myth, by definition, made up? By the by, it sounds like she created most of it herself, starting with the famous shifting birth date."

"The duchess was known to tell a tall tale or four," he said. "But in the words of Thomas Hardy: 'Though a good deal is too strange to be believed, nothing is too strange to have happened.' The most outlandish of her stories are the very ones people swear are fact. What about you, Miss Valentine? Who beguiled you as a wee one? Whose stories filled your mind?"

"I don't know. Harriet the Spy? Mary Tyler Moore?"

"All right," Win said, amused. "Mary's a cute girl. And who wouldn't love Harriet? But newsroom gals and plucky detectives are not the beat I'm after."

"So what is it, then?" she asked. "I feel like I keep waiting for this 'beat' but it never comes."

"Bloody hell. Why am I so cack-handed at explaining this? It's my life's work. Though, as it turns out, I'm horrible with words."

"Here we go again," Pru said and rolled her eyes. "Break out the tissues for the world's most hard-luck writer! For the love of God, Seton, why not do the regular, normal-person thing?"

"And what is that, precisely?"

"Make like a bona fide storyteller and start from the beginning."

Thirty-seven

THE GRANGE
CHACOMBE-AT-BANBURY, OXFORDSHIRE, ENGLAND
JANUARY 1973

"It all goes back to my chum Gads," Win said.

"Gads?" Pru could not help but scoff.

"Ah, the young lady takes issue with my best mate's name. I see how it is."

"Sounds like a half-baked puppet show, is how it is. Win and Gads. Watch as they entertain children in the library at one o'clock."

Win dropped his jaw in feigned outrage. He was not used to getting this much crap from someone not already tired from years of his gaffes and tom-foolery. Astonishingly, Win didn't mind. He'd forgotten a good ribbing didn't always bruise.

"A *puppet* show?" he said, laughing.

"I can already tell this story is going to be ridiculous. Win and Gads. It's absurd!"

"Why, they're jolly good names!" Win said, letting himself in on the joke. "Succinct! Punctuated!" He swung his arm twice, much like someone named Win or Gads might do. "No nonsense."

"No nonsense? *Gads?*"

"They're nicknames. Practical. Not born of romantic notions, *Prunus lauro-cerasus*. I won't even start in on your surname, though I should."

"Both of my names are unimpeachable."

"A matter of opinion, that. If it makes you feel any better, Gads is officially Lord George William blah-de-blah cack-and-cobblers. He's the youngest brother so his title is irrelevant. Since our childhood, and on through Eton, he's always been Gads to me."

"Gads," Pru said a third time. "I can't handle these names. Gads. Egads. *Egads, that's one crazy bloke! Mad as a hatter!*"

"Your British accent needs some work. And whilst you think you're being funny, 'egads' is often ascribed to him by any one of his three wives, past or present." Win shook his head, still laughing. "As with most things, I blame my keen interest in Lady Marlborough—"

"Obsession."

"I blame my diligent duchess scholarship on Gads and his family. Mind you, he's merely the bumbling younger brother. His older brother John inherited the family dukedom, as big brothers do."

"Yes, yes," Pru said. "Happens all the time. If only I had a big brother to inherit ours."

"If you'll let me finish," he said, grinning. "Gads's older brother inherited the family title late last year, after marrying his third wife, the daughter of a Swedish count. Gads doesn't expect it to last long."

"Sounds like he'd know."

"Nevertheless wife number three can say that she was at one time hitched to the eleventh Duke of Marlborough."

"The same Marlborough as in . . ." Pru pointed toward Mrs. Spencer's room. "That one?"

"Yes! Of course 'that one'! There's only one Duke of Marlborough! This isn't a corporate position. It's a title. It's *inherited*. Honestly, Miss Valentine, I don't even know if I can carry forward."

"Stand down, mate," she said. "And please forgive me. We Americans aren't used to inheriting titles. Generally we have to put in a little effort for that kind of recognition."

"Right, right. Nothing for free. Only working to the teeth like the busy beavers that you are." Win rolled his eyes. "In any event, Gads's loaf-about, un-American brother inherited the title from their father, who was the tenth Duke of Marlborough. Because, as you may have learned during your storied tenure at university, ten comes before eleven."

Now it was Pru's turn to roll her eyes.

"Shall I write that down?" she asked.

"Yes, you'd better," he said. "The tenth duke, in addition to being Gads's and John's father, was also the dreaded stepson of our lady of the manor." He jerked his head toward the door. "Mrs. Spencer aka Lady Marlborough, who married the ninth duke. She did not get along with ol' Duke Ten. At all."

"So the duchess is . . ." She paused. "Gads's grandmother?"

Win nodded.

"Mrs. Spencer is your best friend's grandmother?" Pru said. "Have you told her? I feel like she should know."

"Technically she's the stepgranny, but close enough. And, no, the woman isn't aware of my relationship with Gads. Of course she claims she's not the duchess. Gads's *real* grandmother was Consuelo Vanderbilt."

"Coon!" Pru said with a small clap. "Mrs. Spencer's best pal."

"You've got it. As you already know, Gladys succeeded Coon as the Duchess of Marlborough."

"Quick way to end a friendship."

"Eh." Win shrugged. "Coon was thrilled to be done with the highly arranged marriage, as was hers with Marlborough Nine. He went by Sunny, short for Sunderland, which was no referendum on his temperament. The man was quite gloomy. Anyhow, Sunny and Coon married so he could have her cash, she his class. When they divorced, both were relieved to shed the façade."

"Mrs. Spencer told me that she didn't get married until age forty," Pru said. "When did Coon and Sunny divorce?"

"Shortly before Sunny and Gladys wed, though they'd been apart for nearly two decades by the time everything was finalized. Coon remarried within months of signing the papers. So did Gladys and Sunny, who had been traveling together as a couple for a dozen years."

"And Gladys first declared her love for him a dozen years before that," Pru said. "Nearly a lifetime of loving the same person. Can you imagine? How lucky."

"Lucky? Most would disagree. As brilliantly as Gladys and Sunny carried on as lovers, once married they bickered like cats. I think they loved each other so much, and for so long, that their expectations were too lofty. Plus his family hated her. Marlborough Ten, Gads's father, was out of the house by the time they wed but was incensed that the woman weaseled her way into their good name. When Nine kicked it before they could divorce, Ten was livid because Gladys got to keep her title."

"Poor Mrs. Spencer. Lady Marlborough. To have your new family hate you."

Pru knew a little something about that, albeit to a lesser extent. They never made it to the wedding, and Charlie had no sons to bicker with or titles to give away, but the Kelloggs definitely viewed her lack of pedigree as an insult to their name. They never should've let their Golden Son attend such an anarchic college.

"They didn't all hate her," Win said. "Her other stepson, Gads's favorite uncle Ivor, got along famously with the new duchess. But he hardly mattered, what with his outright lack of dukedom."

"No wonder she was so miserable living at Blenheim," Pru said. "She called it a dungeon or a prison or something."

"The phrase you're looking for is a 'monolithic beast of a supposed home.'" Win tapped his desk. "One of the few morsels she's given us so far."

"So Blenheim was their family seat. And because of your friendship with Egads, you summered there as a kid and let yourself get wrapped up in the lore of the duchess. She probably made your family look downright boring."

"That's the short of it," he said.

"Do they still live there? At Blenheim?"

"They do. But each year, the family opens up new sections of the palace to tourists in order to keep the lights on, while they themselves consolidate into smaller and smaller portions of their once massive, private home. Moral of the story? Not even Vanderbilt money lasts forever."

"It's strange," Pru said. "If the Marlboroughs were so vexed by the duchess, why did they keep talking about her? Especially after she left?"

"They *still* talk about her, to this day. Forty years after she disappeared."

"But she was doing them a favor, right? By not hanging around?"

"The dowager duchess definitely did not 'hang around.'"

"She got out of their hair," Pru said, thinking of Charlie's family. "Of her own accord."

Were they complaining about her back in Boston? *That bohemian orphan. What a blight on an otherwise storied family.*

"You'd think they'd appreciate Gladys's efforts," Pru added, with a sniff.

"Yes. You'd think. But Gads's father cursed her name until the day he died, which, as I said, was only a few months back."

"What about Gads and his brother? How did they feel about the duchess?"

"Gads is and was indifferent. He's a reasonable chap, about this anyway. Never met her, so reserved his judgment. John, on the other hand, inherited not only his father's title but also his unending hatred of the woman. His various wives haven't been particularly chuffed either, some dowager duchess with a better name than they could hope to have."

"My head is spinning with all these wives," Pru said. Or maybe it was the wine. "How many are we talking about here?"

"Gads's brother married his third last year, the aforementioned daughter-of-a-count. His second wife, a Greek woman, was a drug addict. Not unexpected when your first husband ditches you for Jackie Kennedy."

"Six marriages between Gads and his brother," Pru said. "Throw in the ninth duke, and I think I've counted eight in your story so far. Sounds like the Marlboroughs have horrible romantic tastes. Or bum luck. Or both."

Pru leaned back onto Win's bed. She normally had more couth than to lounge all over some strange man's bedsheets, but she was also not normally so pissed.

"Most people have horrible romantic tastes," Win said. "Why do you think I remain unmarried?"

"Didn't think it was really your choice," she said sleepily.

"Goodness. Does the so-called second wave of feminism also include browbeating tatty writers? Listen, when you've got a title and a palace to maintain, sometimes you marry for the wrong reasons. If money is a 'wrong reason,' which one could argue either way."

"So is that why everyone hated Gladys Deacon? Because she wasn't a Vanderbilt?"

"That's part of it. Also some believed she put a curse on the castle and the land. It's why the money was never enough. The love was never enough. It's why people left the home more mucked up than when they walked in. As the story goes, shortly after Douglas Fairbanks and Mary Pickford visited, they decided to divorce."

"A curse? And the Marlboroughs think *she* is crazy?"

"Jinxes aside, she flat offended them. Gladys Deacon was brilliant and eccentric and cared little about decorum. She refused to play by their meticulously crafted script. Year after year, they ranted about her, told endless stories of her scandals and misdeeds. Because of these things, as a lad, this hellcat mesmerized me. And as a young man, I picked up on something else. Once you waded through all the shite there remained a begrudging respect. Or as Berenson put it: 'One admires her and one is horrified with her at the same moment.'"

"I experience that very sensation once per day, minimum," Pru said with a tired, eyes-closed chuckle. "Mrs. Spencer and the duchess *must* be the same person. So, did you think the house was cursed? As a kid? I'll bet it was creepy as hell."

"Miss Valentine!" he said, more offended by this than the puppet show comment. "Blenheim is not 'creepy as hell.' It's magical. It was my childhood."

"Geez. No need to get all 'tetchy.' It's just a house."

"JUST A HOUSE! I suppose, if the earth is merely a clod of dirt, the oceans a place for a dip. Blenheim is visually staggering, its grounds enchant. As lads we'd lose ourselves for weekends, weeks even, as we played tennis and shot fox and bumped through the box hedge maze."

"I'll bet you 'became a man' there, too," Pru said.

"I did but that's not the—"

"Uh-huh. Now it all makes sense."

"Anyhow, you randy young thing, as I was saying. Every day was memorable, each night a dream. We held grand balls and watched orchestras play on the lawns. When the weather was nice we took boats onto the canals. We frolicked in the fountains as golden droplets of water sprinkled on us in the late summer sun."

"Uh. Wow."

Pru opened her eyes, then scooted up onto her elbows.

"That doesn't even sound real."

It surprised her that the man was not just gruff and vinegar.

"My fondest memories happened there," Win said. "And through it all threads of the duchess. Stories of her past. Theories about her present. At every dinner and party and hunt she was the topic of discussion."

"Yet you never met her," Pru said. "How come? If you were there so frequently?"

"Despite your uncharitable thoughts on the matter, there is a sizable age gap between the duchess and myself. Gladys Deacon left the palace in 1934 after Duke Nine died. I wasn't even born until 1938. Please reserve your shock."

"Wow. No television then, even."

"Yes, we had to follow our wars the old-fashioned way," he said. "Through radios and newspapers. As dark and backward as the times were, I didn't lay eyes on Blenheim until 1945, eleven years after she disappeared."

"And they still talked about her."

"Obsessively. And among people far more notable than Gads and his family. Sir Winston Churchill, for one. Though he was technically part of the family, too."

"Ah, Winston. Mrs. Spencer's favorite subject."

"Favorite something. Person to torment perhaps. 'He couldn't have done what Hitler did!' " Win trilled in a perfect Mrs. Spencer voice. "The scuttlebutt wasn't limited to the Marlboroughs, either. Guests all parroted the same questions. What happened to the duchess? Was she alive? And what of her personal possessions? The duke and duchess were in the process of divorcing when he died, leaving her his forever wife. The family felt her things belonged to them, even though Nine cut her out of his will and left the estate to Ten. Estate. Albatross. What have you."

"Hmm," Pru said, and settled back onto the bed. "It's amazing how much damage one person can do."

She was half asleep now, the odds of making it back to her room slim. Could she sleep there? On the bed of an unfamiliar man? What would he think of her? More important, what would Pru think of herself?

A few short months ago she was a student at Berkeley, living with roommates who introduced themselves as "lesbian-feminist organizers." Pru dutifully protested the war, but waved the figurative hanky as she sent her fiancé off to fight. Then she left school to get married, a decision she could not reconcile with the desire to call herself a feminist. Alas, it was Charlie. And so love won.

Pru was equal parts independent and traditional. She dreamt of office pumps and also a pregnant belly wrapped in a housecoat. Now, a continent away, among people whose families and traditions went back for centuries, Pru didn't know who she was at all. Already she felt like someone else but couldn't pinpoint in what ways.

"Are you still with me, Miss Valentine?" Win asked in a half whisper as he stood above her.

She nodded, the back of her head rubbing against his pillow.

Pru was beginning to understand the man's obsession. If she was slightly stunted in her forward progression, this chap was doubly so. Thirty-four years old. A man-boy who lived in a world of family stories and fish tales. He said it himself. What grown child wouldn't want to meet his Peter Pan or Wendy? His Alice in Wonderland?

"I get it now," she said dreamily, her mind and good sense already slipping away. "Staying at Blenheim, stories of the duchess bleeding through the years. She grew to fabled proportions, a goddess to those who visited."

Pru fluttered her eyes open. Win remained hovering above, hands on hips, staring down with his puckered blue gaze.

"Scoot over," he said, nudging her leg with his foot. "You're welcome to sleep here but make room for me, and pronto. I'm suddenly feeling quite off my tits and am liable to pass out right atop you."

"Mmm," she replied, and inched to the right. "Can't have that."

"How generous. Thank you for providing me a full three centimeters of space in my own bed."

Pru felt him slide in beside her. Her eyes popped open as she felt his fingers whisper ever-so-slightly against hers.

"Are you okay?" he asked, sensing her body tighten against the bed.

"Yes. Peachy." Pru closed her eyes again and tried to steady her breath. "Win, who are you writing this book for? Do you really think anyone will care about a woman who's been missing for thirty-five years? A woman who was more legend than truth?"

"How can you *not* find her fascinating?" he asked. "A champion spaniel breeder who is also a firearms enthusiast, a kidnap victim, a lover of great men, and the one person who could have prevented World War I?"

"Yes, this person does sound fascinating. If she existed. If that's her down the hall."

"What about a woman who keeps dead cats in the icebox and is famous for running naked through the town center? If you don't find this compelling may I direct you to more plebeian entertainment? An episode of the American comedy *Sanford and Son*, for instance."

"Well," Pru said, breath finally at peace in her chest. "Perhaps you have a point."

Win beamed in return, though Pru's eyes were closed and she could not see him.

A point? He had a point? It was a very rare thing for anyone to say about Win Seton. A very rare thing indeed.

"Do you really think Mrs. Spencer is the missing duchess?" Pru asked before finally nodding off.

"Yes, of course. Otherwise, what am I doing here?"

"But what proof do you have other than a hunch and a handful of rumors?"

"I have photos. And documents. And we have her name."

"Whose name? Gladys Deacon's? That's not exactly top secret information."

"I'm referring to Mrs. Spencer, your oft-naked employer. You see, I've not told you Gads's surname."

"It's not Marlborough?"

"No. It's Spencer. Well, Spencer-Churchill to be specific. And isn't sloughing off the Churchill the very thing our dear friend would do? Winston was no Hitler, after all."

thirty-eight

GD: He was the worst. The absolute worst.

WS: I'm not sure why you have such prejudices against Churchill.

GD: Because he was not a great man! And everyone erroneously thought he was. Which only served to puff him up.

WS: But how well did you know him?

GD: I knew him well enough. He used to come to that place where we were.

WS: Blenheim, you mean?

GD: He liked to lay down the law! No compassion. The

man was incapable of love. He was in love with his own image—his reflection in the mirror. Coon thought he was tiring, too.

WS: To be clear, you're talking about his visits to Blenheim.

GD: Yes, of course I am.

WS: Your family seat.

GD: They're not my family.

WS: Churchill was your husband's cousin. His best friend.

GD: I'm telling you he's not my family.

thirty-nine

THE GRANGE
CHACOMBE-AT-BANBURY, OXFORDSHIRE, ENGLAND
NOVEMBER 2001

When her father passed, he left each of his daughters a sizable trust. Naturally, this sudden influx of riches rendered Gladys Deacon ever more attractive to potential suitors. The "cash for class" business was thriving, this a term invented by Consuelo Vanderbilt herself. Old Coon was quite aware of her position in that particular exchange.

Despite a revolving door of paramours, Gladys saw in the dollars not a dowry but her chance at freedom. She bought her very own Parisian apartment at the Trocadéro and flitted about the best salons, not a care to be had. On weekends she visited Monet in Giverny and consorted with the likes of Renoir, Rodin, and Degas.

Because of this freedom, Gladys endeavored to improve herself in every conceivable way. She understood beauty and money would disappear long before she had a chance to appreciate either. But knowledge, education, and the ability to dazzle at salons, these were qualities age and bad decisions could not erase.

Already a skilled mathematician and almost grotesquely well read, Gladys set out to better understand the art world, an education garnered via a close father-daughter relationship with renowned art critic Bernard Berenson.

What happened to their friendship leaves room for conjecture. They went from touring the world together for months at a time to a permanent severing of communication. Whatever caused the rift must've been monstrous given the friendship ended with such bitter finality. On the plus side, not a single person was shot.

—J. Casper Augustine Seton,
The Missing Duchess: A Biography

"Bite me, Gus," Annie said to herself as she climbed up into the windowsill, breaking and entering without compunction. "And you too, Mom, while we're at it."

She didn't mean it, not really, but it was comforting to say. Gus who told her only half the story, then made her feel silly for wanting the other half.

"So they slept together?" she'd asked, when he finished his tale about the wine-slugging.

"I didn't say that," he replied.

"So they didn't sleep together."

"I didn't say that, either."

Thanks, jerk.

And then there was Laurel, who'd promised a memorable mother-daughter adventure yet they'd spent more time apart than together. Not that their separation didn't have certain advantages, like more time for Annie to snoop.

With a sigh, she hopped down from the window and scanned the room. Everything appeared the same as before. Using much less caution and far more haste than her first visit, Annie made a straight line toward the opposite end of the house, where she bounded up the stairs, taking them two at a time.

"All right, Seton," Annie said as she stepped into his room. She dropped to her knees and peered beneath the bed with a flashlight. "What did I miss the last time through?"

Among the dust and bug carcasses, Annie uncovered little, only a few more sheets of paper, which she dragged toward her with a stick. Another look indicated there was nothing else to find, at least not beneath the bed. Annie leaped to her feet and crammed the transcripts into her backpack.

"What next?" she said with a small hack. Already her throat felt sore and scratchy, her eyes swollen. She'd have to get out of there soon.

Approaching the typewriter, Annie noticed a half-torn, ragged sheet of paper lodged inside. She turned the knob, which caught on its own rust. Using both hands, she pried and jerked until she finally released the words.

"~~Do you remember what you said to me once? That you could help me only by loving me? Well—you did love me for a moment; and it helped me. It has always helped me."~~
~~=Edith Wharton, The House of Mirth~~

"I have nearly died three times since morning."
—Marcel Proust

Annie shoved it into her bag along with the rest of the purloined manuscripts. There wasn't much to learn from dead-writer quotes, but as the Diet Coke incident proved, sometimes there was more to a page than the words written on it.

Before heading out the door, Annie paused to stare at the desk. It had two drawers, she noticed for the first time. She doubled back to case them out, but found both were stuck.

"Hmm," she said, eyes skimming the room. "Hmm. If a thief wanted to bust open a furniture lock, what would he use?"

The bed, she thought with a startling quickness. The very bed where Pru and Win had their maybe-salacious, maybe-innocent drunken evening. Surely there was a loose spring she could use to jimmy open the drawers.

Chin held high, she moved swiftly, assuredly across the room.

"Hello, coil," she said, yanking one from the frame.

With a grimace and a heretofore-untapped physical strength, Annie stepped on one end and pulled the entire spring taut. Then, after only a few minutes, she was able to force open both locks. If fake researcher didn't pan out, Annie had burgling down pat. The CIA wasn't too far from Goose Creek Hill, maybe they needed a new covert operations specialist.

But despite her efforts, the drawers revealed nothing more than a smattering of pencils, several spools of errant typewriter ribbon, and some blank sheets of paper.

After Annie tossed her findings onto the bed, she reached farther back in the drawers, where her hand made contact with a set of plastic cartridges. Audiotapes, eight in total, all of them damaged with thin brown ribbons gnarled and kinked. What Annie might do with broken tapes and nothing to play them on, she hadn't the faintest but she added them to her backpack of thievery nonetheless.

As Annie went to leave, she gave the bed one last look. Poor confused Pru Valentine. A feminist and Victorian lady both.

Smiling, Annie headed toward the stairs, no longer afraid she might fall right through them. Somehow it felt safer knowing Win and Pru had been there first.

After reaching the bottom step, Annie swung around the banister. She skipped forward a few paces then froze.

Something caught her eye.

"Huh?" she said, backing up.

Annie crouched down and saw, lodged in the banister, a tan, rectangular piece of leather, across it a strip of metal. It was a luggage tag, caught on a spindle.

She picked it up and ran her finger along the brass plate. The metal was blackened and mottled but the inscription was decipherable. She'd seen the address before.

JAMES E. SETON
24 QUAI DE BÉTHUNE
PARIS

Forty

Annie stood at the counter, staring down at the luggage tag in her right hand, a cluster of cassette tapes in her left.

James E. Seton. Paris.

Gus had never mentioned the *J* in "J. Casper Augustine Seton" stood for James. Granted, Annie cared far more about what happened between Win and Pru than the details behind their given names, but Gus's ongoing fact embargo needled. It was another hidden tidbit, a plot point withheld.

"Hello, miss, can I help you?"

A man bumbled out from behind a mauve curtain.

"Oh, hello there." Annie slid the tag back into her pocket and extended a hand over the counter. He stared at it with suspicion. "My name is Annie Haley."

She let her arm drop back to the counter, hand untouched.

"Anyway," she said. "Nicola Teepers gave me your contact information. I'm in possession of some damaged audiocassette tapes."

As Annie pushed the cartridges forward, they squeaked against the glass.

"She thought you might be able to repair them," she said.

The man, who was reed-legged but round across the middle, twisted his mouth in confusion. And who could blame him? They were in a clock shop and she was handing him a pile of broken tapes.

"Right," Annie said and dragged them back toward her. "I can see where this would be a crazy place to come. I must've misunderstood. Well, have a splendid day. Cheers!"

"Stop."

He grabbed her hand. His fingers felt cold and dry.

"I can help you," he said.

"Really?"

She slipped out of his hold, then glanced at a cuckoo on the wall. The poor bird was getting himself stuck each time he tried to exit the doors.

"We're mostly watches in this shop," the man said. "And clocks. But I do the odd job here and there."

He pulled a magnifying glass from his shirt pocket and studied each tape.

"I think I can fix these," he said.

"That's terrific news!"

Annie smacked her hands together, which sent the cuckoo once again spiraling out of its hole.

"I do appreciate it," she told the man as he shook his head wearily. "You see, I'm a researcher and trying—"

"It'll take about a week."

"A week? Mister . . . I'm sorry I didn't catch your name. Are you . . . might you be the eponymous Basil?"

"Sir. You can call me sir."

"Mister, uh, sir. I'm grateful for your help but I don't have a week. You see, I'm from the States."

"You don't say."

"I have to go back. Soon. I'm not sure when, exactly, but most likely within the next few days."

"And the town shall weep," he said. "I'll try my best to fix them sooner. No promises, though. You're not the only thing I have going on."

"Got it. Thank you for doing what you can. You can reach me at the Banbury Inn. The name's Annie Haley. Do you need to write it down?"

The man stared at her tiredly, one of his eyes wandering off in some other direction.

"I see," she said. "Well, I'll check back in a few days. Thanks again!"

He was already gone, evaporated behind his mauve curtain.

"Not very jolly, are we?" Annie muttered.

She tucked her hair behind both ears and walked back out the door.

"Okay," she said to herself, under her breath. "This is a start."

Step one was getting the tapes repaired. Step two would be figuring how to pay for it. But she also had to find something to play them on, in the next few days, all without Laurel catching on. Annie frowned. Things were not looking too prospective. Already deflated, she began shuffling back toward the inn.

"Excuse me," she said, jostling between a couple and then around a woman. "Pardon. Sorry."

No. She would not cry. Not there. Not in a foreign country about a set of tapes.

"Sorry." Her eyes ached. "Excuse me."

"Annie?" said a voice.

She tried to shake away the cobwebs.

"Annie? Annabelle! What are you doing?"

Annie whipped around. The woman she'd not-so-politely skittered past was her mother and she looked rather pissed. Not the good kind of pissed, either, as in drunk like the Brits. No, Laurel Haley was full-blown American mad.

Forty-one

"Oh," Annie said, swallowing hard. "Hey, Mom."

"What are you doing?"

"Nothing really. Strolling around town. A walk, you know."

"A walk. Have you given up jogging already?"

"Ha! Good one!"

As her pulse quickened, Annie reminded herself that she hadn't done any-thing especially shady. She didn't even have the stolen tapes on her anymore. The person who should've been acting sheepish was Laurel.

"What is it *you're* doing?" Annie asked, trying to turn the tables though she mostly lacked the strength. "I thought you were in meetings all day."

"Ah, yes, the meetings," Laurel said with a wry smile. "The ones I walked out of."

"You walked out?"

"Indeed I did. Dramatically and in a huff. Not my usual MO, but I was over it. Done. I'm so tired of haggling."

"You? A lawyer? Tired of haggling?"

"I'm as baffled as anyone. But it was . . . I don't know . . ."

Laurel struggled to find the words, a first as far as Annie knew.

"It all suddenly seemed so pointless," she said, puffing out her cheeks. "Every last bit of it. All the hassle, and to what end? The chance to grab a few more dollars? What a waste, especially when offset with lawyer's fees, lodging costs, and the anxiety medication I'm surely going to need."

"Wow, Mom. I'm surprised. It's good, though. I guess. Why stress out over something that's basically a gift?"

"Yes." Laurel exhaled. "Exactly."

"So what now?"

"I think . . ." Laurel started. She looked up at the sky, at the clouds shifting overhead. "I think it means I'll take the lowball offer. What the hell. It's only money."

"You have enough, don't you?" Annie asked. "For retirement? To last . . . until . . ."

"Oh, we'll be fine. I saved plenty while working at the firm and even the deal as it stands is a nice chunk of cash. Plus how much money does a person need? I should've just let my lawyer handle it and waited back in the States for a check."

"Wow," Annie said again, the thought jarring. "Just wow."

What if her mom *had* done that?

What if they'd stayed in Virginia, Laurel continuing to ride her horses while she waited for a check? Annie could barely remember what she did all day before trailing after old codgers and getting herself mired in life at the Grange. If they'd never come to England nothing would've changed yet everything would've been somehow different.

"Why didn't you?" Annie asked. "Why didn't you just collect your money?"

"I ask myself that very question ten times a day. I guess I felt like I had to see it, pay the property its due respect. Not to mention I was more likely to get top dollar if I came in person, which seems preposterous now. I hope you're not disappointed."

"About you not getting top dollar?" Annie crossed her arms, and then uncrossed them again. "No. I'm not disappointed about that."

"I'm sorry, Annabelle. I'm sorry that I couldn't get a higher price for you."

"For *me*? What does this have to do with me?"

"Well, eventually, this, what's here." Laurel gestured with both hands.

"What's at home. It all will go to you. Not soon, of course. That I know of. But one day."

"God, Mom, don't think about it like that."

As if Annie cared about her inheritance. As if she even assumed there would be one.

She wondered if her mom would've gone to the trouble if Annie had a job, or any financial promise whatsoever beyond marrying some dude with a steady paycheck. Military pay wasn't exactly known for its high tax bracket, and it couldn't keep the lights on at Blenheim, but Eric's pay was a veritable fortune compared to the zero dollars Annie made.

"Don't do it for me," Annie added.

"Why not?" Laurel asked. "You're the reason I do anything, period. My sole motivation in life. It's been that way since the moment you were born. Before, even."

"But, Mom, like you said, it's only money."

"That's true, but I've always wanted to give you the most of everything, all the top dollars, literally and figuratively. This is too much, though. The land. The lawyers. The other sellers. Even this town is getting to me."

"Yeah," Annie said, glancing in the direction of the George & Dragon. "I know what you mean. Mom, it won't be like this forever. I know you worry, but I'll get a job. I'll make something of myself. I'm not as lost as I seem."

"Annie," Laurel said, and turned to face her. She grabbed her daughter by both shoulders. "You don't have to do it. You don't have to marry Eric to prove you're a grown-up."

"Geez." She jerked herself out of Laurel's reach. "Is that what you think of me?"

"I don't think that about you," Laurel said and pressed her lips together. "I worry that you think that about yourself."

"Mom . . ."

"A marriage is not adulthood," Laurel said. "And it's not security. In fact, a crappy marriage is the most insecure place in the world."

"I'm sorry that your marriage was bad," Annie said. "I mean that because it would've been awesome to have a father in the picture."

"I know." Laurel's eyes began to water. "I wish I could've given you a good dad and the support that comes with it. He was simply not that kind of man."

"Did you even give him a chance, though? A real chance?"

"Of course I did," Laurel said with a nod. "I wanted nothing more than for us to be a family."

"But you left him before I was born."

"Yes, but we'd been together for many years before that. A family doesn't have to include kids. You rug rats are not the center of the universe," she tried to joke.

"Not funny," Annie said. "I'm trying to have a serious discussion with you."

"Annabelle, simply put, things with your father were bad. Worse than bad. This wasn't about a few fights over bills or a slammed door or two. I had no choice. And I'd do it again, in a flash."

"Maybe things were terrible for him, too."

Annie thought of the transcripts, the story of the duchess and Gladys's own dad. The man was an assassin and she forgave him. The word "forgiveness" had, at its heart, so very much give.

"Absolutely," Laurel said. "Things *were* awful for him but in a way that had nothing to do with us. I tried, Annie. God, I tried. But you can't fix someone else."

"I get it," Annie said with a defiant sniff. "You made the only choice you could. But just because it was bad for you doesn't mean that it will be for me."

"I never said that it would."

"I know what you're thinking," Annie said.

"I'm not sure that you do."

"I'm not marrying Eric because I have nothing else going on. I will have a job. A career. A life outside of him."

"But behind it all you need a safety net. Let me be that person. Not Eric. Let it be me. Listen, Annie, I'm not going to forbid you from marrying him."

"Good. Because you can't."

"Just remember," she said, "that whatever happens, however things pan out when he returns, you can back out. A job, no job. Money or not. Your path is not carved in stone and no agreement is permanent. Not an engagement. Not a land deal. Nothing. Don't let anyone tell you otherwise."

"Eric would never tell me that I was stuck. He says the opposite, that I don't have to keep my promise. I can back out of the engagement, no hard feelings. He claims I'm too good for him, which is patently untrue."

"I'm glad he's not pressuring you," Laurel said.

"He'd never pressure me!"

"But I wasn't referring to Eric. I was talking about you."

Annie squinted in confusion. Her temples began to throb.

"Me?" she said. "Me?"

"Yes. If things are different when he gets back . . . if you change, or if he does, know that you don't have to say 'I do' because you already promised 'I will.' "

Annie continued to stand there, head pounding as Laurel's words played in her mind. Would Annie do it if she had to? If Eric turned out not to be the person she loved, would she say no? Annie believed that she would.

"I know I don't have to marry him," she said at last. "And I won't, unless it's the right time with the right person, which I'm positive that Eric is. Either way, twenty-two or forty years old, one engagement or fifteen, I can wait."

She also understood she didn't have to.

"Okay," Laurel said, nodding. "Great. Though I'd prefer something less than fifteen engagements."

"It was a joke," Annie said. "Something I read in a book."

Laurel smiled.

"A book," she said. "Of course. Look, I'm sorry for bringing this up when maybe I didn't need to. It's funny . . . there's, I don't know, something different about you lately. On this trip you've suddenly seemed older, more grown-up. I suppose that's quite the sad commentary on how much I've been away."

"Don't beat yourself up about it, Mom. I've kept busy and even had a little fun besides."

"I hope so." Laurel sighed. "I'd hate for you to have bad memories of this trip. Or, worse, no memories of it at all."

"No danger of that."

"Good." Laurel sighed again. "So, should we blow this taco stand or what? Or do you want to keep regaling the fine citizens of Banbury with our deepest personal problems?"

"Let's go," Annie said. "But first, I need a favor."

"Anything."

"Mom. 'Blow this taco stand'? Please don't speak that way again. I think it's a form of child abuse."

Laurel closed her eyes and laughed.

It was such a happy sound: light, high, and twinkly. Annie realized then how very long it'd been since she'd heard it. This town *was* getting to Laurel. It was getting to both of them.

"I have to ask," Laurel said as they rounded the corner toward the inn. "Nicola says you've been running around meeting strange people, asking odd questions, borrowing bikes and flashlights. For what, exactly?"

"Um." Annie paused and let her mother walk a few steps ahead. "I've been doing some, uh, research."

"Research?" Laurel stopped, then turned back around.

"Yes. Research. On the town history."

"Oh good grief." Laurel rolled her eyes. "Is this about that old book you found?"

"Well, sort of," she admitted. "I mean, it was the genesis."

Because though it was about the book, it was not entirely so. Not anymore.

"Sweetheart, put it out of your mind. Stop spinning your wheels on this nonsense. Actually, I forgot to mention, but the other day, after you asked about the Grange, I looked into it for you."

"You looked into it?" Annie leveled her eyes on Laurel. "What do you mean you 'looked into it'?"

Did she trespass? Stand outside? See her only child coming and going?

"As it turns out," Laurel said. "The property is gone."

"Gone."

"Yup." Laurel answered with a stiff nod. "Gone. They razed the Grange. Mowed right on over it."

"Where'd you hear that?"

"Oh, um, Nicola?"

Nicola. Nicola who lent Annie the bike. Nicola who told her the address of the Grange and said to bother her best girlfriend next door.

"Are you positive?" Annie asked, a squeak in her throat. "Absolutely certain? Maybe you heard it wrong."

"I thought the same thing. So when I had a few minutes on the way home the other night, I swung by. And the whole thing was . . . pssst." Laurel whistled through her teeth. "Completely flattened, like it'd never been there in the first place."

"Flattened. Really."

"Yep. Don't look so upset! It was just an old house. There are better things to see around here!" Laurel grinned. Annie never noticed how pointy her incisors were. "You know what I'm thinking? We need a big ol' glass of wine. Where can we find some around here?"

"I'm sure Nicola has something," Annie said, disoriented. Her headache had morphed into full-blown vertigo. "She, uh, usually puts out wine and cheese this time of day."

"Yes!" her mom chirped.

Annie started.

"Um, what?"

"Nicola's sundry wines and cheeses!" Laurel sang. "And the cakes. Don't forget the cakes!"

With an exaggerated wink, she did a little gun-shooting motion, the kind of which Laurel Haley had never made in her lifetime. Then she jauntily bounced up the stairs of the inn. Annie remained at the bottom, mouth open, her tongue tacky and dry.

"Uh, Mom?"

At the top step, Laurel glanced over her right shoulder.

"What is it, Annie?"

"Well, it's about the Gr . . ." she began.

Then Annie pulled back. It was not the time to ask. The exchange was too confusing, the pieces inexorably scattered. She didn't even know where to start, or which aspect of the lie was most upsetting.

"Oh, never mind," she said.

"Okay!" Laurel shrugged cheerfully. "Well, let's get a move on! That wine can't be poured too quickly!"

Annie shook her head and silently trailed after her mom, staring at Laurel's birdlike back in confusion. All this time she wanted more information about her dad but it seemed Laurel wasn't so thoroughly known herself. Some safety net. Damned thing was full of holes.

Forty-two

"Well, if it isn't my favorite half-storyteller," Annie said, taking a stool beside Gus at the bar. "Hiya, Ned, what's cooking?"

"Hello, Annie. Fine day, isn't it?"

Lord help her, she was a regular. Annie tossed her backpack to the ground.

"It's fair," she said. "Though I expect the weather to turn to shit at any moment. So, Gustavo, what's going on?"

"*Gustavo?*" The man scowled. "Have we met? Because you look exactly like an amiable young lady with whom I'm acquainted. But you are lacking in her good graces."

"Been hanging out with you too much, I s'pect," Ned said.

He pushed a beer toward her and went to help a patron at the far end of the bar.

"So I have a question," Annie said and sipped her beer.

Ned had given her a new kind to try, something with a dark amber hue. Four years of college and it took hanging out with some geezer in a pub to make her enjoy the taste of beer.

"Actually I have *several* questions," she said. "But let me start with one. Can you think of any possible reason a person might lie about the Grange?"

"In what way did they lie?"

"This person said it was gone, razed, when obviously it's not."

Gus swiveled to face her.

"Someone claimed it was gone?" he said. "Who?"

"Oh. This random person I bumped into at the inn. A stranger, apparently."

"Apparently?" Gus took a sip of his own beer, though the glass was mostly drained. "Can't say, really, without knowing the context. Razing is the ultimate plan, though. Maybe this 'random' got his or her wires crossed. Or is anxious to buy a miniestate when they go for sale."

"Is that a definite?" Annie asked. "That they'll bulldoze the property? I thought you were only speculating about the developers."

"No, they're trying to get their grubby paws in there as soon as practicable. Sadly for them, there's been a holdup with the permit, a local fussbudget is trying to have it designated as a historical site."

Annie thought of the first thing she'd stolen, the note tacked onto the front gate. "Application for Grade II building: House. Early 18th century. Coursed limestone and ironstone rubble . . ."

"Alas, the Grange is changing hands as we speak," Gus added.

"What do you mean changing hands?" Annie asked, looking at him cross-eyed. "Like, it's on the market? Up for sale?"

"Not in the traditional sense, with estate agents and whatnot. Could you imagine an open house? Straight from any homebuyer's nightmare. Anyway, yes, it's being sold—in a private transaction."

"Private transaction?" Annie said, heart thwacking in her chest. "What kind of private transaction?"

"The money kind? I'll sell you my land and you give me a few quid? Is that not how it works stateside?"

"The permit," she said. "It delayed the sale?"

Had it also impeded American ex-lawyers? Ones who sat in meetings all day while ignoring aimless daughters? Because when Annie heard the words "delayed" and "transaction" she could only think of Laurel.

"Yes, it's held up the sale for some weeks now," he said. "Why do you ask?"

"The woman I met. I think she is part of the transaction. Maybe a seller."

"Did she say that?"

"In a way."

"Who was it?" Gus asked, voice coming out like bullets. "Did she give a name? What did she look like?"

"Blond," Annie said. "Petite. American, like me."

Was it possible?

Was Laurel's property the Grange itself? It was family land, she'd claimed. Could Laurel be related to the duchess? Or to Edith Junior? Or to Tom or Win?

"Who inherited the property when the duchess died?" Annie asked.

"I mentioned before, Mrs. Spencer didn't bequeath it to any one person. It's held in a blind trust by a variety of parties. Did you get this woman's name? The petite American?"

"What about Win?"

Annie thought of the address from the transcripts, the same address etched into the luggage tag perpetually tucked in her pocket. She carried it around now, like a talisman, a piece of good luck.

"Does Win own the Grange?" she pressed.

"No," Gus said. "Win Seton does not own the Grange."

"Is there a way I could get in contact with him?"

"Why would you want to do that? I told you—"

"Gus, you're killing me here. Everyone's killing me. Just give me what I want!"

After releasing a frustrated grunt, Annie kicked at the bar. Ned's glare immediately snapped in her direction. Property damage. Another petty crime for the ever-growing list. She gave Ned a feeble smile.

"Annie, calm down," Gus said. "I don't understand why you're so plucked."

She removed the luggage tag from her pocket and slapped it on the counter.

"What do you think about this?" she asked.

Gus's face reddened.

"You have to stop—"

"Stealing things. Yes. I know. I found this lodged in the banister at the Grange. It's clearly the writer's. You said when we first met that Win is in Paris. Is he still at this address? That is in Paris, correct?"

"Île Saint-Louis." Gus nodded toward the tag. "It's one of the oldest sections of the city. Many of the homes have been in families for centuries."

"I know, I've been there," Annie said. "And I'm not asking for the island's history. I want to know if Win Seton lives at twenty-four Quai de Béthune?"

"How am I supposed to answer that?"

"You know, you've made a lot of disparaging remarks about the guy," Annie said. "He's a tosser, a wanker, a ne'er-do-well, on and on. You're not exactly chuffing brilliant yourself."

"You're not using the term properly. It's not a curse word."

"What about Pru?" she asked. "Is Pru in Paris?"

"That would be highly unlikely. The young woman returned to America, eventually."

"Really?" Annie said with a small pout. "She did? I actually thought . . ."

She hesitated and took a sip of beer, though was tiring of it already. What exactly *did* Annie think? What ending had she mapped out for these people, subconsciously or otherwise?

"It's stupid," she said. "I guess . . . I suppose I assumed they fell for each other. That after Win got what he needed from Mrs. Spencer, he returned to Paris and Pru joined him. Eventually."

Annie pictured the transcript, Win's address on the back, written in a woman's hand. She had assumed it was Pru's.

"You thought they ended up together?" Gus said and frowned. "Well, sorry, there's no happily ever after here."

"Wow, okay." Annie sighed. "I'm shocked. I don't even know why since you never mentioned a romance. But they had this sweet rapport."

"That they did."

"So I thought . . ."

"Not altogether unreasonable."

"He went and muffed the entire deal though, didn't he?" she said. "They could've had a happily ever after but Win Seton screwed the pooch, just like you intimated he would."

"I intimated that?"

"Of course you did! Basically, you've painted the guy as a loser."

"Well, now, I never meant to go *that* far," Gus said. "He was daft at times but not so bad a guy."

"Not so bad? Tell me, Gus, how did you wrap up the story last time we spoke? Oh, that's right, he lured Pru into his room and got her drunk on cheap wine. Sounds like a stand-up guy to me."

"He didn't lure her! She showed up!"

"Then Pru passed out, in his bed. Lord knows what kind of mischief he wheedled from her."

"I don't know what you're implying," Gus said, eyes boring into Annie. "But it was nothing like that. Win was often a bumbling do-nothing, and a bit too quick to take the piss out of people, but he was not a monster. Win Seton cared about people. He cared about Mrs. Spencer. And he definitely cared about Pru."

"But Pru was naïve, incredibly sheltered. Win was worldly. He had tricks up his sleeve."

"I'd hardly call the bloke 'worldly.' Did you miss the part where I mentioned he was coddled since birth? Pru was smarter and savvier in innumerable ways."

"Then tell me what happened in the bed," Annie demanded.

"Not a thing. Blimey, have some respect for the two."

"All right. Fine. I'll give them their so-called privacy. But if you're going to claim it wasn't Win who drove the girl away, then tell me what happened the next morning, when they woke up."

Forty-three

Pru wakened to someone depositing two live chickens on her head.

"Miss Valentine!" called the shrill voice she'd grown oh-so-accustomed to hearing.

Even with the decibel level, it was a miracle Pru woke up. She'd become skilled at tuning out the old woman. On top of that, she was spectacularly hungover. Though there were the chickens, which helped.

"Do you know where I found these birds?" Mrs. Spencer asked.

"Um, in the yard?" Pru said, and scooted up onto her elbows.

She glanced over to see Win snoring heavily beside her. So he did sleep. It was a revelation.

Oh God.

Win was beside her.

And Mrs. Spencer was standing over them, surveying what appeared to be a wildly indecent sleeping arrangement though all parties were fully clothed.

"I can take the birds outside if you'd like," Pru said, scrambling to her feet. "Silly chickens shouldn't be in the house!"

"They were in your room, Miss Valentine!"

She felt the woman's voice all the way down to her fingertips. From the moment Pru stepped onto the property, she understood Mrs. Spencer could kill a man at twenty paces. But this was the first time she was well and truly scared.

"I found these chickens in your room!" Mrs. Spencer bellowed. "Roosting because they had plenty of space to do so, my randy assistant having flown the coop!"

"I haven't flown the coop," Pru insisted, using a foot to feel for her shoes. She swallowed, the taste of the wine thick on her tongue. "I was helping Mr. Seton with his, er, writing. And fell asleep."

"Passed out, more like, judging from the smell and your purple mouth. Is there a particular reason you've decided to cop off with my biographer?"

"Cop off?" Win said, immediately prodded into consciousness. "Is someone copulating? That hardly seems fair."

"Lord Almighty!" Mrs. Spencer said and tossed up her hands.

The woman shook both fists at the ceiling, which sent the birds flapping about the room. The chickens spent the better part of five minutes disrupting papers and banging into windows and walls until finally releasing themselves out into the hallway.

"No one's copulating," Pru mumbled and scooped up her shoes. "Not to worry."

With both shoes gripped to her chest, Pru scooted to the room's periphery and tried to slither out the door. Mrs. Spencer kicked it closed.

"No one's leaving until you confess your sins."

"You're not a priest," Pru said. "And I don't have any sins."

"More's the pity," Win said as Pru shot him a look. "Aw, Mrs. S., we're not copulating. Don't you worry, all body parts have remained with their original owners."

Pru scowled again, an error in judgment to be sure. Her cute glower was an invitation, a call to increased cheekiness.

"Don't give me any of your seductive gazes, Miss Valentine," he said with a wink. "This poor old man can't handle your wiles."

"That was a glare, not a gaze!"

"Miss Valentine, I didn't take you for such a harlot!" Mrs. Spencer said.

Pru groaned. Her mistake, thinking Win Seton was a chum for those few minutes. It astounded, his dire lack of social graces. No surprise he was thirty-four and unmarried. The bloke was a fiasco.

"Nothing happened," Pru said. "I was trying to save your alleged biographer from mental collapse. He's being impossible on purpose."

"It wouldn't be accidentally now, would it?" Win said with a chuckle. "Anyway, a harlot is not so bad an insult. 'If a woman hasn't got a tiny streak of harlot in her, she's a dry stick as a rule.'"

It was a quote Pru recognized immediately, but it did not make her any less cheesed.

Okay, perhaps it made her a touch less cheesed. The very slightest.

"Very nice, Seton, with your D. H. Lawrence," Mrs. Spencer said, picking up on the reference as quickly as Pru had. "He was a friend of mine, you know. I have a book of his sexually explicit drawings in my library."

"Please. Show them to me straightaway."

"You are both ridiculous," Pru said. "As I told you, nothing happened and Mr. Seton would be *lucky* to experience one of my seductive gazes."

"Here, here," Win said.

"Edith Junior vowed that you were a nice girl," Mrs. Spencer said. "Tight with one of the best families in Boston. What would the Kelloggs think of these exploits in the boudoir?"

"I don't think the Kelloggs would much care."

"Kellogg?" Win asked. "As in the foodstuffs?"

Pru nodded. She moved from the barricaded doorway and slumped down into Win's writing chair.

"Mrs. Spencer . . . I *am* a nice girl," she insisted, though it didn't sound remotely convincing. "This is a misunderstanding."

"What's to misunderstand about you taking sexual advantage of my biographer! You're not even French!"

"How many times do I have to say it? There's nothing sexual! He wishes there was something sexual!"

"I like the way you say 'sexual,'" Win said and wiggled his brows.

"Oh good grief! Don't you think *he's* more the taking-advantage type? I'm a fresh, young innocent girl of only nineteen. He's a grizzled old bachelor."

"Why, I'm gobsmacked," Win said. "Simply beside myself! Miss Valentine, tell her the truth. Here I was, innocently pecking away on my manuscript—"

"I wouldn't touch you with someone else's hands!" she barked.

The man felt a troublesome sensation across his chest. Regret? Sorrow? The realization that this was all a big joke, that he could never hope to be in the position of fending off her advances?

Not that Win had designs on the girl, not exactly. She was indeed beautiful and he'd welcome the flattery of her attentions. But he'd never try to outright seduce the poor thing. She was too forbiddingly innocent for one, so ethereal with that flowing, glossy hair and her bright eyes.

And liberal education aside, the girl lacked a certain practicality. It wasn't exactly a dearth of sophistication, but something close to it. Pru was polite and mannered, but in the way a schoolgirl might be, as though she were told how to act and had not yet learned it for herself.

Of course Win didn't know about the dead fiancé, or the things she was trying to get over. If he had, he probably wouldn't have mistaken her brave and quiet self-confidence for ordinary cluelessness.

"I'm only playing," Win said at last. He felt bad, as if he'd been caught teasing a scared little girl. "Miss Valentine has acted appropriately at every turn. As you can see, we are both fully dressed."

"You are in your shorts!" Mrs. Spencer said. "I can see the outline of your willy!"

Pru blushed hard and turned to face the window. She didn't want Win to notice that she was giggling. But notice he did. She could feel his grin from clear across the room.

"The outline of my willy? Heavens!" Win swung his legs off the side of the bed. "Well, do enlighten me, Mrs. Spencer. How does my willy compare to, say, the Crown Prince of Prussia? The man who owned the Hope diamond? I can assure you its abilities leave women sparkling far more than the diamond itself."

"Oh please!" Pru said, and bonked her head on the desk. "Dream on!"

Win hobbled toward her, his bones tired from spending all night maintaining an appropriate distance from his unexpected companion. As he walked, Pru tried her mightiest not to catch sight of his legs, which were bare and muscled in a way that brought to mind D. H. Lawrence's book of explicit renderings.

"Up," he said.

"Um, what?"

She could not stop staring at his legs. Better those than the "outline of his willy," of course.

"Up out of my chair, you plotting vixen. I can't be distracted by your sexual aggressions. I have to write my book."

"You're disgusting," Pru said and tried, once again, for the door. Mrs. Spencer swatted her away.

"I can't have this," the old woman said, her voice scratchier by the syllable. "Two of my employees fornicating in my home! We have to contend with enough litters in this place. I'm not sheltering whatever godforsaken offspring the two of you might produce."

"Which would be far less special than the spaniels," Win said, and rolled a piece of paper into his typewriter.

"You don't need to tell me that!"

"Relax, everyone," Win said. "This is all in good fun. I'm merely trying to get a rise out of the two of you."

"Getting a rise is precisely my concern!"

"You don't need to worry about the hired help shagging," he said. "What you see before you are the aftereffects of a couple of mates sharing a bottle of cheap wine and then promptly passing out. Plus whatever Miss Valentine said about my crack-up. That is also true."

"Well, I'm delighted to learn you have so much excess time for drinking and losing the plot. I thought you were writing a book. You're both here to work, by the by."

"I can't speak for the innocent young lodger, but as for me, I do swear by the *Church* on the *Hill*," Win said and winked at Pru, "that I'm working hard as I can."

"Church on the Hill? Not Winston again," Mrs. Spencer said with a snort.

"Here's the rub, though," Win said. "You've given me so little to work with I often find myself facing gobs of free time. Can you blame me for befriending the only other employee of the Grange? I'm quite bored and Miss Valentine makes for excellent company."

"Oh, I'll bet she does," Mrs. Spencer huffed. She sat on the bed. Pru inched toward the door. "You're supposed to be writing *my* story, Seton. Paying attention to *me*."

"Lady, that's what I've been trying to do. Problem is, you're not giving me the chance."

Forty-four

"Fine. Have it your way," Mrs. Spencer said, and took to roost at the end of Win's bed, same as the chickens. "I'll answer whatever questions you please. Though, as I said, I'm no duchess. Where's your tape recorder, Seton?"

"Tape recorder?" Win said, stunned and buggy-eyed. "To be honest, I'd rather transcribe our discussions. I've grown, shall we say, rather embittered by the recorder. Just ask Miss Valentine over there."

He nodded toward where she stood rooted beside the door. Though her exit was no longer restricted, Pru found herself unable to move. Mrs. Spencer's demeanor had flipped. She was at once more attentive, ready to play. Pru wanted to stick around and finally hear the full tale.

"Miss Valentine? What does Miss Valentine know of your recordings?"

"I played her the tapes. Then I promptly reached my limit and chucked the device against the wall."

"You *threw* it?"

"It didn't break!" Pru chirped. "He didn't use enough force to cause damage. It was more like a high lob."

She arched her arm to demonstrate.

"Many thanks for that," Win said. "A bloke can't feel too manly around here, can he?"

"I want to be recorded," Mrs. Spencer said. "I can't trust you to write my words as I say them. You don't seem particularly bright. No offense."

"How could I possibly take offense to that?" he said and rolled his eyes. "You win, Mrs. Spencer. If you provide a single crumb of information not web-footed or feathered in nature, I will gladly record your musings."

He opened a desk drawer. After groping its contents for thirty seconds, Win found an unused tape. He jammed it into the recorder and tapped the red circle.

"Where would you like to start?" he asked.

"I was born in 1881."

"Righto," Win said with a nod. "Just as the Duchess of Marlborough was."

"No," Mrs. Spencer said. "I mean 1892. My apologies. I'm old, you see."

"I use that excuse all the time, too."

"Yes, yes. I was born in 1892, at the Hotel Brighton in Paris. It was on the Rue de Rivoli across from the Tuileries Garden. My first official home was at Fourteen Rue Pierre Charron, a few blocks off the Champs-Élysées. My family was from America but I lived most of my life in Europe and consider myself a Parisian, through and through."

Win jotted a few notes. Pru tried to see them from her place near the door.

"My mother was a known femme fatale," Mrs. Spencer continued. "More than that, she was a *demimondaine*, a bygone being who was equal parts countess and courtesan."

"*Demimondaine*," Win said, addressing Pru. "A prostitute, basically. But higher class."

"A prostitute?" She gawked.

"Oh, Miss Valentine, don't get so prudish about it," Mrs. Spencer clucked. "Why am I even bothering? I can't properly explain this to a woman of the modern era, what with her job-seeking and bra-burning."

"Note to manuscript. Mrs. Spencer glared at Miss Valentine upon speaking the word 'bra.'"

"Believe me, there was honor in the position, in one's ability to use her beauty and charm to make a life. Quite a nice life, it should be stated. The last home Mother lived in was a castle, decorated with unicorns and virgins."

"Not the least bit vulgar," Win said. "Though this is a woman who traded sex for peignoirs and incited at least one death."

"I quite don't know what you're speaking about."

"Note to manuscript: Mrs. Spencer is sniffing haughtily as can be."

"Are you interviewing me or adding your commentary?"

"Both," he said. "Miss Valentine, you look uncomfortable standing around like that. Why not have a seat?"

With both pairs of eyes on her, Pru scuffled against the wall and planted herself at the far side of the bed, near Win's pillow, which still had on it faint traces of his unwashed, musky scent. Her heart rate sped up by a few extra beats.

"Where was I?" Mrs. Spencer asked, watching Pru.

"Your mother," Win reminded her.

"Right. Mother. She was a majestic being. A noted femme fatale, as I mentioned. This got her into a spate of trouble."

"I'll say."

"Mother was . . . her beauty . . . it was a crashing chandelier. She was elegant and graceful and made a scene simply by walking through a door. Her luxurious chestnut hair was envied more than her figure and her clothes, which was saying something given her resplendent serpentine dresses. She had accounts at the finest shops, bills paid by the finest men."

"Like I said, high-class prostitution."

"Mother traveled the world," Mrs. Spencer went on, intent on ignoring the wisecrack, a solid strategy when dealing with Win. "But never without the four of us girls and our accompanying nurses, nursery maids, and governesses. We toured every major country in Europe, and even some minor ones. We summered in Newport, where our American cousins thought us fast merely because they caught us warming our bloomers at the fire.

"We visited Africa. South America. The far Orient. But mostly we stayed in Paris. Sometimes we lived at the best hotels, other times in meticulously appointed flats in the Marais. Either way, Paris was our home."

"Did you study in Paris?" Win asked. "As a young girl?"

"Yes, of course. Mother ensured we were schooled in the arts. All of us were fluent in half a dozen languages by the age of ten. Even Edith, with her head thick as a brick. Mother squeezed the best parts from us. That's what she did.

"My dearest sister Audrey and I both demonstrated early musical prowess so we trained at the Sacré-Cœur. I can still feel Audrey's hand in mine as we promenaded through the wooden-planked entrance and toward the white domes that loomed over the city. We found our greatest happiness inside the basilica's cool towers. So many people hated the Sacré-Cœur, so whipped up were they in Gothic furor. Audrey and I never felt threatened by the building's aggressive Catholicism, though. Mostly the place made us want to sing."

"Tell me about living in Rome," Win said. "With your mum in the aforementioned unicorn castle."

"It was a decline in station," Mrs. Spencer said. "Despite the Renaissance palace. Mother encountered great difficulty in trying to establish herself. Italians are more rigid than their Parisian counterparts, and much less amenable to colorful backgrounds and spotty pasts. Parisians celebrate liveliness and intellect, irrespective of skeletons lurking in the closet."

"Literal skeletons. Ergo, Coco."

"Through it all," she went on, doing a hero's job of trying to hide her vexation. "Mother kept her head high and her elegance intact. She suffered no fools. She suffered nothing, really. Even at her most destitute, at the end of her life when the bills had come due and there was no one left to pay them, even then she lingered on in the palace, blue and white peacocks strutting across the lawns."

"Form over substance, eh, Mrs. Spencer?" Win asked with a sly grin.

"Young man, my mother was nothing but substance. It was only fitting she had the form to go with it."

Forty-five

A few days later, Pru was washing a trio of dogs when she happened to glance out the window. She almost couldn't believe her eyes.

It was Win Seton. Outside. Standing beneath a weeping birch in the honest-to-God daylight. He hadn't even yet disintegrated into a pillar of salt. Pru thought it her duty to investigate.

She approached as Win stood on the embankment, whistling and skipping stones across the partially frozen goose pond. Whether he was trying to hit the geese on purpose or suffering the effects of his poor accuracy, Pru didn't know.

"And the writer emerges from his lair," she said, walking up behind him. "Finally."

He turned to face her, grinning wide.

"Never let anyone—ahem, my father—tell you I'm not a keen outdoors-man," he said as the sunlight shot through his hair. "A glorious day, isn't it?"

Pru nodded, feeling daft and off-kilter. Lord help her. She'd been cooped up in that blasted home too long. Win Seton was starting to resemble a movie star, all golden and radiant. Pru shook her head. This would never do.

"Here," he said, handing her a stone. "Would you like to have a go?"

But, personally, I prefer Mrs. Spencer's later years. Like her relationship with Proust."

"A friendship for the ages."

"I adore the fact that he chased her around the globe, obsessed with befriending her. Demanding it, really!"

"But she relished the chase."

"Without question," Pru said. "Though she did have the good sense to be galled when his dogged pursuit landed her in a Roman jail."

"Well, it *was* illegal for priceless art to leave the city," Win said with a laugh. "And Proust had to find some way to slow Gladys down. He was something, wasn't he? The neurotic basket case that holed up in a cork-lined bedroom for months at a time. What a spectacle those two must've been together."

"I was telling Mrs. Spencer that a few months back I read *À la recherche du temps perdu—*"

"Ha! You're one for slim tomes," Win said, smiling, eyes wrinkling in the sunlight. "You probably read it in French to boot. I never made it through that unwieldy book, though not for lack of trying. Too many pages, too little plot."

"Don't let Mrs. Spencer hear you say that! Proust is not my favorite, but with him, the plot is not the point!"

"Then what is the point?"

"*In Search of Lost Time* is a study on mankind," Pru said, her view on the writer softening thanks to Mrs. Spencer. "Quite revolutionary for its day, or even for now. One of my professors insisted it's hands down the best novel of the twentieth century so far."

"Count Robert de Montesquiou called it 'a mixture of litanies and sperm.' "

"I think that's meant as a compliment, coming from a dandy like him."

"You know the best bit?" Win asked. "Of her stories and anecdotes and tales?"

He skipped another stone across the pond. The geese squawked and flapped.

"The best part is," he said. "I think most of it is true."

Pru chuckled.

"I hope so," she said. "It'd be a shame for the world to miss out on her."

Pru extended a hand and Win placed another rock in her palm. She turned and sent it skittering farther and straighter than even his best shot.

"But she hasn't admitted she's the duchess," Pru said. "Which is annoying and strange."

"I'd love to."

Pru took the smooth, cool rock and with a flick of her wrist sent it ricoch
ing across the water.

"Not too shabby," he said. "Though I think the ice helped."

"Ice, nothing. I realize it's no tape recorder against a wall," Pru replied, a
skipped a second rock, inordinately pleased with her newly discovered ski
"But it works."

Seton grinned again. Hard. It felt almost like a violation though he'd do
precisely nothing wrong.

Pru immediately cranked her head away, flushed once again. She thought
leave but what Win said was true. Right there, in the dead of winter, it *was*
glorious day. It hardly looked like winter at all.

Around them witch hazel abounded, also honeysuckle with its lemon
scented flowers. Viburnum bloomed its cotton-candy pink and bright purpl
irises burgeoned beside the southernmost wall. Across it all, a dusting of snow
and ice, like a swath of glittering tulle.

What was this? Pru wondered. This unfamiliar feeling? Was it some sort
of . . . happiness? It seemed too exotic a thought.

"So what brought you out here on this bright and pleasant day?" Win
asked.

"Oh. Well. I was passing through. Decided to say hello."

She didn't mention that she'd spotted him from Mrs. Spencer's bedroom,
way up in the highest spot of the house. Pru left three dogs shimmying and
spraying water on Mrs. Spencer's gold lyrebird wallpaper, just so she could
check him out.

"And what is it *you're* doing out here?" she asked. "I don't think I've seen
you leave the house."

"Huh. I'm not sure that I have. Well, the answer is I've been writing like
mad and needed a break. A jolly good problem, to be sure. Mrs. Spencer is finally
giving me what I need."

"And probably much that you don't."

"That too. But I'll merrily take it all, even if she is still a bit cagey about her
title. Tell me, what do you think of our old gal? Prostitution? Kidnappings? Murders? To name the things she was exposed to prior to age twelve."

"Ironic," Pru said. "Given she accused *me* of being fast and a bad influence.

"But she's opening up, so for now I don't mind. And you . . ." He pointed at her. "I have you to thank for everything."

"Me? All I did was wake up in your bed, looking like a harlot."

"Precisely. Lady M. is a jealous cat. Bernard Berenson said about her . . ." He closed his eyes, remembering. "Among other things, he said that she had 'the need to dominate, to crush under her heel the heads of those who were weaker than she. Thus no sooner would she see a possible victim than she forgot everything else, even her deepest interests, and would set out to pursue him until she had led him to his end.'"

"So you're the one she's pursuing," Pru said and rolled her eyes good-naturedly. "How big of you to think so."

"It's not a testament to me. Only to my gender. The duchess wanted nothing more than to be loved. By everyone. Always."

"Not so unique a wish, when you think about it," Pru said. "It must've hurt, those words coming from Berenson. She loved him so deeply. For a time anyway."

Win made a face.

"Nah," he said. "She looked up to him, surely, but it was more akin to a father-daughter, mentor-mentee relationship."

"He almost left his wife for her!"

"Which makes him about as unique as a housefly. Gladys Deacon wanted every man to love her, even if she didn't return the sentiment. With Berenson, she had no romantic schemes whatsoever. She simply wanted him to have schemes on her."

"Rubbish, as you would say. Why else would she spend so much time with him?" Pru asked.

"Gladys Deacon deemed herself the most intelligent and cultured woman in existence but her artistic credentials were feeble. In her mind, Berenson was the only person capable of teaching her something new. She used him for her own benefit, to broaden her mind, and develop new skills to trot out at the salons."

"She didn't need Berenson for that," Pru said. "She was friends with Monet! Degas! Name your artist! No, the Old Masters enthusiasm was a ruse to spend time with Berenson. You can tell by the way she says his name. She's never once insulted his sexual abilities. She's insulted Proust's and he was gay!"

"You're living in too many novels, sweet Pru. Those two were eons apart in age. Almost fifteen years."

The same amount of years, as it happened, between Win and Pru.

"Wasn't Sunny eleven years older?" she asked. "And they got married."

"To resounding success."

"I don't see what age has to do with it. You've heard the snide way she speaks about Berenson's wife even though they were once friends. She doesn't do that with Coon and Coon was married to the duke!"

"Coon never tried to crowd her spotlight," Win said. "If she had, well, she would've been done for. You and I, case in point. Not until she found you in my bed did Mrs. Spencer begin to entertain my queries. She'd rather give me attention than allow my attention to wander to you."

Pru blanched.

Attention? Was Win giving her "attention"? It'd been so long Pru didn't even know what romantic interest was supposed to look like when it flashed on her.

"Your mere presence incensed the lady of the manor," Win said. "She needs to be the nucleus of everything, not outshone by some runabout, confused American girl."

"Hmm." Pru smiled tightly. "I don't know that I'm confused. Or runabout. And didn't you just finish telling me that there was nothing between her and Berenson because of the fifteen-year gap? Or are you saying that you're closer to Mrs. Spencer's age than that?"

"Hilarious. Yes. I'm in my late eighties. My liver looks like it in any case."

"Even if I agreed with your hypothesis," she said, "that she viewed me as competition, what would a ninety-year-old woman care about snaring a young man's appreciation? I use the term 'young' loosely, of course."

"Of course! You see, Miss Valentine, that's the problem with getting old. Your body changes but your heart does not. Lady M wants the same things that she always has."

"Mostly I think you like to fancy yourself the center of romantic intrigue."

Win dropped his head back and laughed.

"Oh, my new friend," he said. "You'll make this endeavor worthwhile, no matter what I manage to wheedle from Mrs. Spencer."

Suddenly, Win grabbed for her hand. The effect was far more startling than any gunshot that had ever echoed across the property. As his hand beat inside of hers, Pru took in a sharp breath, hoping he didn't hear the gasp that escaped her mouth.

"Come," he said. "Come inside with me. There's something I want to show you."

Speechless, Pru allowed herself to be pulled along across the heather and thyme. As they went, she squinted toward Mrs. Spencer's bedroom. The wet dogs would be okay for a little while.

Then suddenly she noticed movement in the window. Pru blinked once, and then a second time. She looked down to navigate a series of fallen logs. When she glanced up again, Pru could've sworn she saw Mrs. Spencer's flinty stare shimmering against the glass.

Forty-six

"You wanted to show me the dining room?" Pru said. "Thanks but I've seen it approximately nine hundred times, mostly while carrying wet dog."

As they stood in the doorway, Win slipped his hands from hers. Pru tried not to frown. It was probably for the best. Mrs. Spencer would throw a wobbler if she witnessed bona fide physical contact between them. And she would be down, any minute now.

"I should be getting back . . ." Pru started.

"Shh! Just hold on a moment. First, this is not a mere dining room. It's the Grand Dining Hall."

He pointed to a placard above the door frame.

"Can't you see?"

"Grand," Pru said. "That's a stretch."

The room wasn't small, but neither was it "grand." In it was a dining table that somehow seemed too narrow and too large for the space simultaneously. Around the table was seating for exactly four guests, provided they were of small-to-medium build and one guest didn't mind a stool.

"I'll allow that the room itself is not particularly impressive," Win said. "But that." He pointed to the portrait above the fireplace. "That is a masterpiece."

"Is it . . . ?" Pru took several steps closer. "Is that Mrs. Spencer?"

She'd walked past the painting countless times over the last few months. The Grand Dining Hall was an excellent shortcut between the kitchen and the nesting places of several packs of pups. The painting was sublime, yes, but it had never occurred to Pru that the woman was the same one who motored through town wild-haired, demon-eyed, and screaming at children.

"It is the duchess herself," Win said. "Or Mrs. Spencer, if you please."

The portrait was a flare of color, a winter's sunset of pinks and silver and white. In it Gladys Deacon sat on an upholstered bench, the cushion dipping beneath her. She wore a dress of pink organza, off-the-shoulder, with roses tumbling down the front. Her hair was pulled back in finger waves and secured at the nape of her neck. She rested against a pink pillow, white and black feathers splayed out behind her. The hint of birds, Pru thought with a droll smile. How appropriate.

"She's stunning." Pru felt a little breathless.

If the portrait was any indication, the duchess was the fetchingest woman of her time, just as Mrs. Spencer always claimed.

"Stunning she is," Win agreed. "The artist is Giovanni Boldini, the most famous portraitist of his day. They called him the Master of Swish due to the grace of his brushstrokes."

"I can see why. The painting moves, as though she's alive. I can almost hear her talking to someone off frame."

"The man was gifted," Win said. "Though he had the choicest subjects to work with. Boldini and John Singer Sargent painted all the stunners of the Belle Époque. Sargent sketched Gladys Deacon numerous times, but ultimately never painted the duchess for fear of not being able to capture her true beauty."

"So Boldini was more of a risk-taker, then?" Pru asked.

"That, or he was hoping for a good shag. The man was a known cad." Win gave Pru a quick wink. "Boldini painted Coon, too. The duke was furious both times but had to allow it. A Boldini portrait was a mark of social standing."

Win took a few steps closer to the painting. He studied it for a minute as he ran his hand along a crevice on the wall.

"She was a fine-looking broad," he said.

So this was Mrs. Spencer. Beneath it all, behind the guns and the spaniels, she was a young woman, painted by a celebrated artist, looking toward some nameless companion elsewhere in the room.

"What is going on with this wall?" Win mumbled, still pushing against the crack. "I hope this room doesn't split in two."

"Or the house," Pru said. "Do you think it's her, Seton? Really her?"

Win peered over his shoulder.

"Of course it is! Look at the color of the eyes, the shape of her nose. Can't you tell?"

Pru nodded.

"Yes. I suppose I can."

Win lifted his hand from the wall. He took a step back.

"You're looking well, Lady Marlborough," he said and took a deep bow. "As always, it's a pleasure to see you."

He turned and took a seat at the table

"Sit." He patted the chair beside him. "Have a rest."

Pru nodded and followed his lead, all the while surreptitiously eyeing the door. Surely Mrs. Spencer would barrel through at any second. She'd yell at Pru for not doing her work, and at the biographer for not doing his.

"Where do you go from here, Miss Valentine?" Win asked.

"How's that?"

"After you leave the Grange? Where shall you go?"

Pru cackled, though she was not especially amused.

"What a question," she said.

The embarrassing truth was that Pru had no idea where she'd go. This was her world now, as unglamorous and unkempt as it was. Given Mrs. Spencer could die at any time, life at the Grange was also fleeting. Where did she go from there, indeed.

"So you don't know where you're headed, either," he said with a smirk. "Join the club."

"No. I do. I'll, uh, return stateside."

"Where, though? Rumor has it America is fairly expansive."

"East Coast," Pru mumbled.

It sounded right, for the most part. California seemed an impossibly far journey, in more ways than one. On the other hand, Boston was unthinkable too.

"New York maybe," she added.

"Sounds like you have it well thought out."

"Yes, plans like mesh." Pru locked her fingers together. "I should be leading armies with my tightly constructed agenda."

Armies. Pru dropped her hands as she felt a jab in her ribs, like a long-ago injury acting up. She hadn't thought about Charlie in a while. Or if she had, it was only for a moment. If and when she returned to the States, would he once again infiltrate her days and leak into her dreams?

Pru began to feel a little sick.

"Is everything all right, Miss Valentine? You look pale."

"Yes, yes, I'm fab. And what about you?" she said quickly.

Go away, Charlie. Go the hell away.

"Will you go back to London?" she asked. "Is that your home?"

Win shrugged.

"I have a place in London, yes, a flat I share with two cousins. We also have a family home on the Île Saint-Louis in Paris. Not sure on which doorstep I'll eventually find myself."

"Maybe whichever is closest to your publisher?" she said.

"Come again?"

"Or your editor." Pru pointed toward the painting. "For the biography? Once you finish writing, I imagine you'd want to be near your publishing house. Or does location not matter? I don't know how it works."

"Uh . . ." He snickered bitterly. "As luck would have it, neither do I."

"Well, I'm sure you'll figure it out," she said, trying to appear chipper. "Once your book is a smash hit and you ascend to literati status you'll need to be where you can hobnob with other writers and visit all the best salons. Just ask Mrs. Spencer."

"Lord, other writers. That doesn't sound fun at all."

"So you don't know where you're going, either," Pru said. "Excellent. I don't feel as bad about my complete lack of direction."

"Blimey, never use this old goat as a barometer for ambition and drive. Of all the bars mine's the lowest. It's very nearly on the ground."

"But think of how happy you'll be," she said. "Once you finish writing and release Gladys Deacon out into the universe."

"Will I be, though? It's funny . . . I . . . I . . ." He stuttered. "I've been chasing this dream for so long, I don't know what I'll do if I ever actually catch it."

For the better part of twenty years, Win believed everything would be different once he wrote the book, just as Pru said. But would anything truly change? What was a book but a person's words, read by a few more persons? Once Win accomplished that, would it put his family's misgivings to bed, to speak nothing of the misgivings he had about himself?

"What do you mean 'if'?" Pru asked. "You *will* catch it. And when you do, you'll hang on and ride that accomplishment as far as it can take you. I'll be the very first person in line to buy the book, and all the books that follow. I'll brag that I knew you when."

"Yes, but what if it turns out . . ."

He stared up at Gladys Deacon, who appeared skeptical amid the feathers and pink. *You people are lost causes, aren't you?* she seemed to say. *The saddest crew I ever saw.*

"What if this thing," Win said, "this thing that I've wanted since eternity, what if I don't want it in the end?"

"Well, then you try to discover what it is you're really after."

Win turned and locked eyes with her. Pru felt herself warm under his gaze.

"Actually, I have a better idea," he said. "How 'bout this? How 'bout we hang around here until Mrs. Spencer passes? Then we'll continue on after she's bought the farm. The dogs will keep breeding into perpetuity, no doubt. Someone should look after them. I can write from anywhere."

"Seton, you're bonkers! Mrs. Spencer isn't going to let us stay at the Grange without her. She barely tolerates us now!"

"But she'll never know!" Win said. "A benefit of being dead. Unless she haunts us, that is."

"Which she undoubtedly would."

"Listen, it'll work like this," Win said. "After she's gone, we'll just very quietly . . . not leave. If anyone shows up we'll claim squatters' rights. Who'd want this old flea motel anyway? We'll while out our days bobbling about with no concrete plans of any kind. Just how it suits us."

Pru smiled.

"That doesn't sound half bad," she said.

"It doesn't sound even a little bad."

Win stood. His knees crackled on the way up.

"Although," he said, walking toward the door. He stopped, then looked again at Pru. "I guess we need to take heed, be careful what we wish for and all that."

"What's wrong with a little wishing?"

"Miss Valentine, don't you see? Wishing is probably what landed us both in these messes to start."

Forty-seven

"Miss Valentine!"

A vigorous rapping erupted on the other side of the door. It was Win, of course. Mrs. Spencer never knocked.

"Miss Valentine! Are you in there? Let me in!"

Pru took her time to respond. She was comfortable right then, lounging beside a fire, wrapped up with a blanket and a book. This time it was P. G. Wodehouse's *Love Among the Chickens*. Pru hadn't read Wodehouse before. His works were humorous, lighthearted, not appropriate for a Very Serious literature major. What a bore she'd once been.

"Miss Valentine?"

"Yes," she responded, somewhat reluctantly. "I'm here. I guess."

She'd hardly gotten the words out when Win exploded into the room.

"You have to come with me!" he said, hopping toward her, his hair flapping like the ears of an excitable spaniel. "Now! It's urgent! I need to show you something!"

"Win . . ." Pru said with a groan. "It's late. I'm comfortable and I don't want to get up."

"Don't be a loaf-about," he said. "And it's not that late. Also, a fire? It's hardly cold at all."

"It's January! And this house is draftier than Santa's sleigh."

Plus everyone knew the best place to read was beside a snapping blaze, especially if you were thousands of miles from home. Or if you didn't have a home.

"I'm in the middle of a book," she said.

Win eyed the cover.

"Love Among the Chickens," he said. "Well, I prefer his Blandings Castle series but to each her own. Anyhow, Wodehouse can wait. Trust me. You'll want to see this."

Win reached for her hand. Pru took it with another groan. He lifted her to standing.

"I've a decade and a half on you," he said. "And you're the one bellyaching like an old maid."

"I'm not old. Just comfortable. Preferring to be unpestered."

"Well, you are in the exact wrong residence for that."

He led her down the hall.

"What about Mrs. Spencer?" she whispered as they pattered toward the stairs. "You know she hates it when we 'ride roughshod' around the house after she's retired for the evening."

"We're not roughshodding anything. And why do you care what a ninety-year-old woman thinks?"

"Well, she pays me for one. On top of that, she's already chapped at me for botching a puppy-weaning two days ago. No one told me I was supposed to be weaning him so I can't really be faulted. But naturally Mrs. Spencer doesn't care about such technicalities."

"Not to worry," Win said as he helped Pru over a broken step. "The old bird's out in a purple laudanum haze."

She was out but for how long? The problem with purple laudanum hazes was that when Mrs. Spencer woke from them she was usually seeing red.

"So where are we going?" Pru asked.

When they hit the ground floor, Win guided her around the corner and toward the Grand Dining Hall.

"Oh good grief," she said. "Back to the portrait? It's lovely but can't you moon over it unassisted?"

"Shush! This has nothing to do with the Boldini."

When they stepped into the room, Pru's eyes went straight to Gladys Deacon's silver plume. That's when she noticed the wall beside it. The fissure from a few days before had transformed into a yawning divide.

"Oh my God!" she yelped. "What happened? Is the room collapsing? Do you have earthquakes in England? We should move the portrait so it doesn't get damaged. How do you even move a priceless work of art? A transport company?"

"No earthquakes. I opened the wall with my own two hands."

"Mrs. Spencer is going to kill you! I mean truly kill you! Probably with a gun!"

"Miss Valentine. Look. Stop yammering and *look*."

He dragged her closer. Pru's hands trembled like the earthquake she'd imagined.

"That crack in the wall," he said. "The wall itself. It looked queer when we were in here the other day. So I decided to perform an inspection."

They approached the opening, which was less a hole and more of an entrance, a door, a hatch into an entirely different room.

Pru gasped as they stepped together through the passageway.

"Is that . . ." she started.

"Yes. A secret library. Have you ever seen anything like it?"

"Oh . . . my . . . God . . ."

She took a few more steps. They were suddenly surrounded, on all four sides, by books. Hundreds of books. Thousands, probably.

Pru's breath quickened as she scanned the room.

Shelves ran floor to ceiling, from one corner to the next, all of them tightly packed with books of all sizes and colors. Any other room in the Grange was partially finished at best: a few appliances and minimal dishware in the kitchen, the sparse dining hall, Win's bed on the floor upstairs. But this room, it was curated. And it was full.

"Win!" Pru said and flew to a row of J. M. Barrie. "This is magnificent!"

Peter Pan. The Little White Bird.

"I knew you'd love it." He grinned. "Worth getting off your duff for, isn't it?"

"Yes. A million times over."

Pru spun around to face a collection of Arnold Bennett. She closed her eyes and inhaled, the smell of paper strong in the air.

"I feel a little drunk," she said.

Win chuckled.

"You seem a little drunk besides."

Pru opened her eyes again and spotted an old friend.

"Look!" she said, sliding a book from its spot. "Virginia Woolf! *A Room of One's Own*. Every girl at Berkeley would be swooning at the sight."

She opened the front cover.

"First edition. And it's signed!"

"Ms. Woolf and Gladys Deacon were acquainted," Win told her. "Virginia said of her, 'one does fall in love with the Duchess of Marlborough. I did at once.'"

Win then moved down a row of books, looking for something specific.

"Ah!" he said. "Here it is. A collection from R. C. Trevelyan, the poet. *Polyphemus and Other Poems*, *The Foolishness of Solomon*, *The Death of Man*. He wrote almost nothing in the late teens and early twenties. A horrid case of writer's block. Virginia Woolf said it was Lady Marlborough who released Bob from his misery. She called it 'the legacy of Gladys Deacon.'"

"The legacy being she could get writers out of their slumps?" Pru asked. Then added with a wink, "Looks like she'd better get working on you."

"Hilarious! A real comedy routine from our cherished Miss Valentine. And yes, she was referring to his writer's block but also that Trevelyan lived in Gladys's home for a spell. After leaving the duchess's tutelage, the formerly homosexual poet had a renewed interest in the female sex. Or sex with females."

"Was it necessary to specify that last bit?" Pru asked. She looked back at the shelf. "Hello, *Mrs. Dalloway*."

She smiled but although Pru loved *Mrs. Dalloway*, she bypassed her for the book beside it. *Grand Babylon Hotel*.

"Mrs. Spencer put Woolf next to Arnold Bennett?" she clucked. "Woolf couldn't stand the man. She thought him hideously old guard."

"I'm sure you can take it up with Mrs. Spencer. Perhaps she'll permit you to rearrange the books according to each writer's complaints and position of envy."

"I'll pass, in the interest of my sustained existence. Obviously she doesn't want us in here, if it's hidden away like this."

Pru stroked the spine of a Cocteau, then a sequence of Conrad.

"Wow," she said. "Wow."

"Look what I've got," Win said and raised a book, tall and thin. "The famous collection of sexual renderings by D. H. Lawrence."

"You would find that one," Pru said and rolled her eyes.

She lugged a stool from the corner and climbed on top to examine the upper shelves. Forster, Wells, Shaw, Wharton. The gang's all there.

"Oh!" she said, stretching to the right. "Is that? I can't believe she has this one!"

Pru tugged a book out from between two others, and then held it to her chest.

"One of my favorites." She breathed in its scent. "*Sailing Alone Around the World*. It was my parents' favorite, too."

"I'm not familiar," Win said and took a few steps closer.

Book in hand, she hopped down from the stool.

"It's a memoir by Joshua Slocum," Pru explained. "He was the first person to sail the world alone. His book was an enormous hit when it came out."

She pried open the cover and ticked through several pages.

"His publisher built him an onboard library for the journey," she said. "How neat is that?"

I had already found that it was not good to be alone, and so made companionship with what there was around me, sometimes with the universe and sometimes with my own insignificant self; but my books were always my friends, let fail all else.

"Books were always my friends," she repeated with a goofy yet winsome smile.

"Ah." Win set the literary pornography on a shelf. "You like seafaring tomes. I s'pose it makes sense for a Boston girl."

"I'm not a Boston girl," Pru said, staring into the book. "I grew up in Sausalito. It's a former fishing village just outside San Francisco."

As for myself, the wonderful sea charmed me from the first.

Even a decade later Pru could still picture her home. She could catch glimpses of the wind kicking up water, the morning fog gripping the roads. She closed her eyes to conjure the sun as it rose and cleared out the gloom, washing the world clean. Inhaling through the books, Pru could almost smell the sea.

"It's odd," Win said. "In all of our conversations, I don't think you've once mentioned your childhood. Or your parents. On bad terms, are you?"

Pru shook her head.

"No terms," she said. "As a child I adored my parents. They were beautiful and careless, but oh such fun."

"Gatsby-esque?"

"Something like that. They were sufficiently well off to appear rich, but in absolutely no position to spend with the abandon that they did. I suppose my mother was like Mrs. Spencer's, minus the slain lovers. But, gosh, they made it seem so simple and happy with their clothes, and their boat, and all that champagne spilling into the bay."

"That's why your family was so fond of the sailor," Win said, pointing to the book still in her hands. "You were bred for the sea."

"Or irony. When I was nine, my parents took our boat *Day in the Sun* out onto the water and never returned."

"No!" Win said, mouth gaping. "Surely that's not true."

"Unfortunately, it is."

"That's horrific!"

"They eventually found the boat upturned, bobbing along in the bay, their bodies likely sunk to the bottom, if not eaten by sharks." Pru pitched the book onto the stool. "Joshua Slocum, the author, disappeared on his boat, too."

"Miss Valentine." He clutched his chest. "I'm gutted. Truly. I wish I possessed the slightest of couth. I haven't the faintest clue what to say."

Pru shrugged.

"There's nothing to say, really. I was at school when it happened, which was noteworthy as my parents thought experiencing life was far superior to sitting in a classroom. Luckily, I was a bit of a nerd. Of course I didn't always feel so lucky, having been in school and not with them that day."

"Oh Miss Valentine," Win said and looped an arm around her shoulders.

He felt strong. Steady. Secure.

"I wish there was something I could do."

He squeezed tighter and Pru was surprised to find herself snuffle-nosed and weepy-eyed. It'd been so long since she'd cried about them. Of course, as of late, all her tears had been for Charlie.

"What happened after?" Win asked. "Who raised you?"

"I went to live with my aunt and two much older male cousins," she said. "They might be as old as you are, even."

"And they're still alive? Someone call Ripley's!"

Pru gave him a shaky smile.

"Another aunt soon followed," she said. "Then a relative whose genealogy I can't recall. My parents were viewed as vastly irresponsible but in my first nine years, I lived in one home. In the next nine years, I lived in eight."

"Blimey, this old man's heart can't take it. It's ripping apart at the mere thought of a wee Valentine amid all that loss and upheaval. Those big eyes, the sweet face. Gutted, I tell you. Simply gutted."

"It's fine," Pru insisted. "Everyone was fine. Nothing was awful. At worst, the guardian-of-the-moment ignored me. Sometimes I got a hug, or a Christmas present. It was no love fest, but if you're going to be a foster kid, it was a half-way decent fate."

Pru shimmied out of his grip.

"So," she said. "There you have it. My own story. I'll bet you wish you stuck with the explicit drawings."

"I'm having a hard time digesting this," Win said, his eyes almost glassy. "God, you were an orphan, weren't you? Straight out of a Dickens novel, imp-ish and ragtag to boot."

"A Dickens character?" Pru turned to face him, a smile breaking across her face. "Funny, I thought the same about you. I guess it's no surprise we ended up in the same book."

Forty-eight

They spent over two hours in the library that night, thumbing through books, quoting the masters, sniggering over Lawrence's drawings. He had a knack for making the men appear perfect, the women contorted and deformed.

Finally, even Pru had had her fill.

"Might be time to call it a day," she said. "I'm dizzy from all the books. Or the dust."

Pru looked down at her hands. Her fingertips were shiny, bearing a slight silver sheen from the pages and the type. She wiped them on her trousers.

"What's this?" Win said. "Even the highly literary Miss Valentine can tire of books?"

"I think my brain's not used to all the words. Quick. Get me a spaniel to deworm."

She nudged a first edition of *The Jungle Book* back into its shelf.

"What do you plan to do now?" Win asked.

"Uh. Go to bed? Like a normal person?"

"I was not aware normal and boring were synonymous," Win said. "Come on. You can sleep when you're dead. Let's head out for a pop."

"A pop? Of your dreadful family wine? No, thanks, I don't want to suffer another three-day headache."

"I don't think you can blame the wine quality, it was more a matter of quantity," he said. "But, no, I was thinking we grab a pint at a proper pub. In town."

"In town?"

"Sure. The Royal Oak. The George and Dragon. Take your pick."

Pru weighed the possibility. Other than getting flayed by Mrs. Spencer or ending up in Win's bed a second time, what did she have to lose? Finishing the Wodehouse suddenly didn't seem so important.

"You know what?" Pru said. "Let's do it. Why not?"

"Why not. A jolly good question. Okay. Let's go. No time to waste."

Before Pru could regain her judgment, Win hastily ushered her from the library and out onto the road. Win hoped they'd keep a tab for him at the G&D because he didn't want to bother scrounging up a few quid.

"Are we competing in a race or something?" Pru asked as they clipped along. "If so, I think we're in the lead."

"Ha! Funny as always! No, I only want to get there before last call."

It was nine o'clock.

By the time they bumbled into the George & Dragon, Pru's nose was running from the cold and also their brisk pace. She looked down and realized she had on slippers, lounging clothes, and no coat.

"Uh, Win," she said. "We should probably turn around. Look at me! I'm not even properly dressed. This is a bad idea . . ."

"Of course it's a bad idea, which is exactly why we're doing it. Regardless." He gave her a once-over. "You look rather charming. Quite cute."

Pru blushed, right on time, and he led her to the back of the pub, ordering up two pints on the way.

"This place is very English," Pru noted as they sat down.

"How curious. It's not like we're actually in England or anything."

"And you were heckling me for my 'comedy routine'?"

Without her asking for it, Win yanked off his sweater and tossed it her way.

"The old G and D is a seventeenth-century pub," he said. "It has most of its original beams and fireplaces."

"Well, I love it," Pru said, wiggling into his sweater. "Much better than sitting in your room while you mope about in your underclothes."

"And yet, last time I did that you stayed the night."

Pru chuckled as the barkeep dropped off two pints. They each took a sip. Between the sweater and the beer, Pru thawed at once.

"So," Win said and wiped a line of foam from his top lip. "You've told me about your parents, offered a touch of Berkeley to boot, now it's time to fess up about the rest of it."

"The rest of what?"

"Your life," he said. "But mainly I was referring to the fiancé."

"Charlie?" Pru said, her heart beating fast.

She didn't want to tell Win about Charlie. It felt like two different worlds, compounds that should never mix.

"Charlie." Win took another gulp of beer. "Sure. Okay. Lay it on me. Tell me about ol' Chuck."

"There's nothing to tell. He's gone. We weren't even engaged for that long. That's all I have to say on the matter."

"If you planned to marry the bloke, surely you have more to say."

"Nope," she said. "That's pretty much it."

"Do you want to know what I think?"

"Not particularly."

"I think he's the reason behind your unceremonious university departure. You've made some vague references to a lack of funds and not knowing what you wanted to be when you grew up. But I think the leaving was about him. This fiancé is the lynchpin."

"Former fiancé," she said. "And 'unceremonious departure'? My departure was supposed to be literally ceremonious. As in a wedding ceremony."

"Precisely what I'd gathered," he said. "Tell me more. I'm positively dying to know."

"Dying?" Pru said. "Is that really the word you want to go with?"

"Yes. Your withholding of information is causing me a terminal level of pain."

"You'll regret that word choice, my friend."

She took several glugs of beer.

"You were all torn up about my parents' deaths?" Pru said. "Gutted, I believe, was the word. Well, hold on to your knickers because old Charlie has a pretty wretched tale himself. Long story short, the bastard up and died."

Win's eyes popped open.

"He died? This is not . . . are you trying to be funny? Attempting to take the piss out of me? Teach me a lesson?"

"You think I'd lie about someone dying just to mess with you?"

"No. Never. Aw, shit." Win covered his face. "I'm sorry. No. Sorry is not adequate. Bloody hell." He looked up. "Bloody fucking depths of hell. I hate myself with some regularity, but never like this."

"You didn't know. But I have to tell you. It gets worse."

"AW CHRIST!"

"Remember that exchange we had approximately forever ago?" she said. "Soldiers blasting away the VC and whatnot?"

"MOTHERFUCKING CHRIST." Win dug both hands into his hair and scratched his ragged fingertips into his scalp. "Don't tell me. He was a soldier? Blimey, I should just off myself right now."

"Win, you didn't know," she said again.

"Jesus H. Where is a goddamn revolver when you need one?"

"It's okay," Pru said. "I mean *you're* okay. The rest, obviously, is not."

The peculiar thing was that lately it had been starting to feel if not "okay" at least within firing distance of not-completely-unbearable. And Pru felt as awful about this as Win had for bringing it up in the first place.

"What happened?" Win asked. "He was fighting, yes? In the war?"

"Yep. Charlie was fighting the Charlie in Nam," she said. "And don't apologize for that smirk you're trying to hide. It's funny in its own twisted way. I'm sure there are plenty more Charlies on both sides to go around. The worst part, other than, you know, the death, is that he didn't have to go. His parents got him an excuse, or bought him one."

"How do you mean?" he asked.

"Charlie was diagnosed with a very serious football injury despite only ever playing baseball and tennis. A medical miracle."

"But he went," Win said, taking her hand in his. "Because he had honor."

"He had something. I couldn't have done it. I would've milked my phantom running back career for all it was worth."

"I doubt that."

"He was killed during the Easter Offensive," Pru told him. Saying it felt like a release, an exhale after holding her breath. "They found his body, which I don't think was much of one, outside Kon Tum. His entire company was killed by an RPG, a grenade launched at a closer-than-necessary distance."

"Jesus. What a mess."

"Literally," she said with a weary nod. "It happened almost a year ago and his remains didn't arrive stateside until late last fall. It took a while to sort out the parts."

She slipped her hand from Win's and reached for the beer, though not before gently skimming her fingers over his forearm. Pru meant it as thanks for his tenderness, an assurance that although he'd raised the issue, she didn't hold it against him.

Though Win understood the origin of the gesture—he wasn't a total clod—the feel of something else surged through every last miserable corner of his body. And, for the first time, he saw Pru wholly. She was not the blushing, demure girl he believed he knew.

"There you have it," she said. "The reason I'm here, in a crumbling house, completely without plans. I have no one and nothing to go back to. I'll return to America eventually, immigration isn't going to let me stick around here forever, but even in my own country I don't have a home."

"Pru, there has to be someone for you," he said. "How could there not be?"

"I have a few college friends but . . . hold on. Wait. What did you just say?"

"There has to be someone."

"No," she said. "Before that. Did you call me Prudence?"

"What? Oh. No." He looked momentarily perplexed. "I called you Pru, probably."

"Pru?"

"Sure. Everybody has a nickname. You know that. Me. Gads. GD. Have you not heard me say this?"

"No. Never."

"Ah. Well. Must be only in my mind."

"Pru makes less sense than Gads."

"It's short for *Prunus laurocerasus*, the Latin name for English laurel. I believe you Yanks call it cherry laurel."

Win had teased her about the name before. On the one hand it was no different from her Berkeley friends Petal and Daisy. It was a plant, after all. On the other, its fruits were toxic, its cherries made humans ill. And Lord was it invasive. It grew all over the bloody place, just like a weed.

But of course Win loved the name because it was hers. He loved the nickname too, even if it was made of wishful thinking. English laurel? No, this Laurel was all American. Alarmingly, upsettingly so.

Forty-nine

It doesn't do you justice. there's that tooth effect I don't like. which in you
is certainly not apparent. I, too, think the dress *un peu trop décolleté*.
—Florence Deacon on Giovanni Boldini's rendition of Gladys.
The portrait hung for several decades in the Grand Dining Hall at the Grange.

—J. Casper Augustine Seton,
The Missing Duchess: A Biography

Annie wasn't a snooper by nature.

She didn't have a big brother to spy on, no sisters with hidden diaries to pry
open. Annabelle Haley spent twenty years in a scruffy farmhouse with only one
other person who never seemed worth the effort. As it turned out, Annie hadn't
been looking closely enough.

"Nicola!" she yelled, skittering downstairs.

She glanced around. The lobby was eerily silent. Annie looked past one corner and then the next. She clambered over to Nicola's computer and typed out
an e-mail to Eric.

The words and sentences were jumbled together, the grammar poor. Also Annie used way more caps and demonstrative punctuation than was strictly necessary. But Eric would understand. He always did, and this was huge.

After closing out her e-mail, Annie called out for the innkeeper one more time.

"Hey, Nicola!" she warbled, scurrying toward the back door. "I'm going to borrow your bike. Be back in a sec! K thanks!"

Once outside, she jogged to the shed. In the distance was the squeaky scrawl of Nicola's voice, which Annie took as permission. Sliding on her backpack, she hopped onto the bike and pedaled off.

Earlier that morning, while Laurel showered, Annie had snuck into her purse. The last time she'd done that was probably a decade ago, rooting through her mom's bag to find quarters for the arcade. But it wasn't money she was after this time.

After forty seconds of struggle, she extracted an overstuffed black leather Day-Timer, Laurel Haley's definitive playbook. Annie flipped to the current date. At nine o'clock Laurel was scheduled to meet with an inspector. The time was 8:53.

The calendar didn't include an address and it seemed impossible anyone would voluntarily let an inspector near the Grange. Nonetheless, the old estate had to be Laurel's destination. Without a doubt, her mother was the woman from Gus's story.

"You're telling me the girl you've called Pru all along," Annie said the previous day, after Gus finished the latest chapter of his tale. "You're telling me that her name was Laurel?"

He nodded in confirmation.

"What about the Valentine?" she said.

But even as Annie asked the question, the pieces locked into place.

Laurel Innamorati Haley: Annie's mom. *Prunus laurocerasus*, Pru, Miss Valentine: the girl from the story. Laurel, Pru. Innamorati, Valentine. In Italy, Valentine's Day was known as la festa degli innamorati. Of course Gus wouldn't use Laurel's actual name. It wasn't his style.

"Innamorati," Annie said, winded as if struck in the chest. "Was that Pru's real last name?"

"How did you know? Annie, you look peaky."

"That . . . I think that's the woman I ran into, the one staying at the inn who said the Grange is gone."

"The inn?" Gus said, panic flashing all over his face. "She's at the Banbury Inn? God bless it. I . . . I have to go."

He quickly gathered his things then bolted from the pub, leaving Annie to pay the tab. Gus always footed the bill. Always. But he was dumbed by the news. Thirty years later, the bookish girl was back in town.

Bookish. It didn't sound like Laurel at all, other than the old biography she'd stashed in her office for so many years. Annie never saw her read it and in general, always had the feeling that Laurel thought reading for pleasure was a monumental waste of time. Why dabble in the make-believe when you could run a law firm or teach sick kids to ride a horse?

At least Annie now understood Laurel's tight, fake-smile humoring of Eric. It wasn't that she didn't like him, or thought Annie was too young. Laurel was worried that Eric might die, just as her fiancé had.

"Pru Valentine," Annie said out loud for at least the twelfth time. "I'll be damned."

As she curved around the bend, Annie saw her mom step out of the rental car. She watched as Laurel locked the door, and then adjusted her tweed blazer and the hem of her brown wool skirt.

"Well, well, well," Annie said as she pedaled up. "Fancy meeting you here."

Laurel stepped back, startled. She had not seen her coming. Especially not on a bike.

"Annie!" she said, her voice a mile higher than it had ever been before. "What are you doing here?"

"Came to see the Grange," she said. "And it's bizarre because I could've sworn someone told me it was gone."

"God, I hate myself for that." Laurel sighed and squeezed her eyes shut, as if in pain. "I lied to you and it's been gnawing at me ever since."

Laurel opened her eyes again. Her gaze seemed a thousand miles away.

"Why *did* you lie, Mom? I don't get it. Developers? They 'razed' the property?"

"Developers *will* knock it down. Sooner rather than later."

"Nice try," Annie grumbled.

"Honestly, the place is loaded with so many damned memories, it's easier to believe that it's already gone."

"So this is the family property? You own the Grange?"

"Part of it," Laurel said with a nod. "It's held in a syndicate, hence the problems trying to sell my share. On top of that, someone was trying to have it declared a historical site."

"Did you live here, Mom?"

Laurel paused, her breath held behind her chest. Annie could nearly see her deciding whether to lie again. But she wouldn't. Laurel had told the one, which was one lie too many.

"Yes," Laurel finally said. "I lived here. A long time ago and not for very long. But I did live at the Grange."

"The man who wrote the book. *The Missing Duchess*. He was with you."

Laurel nodded, her eyes glistening.

Annie tried to see her as Win had back then: young, scared, wide-eyed, and ethereal. There was a glimpse of Pru in there among all that drive and capability, but only a glimpse, and only in shadow. Gus had mentioned Pru's quiet strength and that was all Annie saw right then.

"How did you find out?" Laurel asked.

"Well, the book for one."

"I'm not in the book."

"I know, but it's how you reacted to it," Annie said. "I put two and two together."

"Two and two? With only the one book?"

"I fished around town," she said. "Talked to a few longtime residents. Some of them remembered you."

"They did?" Laurel's face jumped. "Who? I didn't get out much."

"You had to go to the store sometimes, didn't you? The occasional stop in a pub?"

"Annie, who did you talk to?"

"Various people. Someone named Gus?"

Laurel stared vacantly.

"I don't recall anyone named Gus," she said.

"Mom, where did you go to college? I could've sworn you went to Wellesley but now I think you might've started somewhere else."

Laurel sighed again, turned around, and took a seat on a nearby rock. She braced herself against her knees with both hands.

"I went to Berkeley," she said. "For a year. A long, long, long time ago. I barely remember it, having ended up at Wellesley, which was the exact opposite in terms of . . . everything."

"After Berkeley you came here. To get over a fiancé."

"That's the short version, yes," Laurel said. "Those years. They were so difficult. At the time I doubted I could even survive them. And now it all seems like a story. A novel read decades ago."

"So the pain goes away," Annie said. "Eventually."

"Or else it just gets covered up by some new kind of injury."

Suddenly a car pulled up. A man stepped out, a thick folder lodged beneath his arm. Laurel stood and brushed off her skirt.

"Ms. Haley?" he said and extended a hand. "The name's Richard Moskin. I'm the inspector."

"Pleased to meet you," Laurel said. "I'm finishing up out here. Feel free to help yourself onto the property. I haven't been inside but it's unlocked, I think. I'll join you in a minute."

"Righto," he said and smiled. The front gate squeaked and he disappeared.

"You're finishing up?" Annie said and lifted a brow.

"I know, I know. We have a long way to go, yet."

"Mom, did you love him?" Annie asked. "The writer?"

"Oh, Annabelle. I suppose I did."

"I'm sorry it couldn't have been more," she said, thinking of the last two decades and their quiet country life. Never a boyfriend in all that time. Or no boyfriend important enough for Annie to meet. "I'm sorry you and the writer didn't see things through."

"Oh. Well."

Laurel flushed and for a moment Annie saw Pru. Only a glimmer, the briefest of snapshots, but there she trembled beneath the stern and polish.

"That would've been nice, in theory," Laurel said. "But then I wouldn't have you. So everything worked out as it should."

"That's a sweet sentiment, even if it's total crap. If you'd stayed with Win, there'd be some other kid you were grateful to have."

"Excuse me!" said a voice. The mustachioed head of the inspector popped up over the fence. "I find myself challenged in accessing the building."

"Huh. They told me it'd be unlocked. I'll come check it out." Laurel turned to Annie. "Do you want to go in with me? It'll be the first time I've stepped inside in almost thirty years."

"Uh, sure," Annie said, neglecting to mention that she'd already been, twice, and that she could get them in without a key.

"All right," Laurel said and exhaled loudly. "Let's do it. This is going to be . . . this is going to be something."

With a watery smile, and as she had so many times for so many years before, Laurel took her daughter's hand and guided her along the way.

Fifty

Subject: **Like lightning**
From: eric.sawyer@usmc.mil
Date: Nov 15, 2001 04:35
To: anniehaley79@aol.com

I'll bet you didn't expect such a fast reply.

I was at my computer when your e-mail came through. That chime was the best dang thing I've heard this year, other than that one time you said "yes." When I got the e-mail I swear I could picture exactly where you were. It almost felt like talking.

Your poor mom. But stop worrying! Charlie Vietnam and me—two different people. Two different Americas. We're better organized now. We have our crap together. That's what they tell us anyway.

Do I think it's weird she never told you about him? I dunno, I guess. But you probably haven't told her everything about you, right? Does she know you've been slinking around town with that old man for instance? Sorry, I'll never not think of him that way.

Y'all are close but she's still your mama. Had a big ol' life before you came around. Prob a mess of secrets, too. You figure to tell our kids everything you've ever done? Every heartbreak you've ever had? I reckon not. Keep me out of it if you do.

I don't know why she won't say more about your dad. Whatever her reasons, I'll wager they have to do with love. Your mama has nothing but goodness inside. You're made the same way.

I guess you have to ask yourself why you care. Why it matters to know his name. You've managed a-okay till now without it. More than okay, as it happens.

Well, love, gotta go. I'm not supposed to be on this machine. Guess what? We're almost there! I'll send you postcards from Kandahar. Sounds like a novel. Maybe you can write it.

All my love,
ES

GD: He was a bastard, wasn't he? Oh, I adored the man!

WS: So he did paint you.

GD: Perhaps. It's all starting to seem familiar.

WS: There's not a person alive who finds creeping dementia so convenient.

GD: You're mistaken, though. About the painting. There's never been a portrait of me on the premises.

WS: You're truly going to claim the Boldini wasn't in your dining room?

GD: It wasn't. Ever. Not for a single second.

WS: Note to manuscript. Writer's assistant looks at GD agog.

PRU: I'm not your assistant.

GD: Who's GD? Surely you're not calling me goddamned.

WS: Simply your initials. Though it's also a highly appropriate coincidence.

PRU: Mrs. Spencer, that portrait was there. I saw it with my own two eyes! Why can't you admit it? What's holding you back?

GD: Boldini painted me, it is true. And he sketched me many times besides, the renditions of which I'm

Fifty-one

WS: Do you care to explain why you've moved your portrait out of the dining room?

GD: I don't recall there ever being a portrait in the dining room.

WS: Come now, Mrs. Spencer. You know the one. The glorious Boldini. It was there a week ago and now, poof, disappeared with the wind.

GD: Boldini? Hmm, the name sounds familiar.

WS: Surely you're not going to lie about this! It's the most fetching portrait the old bastard ever did, as far as I know. Unless there's some other lady in some other country hiding some other portrait in her broken-down home.

happy to provide. But the portrait was never in my home. My former husband kept it, if I recall.

WS: He's been dead, quite a while now.

GD: Probably incinerated the thing. He hated Boldini. Called him a pig. To his face and behind his back. Boldini had a salacious reputation with women and my former husband worried he'd make me look like a tart.

PRU: Mrs. Spencer, I don't understand. The portrait was there. We both saw it.

GD: I don't know what you think you saw but it wasn't me. And so what if I did remove it? Why is it any concern of yours? There are things about me you don't know. Things not even a would-be biographer can weasel out of me with his incessant quizzing. Though, I am sure, that won't stop him from trying.

Fifty-Two

WS: Two bobbies showed up at the door today
while you were out on a very rare afternoon
constitutional. Would you know anything about
this?

GD: How could I?

WS: Mrs. Spencer, I noticed the front of your car is
demolished.

GD: Yes. A goat ran into the fender while my car was
parked in the yard.

WS: Must've been some goat. Unfortunately the
coppers offered an alternate explanation.

GD: I'll bet.

WS: Frideswide's Dress Shop reported that a certain black car smashed into its front window display earlier today. Were there goats in town too?

GD: There might as well have been!

WS: Mrs. Spencer . . .

GD: Fine! I did it! All right? I busted through her window. And I don't regret it.

PRU: But you could've injured someone. That plus the "small fire" you set the other night . . .

GD: Oh please. Frideswide's was closed. No harm, no foul.

WS: The insurance broker believes it some foul.

GD: I didn't want Frideswide infecting this town.

WS: Infecting? Is the sweet clothier ill?

GD: In the brain maybe! Do you know what she had on display in that picture window of hers? Polyester! Polyester trousers! FOR WOMEN. It had to be done, Seton. It positively needed to happen, lest this town fall victim to horrible taste.

Fifty-three

"I'm glad I tracked you down."

Nicola waddled out from her office and to the breakfast table where Annie was piling minicroissants onto her plate.

"Track me down?" Annie scooped up three pieces of cantaloupe. "I'm staying right upstairs."

"Yes, but you seem to flit and flitter all over the place," Nicola said, dancing her hands in demonstration. A passerby ducked to avoid getting socked in the face. "Like a hummingbird."

"I'm generally not one for flitting."

"Further, your mum said you were leaving for the States the day after tomorrow. I couldn't risk not seeing you."

"Excuse me?" Annie said, the plate at once too heavy for her hand. "Leaving? She told you we're leaving? In two days?"

But what about the sightseeing? The promised trips to London and to Blenheim? Not to mention all of the things remaining in Banbury, the pieces of Win's puzzle—and of Laurel's—Annie still had to connect. Laurel said that she was "done" but never mentioned how fast she wanted to get out of town.

"That's what she told me," Nicola said in a clipped tone. "You rushed out of here so briskly *on my bike* I didn't have the chance to tell you."

"Nicola." Annie winced. "I'm sorry. I assumed it was fine."

"S'okay."

Nicola went back to her desk and disappeared beneath it. She remained submerged for so long Annie worried she might've capsized.

"Nicola?" She stretched across the top of the counter. "You still down there?"

"Ope! Here it is!" Nicola popped back up, face reddened and eyes slightly crossed. "Whoa, nelly." She shook her head. "Someone left this for you."

She passed Annie a manila envelope.

"Someone?"

"That older gentleman from the other day? The one with the brother?"

"Oh right." Annie took the envelope. "Gus."

"Is that his name? Well, no matter. His brother is the important one." She wiggled her brows. "That man, easy on the eyes. I've had a crush on him for donkey's years."

"You know Gus's family?" Annie asked. "How well?"

It was worth a shot. Maybe if Nicola knew Gus and his brother, she'd have a string to tie some corner of the story together. Gus insisted he wasn't involved in the tale, that he was an outsider, on the periphery. But outside was still a place. It was part of something too.

"I didn't know him particularly well," Nicola said and pulled at her blouse. "He's much older. But I had a wicked crush on him as a girl. Anyhoo, off I go. I'm leading a band of tourists to Blenheim Castle for the day. Are you familiar?"

"I've heard of it, yes."

"You should check it out. Beyond fabulous," Nicola said. "Did you know the Germans planned to destroy it during the war but Hitler called them off? Fancied he'd assume residence when the Krauts took over the world. It's nice to dream big, I suppose. Well, ta-ta! Enjoy your day! Cheers!"

Nicola spun around and toddled off, leaving Annie amused—another Hitler story for the duchess—as well as alone. Alone with a package from Gus.

Fifty-four

Dear Annie,

Poor timing.

I've been called out of town to contend with a family emergency. Don't worry! Everything is jolly good. For now.

Only as I leave this derelict hamlet do I realize that I want to finish the story. All along I thought I'd tell you only as much as you had the time and tolerance for, and perhaps not even that.

But you should know how things concluded, what happened to Win and to Pru and whether Mrs. Spencer ever revealed herself as the duchess. Of course, titled folks aside, Pru is the true hero of the story, of Win's biography even, though she's not mentioned in it once.

Because I cannot enchant you with my winning personality face-to-face I've enclosed a set of recordings. These tapes, and the accompanying recorder, are provided gratis. You will not have to commit larceny in order to hear them.

Likewise, your bill has been settled at the clock shop. Ah, you'd not told me about those purloined tapes, had you? A little birdie snitched on you. He said a mysterious American girl arrived in his shop with a stash of someone else's recordings. The list of suspects was short.

When you put those recordings together with what is in the envelope you now hold, you'll have a clearer picture of The Missing Duchess. *And by that I mean the story behind the story. A book is nothing without the backstory, the through-line holding it all together. I don't know the full tale myself of course. I'm just one person, one viewpoint, an old bachelor at that. But I've shared with you what I can.*

Finally, Miss Annie, I will answer one of your more nagging questions. The writer does still live in Paris, on the Île Saint-Louis, at the address you discovered. Do with that information what you please.

Until I met you, I hadn't realized what was here. Thank you for showing me, however inadvertently, the narrative's scope. Thank you for researching and for nosing your way into the lives of Win, Pru, and the duchess. And thank you for asking an old bugger some tough questions. I hope I've been of some use to you as well.

Good-bye, for now. Please come see me on your next scholarly expedition.

Cheers and all good things,
Gus

Fifty-five

The biography was coming along.

Win was getting what he needed, if not what he wanted. Maybe this would turn into a legitimate book yet.

"I think she's actually into it," Pru said one night as they went through the library, matching Mrs. Spencer's stories with the books her friends wrote. "I think she likes how this is going."

"Of course she does! Look around!" Win said, waving toward the seemingly infinite library. "This woman is an avid reader. She must gaze upon these, tickled that she will eventually star in one herself."

"Not to mention all the most lauded writers of the day will be only meager players in her story."

Win chuckled.

"You're right," he said. "Conrad. Proust. Mere footnotes. Single entries in the index. 'Please refer to page ninety-three.'"

"But, a piece of criticism if I may," Pru said, lifting a John Galsworthy from the shelf. *The Skin Game.*

"Please, yes. If there's one thing I lack at the Grange it's a constant barrage of flak provided by family and friends. It's like music that's abruptly gone out."

"I didn't realize you were feeling so neglected." Pru coaxed the book back into place. "I'll try to step up my game. Anyhow, if you ask me, the phrase 'avid reader' is too tepid. You've used it at least three times in your book."

"You've a better description, I suppose?"

"Avid is for girls who hide flashlights beneath their pillows so they can finish the latest Nancy Drew after the lights go down."

"Like our Miss Valentine, I presume."

"Yes," she said. "But unlike Lady Marlborough, I never once read so much that I had to spend a week in bed with black bandages over my eyes."

"Fair enough. I'll try to be more descriptive."

Win pivoted around to face her.

"You know, I was thinking," he said. "That here we are writing the duchess's story . . ."

"*We're* writing her story?"

"Yes. We. Did you not just offer editorial notes? So. Here we are penning Gladys Deacon's tale and perhaps somewhere, someone else is writing the story of us."

"The story of us?" Pru balked. "Sounds like a snore. And I'm not a fan of novels with protagonists who are writers. Get some originality, people."

"But, Pru! Think about it!"

Win was starting to get that peppy way about him, the big eyes and spaniel-like bounding. It charmed Pru every time.

"Think of all the great writers Mrs. S. has known," he said. "All the folks in her index. Maybe in an alternate universe someone famous is doing a turn on all of us. The duchess can be in *our* footnotes."

"Did you take LSD or something?" Pru said with a snort. "Some of Mrs. Spencer's laudanum? Because you're not making a lick of sense."

"I'm clean as a whistle! We haven't even partaken of Welsh wine for over forty-eight hours. Humor me. Who would write about the duchess?"

"Uh, I thought *you* were writing about the duchess?"

"I've got it!" He snapped his fingers. "George Bernard Shaw. He would do a bang-up job with the old gal."

"Well, he did hate Winston Churchill, so they have that in common."

"Yes! As G.B.S. famously wrote the man: 'I am enclosing two tickets to the first night of my new play; bring a friend . . . if you have one.' "

" 'If you cannot get rid of the family skeleton, you may as well make it dance,' " Pru quoted, playing along.

"And, by gosh, are there family skeletons."

"He hated hunting, too," Pru added. "Just like Mrs. Spencer. 'When a man wants to murder a tiger he calls it sport; when a tiger wants to murder him he calls it ferocity.' "

"Aces!" Win said. He did a little hop-dance toward the shelf at the far end of the room and pulled from it a red leather book. "Here we go, another Shaw quote! 'War does not decide who is right but who is left.' "

At once Pru's face fell, and with it the temperature in the room.

"Oh fecking hell! Too much. Too much, Seton! Okay. Proust could write her too, you know. Though I suppose that's a stitch obvious."

He shoved the book back into its place.

"Proust should write about himself," Pru said, still smarting from the war comment.

She shook her head, trying to rattle away the feeling along with it.

"No, no, no," Win said. "Where's your originality? Blenheim practically screams Proust!"

"Blenheim?"

"Yes! It's perfect! He could go on and on about that sprawling space in true Proustian fashion. Like his own writing. Interminable. Over a hundred characters per part."

"Mrs. Spencer did call the palace neurotic," Pru said. "And Proust was a total head job. But mostly I find his style introspective and Blenheim is as ostentatious as it gets. Give me more gold! More statues! Paint my eyes on your ceiling in dizzying pattern!"

"Forget Blenheim for a minute. What about Tom?"

"Tom?" she said, gawping.

"Yes, you know, Tom from the barn?"

"I'm familiar with the trope. You believe he really exists?"

Oddly, Mrs. Spencer hadn't brought up his name in some time. Not since Win showed up, Pru didn't think.

"Of course he exists!" Win said. "I've seen his home."

"His home? You mean the proverbial barn?"

"That's the one. I walked through it on my way onto the property. You wouldn't believe the stuff in there. I think the . . ." He batted the air. "Never mind. But, yes, Tom exists."

"Holy cow," Pru replied, dumbfounded by his assuredness.

Tom existed and Win did not seem to doubt this. He didn't even have the good sense to be alarmed.

"Okay, Tom would be written by . . . um . . . Conrad?" she said, still dizzy.

"Conrad?" Win twisted up his face. "How's that?"

"Joseph Conrad. Also known as Józef Teodor Konrad Korzeniowski. He deemed himself a Pole, through and through. Assuming Mrs. Spencer's own Pole exists, he's her longest-standing friend and she simply cherishes Conrad."

"Oh! I used to revel in his books," Mrs. Spencer told Pru once, before Win Seton stumbled onto the scene. "I wanted to take to the sea at once!"

No wonder the woman had a copy of *Sailing Alone Around the World* in her collection. The longer Pru lived at the Grange, the more simpatico she felt toward Mrs. Spencer. Maybe, in the end, they'd need *two* beds at the O'Connell Ward, side by side.

"Ah, Conrad," Win said. " 'We live in the flicker.' That's a good one."

He whipped out a notepad from his back pocket and began to scribble.

"You're writing this down?" Pru asked.

"Yes, this might be the best interview I've conducted to date. Naturally, Edith Wharton would write you."

"Me?" Pru squawked. "She writes about the privileged class!"

"The Kelloggs are pretty privileged, far as I can tell."

"Doesn't count. I was never part of their family. I'm an orphan, remember?"

"The fetchingest orphan to ever exist. Sorry, Miss Valentine, I'll have to overrule you. Wharton is a prime choice. She wrote with humor, wit, and warmth. Her characters were always beautiful."

"I do adore her stories."

Pru sighed, conceding that perhaps the reason she loved Wharton was because she wanted to live in the worlds she created, which happened to look a lot like Charlie's.

" 'Set wide the window,' " Pru quoted. " 'Let me drink the day.' "

" 'If only we'd stop trying to be happy, we could have a pretty good time.' "

"That sounds more like Mrs. Spencer than it does me," she said. "I'm closer to Henry James. His protagonists are often young American women enduring oppression and abuse."

"Somehow I don't like where this is headed."

"Oppression." She pointed directly at him. "And abuse. All wrapped up in one writerly package."

"Ah!" he said, laughing now. "So I'm the antagonist in this story. Domineering you with my tyranny!"

"Yes. Exactly. And as for you, Evelyn Waugh is the clear choice. His novels center on the rise of mediocrity in the common man."

"There's nothing on the rise about my mediocrity."

Bump. Bump. Thump. Stomp.

"What in the world?" she said.

Thump. Stomp.

Together Win and Pru wrenched their heads toward the door. They'd been too loud, too aggressively spirited in their repartee. There was no telling how Mrs. Spencer would react, catching the two of them in her sanctuary, in the hidden den of books.

"We're in the shit now," Win murmured.

At once, the Duchess of Marlborough burst through the door, the purple silk gown wafting out behind her like a sail on a ship. In her hands she held a radio.

"Mrs. Spencer, let me explain," Win said, speaking fast. "We stumbled upon your impressive library—"

"Shush!" she yipped, scrambling about for an outlet. "I knew you two were prowling around in here. Someone moved my Bennetts."

She fiddled with the radio knob. Pru winced at the shrill of the static.

"Well, we're glad you've joined us," Win babbled on. "Not to worry, nothing dodgy happening here. We're having no fun a'tall without your observations and clever bon mots."

"Enough!" Mrs. Spencer said. She looked up. The muscles in her neck twitched. "Listen, you fool. Something is happening."

"What do you mean 'happening'?"

She turned to face Pru.

"This war of yours. I think it's about to end."

Fifty-six

RADIO BROADCAST

If you're just joining us, today at the Majestic Hotel in Paris, the governments of the Democratic Republic of Vietnam, the Republic of Vietnam, and the United States signed an agreement to end the Vietnam War.

Beginning on twenty-eight January a cease-fire will go into effect. North and South Vietnamese forces are to hold their locations and American troops will withdraw within the ensuing sixty days.

Prisoners of war on all sides will be released and allowed to return home. The parties to the agreement will assist in repatriating the remains of the dead. Reunification of Vietnam will be carried out step-by-step through peaceful means. And now, a word from the president of the United States, Mr. Richard Nixon.

"At 12:30 Paris time today Tuesday, January 23, 1973, the Agreement on Ending the War and Restoring Peace in Vietnam was initialed by Dr. Henry Kissinger on behalf of the United States, and Special Adviser Le Duc Tho on behalf of the Democratic Republic of Vietnam.

"The agreement will be formally signed by the parties participating in the Paris Conference on Vietnam on January 27, 1973, at the International Conference Center in Paris.

"The cease-fire will take effect at 2400 Greenwich Mean Time, January 27, 1973. The United States and the Democratic Republic of Vietnam express the hope that this agreement will ensure stable peace in Vietnam and contribute to the preservation of lasting peace in Indochina and Southeast Asia."

Fifty-seven

GD: During the war, I remained in Paris.

WS: It must've been a time of great challenge.

GD: You're telling me! You couldn't get a cab at all to come to that quarter.

WS: I was referring to the general living conditions. The men off to war. The women home and nervous. Rationing. The lines for food. Not to mention the threat of German occupation.

GD: Oh, Germans. [Snort] And I never had issues with rations. There were plenty of men left in the city happy to share their spoils.

WS: I'll bet. So you stayed in Paris for the

duration? That's a long time for someone like you to
remain in one place.

GD: The first German shells didn't even hit Paris
until March of 1918. I was in the city when it
happened. One landed thirty yards before me. My
skirt was blown straight over my head!

WS: That must've been quite the sight. Especially
for the sugar-sharers. Ha. That's a good euphemism.
Pru, write that down.

GD: You think it's funny that the city was bombed?
That I was thrown to the sidewalk, which was
nothing compared to the four people I saw in front
of me, blown to atoms.

PRU: Blown to atoms. Her favorite wartime anecdote.

GD: Later that night, I found shrapnel lodged in
my sable shawl. The fur saved me from certain
death.

PRU: I'm just going to leave you two alone . . .

GD: Sit down, Miss Innamorati. I'm not finished and
it would serve you well to hear my tales.

PRU: But I . . .

GD: Not to worry. I won't talk any more of people
being blown to bits. I'm well aware of your
background in that area.

PRU: You told her?

GD: He didn't have to tell me. Return to your seat. Can we jettison your theatrics for now and return to my story? Good Lord.

WS: Please, Mrs. Spencer. Proceed. I'll keep her theatrics in check.

PRU: HEY!

GD: It wasn't too long after this that they found Mother's body in the salon at her palace, left rotting for a fortnight.

WS: Sickening and tragic.

GD: Who found her and how she died I never learned. It took eleven days to contact me, which the Italians blamed on the war. I'll tell you something. This news hit harder than the metal to my mink. Mother was no longer in the world. She died in a way she would've despised. Undressed. Old. And inexorably alone.

[Tape is silent for ninety seconds]

WS: I'm very sorry, Mrs. Spencer.

GD: She never got to see me married. Mother always believed I'd end up with Sunny.

WS: Sunny . . . as in the Earl of Sunderland. Are you finally admitting . . . ?

GD: Yes, you've won the battle, all right? I was married to the Earl of Sunderland. The Duke of

Marlborough. Congratulations. You beat an old woman
into submission. I hope you feel quite proud of
yourself.

[GD's eyes glisten in the candlelight]

WS: Mrs. Spencer, my apologies if I was being
insensitive or if I've hurt you . . .

GD: [Ignores writer] It's what Mother wanted for me.
A marriage like that. But she never saw it happen.
Unless, you know.

[GD looks heavenward]

WS: She knew. I'm sure of it.

GD: I never took you for a religious man Seton.
[Deep sigh] Her death changed everything for me. I
decided to hell with it. Time to toss propriety out
the window.

WS: In what way, exactly, did you toss it out the
window?

GD: I went straight into Sunny's arms, just as
Mother would've wanted, though he was not yet
divorced from Coon. We began traveling together, not
bothering to conceal our relationship. Those were
some of the best years of my life.

WS: He was your destiny.

GD: If you want to get unnecessarily romantic
about it.

WS: And how did Coon feel about all of this?

GD: After the war our friendship petered out. But, not to worry, she was thrilled with her fresh new life.

WS: Why didn't you two get married right away, then? If Coon was so happy without Sunny?

GD: They weren't formally divorced. And we weren't in a particular rush.

WS: You were thirty-seven when the war ended.

GD: Twenty-seven!

WS: Sure. Yes. Most women of your standing would be anxious to marry at either of those ages, especially to a renowned duke.

GD: Oh, I don't know. [Audible sigh]. I always found the prospect of being a mistress far more alluring than being yet another duchess. In the words of Edith Wharton, "I don't know if I should care for a man who made life easy; I should want someone who made it interesting."

Fifty-eight

"I'm not even sure what it means," Pru said, Nixon's words being kicked around by her brain. "It's over? Is that what he's telling us? That soon the troops will return?"

"That's what he's telling us, yes," Win said. "Though it'd unlikely work as fast as all that. My best guess anyway."

Remarkably, Win's best guess was the right one. The war would drag on but of course they didn't know that then. The reports, they sounded final enough.

"It's done?" Pru said, inhaling deeply. "I can't believe it's over."

Win put a careful hand on her shoulder. He could feel Mrs. Spencer watching them from across the room. She made no move to disrupt the gesture, despite not being party to it. Instead she remained an observer, for perhaps the first time in her life.

"In addition to the cease-fire," the radio voice droned on, "both sides promise to release prisoners of war. The American government estimates that over thirteen hundred United States citizens are currently being held by opposition forces."

The men were finally coming home.

Was Pru happy for the families waiting? Chapped about the timing? A day late and a dollar short, to be sure. She had a lot of emotions right then, all of them jumbled together, not a one that stood out.

"Pru?" Win said in a whisper. "Are you okay?"

She nodded, and then shrugged, unsure what to feel.

"Well," she said at last. "A lot of weed will be smoked at Berkeley tonight."

Win spat out an awkward laugh. He looked to Mrs. Spencer as a gauge, which tells you something about his state of mind. On the other hand, the old gal had lived through two wars and had seen people "blown to atoms." Gladys Deacon was not unaccustomed to war.

"She's in shock, Seton," Mrs. Spencer said. "Leave her be."

"In shock?" Pru looked up, her face drawn and whitewashed. "Why would I be in shock? The war was going to end, one way or another. Eventually."

"The North Vietnamese returned to the negotiation table," said the man on the radio. "Likely at the urging of the Soviet Union and Red China."

The volume was turned up, but none of them were fully listening.

"I'll take my leave," Mrs. Spencer said as she moved toward the door. "Let you two sort this all out."

With her words, Win was suddenly gripped with panic. He was supposed to help "sort it out"? What did he know about sorting anything of this magnitude? He scarcely had the resourcefulness to pay bills on time and buy toothpaste when he ran out. The bloke had half a mind to follow Mrs. Spencer straight out of the room.

"You'll know what to do, Seton," Mrs. Spencer said, reading him flawlessly.

The door clicked behind her.

Several uncomfortable moments passed. And then, several more after that. Win broke into a cold sweat.

"So—er—I hear the Dolphins won the American Super Bowl," he said, finally, in a magnificent display of verbal acuity. The man had all the empathy of a lab rat. There wasn't a situation he couldn't make more awkward. "First team ever to have a perfect season. Nineteen and zed."

"The Dolphins?" Pru looked at him walleyed. "What are you even talking about?"

"Sorry, sorry. Gads swears that when running out of things to say to Yanks it's best to bring up American football. Or baseball. Catfish Hunter, Rollie Fingers? Yes? No? Baseball players have the cheekiest names."

"You have problems," Pru said, annoyed but also grateful. His ineptitude was a good diversion. "Your mental issues are severe."

"Devastatingly accurate. Pru, I haven't the vaguest notion what to say. Other than, I'm sorry. I'm so bloody sorry for the news."

"Win, that's sweet," she said. "But what, exactly, are you sorry for? A war ending?"

"I flub all kinds of things. Approximately ninety-two percent of what comes out of my mouth is a bungle of some sort. But 'sorry' is the proper word here. It hasn't been a year since Easter. Not one fecking year. Shit timing. Out-and-out shit."

What he said, this was Pru's very problem.

Because Win was right, which was tricky on a number of grounds. Not one fecking year. A handful of months were the difference between life and death, for Charlie and for who knew how many other men.

Each month tacked onto the skirmish added nothing to the story. It served only to lengthen the mess, no additional plot but ever more body bags. If it were a film or a book, critics would call the deaths gratuitous, unnecessary. Because of this, anyone would understand if Pru was glad the war was ending but still felt enraged by the timing. Unfortunately this was not the emotion that Pru had.

When she first heard the news, her heart plummeted. And then it whispered something to her brain. It said: thank God the war went on a bit longer. Thank God everything happened as it did.

Fifty-nine

Pru had fallen for Win.

Arse over tits, he'd say, if speaking about someone else. Either way, she had fallen, and hard. It seemed impossible but there was no other explanation for Pru's reaction to the cease-fire.

The whole thing felt like a harmonious convergence of circumstance. She ended up with Win! At a remote estate on another continent! How lucky they were to find each other in this big, mad world.

Of course Pru appreciated the level of selfishness required to believe fate might intervene in such cruel fashion. Her romantic interests were not important to the world order and there'd been far more to Charlie than who he planned to marry. Most would argue it was the very least of him.

As for Win, the lucky bastard didn't even comprehend her feelings, or see that she was trying to express them in her quiet Pru way. Yes, he had some inkling but the scenario seemed too far-fetched, too "dream on, bugger," and so the man shucked off the thought whenever it poked its head through the door.

At any rate, Win didn't have time to ponder the love of beautiful girls he didn't deserve. There was a book to finish and the duchess was once again unco-operative. They were back to her old sidewinders and geese.

In some ways it wasn't as bad as before. She had admitted to being the duch-ess after all. Yet in other ways it was far worse because of what they'd already gone through. They were in the middle of the story. Too far to turn back but with ungodly lengths to go. Middles were daunting, insurmountable. Middles were the very reason Win Seton had yet to finish a book.

"Mrs. Spencer," Win said one night as they sat in his room, dining on cod-fish. "I want to hear more about your marriage to Sunny."

"What do you want to know? It was properly awful."

"I'm sure there were some good times. What about the sixtieth-birthday party you threw for him? I have a quote from one of Blenheim's neighbors."

Win flipped open his notebook and flicked through the pages.

"Ah! Here it is!" he said. "'The Blenheim dinner and dance was most amus-ing. They had got H. G. Wells of all people, and the duchess made him dance, a most comic business.'"

Mrs. Spencer giggled.

"Sunny was acting like an utter bear that night," she said. "But Wells did lighten the mood. 'We all have our time machines, don't we. Those that take us back are memories . . . and those that carry us forward, are dreams.'"

"A Wells quote?" Win asked to Mrs. Spencer's pleased nod. "Sounds like a memorable night."

He did not mention other reports from the festivities, including Evelyn Waugh's view of the partygoers: "about forty hard-faced middle-aged peers and peeresses." Mrs. Spencer herself was described as "very battered with fine diamonds." The night was supposed to be grand, over the top, but the consen-sus was that it smelled of desperation and last-ditch efforts. Already their marriage was frayed.

"We had *some* fun," Mrs. Spencer conceded. She pulled her lips into a tight and distant smile. "But it was such a confusing night."

"Tell me more," Win pressed. "Tell me everything about the guests. The decorations. The food. It must've been marvelous."

"I've said all I want to on the subject."

"Mrs. Spencer . . ."

Pru shot him a look. As much as she cared for him, as much as her heart squeezed at every one of his rakish, crinkled grins, the man had learned little in their weeks at the Grange. For one, he still had the appalling propensity to push when it was very clear Mrs. Spencer needed to be pulled.

"I think the young lady wants me to back off," Win said, locking eyes with Pru.

"The old lady, too," Mrs. Spencer said. "By the by, you should know there's been a mix-up in town. They claim I stole a can of gooseberry pie filling and some drinking chocolate from the market."

"So we can expect another visit from—"

Suddenly thuds and crashes erupted throughout the house, as though someone were trying to roll a bookcase down a flight of stairs.

"What in the world?" Win said and stood. "The police again?"

Mrs. Spencer flew to the window.

"Who is that?" she said. "What's out there?"

"Probably a cat," Pru said, pulse screaming. "Or a dog."

"Helluva cat," Win said.

"They're coming for me! They're here! I saw them."

"Who?" Win asked. "The coppers? Perhaps if you stopped instigating calamities in town . . ."

"Not the police, you clown!" Mrs. Spencer said, slightly out of breath. She took to pacing by the window. "Yesterday a man showed up at the door."

"Someone was here?" Pru said. "At the Grange?"

"Yes. And he drilled me with all kinds of questions about my health, my welfare, and even about you."

"ME!"

"You answered the door?" Win said. "Without firing any shots? This is an interesting turn of events. Do I need to fish some poor bloke's body from the pond?"

"No dead bodies. This time. And I didn't shoot the intruder because he was holding a bitch."

"He picked you up?" Win said. "All the way off the ground? Why, the nerve! But please don't speak so harshly of yourself."

Mrs. Spencer glared at him, the corners of her mouth quivering as she tried to keep away a smile.

Meanwhile, Pru began to fidget and pace. Had this man really been asking about her? Mrs. Spencer had been "acting up" lately and the last time she regularly vexed authorities the family hired Pru. Maybe this time they'd hired someone who could actually keep Mrs. Spencer in check.

"Bitch," Mrs. Seton said. "So very droll, Seton. Alas, of every living creature in this house, including the dogs, you are the bitchiest. For your information, I allowed the stranger on the premises because he looked familiar and I thought he was a spaniel showman. I've been in the market for another."

"More dogs?" Pru yawped.

"Alas, he was holding one of mine that allegedly escaped. After dumping Jangles on the floor, the man immediately took to quizzing me about my health. Naturally I informed him that the only medical assistance needed would be to get my cane removed from his bum. He was gone in a flash."

Mrs. Spencer checked the other window.

"Don't see anyone now," she said. "Maybe Tom scared him off."

"It was probably some tramp," Win offered. "Who heard there's an old duchess around and figured he could swindle you for a pound or two."

"Who you calling old, Seton?"

Mrs. Spencer paused and crossed both arms over her chest.

"Oh, you're right," she said with an exhale. "It probably *was* some filthy drifter looking to make a fast quid."

"Nothing more," Win agreed with a nod.

Though he and Mrs. Spencer both felt satisfied, Pru sensed the true explanation was not so simple. Whether the man was there on behalf of Edith, or the mental hospital, or some different entity altogether, it didn't matter. At that precise moment Pru understood, without the slightest hesitation, that her time at the Grange would soon come to an end.

Sixty

"She hardly talks about Sunny," Win said, sliding a half-bitten pencil behind one ear.

A week had passed.

No further men showed up looking to compile medical dossiers. Not a single constable appeared at the door. Things seemed calm, even as Pru's insides coiled and turned. It was all she could do to stop herself from grabbing Mrs. Spencer and pleading for her life.

I beg of you, keep on your best behavior! Or they'll replace me with someone who can handle the job!

And she would've done it too, had Pru felt at all assured that Mrs. Spencer wanted her to stay. More likely she'd cackle and promptly toss Pru's baggage out onto the pavement. *Cheers and good luck!*

"Why won't she discuss him?" Win said. Sunny, the latest topic he tormented himself with. "They were together for eons. Before the marriage. A dozen years after. Yet she treats him like a slightly dim and irritating neighbor best left ignored."

"I'm not sure that's wholly unique," Pru said. "When talking marriage."

"She chased him for decades, though! Relentlessly! From the time she was a young girl!" Win slammed a pencil onto his desk. "That's it. I've determined Gladys Deacon is incapable of love."

"She's had fifty-plus lovers and *that's* the conclusion you've made?"

"Lovers and love are two vastly different concepts. She's too cold for true love. Too calculating."

"Come on, Seton," Pru said. "Mrs. Spencer has been in love. She's fallen out of love and she's also had her heart broken more than once. You can't blame her for being a little cynical."

"Who, exactly, did she ever love? Other than herself, of course."

"Jesus, you really are thick," Pru said. "Allow me to quote from *your* research. 'You are not a person to me. You are an *état d'esprit et d'âme.*' In English: you are my spirit and my soul."

"Bloody hell. You're back at it with the Berenson rubbish," Win said, turning away from his typewriter and toward her. "Why are you so hung up on him?"

"I'm not hung up on him, but the duchess was. 'Her spirit and her soul.' Surely you can see it."

"It's all for show. GD's an unmitigated bootlicker. You know this. She called Berenson's wife a honey bear or some treacle. It's part of the veneer. She always ingratiates herself before moving in for the kill."

"She is indeed a sweet-talker," Pru said. "When she wants to be. But the buttering up of Mary was a case of keeping one's friends close and her enemies closer."

"I can't buy it."

"Mrs. Spencer called herself Maenad when she was with Berenson. *Maenad.* A mythological creature frenzied with wine and lust."

"And he called her 'mannequinlike and repellent.'"

"Yeah, after it ended," Pru said. "You've seen the love letters."

"As well as the thistle she mailed him to demonstrate her prickly disposition."

"Okay, then, whom did she run to after the war ended?"

"Her mother's corpse. Dead in the salon at the unicorn castle."

"And after that?"

"She went to find her sister," Win said.

"Exactly. She showed up at Edith's door, not to break the sad news of their mother's death, which she'd already done via telegram, but to coax Edith into helping her find Berenson, who'd gone to America for good by then."

"You're right, she did try to find BB," Win said. "But you're looking at it the wrong way. Distraught by the war's fallout, GD first went to her mother, who was already dead. And then she went to her father. Her de facto father in the form of Bernard Berenson, since her real one was long since gone."

"Jesus!" Pru said and smacked her hands on his desk. "Cut it out with the father figure nonsense. You're using it as an excuse. Fifteen years' difference. That's nothing."

"I wouldn't call it nothing. It's a whole person. An almost-debutante."

"There is no amount of time, of years, that love can't bridge."

"Love? Bridging? You're not getting whimsical on me, are you, Valentine? I need one normal-acting person around here."

" 'We will make long walks,' " she started.

It was a quote, from a letter written by Mrs. Spencer, which Win had in his desk. Several months before arriving at the Grange, he'd traveled to I Tatti, Berenson's Italian estate, which had been donated to Harvard upon his death.

Win flattered the woman in charge of the Berenson papers into letting him make copies and so all the evidence Pru needed was in Win's very possession. But when it came to Berenson and Mrs. Spencer and fifteen-year age gaps, it was as though Win was suddenly illiterate, unable to read.

" 'We will make long walks,' " Pru said again.

"Miss Valentine, that's enough . . ."

" 'You will tell me everything. In the aftermath we will come home bringing to your comfortable armchairs that slight weariness exquisite at twilight and it will be a year before dinner is served.' "

Pru paused, hand on hip. Win fought the urge to return to his typewriter. There was something about the way she quoted the passage that made his skin feel like it was burning.

"Nothing," she said. "You have nothing to say to that?"

"The words are lovely. Dreamy, even. But that's all they are. Words. Now if you don't mind, I have to create a few of my own."

"You are maddeningly dense sometimes."

"Pru, she *married* the duke."

"Yes! I know! Because he was the duke! And it's what she thought her mother wanted!" Pru flipped around to face the far wall, tears threatening her eyes. "She told us outright that she'd rather be with someone interesting than become yet another duchess."

When she turned back around, Win was crooked over his desk, banging away.

"Look at me," she said. "Look."

"No time, luv. Gotta get this story pecked out," he said, steadfastly maintaining his over-the-typewriter hunch. "We can chitchat about dukes and art connoisseurs later. I'm on a deadline here."

"Stop typing and look at me," Pru said. "If you have a single ounce of humanity in your entire godforsaken body, look at me."

"Unfortunately I do not."

"Win."

Finally he removed his hands from the keys. Then he looked up.

"Can't you admit it?" Pru said.

She stared at him with such intensity, such a mixture of power and fondness, his heart began to flounder all over the place.

"Admit what?" he said with a squeak.

"That there was some chance Mrs. Spencer loved Berenson. That she has some modicum of regret about the way she conducted her romantic life. Does that?" She pointed toward the door. "Does that seem like a woman happy with whom she's loved?"

"I suppose it's possible . . ." Win said with a small gulp. "But their age difference."

"Enough with their ages!" she cried out. "How can you say that when you know how I feel about you?"

"How you feel about me?" Another gulp. It was growing increasingly difficult for Win to breathe. "You called me tyrannical. Is that what you're referring to?"

He was trying for a laugh but falling short, like he so often did.

Dear God, he wanted her to say it. Win desperately wanted Pru to jump out of her reserved, smooth skin and make a passionate declaration about how much she loved him and how they'd be together, whatever it took. Screw the age difference. Sod off to visa expirations and return trips to America. They were meant to be together.

He needed her to say it because he could not.

"Is that how you're going to be?" she asked, the disappointment like gray paint spilling across her face.

"Well, ha-ha," Win said. "If there's one thing you can count on with thirty-four-year-old bachelors it is their complete inability to break a pattern."

"You're going to make me say it, aren't you?"

"Say what? Miss Valentine, I really need to get back to writing."

"Fine, you pansy. I must be a lot more damaged than I give myself credit for because for some inexplicable reason I've fallen for you. I don't even care that the war is ending now instead of before and that Charlie is out of the picture. I don't! Because I'm a horrible person."

"You're not horrible," Win said in a whisper. "You're the greatest person I've ever known."

"I'm supposed to be in mourning. But somehow, in this wreck of a house, in my wreck of a life, I've fallen in love. I've fallen in love with a salty, ornery writer who doesn't know his ass from a hole in the ground."

"Well, that is certainly true. Laurel . . ."

"I've fallen in love with you. And it pisses me off."

Sixty-one

On the twenty-fifth of June in the year 1921, Gladys Deacon became the Duchess of Marlborough. Gladys was forty years old to the duke's fifty-two.

In the months leading up to the nuptials, Gladys was headline news, mostly thanks to her own efforts. If she was going to retire to the marriage pasture, the duchess-to-be wanted to go out with fanfare.

And so she reveled in her waning glory days. Gladys invited sculptors and painters to her home. She arranged salon after illustrious salon and made Proust sign a blood oath promising he'd visit Blenheim no less than once per season. The First World War put an end to the Belle Époque but Gladys Deacon wanted to bid proper farewell to the Gilded Age.

Finally their June wedding arrived, twenty-seven years after Gladys first started pining for the duke. For the event, Sunny donned a gray, double-breasted suit with cutaway tails, a style that heralded a new trend in menswear.

Gladys wore a dress of old lace cut from a single piece, with a wreath of myrtle and orange blossom in her hair. Later in the day, she changed into a navy blue embroidered chemise.

Guests included Princess George of Greece, Gladys's youngest sister Dorothy (sister Edith was absent), the Maharajah of Rapurthala, Princesse de Polignac, Princesse Murat, and Edith Wharton. Proust also attended, dressed in a snakeskin gown that hung to his ankles.

Despite promises made in blood, this would be the last time Gladys saw Proust, her companion and closest friend. Shortly after the duke and duchess wed, Proust fell ill. He died in 1922, never once able to visit her as Lady Marlborough, never able to save her from Blenheim, or from herself.

—J. Casper Augustine Seton,
The Missing Duchess: A Biography

They stood in the train station, staring at the departures board. London Marylebone 10:07.

"Are you sure you don't want to come?" Laurel asked as she clung to the strap of her honey leather tote. "It's only a day trip but there's a lot you can see in a day. Or are you going to rebuff my London offer a second time?"

"I'm going to rebuff," Annie said, feeling woozy as a result of too much wine at the previous night's dinner. "I'm pretty tired."

Also, she didn't want to go to London. Not in that way. Short. Brief. A passing-through while Laurel signed the papers, disposing of the Grange forever. In twenty-four hours they'd be on a plane to Virginia. But in Banbury, backhoes and bulldozers would start rolling in.

"Tomorrow?" Annie had balked earlier that morning, as Laurel stood in the bathroom doorway wearing only a towel. "We're leaving tomorrow? Just like that, the negotiations are done?"

Nicola had given her advance warning, but it still felt like a fresh blow.

"Yep, all parties have come to an agreement," Laurel said. "I was the last holdout and I finally caved. I'm practically giddy to be rid of that eyesore."

Sure, Mom, Annie thought. *Eyesore. That's all it was.*

How Laurel felt about the building was as obvious as if she'd written it down, or recorded it on tape. When her mother walked into Win's room she clasped her stomach, then immediately dropped to her knees by the bed.

"Mom!" Annie shouted, unable to hide her surprise, despite knowing the story behind the room and the man who once lived in it.

Laurel was not the type for swooning, or vapors, or whatever it was that was happening. Annie had never seen her mom so weak.

"Are you okay?" she'd asked.

"Ha-ha! Yes!" Laurel jumped to her feet. She looked at Annie like she hadn't remembered she was there. "Yes, yes, I'm fine. I tripped. Clumsy me."

The only clumsy thing was Laurel's struggle to hide her reaction.

"Annie, I'm sorry this trip has been such a debacle," Laurel said, at the train station, as the board flickered overhead. "I didn't think it'd be like this."

"It's not a debacle but I'm kind of ticked we're leaving. What about the 'girl time' you promised? All the touristy stuff? And now we're going home? To-morrow? What a waste of a trip."

"Annie, we can't stay indefinitely."

"Why not? You're retired. I'm unemployed as we all know. Seriously, we could hang around for another week. Two weeks! What do we have to get back for?"

"My riding students?" Laurel offered.

"They're in good hands with Margaret," Annie said. "You've already talked about transitioning more lessons to her anyway. Come on, we can extend the trip. At this point, the horses are just an excuse."

"No," she said. "They're not. I promise we'll do a big trip in the spring to make up for this. Wherever you want! Turkey? Greece? New Zealand? Bangkok?"

"Bangkok?"

"Yeah, you're not really a Bangkok type."

"Mom," Annie said. "I want to be here. Taking this trip. Now."

"Come with me to London, then! Or stay here and explore on your own. You have the rental car. Check out Blenheim Castle. The day is yours to do whatever you want!"

"What I want is to stay longer than a day."

"I'm sorry, I can't do it. We have to go home. I don't know how else to ex-plain it to you."

"It's the writer, isn't it?" Annie said. "Memories of him. The home you're giving up. I think you feel guilty."

Laurel shook her head, then nodded. She sighed and shook her head again.

"Guilty's not the right word," Laurel said. "It'd be silly to hang on to a house just because of a few good months." She snorted. "They weren't even that good. It's a miracle I didn't end up with pneumonia or Lyme disease."

"Mom, I have to ask," Annie said. "Do you know where he is? The writer? Have you tried to track him down?"

"I did try once," she said. "Long ago. It ended badly."

"That sounds like something Mrs. Sp—the duchess would say."

"Oh, Bernard Berenson? Yes, that did not end well. Quick, let's change the subject."

"Ha," Laurel said. "You're right. She would say that."

"Do you think the duchess loved Berenson?" Annie asked.

"What?" Laurel wrinkled her forehead. "Berenson? Where is this coming from?"

"You thought she loved Berenson, didn't you? The art critic not the duke."

Laurel nodded.

"That's what I believed, yes. Still believe, I suppose, though I haven't thought about it in years. But, you're correct. In my opinion, Gladys Deacon only married the duke because she'd acted as his mistress for so many years. And she only did *that* because Berenson chose to move to the States with his wife." Laurel exhaled, blowing a long, wavy lock of hair from her face. "But who knows. It's only a theory. And probably a biased one at that."

"Well, I have my own theory," Annie said as her mom glimpsed repeatedly at the board.

"Honey, I have to get to the track . . ."

"Here's what I think. In the end, the duchess didn't love either. She wanted to love one or both, to love anyone really, but after a hundred years came up short."

"Wow," Laurel said. "That's depressing."

"It happens."

"Geez, I'd expect a newly engaged girl to have a more idealistic view of the world." Laurel reached in for a hug. "I'm sorry. I have to run. My train is arriving."

As Laurel squeezed her, Annie felt like she was touching some other person, not the woman she'd lived with for a lifetime.

"Do something fun," Laurel said. "You have the credit card. Use it however you want."

"Bye, Mom," Annie said, confused and hurt and not sure why. "Safe travels."

As Laurel walked away, marching at her typical Laurel Haley quick clip, Annie remained in place, staring at the departures board.

Kings Sutton.

Bicester North.

Haddenham & Thame Parkway.

She turned and walked toward the ticket booth.

"Hello there," she said to a woman in a blue smock. "Do you have a train to Paris?"

The woman snickered.

"Wouldn't that be nice," she said. "I'd love a one-way ticket to Paris myself right about now. No, dear, if you want to get to Paris, it requires a bit of a rigmarole."

She leaned out her window and pulled a map from its bin on the wall.

"Here." She laid it out in front of Annie, and then made several circles with a black Sharpie. "First you take the train to London Marylebone. About an hour's ride. Then Marylebone to St. Pancras. Change trains there and two and a half hours later you'll find yourself at Gare du Nord in Paris!"

"That doesn't sound too complex," Annie said and folded up the map. "When's the next train to Marylebone?"

"We have a 10:40."

"Oh! No! That's too soon."

Annie didn't want to risk running into Laurel at the station.

"Okay . . ." the woman said, eyeing her dubiously. "There's also the 11:04, and the 11:40 . . ."

Paris. Could Annie really go to Paris? Gus said the writer was there, and she still had Win's luggage tag in her jeans.

"Would you like a ticket, dear?" the woman asked.

"Um . . ."

So far there was Gus's story on the one hand, and Laurel's on the other, but what about Win's? His story was in print but *The Missing Duchess* and the tapes in Annie's backpack were surely not all he had to say.

"Miss? There's a queue forming behind you. If you don't mind terribly—"

"You know what?" Annie thwacked her mom's credit card on the counter. "Yes. Please. One ticket to Gare du Nord by way of London. Paris, here I come."

Sixty-two

"Miss Valentine! Seton!"

Mrs. Spencer stood in the doorway, looking rabid.

"They're here! The people! They're back!"

Pru was in no mood for another one of Mrs. Spencer's fits. She'd just told Win that she loved him and he'd given no response. How was it possible for a full-grown man to be so thick?

"You don't have anything to say?" Mrs. Spencer howled.

Pru was thinking the exact same thing.

"Mrs. Spencer," she said. "Now is not a good time."

"Actually . . ." Win glanced at Pru with a jittery smile. "I think you arrived at the optimal time. Saved by the bell. Close one, Miss Valentine. You'll thank Mrs. Spencer later."

"You really are something else," Pru said.

She was not one for middle fingers but desperately wanted to use both right then. As usual, Win was under the boundless misconception that he had sufficient humor to get himself out of a thorny situation. With one well-timed joke, everyone might tee-hee along and forget what transpired. Unfortunately he'd never done the math, thus didn't realize this worked for him zero percent of the time.

"Something strange is going on," Mrs. Spencer noted.

"As a matter of fact, yes," Pru began.

"That's nice. But I don't actually care. I have bigger problems than the two of you."

"I love him," Pru blurted.

"Beg pardon?" Mrs. Spencer's eyes bugged.

"That's what he meant by 'saved by the bell,'" Pru said. "I told Win that I loved him and he clammed up. You saved him from admitting he is capable of real, genuine feelings."

"This is ridiculous," Mrs. Spencer said. "Of course you love him. And he loves you. But if everyone can stop making googly-eyes at one another, we need to focus on me."

"Look at him!" Pru said. "Just look at him! He has that stupid dumb look on his face. Ugh, I am so disgusted with myself."

"He displays many dumb looks on his face, dear. And this type of behavior is why he's unmarried and living with us."

"Don't mind me. You two carry on like I'm not here," Win said. "Alas, it's true, I'm a horrible, sophomoric individual who deserves the station in which I find myself."

"Don't flatter yourself," Pru said.

"Now that we're all in agreement," he said. "Mrs. Spencer, what's wrong? I've never seen you this out of sorts. And that's saying something. Also, are you aware that your shirt is on backward?"

"I had to take my clothes off in town so they wouldn't recognize me."

"Great. Another visit from the police," Pru moaned.

"Er, um . . . don't you think disrobing might've had the opposite effect from what you intended?" Win asked.

He desperately wanted to share his astonishment with Pru, but of course she wouldn't accept any of his lame attempts at camaraderie. He'd cocked up the whole thing as he so often did, their brief, tenuous friendship already strained.

"It was the only way to hide," Mrs. Spencer said.

"Righto. Hide in the buff," Win said with a firm nod. "Makes sense. Tell me, who were you hiding from, exactly?"

"The Marlboroughs!"

"Wait," Pru said. "The Marlboroughs? Sunny's family? I thought it was Edith Junior you were concerned about."

"Her too. They're in cahoots."

"Are you sure?" Pru said. "Are you sure it was them?"

"I can diagnose that terminally weak Marlborough chin and lemon-frown anywhere. They're here. They want me out of the way so they can wrest my things from me."

"Your things?" Win said, eyes flicking around the room: to the books, the broken bed, the single typewriter, much abused. "What things?"

"You don't know the half of it."

"Apparently I don't."

Suddenly they heard a distinct stumping noise, the sound of boots clomping up wooden stairs. Without a thought, Pru bolted to Win's side and clutched his arm.

"Mrs. Spencer?" said a voice.

She gripped tighter. Win placed one hand over hers.

"Should we hide?" Pru whispered.

"The gun," Win hissed. "Where's the revolver?"

"Calm down, you two," Mrs. Spencer said, for once the voice of reason, the sole unruffled duck. "It's only Tom."

"Tom?"

Pru took in a giant swallow of air. Her heart pounded so hard it left little space to breathe. She tried to catch Win's eyes but looked away again, remembering she was livid.

"Yes," Mrs. Spencer said. "Tom, my Pole. Normally he stays in the barn but desperate times and all that. Oh, Tom! We're in here! Come meet the rest of my staff!"

Sixty-three

One might say Tom materialized in the room, but his entrance was more lumbering than that.

The man was two meters tall, or six and a half feet by Yank standards. He was no rangy thing either, weighing in at around twenty stone, the size of an American football lineman. He moved like one too.

"Tom?" Pru said, gaping.

Tom the Pole was fair-skinned, made almost exclusively of beige. His brow bone was heavy, a hard shelf above his face.

"Tom?" she said again.

His eyes skipped over her with some degree of apprehension. He seemed nervous, almost. Interesting for a man whose hands were the size of Pru's skull.

"I'm sorry to come inside, Mrs. Spencer."

"Please, Tomasz. I'm the one who should apologize! I'm so very embarrassed." Mrs. Spencer grabbed at her throat. "I haven't had a chance to tidy up this week."

Pru lifted her eyebrows. *This week?* As far as she could tell, Mrs. Spencer hadn't tidied up this year, or that decade, or even the one before it. The home had more litter in it than any given public park. There was a pile of dog feces that'd been in the room so long it didn't even reek anymore.

"Mrs. Spencer," Tom said. "I regret to report the Marlboroughs are in town. Not to worry, I shooed them away. But my guess is they'll be back."

"They're here?" Win said. "In Banbury? Are you quite certain?"

"Yes, I'm certain." Tom narrowed his eyes, though the distance between them remained wide. "Who are you?"

"Don't worry about him," Mrs. Spencer said. "He's just a writer."

"The name's Seton." Win extended a hand, which went ignored. "They don't teach manners in Poland, I gather. In any case, are you sure the people you saw weren't trying to sell knives or encyclopedias? I know our girl Gladys likes to stir it up, but just because she claims to see the Marlboroughs, does not make it so."

"You saw them too?" Tom said and turned to Mrs. Spencer.

In the new light, his eyes darkened, changing color like a hologram.

"Yes, that's what I was trying to explain to these two nitwits," she said. "I saw the Marlboroughs lurking around Banbury proper. They even sent an emissary to my front door, replete with stolen pup. Where did you see them?"

"Near the front gate. I chased them off with a hammer."

Win batted a piece of hair away from his eyes.

"Remind me to stay off your bad side," he said.

"It was the eleventh duke," Tom said. "And various family members. They also had a barrister with them, plus a *lekarz* from St. Andrew's."

"A doctor." Mrs. Spencer sighed. "Christ. What are we going to do?"

She looked back and forth between Pru and Win. Somewhere in the distance, a grandfather clock chimed.

"It might be time to . . . disappear," Tom said, making some sort of gesture with his fingers. It looked like he was wagging kielbasa in the air.

"Hmm . . ." Mrs. Spencer said. "You may be right."

"Disappear?" Pru said. "Where?"

Were they going to ship her back to America? Already? Her heart galloped. Then again, perhaps the farther away from Win the better. "Saved by the bell." For the love of God. He had a perilous level of stupidity.

"Seton," Mrs. Spencer said, spitting his name through her teeth like a particularly satisfying swear word. Pru knew exactly how she felt. "Didn't you mention Paris? You have a home in Paris? Or something? I can't believe they let you into that city."

"Yes, Lady M., I do have a flat there."

"Brilliant. We're moving in."

"Er, hold up. I'm not so sure that's wise. Also, I'd prefer to stay at the Grange and finish your biography."

"You'll get your damned book," Mrs. Spencer said. "As if I'd waste all this time with nothing to show for it. I'm only thinking of a different venue from which to conduct your work. Your home, is it large?"

"It's a fair size," he said. "About two hundred seventy-five square meters. Mrs. Spencer—"

"How many people live there? Parents? Siblings? Staff?"

"It's been some time since we've had any staff," Win said. "And my parents are dead. It's only my brother at present."

"Excellent!" Mrs. Spencer spun around. She pushed past Tom and out into the hallway. "We leave tonight!"

"Tonight?" Pru gulped. "You're leaving tonight?"

"*We're* leaving. The three of us. You, me, the writer." She rolled her eyes. "We're off to Paris. Seton, ring your brother. Tell him to make up the beds."

Sixty-four

ÎLE SAINT-LOUIS
PARIS
NOVEMBER 2001

Almost immediately after Gladys and Sunny's wedding, the duke became a royal pain in the arse. He grew so quarrelsome Gladys took to bringing a revolver to the dinner table just to keep him in line.

On top of this, he began paying undue attention to a fifteen-year-old girl named Theresa Jungman, whom he sickeningly called Baby. Though Sunny professed his undying love for this Baby, he went on to have many other mistresses, including Canadian actress Frances Doble. After many years of trysting, he promised to marry Frances and asked Gladys for a divorce.

And wouldn't you know it, Gladys obliged. What did she need with Sunny and a title anyhow? They'd been wed for over a decade by then but in that marriage and throughout their home, Gladys proclaimed, "I still feel like a tourist."

Alas, a third marriage for Sunny would not come to pass. He developed liver cancer and died in 1934, leaving Gladys with a permanent duchess title and most members of his family up in arms about her immutability in their lives.

Not that Gladys longed to hang around playing duchess. She high-tailed it out of Blenheim as soon as practicable, loading up a half-dozen lorries, and spiriting her possessions out of town.

—J. Casper Augustine Seton,
The Missing Duchess: A Biography

Annie arrived in Paris in the late afternoon.

Winter was approaching. The sunlight fell low and flat across the city, casting long shadows, making the ground look as if it were perpetually dusk. Paris. She'd returned.

Annie's breath caught as the cab turned away from Gare du Nord and onto Rue Saint-Martin. It'd been eighteen months since she was last there, which somehow felt like both yesterday and forever ago. That's the way Paris was.

Had her French been less rusty, Annie would've asked the driver to take the scenic route: a jaunt down Rue Lafayette, with a quick circle around the Opéra and its stunning green dome and golden statues. She never tired of the building, even if it was a little too close to the harried Galeries Lafayette, a place forever socked in by buses and tourists toting wheeled suitcases crammed with newly acquired clothes.

Had they gone that way, past the Opéra, it would've been a relatively straight shot toward the Tuileries and la grande roue, the city's famous Ferris wheel. No matter how tired, physically or otherwise, Annie couldn't watch the carriages lift over the trees without feeling the lift of her heart.

Accessing the Île Saint-Louis from there would require only a short trip along one of the roads running parallel to the Seine. Rue de Rivoli, for example—the very first street Mrs. Spencer ever called home.

As they traveled across the bridge and onto the island, Annie glanced toward Notre-Dame and smiled in remembrance. When she studied in Paris, her roommate was an aspiring architect. Because of this, the girls spent untold hours in and around the cathedral, pointing out its gargoyles and flying buttresses, studying the gallery of kings and the spectacular rose windows. At once, Annie felt every second of those months. Why had she waited to come back?

"Where are you staying, mademoiselle?" the driver asked as they crossed the Pont Marie. "Which hotel?"

"Oh, I'm staying with a friend."

A "friend" she'd never met. One who didn't know she was coming. One who would be puzzled to see a girl show up on his doorstep in jeans, a slightly frayed T-shirt, and a backpack filled with cassettes. What the hell was she doing?

"The address, mademoiselle?"

"Yes, sorry. Twenty-four Quai de Béthune."

Really. What the hell was she doing? Annie shook her head, at herself, at her folly, at the ridiculousness of the situation. Well, if nothing else, she was in Paris. As Mrs. Spencer would say, it was the best place to make a bad decision.

Annie turned toward the window as the roads narrowed and the buildings became less ornate. Though Napoléon III tasked Haussmann with turning Paris's crowded streets into wide avenues with parks and squares, Île Saint-Louis maintained its medieval vibe. It was her favorite neighborhood in the city. Annie never could've fathomed the events that would lead her back.

"We have arrived," the driver announced, stopping before an elegant seventeenth-century town home, one of the many lining the quays along the Seine.

"*Merci*," she said, fumbling for her wallet. She'd taken out forty euros at the train station and hoped her mom wouldn't notice the missing funds.

After paying the driver, she slammed the taxi door and looked up at the building's tawny stone face, its white shutters, and wrought-iron balconies. So lovely, so simple, yet the interiors were probably grander than anything she'd seen in that city. Student housing was decidedly more pedestrian, even in Paris.

"All right," she said to herself. "Let's see what happens."

Just as she was about to ring the intercom, a smartly dressed couple punched a code into the keypad. They popped open the black door and Annie slipped in behind them. They didn't even notice she was there.

The couple kissed once in the lobby and then tumbled together into a ground-floor flat. Annie reached out for the second set of doors but found them locked. She glanced toward the brass-mounted directory, her eyes scanning the list. There he was. Seton, number six.

With an inhale that reverberated through the building's stone lobby, Annie pressed the black button beside his name and launched a quick prayer up to the sky.

"*Allô?*" said a voice.

Allô. A small word, three quarters of a word even, but enough to send Annie's stomach tumbling.

Once again, what the hell was she doing? Traveling to another country? Ringing the doorbell of a stranger? Granted, he was a man her mother once loved, but he was foreign to Annie. And probably to Laurel as well, decades having passed.

"*Allô?*" the voice said again.

Annie's mouth felt gummed up and thick. The words were there but she could not spit them out.

Then, suddenly, she heard a loud buzz.

"Why don't you come up?" he said. "Top floor."

Sixty-five

ÎLE SAINT-LOUIS
PARIS
NOVEMBER 2001

"It's been a long time since I've had a pretty girl show up unannounced on my doorstep," the man said.

Annie stood in the doorway, dumbfounded.

He was tall, over six feet, and thin, almost awkwardly so. His eyes were dark, his features sharp, and he had a tangle of curly black hair. The man was attractive, in a goofy sort of way, but his looks were not what left her stupefied. He was familiar. Annie had met him before.

"Hello," she said.

Where? Where had Annie seen him? Was this Win? Or some other person?

"You don't know me," she went on. "But I know you. I think. You see . . ."

"You must be Annie. Come on in."

"Um, what?"

Despite her confusion, or because of it, Annie stepped through the doorway. If she ended up hacked to pieces it would be her own damned fault. She'd not mention this in her next e-mail to Eric. That is, if she made it out alive.

"Yes, I am Annie," she said. "Annie Haley."

"Haley. Really?"

"Yes. And . . . how did you know who I was? I'm . . . I honestly feel like I'm about to pass out."

The man laughed. Even *that* was familiar.

"My brother," he said with a grin that also somehow rung bells. "I'd been informed there was a chance you'd show."

"Your brother told you I was coming? Who's your brother? No one knew about this, not even me. The trip was very spur-of-the-moment."

"Welp, somehow he knew. The old tosser said that a pretty American had my address and might try to make an adventure out of it. He never imagined you'd go through with it, mind you, but felt I needed due warning."

Perhaps it was the smile, or the laugh, or the use of the word "tosser," but suddenly it struck Annie. She *had* seen this man before. He'd been at the George & Dragon, talking to Gus.

"And that, my dear," Gus had said at the time, "was no friend. That was my brother Jamie."

Jamie. Gus's brother.

Jamie as in James as in James E. Seton. Annie felt for the luggage tag, her trusty good-luck trinket. All this time she'd been talking to the wrong brother. No wonder Gus was so dismissive of Win. Typical sibling rivalry, not that she knew anything about it.

"Well." Annie exhaled and threw out a rigid, unpracticed smile. "You'll have to tell your brother he misjudged my fanatical interest in the story. Though I suppose you're acquainted with that level of zealotry. The chasing-down of Lady Marlborough, for instance."

Jamie laughed again, same as before, same as Gus.

"Indeed I'm acquainted with that story," he said. "Quite well as it happens."

"I'm sure you're busy, but if I could steal a few minutes of your time."

"Not busy at all. I'm pleased to have you here. Come. Let's go to the kitchen."

Annie nodded and followed him deeper into the apartment, trying to concentrate on the gleaming parquet floors and ornate crown molding. Better to appreciate the architecture than remember she was in a stranger's home and that there wasn't a person alive who knew where she was, or that she was even in France in the first place.

"Your apartment is beautiful," Annie said. "Mr. Seton . . ."

"Jamie, please."

"Jamie, you must wonder why I'm here. I don't know what your brother told you. I don't even have a sense of how much he knows."

"He had a few guesses as to why you might appear," Jamie said as they walked beneath one chandelier, and then another. "Then again, he scarcely knows his arse from a hole in the ground."

"I've heard that one before," Annie said with a smile as her shoulders loosened.

They stepped into the kitchen.

"What can I get you?" he asked. *"Café? Vin?"*

"Coffee for now, thanks."

"Espresso okay? Have a seat."

He gestured toward the long, oak farm table as Annie lowered onto a gray linen chair.

"So," Jamie said, grinding the espresso beans. The smell was sharp and warm. Annie's shoulders relaxed. "Let's get to it, shall we? Why are you here, exactly?"

He packed the coffee grounds into a sleek, silver machine.

"It's about the book," Annie told him. *"The Missing Duchess."*

"Ah, the book," he said. "The famous book. Only joshing on the famous bit." He fiddled with something on the espresso maker. "Rather, it was the white whale. The fool's errand of a lifetime. I presume you've read the dreadful tome." He peered over his shoulder. "What did you think?"

"I enjoyed it. The writing is . . . excellent. Clever, funny at times."

"Humph," he said.

"But it's not about the book. I mean, the book started everything, but it's the story behind the story that I'm after now."

"Always the best part."

"Your brother has been telling me about the duchess and the . . ." She cleared her throat. "The man who came to write about her."

"And the girl," Jamie guessed. "Laurel."

"That's the one. Full disclosure, Laurel is my mom."

"Yes." Jamie nodded. "I've gathered."

"You've gathered?" she said as he delivered the coffee. "From what? We don't look anything alike and I only just figured it out myself."

"You introduced yourself as Annie Haley. Another nosy and animated American with that particular surname. It all made sense."

Annie looked at him cross-eyed.

"How did you . . . Haley is my mom's married name. You've been keeping track of her all these years?"

"Not especially."

As Annie waited for him to speak, to describe how he could know the "Haley" without keeping track, her stomach roared. When was the last time she'd eaten? Had she even had breakfast that morning?

Jamie spun toward the refrigerator.

"You seem hungry," he said, pushing aside wine bottles and lemons.

"Oh, um, I just ate," Annie lied, a blush spreading across her cheeks.

"Rubbish! Your stomach speaks louder than you do. Hmm, my fridge is in a sorry state. I have positively nothing to eat unless you like olives or gherkins."

"Really, I'm not hungry."

"A tall tale if ever I've heard one. And I've heard a few. I have a proposition for you." He spun back to face her. "Why don't you relax, watch some telly, enjoy a drink. Wine is one provision I have. In the meantime, I'll scamper over to the market and pick up a few supplies for dinner. It's early, but I'm happy to eat now."

"That's very kind, but you don't have to feed me."

"It'd be my distinct honor." Jamie placed a hand to his heart. "I love to play amateur chef and since my wife left I haven't a person to cook for."

With the words "wife left," a sneaky, tight-lipped smile crossed Annie's lips. Win was unattached and so was "Pru." Was it too ridiculous to think . . . ?

"You have a wife?" Annie said.

"Believe it or not, yes. Alas, the ole ball-and-chain's been in Gstaad for two weeks visiting her parents."

"Oh."

Annie frowned. So much for that fantasy.

"Miss her like hell," Jamie said. "But she didn't make me accompany her, thank heavens. Bloody awful people, those parents of hers. Extraordinary that they produced such a primo child. So what do you say? Meal for two, made by yours truly?"

"If you're sure . . ."

Annie was hungry, famished even. She'd have to eat at some point. Maybe it'd slow the spin of her brain.

"Bien sûr!" Jamie said. "Of course I'm sure. You'd be doing me a favor. Will you be all right alone for a spell?"

"Yes, of course," Annie said, thinking of the tapes in her backpack. "I have some work to catch up on. So I'll be just fine."

"Brilliant. Well, young lady, I shall return. I look forward to a delicious meal and an even more delectable chat. Sounds as though my brother's not talking so I will fill in the gaps. And, believe me, I have plenty to say."

Sixty-six

The moment Annie heard the creak of the door she snapped a cassette into the player. It was a tape from the desk drawer at the Grange, freshly repaired by a grumpy man from a clock shop.

With a thundering heart and the shakiest of hands, Annie swallowed hard and hit Play.

FROM THE RECORDINGS FOUND AT THE GRANGE

A voice, male: This is a first interview conducted by writer Win Seton.

A voice, female: Also, the last.

Male: We'll see about that. I have with me the lovely and talented Pru Valentine.

Female: Laurel Innamorati. Let's get our facts straight.

Male: Yes, okay. No aliases. I am here with Miss Innamorati at a decayed estate in the derelict hamlet of Chacombe. The last time we were in this location a grievous injustice was committed. Miss Innamorati, how does it feel to return to the scene of the crime?

Female: Interesting question. Now that you mention it, I am a touch sick to my stomach.

Male: The interviewer will assume it's not the company making you ill.

Female: Feel free to assume what you wish. It won't make you right.

Male: Why do you think your stomach is upset? Is it due to "fear" perhaps?

Female: Yes. I am worried I'll fall victim a second time.

Male: Lightning doesn't strike twice.

Female: Actually, it often does. I'm quite afraid I'm in a great amount of moral danger.

Male: You mean mortal.

Female: No, I mean moral.

Male: Tell me, what happened the last time you were at the Grange?

Female: I encountered a suspicious character. He called himself a writer.

Male: Suspicious indeed.

Female: This so-called writer, he started out as your basic prowler. Then he ingratiated himself to the woman of the manor. He secured free room and board to boot.

Male: A real swindler sounds like.

Female: If you're being generous. Anyway, he tried to befriend the woman's guileless, wide-eyed assistant.

Male: Wide-eyed! Ha!

Female: The girl didn't know what she was getting herself into, being sweet and innocent as a lamb.

Male: Now I think *I'm* getting sick.

Female: Within days, the writer began weaving a web of lies and wickedness around her.

Male: Sounds wretched! Don't tell me this man is permitted to freely roam the streets?

Female: He's free as a bird. This known confidence trickster duped the poor girl into a friendship and then . . .

Male: Yes, Miss Innamorati?

Female: Oh, it's too horrible to go on!

Male: But you have to! I insist upon it!

Female: Well, this con man bamboozled me into falling, GULP, in love with him.

Male: No! You're the conned girl!

Female: I am.

Male: Please, I must know more details. How did it all start?

Female: In this very room, less than a fortnight ago, I told him the truth.

Male: Which was?

Female: That I loved him.

Male: Sounds like a very bad decision.

Female: The worst. But it was and is true and so I had to say it. Even though he is an unclean, unshaven, uncouth cad of a man, I love him. I told him this and then he committed a grievous crime against humanity.

Male: Which was? I'm almost afraid to hear it.

Female: He did not return the sentiment.

Male: What? But you're so beautiful! Utterly enchanting!

Female: I know! And, what's more, he committed this crime in broad daylight, in front of witnesses.

Male: Dear God. Witnesses? And no one did anything?

Female: Not a soul.

Male: The man must've lost the plot. Tell me, what happened next?

Female: Well, we went to Paris.

Male: You and he? Together?

Female: Yes. And a third person too.

Male: You traveled abroad, voluntarily, with a hardened criminal?

Female: There were extenuating circumstances. We had to help a friend. It was an emergency.

Male: Oh dear, I hope your friend is okay.

Female: Yes, she's fine. She will be anyhow.

Male: What happened after you got to Paris?

Female: Well, this man, he continued his crime even as we cavorted—

Male: Cavorted!

Female: As we cavorted throughout the city.

Male: Did you cavort any other places besides?

Female: I'm not going to dignify that with an answer. What I mean is we dined in cafés, strolled through the quiet, cold gardens, spent hours gazing at da Vincis and Rodins.

Male: Sounds splendid. "Where we are would be Paradise to me, if you would only make it so."

Female: Wharton?

Male: Hardy. Well, surely after all this so-called cavorting the man finally rectified his crime and declared his love in return.

Female: He did not!

Male: I'm gobsmacked! How can that be?

Female: Truth be told, he's a bit of a cheese weasel.

Male: What now?

Female: A cheese weasel. An idiot. I also believe the man is slow. Socially and mentally. He doesn't recognize what love is, even when it's knocked him upside the head.

Male: And you yourself are an arbiter of the feeling?

Female: Well, if I'm wrong then the only other explanation is that he didn't say it because he doesn't feel it.

[*Long pause*]

Male: Ah hell, Pru, you know—

Female: Laurel! No aliases.

Male: Fuck. [*Pause*] Well, in regard to the writer's feelings, you are well aware that the two of you are of the same mind. I don't need to tell you.

Female: Yes. You do. That's how this works.

Male: But you already KNOW it, being a wise woman with vast experience in love.

Female: Not vast. Very limited, honestly. I thought I knew love—before—but this is something else.

[*Long pause*]

Female: You know, this is an awfully elaborate apology, Mr. Seton. Or are you not planning to apologize at all?

Male: I have, I believe?

Female: You're a shit, you know that? You put me through all of this back-and-forth, saying you wanted it recorded. And for what? You're not even going to say it?

Male: Pru . . .

Female: No. Screw this. Turn off the tape. You act playful but it's only because you can't . . . you can't . . . you can't have real feelings!

Male: I have many feelings. Every day even. But I'm a Brit. We'd rather not express them.

Female: You have big-time problems, Seton. Big. Time.

Male: I agree. My problems are many and they are big. The greatest of them is that I do love you, Laurel Innamorati, my Valentine. I love you more than I can satisfactorily say, which is why I haven't been able to say it. Love. It feels so . . . insipid, wishy-washy. I want a better way to tell you.

Female: Just tell me the real way. Like a normal person.

Male: I love you, Laurel.

Female: I love you too. Now turn off the damned tape.

Sixty-seven

Dead air ran for several minutes.

When Annie was sure she'd heard everything, she turned off the tape, then swapped it with one of Gus's recordings. Her eyes were wet but she had a smile on her face. That was her mom, on the tape, professing her love to a man.

A man who sounded an awful lot like Gus.

Annie stood. She peered out the kitchen window toward the street. No sign of Jamie so far. After wiping her eyes with the hem of her shirt, Annie sat back down and, once again, she pressed Play.

Sixty-eight

"This place isn't half bad," Mrs. Spencer said as she promenaded through the front door like the duchess she was. "It'll do quite well in fact."

She shucked off her sable coat and handed it to Win.

Back in Banbury, Mrs. Spencer stuck with dirty trousers and her ever-present threadbare button-down shirt, when she actually wore a shirt. But her appearance was decidedly less ragtag when donning what she called "traveling attire."

In addition to the sable, the century-old debutante wore a peach-colored chemise and was thoroughly decked out in jewels. It must've been what Evelyn Waugh meant when he called her "very battered with fine diamonds." She'd even gone to the trouble of a wig, which hung off the back of her head like an inquisitive but friendly raccoon.

"Welcome to Maison Seton," Win said. "I'm glad you find the accommodations acceptable. Young James! We're here!"

A pair of feet clopped down the long parquet hallway. Soon a tall and gangly man appeared. To Pru he seemed comprised mainly of dark ringlets and nose. Win tried to remember this, the schnoz, whenever he felt inadequate, though he had to admit Jamie possessed a certain beatnik allure that drove girls bonkers. He was probably the very kind of bloke Pru preferred after her stint at Berkeley.

"Hello!" Jamie said, grinning.

In addition to the nose and curls, he was also made of teeth. Jamie was so different from Win who tended toward clean-cut and brawny, his smiles mostly closemouthed.

"You must be the dazzling Gladys Deacon." Jamie took Mrs. Spencer's hand and kissed it. "Oh Lord, you give your former husband's family a decent name. They should thank the heavens for you. How old are you now, Lady Marlborough? Have you even reached fifty yet?"

"She goes by Deacon, mate," Win said. "Or Spencer."

"This lovely man can call me whatever he pleases!" Mrs. Spencer sang as she danced down the hallway.

Win and Pru rolled their eyes in harmony.

"And you must be Pru," Jamie said and kissed her on each cheek. "I'm James. Jamie. The preferable of the Seton brothers."

"Her real name is Laurel," Win said, voice coming out like jelly. He did not like his pet name being manhandled by his little brother.

"Righto. Well, old chum." Jamie pounded him on the back. "I'm tickled to see you. Thought you might end up staying in Banbury forever. Alas, the favored son has returned. I suppose you want the flat back."

"Favored?" Pru couldn't help but blurt, Win still mostly in her bad graces. "That's a scary thought and doesn't speak very well to your own attributes, James. No offense."

Jamie chuckled. Mrs. Spencer heard the merriment and wandered back down the hall.

"You are a very perceptive young woman," Jamie said. "And I'm pleased to know you've not bought any of the rubbish my brother, the venerable Lord Winton, has undoubtedly tossed your way."

"*Lord* Winton?" Mrs. Spencer said. "What do you mean by that?"

"My brother has a title, dontcha know?"

Mrs. Spencer turned to Win, then bopped him in the chest with a panther-hair clutch.

"Of course I didn't know!" Mrs. Spencer said.

"Well, well, well." Jamie whistled through his teeth. "I'm aghast. Usually our lordship doesn't let an hour pass without reminding someone. I'm surprised he doesn't have it embroidered on his shirt. Ladies and ladies, before us stands a bona fide earl."

"No!" Pru said. Her jaw fell open.

"Yes, indeedy. The Right Honorable Earl Jerome Casper Augustine Seton of Winton, hence the deplorable nickname Win. Ironic, isn't it? Like a three-legged dog named Lucky."

"Aw, sod off," Win said, smiling. "You jealous bastard."

"Lord Winton," Pru said under her breath. "It doesn't seem possible."

"James, before your brother further abuses my precious ears with his rough language, can you please show me to my rooms?" Mrs. Spencer asked. "An earl. Honestly, you'd never imagine it."

"Please follow me, Lady Marlborough," Jamie said. "I'm chuffed to have some company. Because of your vast esteem, I shall offer you the master suite. It has the most sensational views of the Seine. A person can spend entire days simply watching the barges pass." He leaned down and grabbed the handle of her tattered croc suitcase. "My room is right next door. Anything you need, just ask."

"*Merci, Monsieur Seton. Je vous remercie de tout mon cœur,*" Mrs. Spencer said. "And what about those two?"

She crooked a thumb toward Win and Pru.

"Ah, let's allow Lord Winton and his lady friend to divvy up the space in the third bedroom. Thankfully Miss Innamorati is petite because they will have to contend with an exceptionally narrow bed."

Sixty-nine

Pru chucked her bag into the closet and heaved herself onto the bed. She sighed and let her arms and legs sprawl the width of it.

"Any room on there for an old friend?" said Win's voice from above her. She could nearly hear Mrs. Spencer tittering from down the hallway.

"Earl of Winton, huh?" Pru said, one arm thrown over her eyes. "Lord Winton. That is an interesting tidbit you managed to avoid."

"It doesn't mean anything."

"The 'Earl of Winton' doesn't mean anything? The title has no significance whatsoever? Nothing?"

"To me it's just a name. Something handed to me without any effort on my part. Why? Does the title matter to you? Do you find it important?"

"Oh yes. Endlessly so. As you have rightly assessed."

Pru turned on her side to face a brown lacquered desk. That no woman lived in the home was abundantly clear. The place was filled with heavy, ornate antiques interspersed with pieces of cheap modular furniture. Between the shag rugs and velour upholstery, any visitor would be treated to a full compendium on the permutations of the color brown.

"Had I known it was an earl I was dealing with," Pru said. "I would've expressed my unreturned devotion to no response three times instead of merely the two."

"Don't be like that, Laurel."

She felt the bed sink with his weight.

"No problem there," she said. "Being 'like that' was my first mistake."

"You know how I feel."

"I don't, actually."

"I can't . . . you're too young. Vibrant. You have the world ahead of you. It'd be wrong, don't you see? To return the words? Even though I feel them?"

"Too young and vibrant. It's Berenson and Mrs. Spencer all over again. Win, you know about Charlie. You know about my childhood. And because of this you know I've probably dealt with more hard knocks in my two decades than you have in three and a half."

The bed shifted again. Pru inhaled and closed her eyes, as if fortifying herself against some kind of blow. She felt Win's body inch closer to hers.

"Win," she said. "What are we doing here? Why are we even in Paris?"

"It was GD's idea, remember?"

"Right. Which makes all the sense in the world. Who wouldn't let a ninety-year-old, marginally sane woman dictate what country they're in? I think this is how adults end up missing."

"It's the Marlboroughs," he said. "She's afraid of them."

"You see, this doesn't sound like a real problem," Pru said. "It sounds like paranoia. What would they be trying to steal from her anyway?"

"Tom exists. She was right about that."

Win scooted closer, the barrier between them so thin it was more awkward than if they'd actually been touching. As a test, Win gently rested his fingers in the nook of her bent elbow. She did not shake him off.

Did Win love her? Of course he loved her, this girl who was some balled-up mix of innocence and wisdom, delicateness and strength. The truth was he loved her so damned much it went past that one trite feeling and into something else.

And because of that, there was no use pursuing it. The whole deal would go tits-up at some point and the poor girl would have to suffer yet another heartbreak. Not that Win fancied himself anywhere close to the league of Charlie but that bloke had reason for leaving.

"So what happens next?" Pru asked.

"Um . . ." Win glanced at his hand, and her skin below it. "I guess we wait."

"Perfect. And how long will that take? To be clear, what are we waiting for? Mrs. Spencer to come to her senses? For her to die? What?"

"What's the big hurry? Do you have someplace to be?"

"We can't stay here forever," she said.

Can't we? Win thought.

"We obviously need to get her home," Pru added.

"And how do you propose we accomplish that? Mrs. Spencer only does what she wants, nothing more. Which is why we find ourselves in Paris, by the by."

"We need to assure her that there's nothing to worry about," Pru said. "That no one's out to get her."

"Don't you think we should first make sure it's true?"

"You could talk to them," Pru said.

"Talk to whom?"

"The Marlboroughs. Convince them she doesn't need hospitalization or whatever it is they're thinking."

"Once again, I ask, shouldn't we make sure that's true?"

"I don't get it," Pru said. "I understand why Edith would care about Mrs. Spencer's mental health. Or at least feel some sort of obligation toward her. But why do the Marlboroughs care if she's wasting away in some ramshackle house? Heck, you'd think they'd want her dead. A duchess no more."

"You have compassion for miles."

"I'm serious. Tell me, Win. Why do they care?"

"How am I to know?"

"Well, you are of their kind," Pru said with a snort. "Seeing as how you're a peer."

"I'm not a duke. Furthermore, Marlborough and Winton are hardly the same. No Blenheim for this crew. Thank God."

Pru jerked away. As Win reached for her, she rolled over to face him. Their noses were but five centimeters apart.

"Blenheim," she said, green eyes shining in the stream of streetlight coming through the window. "You told me that place is a money pit."

"Yes. Blenheim costs more to run than most countries. And it doesn't even have its own army anymore. If the Grange is a money pit, Blenheim is ruinous."

"Maybe that's what they want," Pru said. "Her money. You've seen the diamonds. And the minks." She flicked her hand in the direction of the master bedroom. "If they declare her incompetent can they get access to her estate?"

"Huh, that's not out of the question," Win said, noodling on the concept.

"If those are her *traveling* diamonds, can you imagine her black-tie jewels? And the Grange might be a total heap but it has to be worth something."

"And the paintings," Win said. "Nearly incomprehensible value."

"You mean the Boldini? The one that disappeared from the dining room?"

"Yes. That. But also." His gut began to churn. "The barn. Tom's. It's, I think, filled with artwork. Pieces stacked wall to wall."

"You went into Tom's barn? You are even stupider than you look."

"That barn is how I accessed the property the day I met you. Tom wasn't in there, thank heavens. Probably would've bludgeoned me with a hammer if he had been. Nevertheless, given the nature of my visit—"

"Trespassing, you mean."

"Precisely," Win said, his smile glinting in the dark. "Due to the trespassing, I didn't tarry. But along the way I pulled back a few drop cloths. Artwork, prime artwork, each with a personal note from the artist wedged into the frame. The first three I checked: Degas, Monet, Gauguin. One. Two. Three."

"Holy crap," Pru said.

"Holy crap is right."

"Maybe that's what the Marlboroughs want," she said. "The sale of those pieces could keep the old homestead running for a few more years. Who knows, maybe even the books would draw a pretty penny. There must be thousands in that library of hers. Most are first editions, and signed."

"An influx of cash would definitely be welcome by that crew. No more cafeteria lines and tourists in their backyard."

"You have to talk to him!" Pru said. She swatted Win on the shoulder. "You have to call Gads tomorrow."

"Gads? Why? Do you have a puppet show you'd like to produce?"

"Gads is a Marlborough! He can tell you what's going on."

Win deliberated this.

In addition to being a Marlborough, Gads was also a barrister. Whether he might be on the side of his family or on the side of law, Win couldn't guess. Gads had never been particularly motivated by integrity. On the other hand, he called any gathering of three or more family members "the arse and pansy show." And he was not above doing something out of spite.

"I'll reach out to him in the morning," Win said.

"Brilliant." Pru yawned. "As you would say. Simply brilliant, ye olde bloke."

"I would not say that."

Pru let her eyes go heavy.

"You're really going to sleep here?" she said and yawned again. "Next to me?"

"I'm not sure I have a choice."

"There's always a choice," she said with another yawn, wider this time.

"Fair enough. Well, the answer is yes. I do plan to sleep here."

She nodded, her hair scrunching against the pillow.

"Good night, Lord Winton," she said.

"Good night, sweet Pru. I'll see you tomorrow."

Tomorrow.

A simple concept, a short-term promise, a word to throw away almost. If only Win and Pru had understood the problem with tomorrows. Namely, that they had so very few of them left.

Seventy

As it happened, Mrs. Spencer's floor-length sable was merely the start.

It was as though with one step off the train and into Paris, the woman returned to her former splendor, the Gilded Age all over again. Oh sure, Mrs. Spencer's movements were sometimes jerky and crude. Her eyes flashed between maniacal twinkles and clouded blue confusion. But damn, the old bird was back.

Lady Marlborough was back to her clothes, the cocktails, and an unending social calendar. The closet, her glass, her datebook all filled. The glimmer of Paris fell on the woman like the first dusting of snow.

"I dunno, mate," Jamie said to Win early in their stay. "You'd see more of her if you rose at a reasonable hour. By the time you two miserable tramps stagger out of your bedroom, Lady Marlborough's already out shopping or calling on an old chum. It's a marvel she still has friends, that she hasn't outlived them all."

"Give her time, yet," Win said.

Because Mrs. Spencer was so constantly occupied, Win and Pru were left to their own devices, forced to play tourists in the very best city of all.

Donning scarves and overcoats, the two braved the biting air and relentless sheets of drizzle to hoof about Paris. They visited cafés and museums. They paid homage to the *Nymphéas*, Monet's water lilies at l'Orangerie, as well as the new La Tours at the Louvre.

At the Bibliothèque de l'Arsenal, they spent hours ogling artifacts of the French Revolution, combing through prisoner dossiers and private papers from officers and the royal family.

They visited the Diocèse de Paris, where they dug up Abbé Mugnier's fifty-seven *cahiers de moleskine* and hunted down each mention of the duchess. Afterward they spent the night dancing at Le Sept, a small, fusty, and raucous gay nightclub.

And they dined. They dined in two-bit cafés and at those with more repute. Win took Pru to Café de Flore in Saint-Germain and La Closerie des Lilas in Montparnasse, the latter a favored stomping ground of Wilde, Fitzgerald, and Sartre. Hemingway wrote most of *The Sun Also Rises* at its mahogany bar.

When they ate together it was for hours, one meal bleeding into the next. Sometimes there was coffee, other times wine, though most often they had both. Waiters tried to shuffle them on but Win and Pru lodged themselves too thoroughly in their chairs and in each other.

One would think that in all this time and closeness Win must've returned Pru's previously declared feelings of love. Alas, he did not. The man was a prat, a wanker, a no-good sissy, a chump. He lacked the balls and Pru had the politeness to let the matter slide.

Tacit contracts to ignore hairy topics notwithstanding, Win understood he was bungling this irretrievably, even as they sat beside each other in cafés and danced near in clubs.

But Win saw how Pru looked at him, with faraway eyes, their distance increasing by the day. Each time they spoke, there was no shortage of laughter, but Win could see a wall forming, a new brick added with each conversation. Through it, he clung tightly to what they had.

"I'm working on it," Win said whenever Pru asked how they might entice Mrs. Spencer back home, and how they should handle the Marlboroughs. "I'm doing my best."

Naturally, Win took his time.

He'd call Gads, eventually, but was in no great hurry to leave Paris, or to finish the biography, or do anything that might chase away their moment. All those years Win thought a book would make him happy, that he needed some modicum of commercial success to feel content. But he was wrong. In the end, all Win needed was a paranoid old broad, Paris, and the attentions of a girl called Pru.

Seventy-one

In early March a frost settled upon Paris.

Though it made for slippery sidewalks and drafty homes, at dark, beneath Paris's glittering lights, the city shimmered.

Win and Pru walked home late one night. Both were decked out in coats and scarves but they bunched together tightly, succumbing to a need for closeness that had little to do with keeping warm.

"I'm beginning to wonder," she said as they crossed the footbridge near the Notre-Dame. "First you took me to Le Sept. Now this play. Do I need to start questioning your sexual preferences? Or does anything go in Paris?"

They'd come from the Théâtre du Palais-Royal, where they watched a production of the new play *La Cage aux Folles*, a story centered around two gay men. It was the first of its kind.

"You're questioning my sexual proclivities?" Win said with an abrupt halt.

They were at the center of the bridge, the Seine dancing below, the grounds around them still. There were no tourists that time of night or even that time of year. In the summer, people flocked to the square outside Notre-Dame along with the pigeons. Win's island was not the tourist mecca it'd one day become but it had its fair share of guests. Yet in that moment the city felt like theirs alone.

"Yes," Pru said. "I *am* questioning it. Don't look so glum! I used to live in San Francisco. You'll get no judgment from me."

"How can you doubt the persuasion of such a strapping man?"

"There's the insistence on gay nightclubs for one," she said, smiling.

"Hmm. I seem to recall a certain American sweaty and winded from all the fun *she* was having at such places."

"I wasn't sweaty! Maybe a touch damp."

"You were a lot damp."

Pru rolled her eyes.

"What's more," Pru said. "Tonight you took me to a gay-themed play. Are you trying to tell me something, Lord Winton? Don't be shy. This is the seventies. You no longer have to hide your true feelings. It'd probably make you more interesting to the general population in any case."

She tried to walk on, but for once Win refused to let a pointed comment go ignored.

"Pru," he said and grabbed her arm.

He pulled her back around.

"I'm not gay," he said with more earnest than necessary.

"I'm only kidding—"

"It'd be easier in some respects. My family would hate it but at least they'd be able to more easily pinpoint their dissatisfaction. Alas, men are selfish, hideous, hairy creatures and it'd be terrifying to crawl into bed with such a monster."

"Hmm, you are a monster, yes," Pru said. "Honestly, though? I sort of wish you were."

She tried to smile, though her eyes were too forlorn to pull off the cheer.

"What do you mean?" Win asked, already regretting the question.

"Well, for one, it would explain why you seem to enjoy my company while summarily rejecting my romantic advances."

"Sounds like you've caught the batshit insanity bug from Lady M.," he tried.

"I'm struggling to not take this personally," Pru said as her mouth began to quiver. "I'm putting everything into brushing off what happened, or didn't happen. I don't want to be some tiresome girl boring you to death with my insecurities, but you have to understand . . ."

"Pru."

"What?"

"Just . . . Pru . . ."

"You can't keep doing this—"

Then suddenly, to his great surprise, and especially to hers, Win leaned forward and kissed her. He felt her gasp as their lips met.

It was a simple kiss, a sweet one, but Win thought that if he never had another in his lifetime, this one would suffice. Pru's kiss was enough to carry him through the next ten thousand tomorrows.

Later, Win would remember this feeling and think maybe he turned it into his very own curse. One kiss. One chance. Perhaps the mere thought cemented their fate, launching Pru out of his grasp completely and forever.

Seventy-two

When the kiss ended, Win wrapped both arms around Pru's waist, replacing one contact with another, afraid to let go. The press of her body against his was almost too much to bear, even though their coats remained a barrier between them.

Without a word or even much thought, Win grabbed Pru's hand, a tad gruffly, and led her off the bridge.

Control yourself, Win thought at the time, *no proper woman wants her clothes ripped off in the middle of Paris.*

Good thing it was so damned cold.

After crossing the bridge, they hurried along the quay, Pru too bewildered to speak. Win checked his watch. It was just after midnight. Would Jamie be awake? Fifty-fifty odds.

As for the duchess, she was probably gallivanting throughout the city. They'd already contemplated whether Mrs. Spencer might've chucked the biography idea altogether to instead reel out her days re-creating her former Parisian salons. The notion, it wasn't half bad. Win was close to chucking the story, too.

When Win and Pru arrived in front of his building, they looked up together, searching for lights in windows, evidence of life. Win allowed himself to look at her then. With Pru's eyes lifted heavenward and the moon illuminating her cheeks, Win found he couldn't hold back a heartbeat longer. He grabbed Pru's chin and turned her face toward his.

Then he kissed her. Harder this time, and Pru kissed back, no hesitation on her lips.

Still soundless, they made their way inside the building and up the marble staircase. Their legs felt shaky, anemic. The top floor seemed miles away.

Inside the apartment, all was calm, the only light from the hallway, the only sound the hum-tick of the old refrigerator. Win laughed in relief.

"Thank God," Pru said, knowing his thoughts exactly.

Thank God. They were the first words spoken since their kiss.

In a flurry, they ditched their coats, their gloves, their scarves, and stumbled toward the back of the flat. Though they were still fully clothed, they felt almost naked, their top layers having been shed.

On that night Pru wore a long dress. It was semisheer and dotted with pin-point flowers, the whole getup cinched around the waist with a belt of string she called "macramé." The outfit was not appropriate for winter or, really, for any season in Paris. She was Win's misplaced California girl and he loved her all the more for it.

"Stop," he said as she removed her belt. "Stop." His voice softened. "I want to see you like that."

"Like this?" Pru laughed. "You realize I'm still dressed, right? Oh Lord, maybe you *are* gay."

Still smiling, she undid the top two buttons of the dress, and then the third and fourth. Win tried to appear undaunted by the full, round tops of her breasts, breasts much fuller than he'd expect for someone of her tiny frame.

Eyes fixed on Pru, Win labored to extricate himself from his own clothes. His pants caught on his knees and he had to brace himself against a dresser to stay upright.

"You are outstandingly uncoordinated, aren't you?" Pru said as she threw her dress overhead, revealing gauzy pink underpants beneath. As it turned out, she wore no bra.

Win was in his undergarments but it hardly mattered, so obvious was his, *ahem,* reaction to the display. Poor bastard, acting like a bloody rookie.

Within seconds they were both stripped to nothing and on the bed. Her skin, it was so damned warm. And soft. It almost tasted that way too. How she felt beneath him, and him atop her, it was as if they'd practiced, studied, and hired private tutors to get it so astoundingly right.

And then.

"Win!" said a voice, followed by a thud on the door. "Win! Open up!"

The couple froze. A piece of Win's hair dropped down and tickled Pru's forehead. She wiggled out from under him. He lifted up onto an elbow but kept one hand protectively on the soft, low part of her belly.

"Is that your brother?" she whispered.

"Jamie, now is not a good time," Win barked. Then added: "The worst possible time, actually."

"It's important. Might I come in?"

He was already walking through the door as Win said, "Absolutely not."

"Sorry, mate," Jamie said. "You can get back to the shagging in a jiff."

Pru groaned and threw both arms over her eyes.

"Someone had better be dying," Win said.

"A very urgent-sounding fellow rang about an hour ago. Called himself Tom."

"Tom?" Pru removed the arms from her face. She turned toward the tall, mop-haired figure in the doorway. "Tom? Mrs. Spencer's handyman?"

"That's the chap," Jamie said. "He was calling from Banbury. And wouldn't you know it, the old bird is there too."

"Mrs. Spencer is in Banbury!" Pru gasped.

She looked at Win.

When was the last time they'd seen her? Neither could remember exactly. It could've been that morning, or last Tuesday. Pru was embarrassed by how myopic she'd been, traipsing around the city with Win. She was an employee of the Grange and there she was, in Paris, drawing a salary to flirt and dance.

"Did she take her luggage?" Win asked. "Her minks?"

"I checked her room and there's not a personal effect in sight. But, here's the kicker, the bloody place is socked in by wooden crates. A damned storage unit, right here in our home."

"Christ," Win said. "Do you know how long she's been away?"

"Several days, apparently. All that and she's had herself some visitors."

"The Marlboroughs," Win guessed.

"Righto. There's also an American looking for you."

He pointed at Pru.

"Shit!" she said.

Edith Junior. Come to take her home. Now Pru could never make a case that she was vital to Mrs. Spencer and had to stay on given that caregiver and charge were in two entirely different countries and Pru hadn't even known.

"Goddamn it," Pru said, inching up into a seated position. She pulled the sheet taut over her breasts. "She tricked us. Mrs. Spencer tricked us! I don't know how or why, but she did!"

"Luv, it's okay," Win said and ran his hand along her leg. "I'm sure she had her reasons. Jamie, thanks for the information. Now feel free to take your leave."

"Have fun, you two. But keep it down, would ya? I have an early morning."

As Jamie slunk away, Pru turned toward Win.

"This is not good," she said.

Pru was worried, and not only about her employment prospects or immigration status.

"Those people in Banbury," she said. "Something's not right. What if Mrs. Spencer gets taken advantage of? Or injured in some way?"

"You were the one who said she was being histrionic."

"Well, they showed up, didn't they? Just as she said. And she was also right about Edith and the Marlboroughs being in cahoots."

"We don't know that," he said.

"They'll take her away!"

"Why are you so up in arms? Having kittens over a few uninvited guests? No one wants to take her away. Even if they did, she's probably better off under the care of a doctor. She broke a leg three years ago and never got it fixed!"

"Don't you get it, Seton?" Pru said. "If she goes, so do I. She's the only reason I'm even here."

Win jolted, as if slapped. He'd never considered a situation in which Pru would be gone.

"Have you and Gads worked things out?" Pru said, her voice climbing. "This mysterious plot you're cooking? Because it'd be most helpful if Gads could tell us what's going on. I'm afraid I'll . . . I'm just afraid."

"Er . . . I'll ring him in the morning."

Pru threw off the covers and stood.

"We have to go back!" she said. "To Banbury!"

"Pru . . ." Win reached for her arm.

"We can't leave Mrs. Spencer alone there."

"Please. Let's forget about Mrs. Spencer and the Marlboroughs for tonight." We'll deal with this catastrophe tomorrow.

"Win, she's alone!"

"Tom is there, remember? He's scarier than we are anyhow. I wouldn't want to meet him in a dark alley, or even a lit one."

Pru sighed and slumped down onto the bed.

"I guess you're right," she said.

"Of course I'm right." As Win glided his hand up her side, she shivered. "We'll engage that mob of nutters tomorrow. For now." He skimmed his fingers across her left breast. "For now. Just us."

Pru smiled, at once filled to the neck with a foreign, indescribable sensation. Perhaps, when you got right down to it, the feeling was exactly that, one of fullness, the emptiness finally gone.

"You're right," Pru said again and moved her body flush against Win's. "We'll handle it in the morning."

And with that, Win and Pru took up from where they left off.

Seventy-three

ÎLE SAINT-LOUIS
PARIS
NOVEMBER 2001

"To leave a message for the guest in room five, please speak at the tone."

"Hi, Mom? It's me. You might be wondering where I am. Don't freak out, but I'm in Paris. I hopped on a train right after you did.

"You might've heard me mention my friend from Banbury named Gus. Well, I just found out his full name is Jerome Casper Augustine Seton. He calls himself the Earl of Winton, mostly as a joke but it is also the truth. I am at his apartment now, with his brother Jamie. I think you know the place and the people I'm talking about.

"Honestly? I'm more confused than ever. About you. About me. Why did you keep this part of your life hidden? I feel like it has to do with my dad, but I just can't get the math to pencil out. What happened in those years? Between when you left Paris and I was born?

"Mom, I'm not going back to Virginia until you come here first. You say I was an easy toddler, that I never threw a tantrum. Well, I'm doing it now. This is my tantrum. I'm planting my feet in Paris until you arrive.

"Okay, that's it. Sorry for the long message. And sorry for doing it like this but there's no other choice. So. You know where to find me . . . on Quai de Béthune. Good-bye, Mom. Miss Valentine. I'll see you in Paris."

Seventy-four

ÎLE SAINT-LOUIS
PARIS
NOVEMBER 2001

"To be clear," Jamie said as he dumped a handful of diced shallots into the snapping skillet. "When I claimed to love cooking I did not promise to be especially talented."

"Well, it smells great," Annie said.

"Those are the shallots talking."

She nodded absently, her mind on Gus's tape, likewise the needless description of her mother's underwear and naked breasts.

"Is it drafty in here?" Jamie asked, mistaking her shudder for a shiver. "I can crank up the heat."

He opened a can of tomato paste, and then spooned it into the pan.

"The temperature's perfect," she said and sipped her Bordeaux. "Listen, Jamie, I have a confession to make."

"A confession?" He glanced over his shoulder and waggled his eyebrows. "One of my favorite things to hear."

"Don't get too excited. It's nothing steamy."

Gus's erection. Laurel nude. Annie was just about maxed out on "steamy."

"It's about your brother," she said. "Gus. He's been telling me the story behind the book, the story of Win and Pru."

"Of your mum."

"Yes, my mum," Annie said, thinking of Laurel who was probably right then stepping into an empty hotel room and also into a cold panic. "I had no idea who Win was until about twenty minutes ago. I never realized Win and Gus were the same person. For a second there I thought Win was you."

"Really?" Jamie turned to face her, his back pressed against the counter, a curious smile playing at his lips. "Me?"

"Only for a second."

"The name didn't tip you off?"

"J. Casper Augustine Seton?" Annie said. "I assumed the *J* was for James."

"It's for Jerome. Also, there's a 'Gus' in there."

Annie repeated the name in her head.

"Augustine?" she said. "That's, like, barely a Gus."

"Didn't he tell you that he was the Earl of Winton?"

"Yes, but . . ."

Gus *had* told her that early on, but Annie thought it was a joke.

"It goes without saying Win refers to that," Jamie said.

"Our nicknames are more straightforward in the States, I guess."

She pictured Gus, sitting across the table, or beside her at the bar. Gus with his wavy, white hair, his pressed trousers, that slippery smile. She recalled how he'd tip his head toward her when getting to the good stuff, taking on and off his glasses as he spoke.

The glasses. He wore them to read the newspaper, or a transcript, or the bar tab from Ned. But he never needed glasses to read the book. He didn't have to. The words were his.

"Damn," she said. "I like to think of myself as pretty perceptive. But I honestly never figured it out."

"No worries. The bloke's a roguish sort."

"In my defense," Annie said. "Gus . . . Win . . . whatever his name is, he told me that the writer lives in Paris. Plus he was always so disdainful of the guy."

"My brother is his own worst enemy."

Annie reached deep into her pocket.

"Here," she said and tossed the luggage tag onto the table. "I found this at the Grange. It appears to have your name on it."

"No!" Jamie picked up the tag. He held it to the light. "Well, I'll be. Those two bastards used my very nice set of matching baggage for their return trip to the Grange. Brought it back worse for the wear, as you can see."

Jamie kissed the tag and then dropped it into his own pocket. Annie bristled. That was supposed to be *her* good-luck charm, even if his name was on it.

"So they went back?" she asked. "Win and Pru? To the Grange?"

Jamie nodded.

"They did," he said.

"Because of Tom."

"Criminy, I forgot about that old Pole." Jamie chuckled. "That's what old age will do to a person. But, yes, his call precipitated their return."

"When they arrived," Annie said, "were the Marlboroughs there, too?"

"Those are the events as I know 'em."

Jamie moved to a larger pot and examined the potatoes boiling inside. This dinner was starting to look more Virginia and less Paris.

"So that was it, then?" Annie said and took another sip of wine. "They went to the Grange, end of story."

"End of story?" Jamie said. "What makes you think that?"

"The Marlboroughs were at the Grange."

"They were."

"They—and Edith—wanted to have the duchess hospitalized."

"They did."

"If Mrs. Spencer ended up in a hospital, there was no reason for my mom to stick around. And we both know that she ended up back in the States, alone."

"Your mum did return to the States," Jamie said. "But not right away. Their story went a little longer. You see, Win and Pru managed to find their way back to Paris. Thanks to a little help from a bloke named Gads."

Seventy-five

The duchess was at sixes and sevens when she saw their two faces show up in her parlor-turned-veterinary-clinic.

"Get out! Scram!" she howled, chasing after Win and Pru with some ungodly combination of pitchfork, broom, and backhoe. "Get off my land!"

"Mrs. Spencer," Pru pleaded. "It's only us."

"I know it's you! What in Sam Hill are you doing in England? You think I dragged you to Paris for my own good health? You were supposed to stay there. ALONE. Jesus. How come people can't accept a goddamned gift when they're given one?"

The cleaning and yard implements were one thing, but the collection of guests was no less threatening. For one, there was Tom. And Gads. And a butler named Murray, there at the behest of the duchess's niece. Pru recognized him from her initial trip to the Grange.

All that and Gads had with him his brother, the eleventh Duke of Marlborough, and the duke in turn had his crew of solicitors and physicians. Wife number two was also present due to some vagary of their prenuptial agreement. She herself brought her own legal battalion.

"Greetings, comrades!" Win said, grinning like a dope. "Holy hell. There are a lot of you."

"Why are you here?" Mrs. Spencer demanded.

"We were worried about you," Pru said. Her eyes scanned the room. "For good reason, it seems."

"You should be worried about yourself! I can take care of these buffoons. You need to leave immediately. You're so close to screwing everything up, you have no idea!"

"But, Mrs. Spencer, your niece hired me to look after you," Pru said. "She expects me to be here. I apologize for my misstep but I'm sticking with you from here on out."

"Jesus, don't do me any favors," Mrs. Spencer grumbled.

"Hello there," a man said and stepped forward. "Pleased to meet you, Laurel. The name's Gads."

Pru smiled wide and shook his hand. Gads was short and raggy-haired, every bit the aging scamp she pictured. She adored him on sight.

"George," his brother warned. The man was a duke but looked like an ordinary bloke, including the "terminally weak chin" Mrs. Spencer described. "I've asked you seven times not to get involved."

"As Lady Marlborough's solicitor," Gads said. "It's my very duty to get involved. Now, dear brother, I have to ask you to leave the premises."

"If she is the Duchess of Marlborough, then I am the duke, and that makes all of this mine."

"And mine as well," said the ex-wife.

"Sorry to report, but you're wrong, both of you. This property belongs to Gladys Deacon alone. I have the paperwork right here."

Gads tapped his briefcase.

"You two," Mrs. Spencer said, pointing one craggy finger first at Win and then at Pru. "Are supposed to be in Paris."

"Yes, you mentioned that when you stabbed me in the rear with a pitchfork," Win said.

"If you're here about your stupid book . . ."

"What book?" the duke said.

"Don't worry, my darling grandson," Mrs. Spencer said. "Merely a thorough detailing of my past. You are featured prominently and in bad light. Seton."

She punched at the ground with her cane. "I'll help you finish your precious life's work, but you and Miss Valentine must leave. Now. Go back to Paris. And don't tarry. Time is of the essence."

"While we're at it," Gads said. "The rest of you should likewise decamp."

"I'm not leaving until I get what's owed to me," said the ex-wife, sniffling up to the duke. "And you know exactly what that is."

"Stop it!" Mrs. Spencer yelled, clonking the cane again, this time right beside the ex-wife's foot, which caused her to pop a half meter off the ground.

The duke's former wife was already besieged by a nervous disorder and all that pounding and shrieking only compounded the problem.

"Stop it right now!" Mrs. Spencer said. "Everybody stop grabbing at the people and things in this house!"

She reached for her holster. Like a receding tide, everyone in the room stepped back in chorus. Everyone, that is, except for Win and Pru. They were used to this show and knew Mrs. Spencer was, for the most part, all mouth and no trousers. And sometimes the no-trouser situation was literal to boot. Also, they recognized that of the people in that room they had the least chance of getting shot.

"You." Mrs. Spencer pointed at Pru with the gun. "You, you, and you." Win, Gads, and Murray. "You stay here."

"I thought you wanted us to go to Paris?" Win said.

"To you remaining cretins," she went on, ignoring Win as she loved to do. "Find a place to stay. The Banbury Inn. The Chacombe Motor Hotel. In the bushes, for all I care. Return at nine o'clock tomorrow morning. We'll sort out everything then. My attorney Gads will supervise the proceedings."

"I'm not leaving," the ex-wife said again. "I'm not setting foot off this property until I take possession of my rightful assets."

"Which are a subset of my rightful assets," the duke reminded her.

"What assets are you people talking about!" Pru said with uncharacteristic gusto.

Usually, with folks like these, she was content to remain in the background, especially if possible deportation was in the offing.

"Do you people have eyeballs?" Pru asked. "Look around! This place is a dump! No offense, Mrs. Spencer."

"I'm very offended but am rather enjoying this, so carry on."

"Don't you people live in Blenheim? With fountains and grottos?"

"As if anyone cares about this crap house," the ex-wife said. "We're here for the art."

"Art?" Pru said. "What art?"

"You tell her, Peter," she said to a solicitor. "The art Gladys acquired after she became the duchess is ours. In other words, everything collected in the last forty years."

"Yes. Well. That's an argument to make," this Peter said and then, remembering his audience, added, "and it shan't be too challenging to prove!"

"These people have the ridiculous notion that I'm sequestering priceless art," Mrs. Spencer said.

"Don't let them search your home," Pru said, at once thinking of the Boldini as well as the Monets and everything else Win saw when he first came through the property. "They have no right. Gads, tell her. She's not obligated . . ."

"Sweet girl, it's fine," Mrs. Spencer said, smiling prettily. This action was somehow more threatening than if she'd drawn a gun. "They are free to snoop about until their snaky hearts are content. They won't find a thing."

Mrs. Spencer gave a wink and that's when Pru remembered the crates in Paris, piled up in the spare bedroom. No wonder she needed the cane. The old broad was no doubt quite sore from moving things about. Pru smiled in admiration. Mrs. Spencer knew what she was doing. She almost always did.

"Tom will be pleased to show you out," Mrs. Spencer said, brandishing her weapon once more. "Don't stall! Unless you want to be shot in the knees!"

After much squalling, the assemblage of nimrods and mutton heads collected itself. Win and Pru watched as Tom frog-marched the crew outside. Gads waved farewell and slammed the door behind them.

"Well, old buddy," he said and turned toward his friend. "You're looking positively adequate, which is an upgrade from the last time I saw you."

"Thanks, ya bastard," Win said, eyes sparking. "You always make a guy feel like a million quid. Which is funny since you wouldn't know a thousand quid if it bit you in the arse."

"Wait until you see my bill for these shenanigans. We'll keep the tourists out of Blenheim yet. Laurel," Gads said and gave her a quick hug. "Or Pru. Or whatever my half-witted friend calls you. I'm chuffed to meet you, despite your wretched taste in men. Shall I take your luggage upstairs?"

"They need to get out of here!" Mrs. Spencer said. "Posthaste!"

"All right, all right. But we have some matters to discuss first. Come, let's conference in the library. Lady Marlborough tells me you two are sneaky little bookworms. How appropriate. I've brought you one helluva read."

Seventy-six

THE LAST WILL AND TESTAMENT OF
HER GRACE THE DUCHESS OF MARLBOROUGH
GLADYS DEACON SPENCER-CHURCHILL

I, Gladys Deacon Spencer-Churchill, an adult
residing at 4 Banbury Road, Banbury, Oxfordshire,
England, being of sound mind and marginally
serviceable body, declare this to be my Last Will
and Testament.

1. I revoke all wills and codicils previously made
by me.

2. I appoint my stepgrandson Lord George William
Colin Spencer-Churchill, known colloquially as
"Gads" for some inexplicable reason, as the executor
and trustee of this will (hereafter referred to as
"my Trustee").

3. To each living direct descendant of my late husband Charles Richard John Spencer-Churchill, the ninth Duke of Marlborough, Earl of Sunderland, and Marquess of Blandford, I give the sum of ten thousand pounds, free of tax, but only to those descendants who have not yet reached the age of twenty-five at the time of my death.

4. To my longtime handyman Tomasz Kosinski I bequeath the sum of one hundred thousand pounds, free of tax.

5. To Laurel Innamorati I bequeath the primary residence at 4 Banbury Road (hereafter referred to as the "Primary Residence") located in Oxfordshire, England, as well as all objects and personal effects remaining therein, including but not limited to my collection of literature. This Primary Residence is circled in red on the map provided in Appendix A to this will.

6. To Jerome Casper Augustine Seton, Earl of Winton, I bequeath the land surrounding the Primary Residence and all ancillary buildings, barns, outhouses, artist studios, and other structures not considered the Primary Residence. This parcel is outlined in green on the map provided in Appendix A to this will.

7. To Laurel Innamorati and Jerome Casper Augustine Seton, Earl of Winton, I bequeath the thirty-three Impressionist and other paintings (the "Collection") enumerated in Appendix B to this will, subject to the stipulations outlined in clause 8. All thirty-three pieces of the Collection are currently housed

at Lord Winton's residence at 24 Quai de Béthune,
Paris, France. Miss Innamorati and Lord Winton shall
give to Mr. Kosinski one painting of his choosing as
repayment for his assistance in transporting the
Collection to Lord Winton's residence.

8. Of the remaining thirty-two pieces in the
Collection, Miss Innamorati and Lord Winton shall
select exactly one dozen to bequeath to a museum
or other nonprofit entity. There shall be no
territorial, religious, or other restrictions as to
the recipient of these donation(s). Miss Innamorati
and Lord Winton shall then divvy up, at ten apiece,
the remaining twenty pieces of the Collection as
they see fit. If there is a dispute between parties
as to which paintings shall be donated or to which
organization(s), or the divvying amongst parties, my
Trustee has the final say.

9. Should either Miss Innamorati or Lord Winton not
survive me by thirty days, his or her share shall be
distributed to his or her then-surviving children in
equal shares. If the deceased has no surviving
children, his or her share shall be distributed to
the other beneficiary.

10. To the Marlborough family I bequeath the
portrait of me as rendered by Giovanni Boldini,
which shall be hung in the grand Saloon at Blenheim
Palace so that the Marlborough family and the
tourists who pay its bills will be permitted to gaze
upon my face daily.

11. Subject to the payment of my funeral and
testamentary expenses and the legacies outlined in

clauses 3 through 10 above, I give my residuary estate to the Oxfordshire Spaniel Sanctuary.

12. I wish to be buried after a Roman Catholic service. During the service, the hymn "How Great Thou Art" shall be sung. I request a reception following in the grand Saloon at Blenheim Palace.

To those reading this will, or benefiting from the will, or inspecting it for one's own prurient interests, I shall close with a quote from my dear, departed friend Marcel Proust.

"Let us be grateful to the people who make us happy; they are the charming gardeners who make our souls blossom."

Be happy. Love one another. Chase joy. There is so little of it to go around.

[signature: Gladys]

Her Grace the Duchess of Marlborough
Gladys Deacon Spencer-Churchill

SELF-PROVING AFFIDAVIT

The instrument, consisting of this and two (2) typewritten pages was signed and acknowledged by Testator as her Last Will and Testament in our presence, and we, at her request, and in her presence, and in the presence of each other, have subscribed our names as witnesses.

We, the undersigned Testator and witnesses
declare:

1. That the Testator executed this instrument as
her Will;
2. That in the presence of witnesses, the Testator
signed or acknowledged her signature already made;
3. That the Testator executed the Will as a free
and voluntary act for the purposes expressed in it;
4. That each of the witnesses, in the presence of
the Testator and of each other, signed the Will as
witness;
5. That the Testator was of sound mind; and
6. That the Testator was at the time eighteen (18)
or more years of age.

All of which is attested to this 5th day of March
1973.

Gladys

HER GRACE THE DUCHESS OF MARLBOROUGH
GLADYS DEACON SPENCER-CHURCHILL, Testator

Tomasz Kosinski

TOMASZ KOSINSKI, Witness

George W. Spencer Churchill

GEORGE WILLIAM COLIN SPENCER-CHURCHILL, Witness

Seventy-seven

ÎLE SAINT-LOUIS
PARIS
NOVEMBER 2001

"So they left right after reading the will?" Annie asked as Jamie pulled a long glass dish from the oven.

Meat on the bottom, mashed potatoes on the top: Parisian cooking wasn't so snobby. Or maybe Jamie shared her pedestrian tastes. He *was* the untitled brother, Annie thought with a smirk.

"Yes'm, that's when they left," Jamie said and refilled her wineglass. "They read the will and then Mrs. Spencer kicked them out in the middle of the night."

"Guess they didn't need to borrow your luggage after all. So, why was Mrs. Spencer trying to get rid of them so urgently?"

"She had her reasons."

"Which were?"

"My dear, we've not approached that part of the story."

"You're as bad as your brother," Annie groused.

"An insult, but I won't protest," Jamie said with a grin. "For now, let's just say Mrs. Spencer had great foresight. She understood Win and she understood your mum."

"Well, that makes one of us. I barely recognize her from the story. It's like she left every ounce of romance and whimsy back at the Grange. Or in Paris."

"It was the time," Jamie said. "The era. Things were more fluid then, the people more adventurous, even those who weren't by nature. It's why your mum absconded to Paris with my brother, threat of immigration charges and all. She wasn't convinced Gads could keep Mrs. Spencer out of the loony bin, but at least a visa violation and its ensuing jail time would impress her old Berkeley chums, or so she joked."

"It's hard to picture my mom at Berkeley. To me she's all headbands, collared shirts, and Wellesley."

"People change. Or they try to anyway."

"So everything was in the apartment?" Annie said, her stomach grumbling.

When, exactly, did Jamie plan to serve the food?

"The entire collection was in your house?" she asked.

"Was it ever," Jamie said and blew back his hair. "You would not believe the scene. Somehow the old bird crammed eight large crates of artwork into that bedroom. Tom was obviously involved. How or when, though, we never knew. I was working and Laurel and Win were so inexorably . . . how do I phrase this?"

"In love? Wrapped up with each other? Heads lodged up their asses?"

"Yes! Ha!" Jamie snapped his fingers. "The last one. Now you're getting it."

He pulled a spatula from the drawer.

"What happened to the artwork?" Annie asked.

"It stayed in my damned flat for six years. My then-fiancée-now-wife thought I was some kind of nutter when she accidentally stumbled upon it." Jamie cleared his throat. " 'Yes, dear, just holding on to priceless art for a duchess until she finally kicks it! And then it's into the hands of my wastrel of a brother and the peculiar American fairy-nymph he adores.' It's a wonder she didn't ditch me on the spot."

"And after Mrs. Spencer died? Did Win—Gus—and my mom take possession of their requisite pieces?"

Annie thought of their farm in Virginia and its uninspired décor, the excessively ordinary art hanging on the walls. She couldn't recall a single piece that didn't feature a horse jumping over something.

"Yes, they did," Jamie said. "The two nabbed their chosen pieces, donated the rest, and proceeded on their not-so-merry ways."

"I wonder which ones my mom chose, and where they went. They're definitely not in our house."

"You'd have to ask her," he said with a shrug. "According to Gads, he ended up needing to invoke the 'Trustee has the final say' clause."

"They argued?" Annie crinkled her face. "Over art? That does not sound like my mother."

That did not sound like Win either, she nearly added.

"Quite the opposite," Jamie said. "They wouldn't decide." He pulled a salad bowl from the cabinet. "So Gads picked for them. A real pain in the backside, those two. Do you like anchovies?"

"No, thanks," Annie said, fiddling with a napkin.

Jamie placed the salad tongs on a paper towel and paused. He glared into the bowl as if trying to find meaning in the lettuce.

"I have to ask," he said. "Is your mum still married?"

"My mom? God no. She has been extremely unmarried for my entire life. It's absurd for me to even imagine her as anyone's bride."

"So she didn't stay with your father?"

"I've never even met the guy. And he's dead now. Apparently."

Jamie blanched.

"He is?"

"That's what I've been told. It's not why the marriage ended, though she left him when she was pregnant with me. But, like I said, he's dead now."

"Which was . . . ?"

"Which was what?"

"When were you born?" Jamie asked and set two salad plates on the table.

"Nineteen seventy-nine," Annie said.

"Interesting."

"Why is that interesting?"

She glanced up. Jamie looked apprehensive, as though she'd caught him committing a minor crime.

"Oh. Well," he stuttered, and retrieved two more plates. "It's hard to explain. And it's not really my place . . ."

All of a sudden they heard the click of a key in a hundred-year-old lock, followed by the creak of the door.

"Do you . . ." Annie started. "Guests? Your wife?"

"Well, Miss Haley," Jamie said, and handed her a blue and white dish piled high with meat. "Here's your *hachis Parmentier*. And that, I believe, is the sound of my brother."

Seventy-eight

ÎLE SAINT-LOUIS
PARIS
NOVEMBER 2001

Gus took one glimpse of Annie and looped back out of the kitchen and down the hall toward the front door.

"Lord Winton!" Jamie yelled. "Get your arse back in here! Is that any way to treat a lady?"

Jamie disappeared, the clunk of his footsteps echoing down the hall.

Annie braced herself, heart thumping at a million beats per minute as sweat beaded along her hairline. If Jamie didn't catch his brother, it was a-okay by her. Annie didn't know what she could possibly say to the man.

"That doesn't fit the legal definition of entrapment," she heard Jamie say. "The girl showed up looking for you but not knowing it was *you* . . . oh, no, no, no. You will go in there and talk to her . . . I guarantee you'll come across far more favorably in your version of events than you would in mine."

Annie strained to hear the rushed-whisper of Gus's words, while thinking of the message she left for Laurel at the inn. Would her mom come to Paris? Did Annie even want her to? God, what a disaster of a vacation. She should've just stayed in her room and eaten cakes.

"Anyone know where a fellow can get a little meat and potatoes round here?" said a voice.

Annie looked up, a smile crashing across her face. Gus, her old pal Gus.

"Hachis Parmentier," she said and frowned.

No, she was not happy. She was mad. The man had lied. Or maybe he hadn't. He had led Laurel on. Or so it seemed.

But, at the very least, he broke Laurel's heart, or broke her altogether, otherwise she would've stayed in Paris. Everyone knew the best way to solve an immigration problem was with a wedding. The Laurel in Gus's story wouldn't have left unless she had to.

"Well, well, well," Annie said. "If it isn't the Missing Writer of *The Missing Duchess*. What was it you said to me on that first day? 'The man who wrote that book is long since gone.'"

"The old fella went to Paris in 1973 and in Paris he remains."

"We were acquainted at one time."

"That man is unknowable."

"Long gone," Annie said, eyes narrowing as she poked at her dinner. She was suddenly not that hungry. "Or right in front of my face. Oh, thanks for the tape recordings, by the way. Jolly good time listening to the details of my mother's Parisian sexual awakening. I suppose it's nice to know she hasn't always had her shit together."

"Whoa," Jamie said, entering the room. "You told her about having sex? With her mum? You've some balls on you, guv'nor. Of course, telling Annie about said balls was probably in poor taste."

"Probably?" she said.

Jamie took a seat across from her. He placed a napkin on his lap, as if this were an ordinary meal and not the start of some kind of very jacked-up dinner theater. The man had expended great effort on making the *hachis Parmentier* and evidently nothing was going to keep him from it.

"You told me the writer was long gone," Annie reminded Gus, who remained fixed in the doorway. "You said he was in Paris."

Jamie motioned his brother toward the food but Gus waved him away.

"So, nothing?" Annie said. "You have zero response?"

"Are we not in Paris?" Gus asked. "Funny, as I was sure I saw the Notre-Dame across the way."

"Smartass is not as cute on a sixty-year-old as I'm sure it was on Win Seton the writer. If it was even cute back then at all."

"My guess is no," Jamie said.

"Annie," Gus said with a deep sigh. "I meant every word. The man who wrote that book, who loved your mother, he is gone. Win . . . he was the best part of me. A sad referendum on my true nature, of course, as Win was nothing to get excited about. But that's the God's honest truth."

"Enough with the self-deprecating crap." Annie speared a piece of meat. "It was funny and even charming at first. Before I knew you were completely full of shit."

"Aw, Annie," Jamie said. "Cut the poor bloke some slack. He's only a little full of shit. A half tank. Maybe only a quarter full."

"I haven't uttered a single lie," Gus insisted. "That man. That life. It's gone. When your mother left Paris, Pru disappeared and so did Win. What you see is his shell, the husk of a man. The rest of him remains forever in Paris, stuck in 1973."

"That is completely pathetic," Annie said, even as she felt her heart soften at the thought.

"Probably. But that's how I see it. And that's why I ended the tapes where I did. You want the truth? The epilogue? What happened after? Well, listen up, I'll tell you exactly where Win and Pru went from there."

Seventy-nine

ÎLE SAINT-LOUIS
PARIS
APRIL 1973

We believed Paris was the start of us.

It's the kind of city that makes you think of beginnings, or even juicy middles. Paris is a book to savor, in whole or in part, at any time and in any season. At age ninety or at thirty-four, you can open any chapter and read from there.

Seeing Paris with Pru was like turning up the city's volume, brightening its lights, painting the sky bluer. F. Scott Fitzgerald said "The best of America drifts to Paris." Pru was the best of America, the best of everything.

In between the dispatches from the Grange, tidbits to help round out my book just as Mrs. Spencer promised, Pru and I gulped in the city. We frequented every worthy café, watering hole, underground club, and place to be seen and unseen. We clinked glasses at the Ritz, ferreted out underground discos, and paid more than a few visits to the gay nightclubs Pru still joked were merely colorful closets from which I refused to emerge.

On weekends we went to Brittany, or to Banbury. A half-dozen times we went with Gads to Blenheim, where Pru learned to ride horses and quickly became a foe to the indigenous fox population. You told me you lived in hunt country. I'd like to think Blenheim gave your mom a first taste.

My brother graciously employed Pru as a sometimes-courier at his bank. It was not for want of money but for want of not getting deported. In actuality the only things she ever couriered were the various sunglasses and wallets he'd left scattered throughout town.

Why did I not marry her then? Shed the courier façade and make a proper wife out of her? I don't have an answer other than it didn't seem necessary. Something about superfluous paperwork, unneeded red tape, and a declining institution. Getting married in 1970s Paris was a bit like wearing a tuxedo just for the hell of it. Plus look at the duke and duchess. Things were fantastic, until they wed. They remained a cautionary tale lodged in our minds.

Soon it was April. Paris was coming out of its slush and gloom. In the States, the last batch of the six hundred POWs released under Operation Homecoming returned to American soil. Nixon was knee-deep in post-Watergate conspiracies and cover-ups. Mrs. Spencer's chum Picasso died at his home in France.

It was early afternoon. We'd come from the Luxembourg Gardens, where I'd written the last lines of *The Missing Duchess*. Some claptrap about the duchess unknowing of true love. I'd go on to change these words, the book not published until after her death, but at the time I viewed the biography as good as done. It was the shortest distance between us and the sunset.

"Who are you going to write about next?" Pru asked as we bounded our way up the steps of my flat. "You spent twenty years chasing this broad. You'd better get cracking on the next." She tapped her wrist. "Not a moment to waste."

"The only broad I want to chase is you."

I'd playfully nipped at Pru's backside as she opened the door to the flat. It was two o'clock. Two-ten, to be precise. We knew instantly something was wrong.

"Jamie?" Pru called, tiptoeing down the hall.

He was not supposed to be there. He should've been working banker's hours like the banker that he was. But his unmistakable inflection rang throughout the home. He was entertaining a guest, someone he didn't know.

"In the living room!" he called, voice feeble. "Is my brother with you?"

Jamie stepped out into the hallway, his face green as a witch.

"Jamie?" Pru walked toward him. She placed a hand on his elbow. They'd become close. He was now like a brother to her. "You look peaky. Is everything . . . ?"

"Laurel." He took her hand, panic in his eyes. "Fecking hell. I don't know what to do. There's someone here to see you. Mrs. Spencer . . ."

"Mrs. Spencer's here?"

Pru's face brightened.

"Where is the old gal? I hope Tom's taking good care of her. Is he here too?"

Pru tried to step around the corner. Jamie yanked her back.

"Cor blimey. She warned us! She did!"

Pru gently pushed Jamie out of her way, and then walked into the living room where she saw a figure sitting on the couch. A figure that was decidedly not Mrs. Spencer or Tom. Lord, what Pru would've given to see Tom's menacing glower right then, the hammer in his hand.

"Who are you?" Pru said, though she knew the answer already. "Who are you? Why are you here?"

Every organ inside her body plunged to the floor, Pru would later describe. Here was a ghost. An apparition. Death at her doorstep.

Run! Pru's mind told her, though her feet refused to move. *Run! Leave! Get out!*

The person before her should've been a welcome sight, a miracle, a reason to celebrate. But in fact there sat the worst possible news—for Pru, and especially for a bloke once known as Win.

Eighty

"Laurel Innamorati. You are a tough one to track down."

The man stood. It was not so easy as he had but one leg.

"Here you are though," he said. "At last. I swore that no matter what, I'd go to the ends of the earth to find you and Paris is close enough. Paris by way of a shit shack in the English countryside. What the hell is up with that place?"

Pru would later say that at that moment she genuinely thought she was back at Berkeley. Maybe she was with Petal, finally agreeing to partake in her room-mate's penchant for acid. What felt like a year of grief and turmoil was instead one wretched, upside-down, and backward trip. It made more sense than accepting what she saw as true.

"No," Pru said, and tried to shake away the vision. "You're not real. This isn't real."

I tried to reach for her but she swatted me away. Tears filled her eyes.

"You should probably scram," the one-legged man said to Jamie and me. "She's obviously in shock. Leave her be. Give her time to adjust."

"Sorry, mate, I'm not going anywhere," I said.

"Me neither," Jamie agreed with a nod and a tight-lipped look of solidarity.

"Fine. Have it your way. We can make it a party. Laurel?"

The man tried to walk toward her but, thanks to his lack of balance, fell onto the couch with a thud.

"Laurel?" he said again.

The stranger's eyes latched onto Pru's drawn and waxen face. He scowled at and into her, as if this might get her talking. Pru did open her mouth for a second, but then closed it back up again.

"Well, this has been a hell of an adventure," the man said. "Mom told me you were at some estate in England. Then I showed up and it's a friggin' hovel. I rang the goddamned doorbell and some naked geezer started shooting at me. As if I haven't had my fill of that."

Pru made an odd smacking sound, like a puppet without a voice.

"The bitch was paranoid as hell," he went on. "Wouldn't tell me where you were. Luckily she had some family members willing to be a little more honest." He shook his head, then laughed sourly. "I've seen some crazy shit in the past year, but this might take the cake."

Pru whimpered but I was the only one to hear.

"So old chum," I said, working up the mettle, trying to sound at ease. My stomach, though, was roiling like a storm. "You're sitting in my living room but I don't recall you making a proper introduction."

"Win . . ." Jamie said plaintively, a warning.

"I'm *Charlie*," the man replied, giving his name a kick. "Charles Edgar Haley, Junior. Laurel's fiancé."

He didn't need to add the fiancé part. My heart had already smashed into a trillion pieces.

This man, this skinny, tan-necked, buzz-headed, one-legged foreigner was Pru's fiancé. The one who was dead.

"You told me he'd been killed," I said to her, eyes blazing.

Pru looked back, face as startled as if I'd struck her, which is what she said it felt like. I called her a liar, but I didn't care about the lie. One lie or a thousand, if this man disappeared all would've been forgiven.

"He *was* killed," she sputtered. "That's what . . . no. Everyone go away." She grabbed at the sides of her head. "This is not true. None of you are real."

"Oh sweet Laurel." Charlie lunged forward and grabbed her arm. "My poor girl."

He pulled her onto the couch beside him. And, wouldn't you know it, she let herself be pulled. Once she made contact with the cushion, Pru buried her head in both hands.

"This must be surreal for you," Charlie said. "We tried to find you but no one picked up the damn phone at your supposed number. Some friend of Mom's . . . Edith, I think . . . we thought she was messing with us. Giving us bogus information. So I flew over myself, as soon as I could. We were going to send a private investigator but I wanted to be the one to hunt you down. You are one hell of a slippery girl, I'll tell you that."

"Hunting down women," I said, trying to be funny, trying to be mean. "You Yanks are crafty, aren't you?"

"Who are you again?" Charlie said, squinting.

I noticed then his rumpled clothes, the scarred face. The man was a long way from posh Boston, to be sure. He did not look like someone who fit with Pru. Hell, he thought she was Laurel, when she'd come so far from that.

"The name's Win Seton. And I'm going to have to ask you to leave."

"Whoa, that's quite a bold directive when a man's come back from the dead to find his true love."

"True love?" I said. "The girl who waved good-bye as your ship sailed off no longer exists."

"I was never on a ship."

"She's not the same person."

"Like I said, who are you again?"

"I'm Win Seton."

"Yeah, I got that part. I might be missing a limb but my ears work."

"I'm the owner of this apartment," I said. "And she's my girl."

Pru looked up then. Her eyes were red and streaky. I saw in them what I mistook as a promise but was instead a plea.

"They told me he was dead," she said, voice quivering. "I saw him." Pru turned back to Charlie. "Your ashes. Kon Tum. They buried you! There was a funeral!"

"I know. It's hella fucked up. A real botch job. The short version . . ." Charlie shrugged. "Wrong body."

"*Wrong body?*" I said, as disgusted as I'd ever been in my life. "How is that even possible?"

The explanation was horrific enough but, on top of that, he was talking about it like someone muffed his lunch order and he was therefore forced to eat chicken salad instead of tuna.

"Don't get me wrong," Charlie said. "A bunch of men did die in the blast. The rest of us were captured. Uncle Sam tried its damnedest to match body parts with the list of those missing. But . . ."

He shrugged again. I wanted to punch him in the face.

Sixteen bodies were found after the attack, Charlie explained. Twelve were positively identified. The Department of Defense tried to sort out the leftover four and eventually used their best efforts to pin the parts on Charlie and three other men.

"Some guys reported as dead, like me, were POWs," he said. "Some guys thought missing were already dead. A clusterfuck. No better way to explain it."

It sounded so damned unbelievable at the time. But in the following years I'd come to learn this was not a one-time screwup. Bad luck, horrible luck, though not singular luck. Other misidentified bodies have been uncovered from that war, in the new millennium even, thanks to better forensics.

"They mixed up body parts?" Pru said, green-gilled and looking like she might vomit. "How does that even . . ."

"I guess, fundamentally, we were interchangeable."

"And so you've been . . ." she stammered, trying to get a hold of what he was saying.

"In a POW camp," Charlie finished for her. "Goddamned hellhole. Makes that decrepit mansion of yours look like the fucking Ritz. The shit I saw. The shit that happened. I can't even tell you. I will never tell you. But I will say this. On a good day I only ingested twenty maggots, and the pus on my wounds was allowed to ooze unfettered, no new wounds piled on."

Charlie said nothing else, locking up the details in the steel clamp of his mouth. I was unnerved to see hostility in his eyes, which I attributed to my own demented jealousy. He was a romantic rival, infinitely more sympathetic and brave.

"So they let you out?" Pru said. "Just like that?"

Though she'd heard of Operation Homecoming, Pru had not been one of the four million people glued to a television watching the POWs come home. She had been in Paris, in love, with no time to brood over world affairs.

"I wouldn't say they let me out 'just like that.'" Charlie smirked. "If you're curious, I had both legs when I went into camp."

"God," Pru said, and made a small gagging sound.

"No, miss. There was no God where I was. Not a hint of Him to be found."

"I'm . . . I'm glad you survived," Pru managed. She looked unsteady, unsure, a woman in high heels walking across the deck of a careening boat. "Your parents must be thrilled."

Jamie and I exchanged looks. I'd never seen a homecoming that looked so far from home. In this I found hope, however short-lived. Pru was not overjoyed to see him. She didn't even seem especially relieved.

"They're happy of course," Charlie said. "But, baby, it was *you*. Your face kept me going. I was only in the camp nine months, nothing compared to some of the guys, but it was pure hell. I thought of you the whole damned time. Hell, I thought of you before I was captured. The horrors I witnessed, the ones I committed myself."

As Charlie spoke, veins lifted off his temples.

"You were right," he said. "I never should've gone. But visions of you kept me alive. When I finally got out of the hospital and you weren't there . . . fuck. I wished I'd died. This time, for real."

Pru struggled to inhale. She could not catch her breath.

"But that's over," he said. "Because I found you and we're together at last."

Charlie uncurled his fist, which was until that time balled into a knot. He stretched his fingers, reaching his hand toward Pru.

In the middle of his palm sat a ring. A platinum band with a four-carat diamond in the center, two-carat baguettes on either side. The privileged in England inherited titles. In America, it was grandmother's jewels.

"I'd ask you to marry me," Charlie said, and let his eyes flick briefly in my direction. "But you already said yes. Nothing's changed. Unless you have something against cripples."

"Charlie . . ." Pru said in a whisper. "Don't . . ."

"Come back with me. I've never loved you more than I do at this moment. We'll start over. I'll work at a goddamned desk, the biggest bodily threat a paper cut. Isn't that what you've always wanted?"

As Pru remained in a fog, Charlie leaned into her and glided the ring onto her finger. It was far too big. The diamond fell immediately out of sight.

"Come back with me," he said again. "Paris is nice, Laurel. Paris is great, but God Bless America."

Eighty-one

There wasn't a person in that apartment not floored to see Laurel standing in the doorway. Even Annie, who'd called her in the first place.

"I don't know what you're trying to pull," Laurel said, face beating and hair chaotic around her. "But you don't go running off to foreign countries without telling me."

Laurel ranted on for several more minutes, sounding like a top candidate for Strictest Mom on Earth. But Annie understood it was for show. Mostly Laurel lit into her daughter so she didn't have to acknowledge the other people in the room.

"I left you a message," Annie pointed out. "So I did tell you. And what choice did I have? And, P.S., I'm an adult."

"This is not like you, Annabelle. What were you planning to do? Sleep in some strange man's apartment?"

"He's not a strange man."

"Well, we're both a little strange," Jamie tried to joke.

Laurel closed her eyes. Around them the apartment creaked and sighed. Annie felt Gus quaking behind her.

"Well, now I finally get why you're so anti Eric," Annie said. "Charlie? The dead soldier? He was my dad?"

"He was. And I am not anti Eric. I'm pro you."

"These past few weeks," Annie said. "I thought you didn't want us together because we didn't know each other. Then I thought it was because you were afraid I'd lose him. You had me questioning everything—me, him, whether we should even be together. But now I know. It's not that you were afraid he'd never come home. You were afraid that he would and I'd marry him anyway."

It couldn't have been clearer if she'd written it out, or engraved it on a luggage tag. Laurel didn't love Charlie when she married him. She left with him out of guilt. Or nostalgia. Or because she'd loved him once.

Oh, her mother had tried. Laurel tried her hand at a bohemian Parisian lifestyle, but she couldn't make it stick. She was forced to act like an adult from a young age, after losing both parents, and then losing Charlie the first time. Responsible adult was how Laurel behaved, "doing the right thing" her default mode. Laurel's character and her personal history were too ingrained to overcome.

"Annie," Laurel said, eyes avoiding Gus as if he were the sun. "Whatever you think right now, you're wrong. You don't know the whole story."

"So where is he?" Gus asked.

Annie whipped her head in his direction and was surprised to find a different man standing there. She thought of Gus as tall, broad-shouldered, and strong. But he suddenly appeared thin, anemic almost. She wondered if he was ill.

"Where is Charlie?" he asked.

The muscles in Laurel's neck rose as she strained to keep her head from turning.

"Please warn me if a third member of this esteemed family is going to show up," Gus said. "I can't do that again."

"Not bloody likely," Jamie mumbled. "Mate, he's dead."

"He's dead?" Gus said, gaping. "When? How? *He's dead?*"

For real this time was the question hanging in the air. But Gus did not dare ask it.

"January 1980," Laurel said and at long last turned in his direction.

Gus jolted when her eyes landed on him. What must they look like to each other? As though they'd aged thirty years in one day? Or did they seem exactly the same?

"Pru," he said in a whisper.

"Wait a minute," Annie said. "He died when I was a baby? You made it sound like you left him."

"I did," Laurel said. She pulled her gaze away from Gus. "I left him when I was pregnant. I was alone when I had you and then I came here. Perhaps you two gentlemen remember the baby who was with me, though her hair is much better now, in that she actually has some."

"Bloody hell," Jamie muttered.

"So Charlie was gone?" Gus said. "When you came back?"

"He was alive but we were not together."

"Listen, folks," Jamie said. "I have a brilliant scheme. Annie, you come with me."

"No way," she said. "I'm staying."

Annie wanted to see how this was all going to pan out. Not to mention, she had about a million questions to ask.

"Sorry, little lass," Jamie said. "You're coming with me. We'll enjoy a glass of wine or three, let these two long-lost chums reconnect."

"I want to know—" she started.

"And you shall know." Jamie took her hand. "But they need to know first."

While Annie's mouth remained open, he led her down the hallway and through the front door. As it closed behind them, she heard her mom let out a small cry.

"We'll give them an hour," Jamie said. "It's the least we can do. After all, they have a lifetime to catch up on."

Eighty-Two

BOSTON, MASSACHUSETTS
1973

And so Laurel went back to Boston with Charlie.

Charlie thought it was inevitable, this return. But as for Laurel, maybe she would've stayed in Paris had he not brought his grandmother's ring. Or if he'd asked for her hand a second time instead of reminding her that she'd already said yes.

Perhaps Laurel would've stayed if he'd shown up with two legs instead of only one. Or if he still displayed that old Charlie Haley swagger. Laurel saw from the start he had a few chinks in the armor, a handful of wires shorted out. Some part of her didn't want to tinker with the already-damaged man.

"I understand," Win assured her when Laurel announced that she was choosing Charlie. "I understand completely."

She was a runny-nosed mess as they sat on his bed—their bed—Charlie clomping up and down the hall outside the door as they said their good-byes. Laurel tried not to think of Win and instead her old feelings for Charlie. But they were too far down to reach.

"Don't cry," Win said. "It's the right thing to do."

He was strong. Stoic. Realistic. Nothing like the man Laurel loved. As Win would later tell his brother, he was a better actor than he was a writer. A better actor than he was a man.

"Win," she said, crying into his shoulder, hands wrapped around his neck. "Convince me to stay. Convince me to hide out in this room until he leaves."

If she had been looking at his face, Laurel would've noticed his lips trembling uncontrollably.

"I can't do that, luv," he said, for Win truly believed she was making the best decision—for her. For him it felt like the end of the world.

"But he can find someone else," Laurel said. "Women love him. They fawn over him. It's actually quite annoying."

Where was it? Where was the love she used to have for Charlie? Of course, even at its best, it paled compared to how she felt about Win.

"He can find a girl much better than me," Pru went on. "More pedigreed. You said it yourself, I'm an orphan."

"A girl better than you? Impossible."

"But his family hates orphans! They told me that! Tiggie Haley thinks they should be put in work camps instead of milking the dole. I'm not even kidding. That's a direct quote!"

Win peeled Laurel's fingers from his neck. He had to. Otherwise, he'd never let her leave.

"Laurel," he said. "I'm no good for you. Just a grown-up writer-boy with nothing to offer. You have to go. Boston is where you belong. We can't ramble about Paris forever. No one lives like this for long."

This, an echo of her prior thoughts. In other words: they were too good to be true.

"So that's it?" she said. "I leave with Charlie and never see you again? And you're fine with this?"

"I'm nowhere close to fine," Win said. "And we will see each other. When GD finally buys it you'll have to fetch your art and dispose of your share of the Grange. We will meet again. The old gal's practically written it into law. Maybe you were right. Maybe Lady Marlborough does believe in love."

It was comforting to think that they had this promise for the future, thanks to Mrs. Spencer.

"Who are we kidding?" Pru said. "Mrs. Spencer's going to outlive every person on this damned planet."

Win managed a laugh, even as some part of him thought it might be true. Gladys Deacon Spencer-Churchill, aged ninety-two yet ageless all the same. They should've made out their wills to her, instead of the other way around.

"You can always come back," Win said. "You know that, right? If things don't work out. Or even if they do. I will wait here, in this spot, forever."

"Forever is a very long time," Laurel said in a whisper.

She thought of the duchess, and of the duchess's mother. Florence Deacon chalked up Coco Abeille to standard Parisian flirtation. Laurel would try to convince herself that Win was the same.

"LAUREL!" Charlie shouted.

He clobbered the door with his hands. Laurel jumped. This would become a reflex for her. In the years that followed, she would very seldom feel at rest.

"The car is downstairs," Charlie said. "If we're going, we need to go now."

She inhaled, her breath rocky on the way down.

"I love you, Laurel," Win said. "I always will."

"*Laurel?* Since when do you call me 'Laurel'?"

"Since this very second. Pru? Well, she's not here right now. She and Win, they're at the Café de Flore, walking through the iron and glass door. Tonight they'll go to Le Sept. Or that new cabaret show with the Brazilian transvestites."

Pru—Laurel—gave a runny smile.

"Sounds perfect," she said.

"You see, dear Laurel, Win and Pru are in Paris. And in Paris they'll remain."

Eighty-three

The Charlie that Laurel married was not the person she met, or the boy whose proposal she accepted.

From the start the man was angry, violent, often drunk. The slightest door slam sent him reaching for a baseball bat or a gun. He cried out at night so frequently Laurel started sleeping in another room. She felt bad. It wasn't his fault. But she was afraid to lie beside him.

Charlie was quick to paranoia, quicker to fury. They had so many holes punched in the walls of their Back Bay town home, Laurel took a sledgehammer to them all and called in a contractor for a remodel.

What a successful and enterprising young couple! Renovating their Boston home to keep up with the latest trends! It's what their family and friends thought when they surveyed the mess.

Charlie had a position with the family business, his job duties and title a mystery. If Laurel had to guess it would've been something along the lines of vice president of boozy lunches and hours that happy forgot.

"Is he doing anything?" Laurel once asked her mother-in-law. "At the office?"

She tried to sound nonaccusatory but she couldn't imagine anyone trusting him to do actual work.

"Give him some time to adjust," Tiggie Haley said. "He's been through a lot."

Was still going through a lot, as far as Laurel could tell. It would not be a recognized affliction until the eighties, but post-traumatic stress disorder was a real thing for them.

During this time, Laurel wanted to go back to college, finish her degree. They were in Boston, with no shortage of universities from which to choose, but Charlie wouldn't hear of it. A proper wife stayed at home. His parents agreed. Each day the family, like a vise, closed more tightly around her.

"Charlie and I have something in common," she wrote in her journal one evening after he'd passed out beside her on the couch. "We've both been POWs."

As soon as the words were on the paper, Laurel felt ashamed. Likening a fancy home and ample food to what her husband endured? She was a horrible, small-minded person. Laurel ripped up the page. She never wrote again.

They tried to have children. Charlie himself was the oldest of five and so there were expectations, particularly to produce at least one son. Their love-making was a hurried, angry, sloppy affair, after which Laurel would pray that the sperm made union with a plump and healthy egg. Not that she particularly wanted kids, but maybe her husband would be kinder with a baby or two in the home. It seemed to be the only thing he desired, other than more booze.

Between 1973 and 1978, Laurel got pregnant five times. Babies lost at seven weeks, then ten, twelve, eighteen, and a gorgeous, dark-haired son stillborn at twenty-nine. Charlie blamed Laurel.

"Cut him some slack," one of his sisters said when Laurel confessed she was thinking of leaving because their life felt toxic. The vanishing babies seemed proof of that. "He's been through so much. Be grateful for what you have."

Be grateful. This was solid enough advice. What was she thinking? Laurel could never leave Charlie Haley. It simply wasn't an option.

When Charlie had been out of the war longer than he'd been in it, Laurel suggested medication and psychiatry. The summer she tried to more actively help, their home underwent another full-scale renovation.

As time pressed on, Laurel began believing that perhaps she *was* a tough shrew of a wife, just as Charlie said. How did you ask a person to "get over" the shooting of men or nine months of daily beatings and starvation? She hated herself for not being able to tolerate his moods.

Still. A hundred times Laurel thought of leaving, but where would she go? And who with? She had precisely no one in her life who wasn't Charlie's first. Her only true family was on some other continent, wrapped up with a girl named Pru.

She considered calling Win, or the duchess, or even Jamie. But there was no way to do it without leaving evidence. Charlie already accused her of slutting around and he inspected every canceled check and phone bill with exacting diligence. There was no way to reach out behind his back.

Then, one morning, Laurel received a telegram.

At the time, she was desperately sick with her sixth pregnancy, the vomiting so violent she hoped the inevitable miscarriage would happen sooner rather than later. If she'd never get a baby out of it, then what was the point of the suffering?

"A telegram?" she said when the man handed her a piece of paper. "For me? Are you sure?"

"If that's your name at the top, then yes."

Was she Laurel Haley? They'd been married five years and she still didn't know.

"Uh, thanks," she said.

With rickety hands, Laurel opened the envelope.

WESTERN UNION
TELEGRAM

2/22/1979
MRS LAUREL INNAMORATI HALEY
410 BEACON ST
BOSTON MA 02115

DEAR LAUREL
THIS IS A PRIVATE TELEGRAM FROM GADS TO NOTIFY
YOU OF THE RECENT DEATH OF MRS SPENCER THE
DUCHESS. A SUM OF 86200 USD HAS BEEN DEPOSITED

IN YOUR NAME AT BANC OF BOSTON ON BOYLSTON ST.
PAPERWORK FOR ART, PROPERTY IN SAFETY DEP BOX
OF SAME INSTITUTION. COLLECT ART AT YOUR
LEISURE. WISH YOU LUCK. YOU ARE MISSED. WARMEST
REGARDS GEORGE WILLIAM COLIN SPENCER–CHURCHILL
FONDLY KNOWN AS GADS.

Heart pounding, Laurel folded up the telegram and stuffed it down the front of her dress. She cringed, her breasts sore from the difficult pregnancy.

"Rest in peace, Mrs. Spencer," she said with a smile, for she was not sad because the woman was probably right then in the most glittering salon in all of heaven, holding court over the lauded and the famed.

"I've thought about you every day," Laurel mused.

She hurried toward her room, a hop in her step. On her way, Laurel flipped on the record player. The Steve Miller Band played. Her smile only grew. Mrs. Spencer had answered her prayers. She'd interfered in her Gladys Deacon sort of way.

"'They got the money, hey,'" Laurel sang, reaching into the back of her closet for a suitcase. "'You know they got away. They headed down south and they're still running today.'"

Singin' go on take the money and run.

Go on take the money and run.

And that's exactly what Laurel did.

Eighty-four

Thanks to Mrs. Spencer's generosity, Laurel was able to prepay a year's worth of rent in a building with a doorman and a guard. A week later, she enrolled at Wellesley.

Though she'd been a literature major, Laurel transferred all the credits she could and switched her concentration to finance. When she thought of novels and biographies and the great literature of the world, she thought of the duchess, and she thought of Win. She'd never graduate if she let herself get mired in the story of Pru. The season for burying herself in books had passed.

After she moved, Laurel tried calling Win. Twice. Both times a woman answered, identifying herself as Mrs. Seton. So much for "waiting forever," she thought. Not that she truly expected he would.

Pregnant and fattening by the day, Laurel worked to finish her degree and also to formalize her break from Charlie. He refused to grant the divorce and took to harassing her, materializing on campus and appearing outside buildings late at night. Laurel lopped off her hair and dyed it brown, hoping the disguise might suffice, praying he'd eventually give up.

Former golden boy Charlie Haley soon became quite the adversary of campus security, who escorted him off the grounds on an almost daily basis. Charlie was by then a full-blown drunk, which meant he was mostly relegated to a wheelchair. The students who didn't know Laurel would forever remember him as the homeless wino that terrorized the Wellesley girls.

Laurel never told Charlie that she was pregnant, even before she left, but suspected he knew. As her due date approached, he circled closer, tighter, like a shark around its prey. Laurel dressed in baggy, flowing clothes but at some point the wind would've blown and revealed the budding Annie hidden inside.

On August 31, 1979, on the fifth floor of Massachusetts General Hospital, Laurel Innamorati Haley gave birth to a bald-headed, blue-eyed, seven-pound baby girl named Annabelle. She was so delicious this girl, slept six hours a night straight out of the gates. She hardly ever cried.

The only witnesses to the birth were one doctor, two nurses, and an Eastern European woman named Blanka who sometimes cleaned Laurel's apartment when she was too spent or sick to do it herself. On the birth certificate, Laurel wrote "unknown" in the place a father's name would go.

Shortly after Annie's arrival, Blanka, the maid who knew nothing about Charlie, told Laurel stories of a handicapped grifter who hung around the build-ing's lobby. One morning she watched him argue with the security guard, a well-heeled older couple standing behind him.

"That's odd," Laurel said, trying to hide her panic.

Charlie knew where she was and had the support and backing of his parents. The mere thought petrified Laurel. Bad dye jobs and ill-fitting clothes would serve no bulwark against the levels of wealth and fury Charlie's family had.

Could his family assert any sort of claim on Laurel? Her apartment? The chubby, happy, rosy-cheeked babe of perfection? Laurel was technically still Charlie's wife and Annie his child. Because of this, Laurel existed in a constant state of medium-grade fear, which was the very worst fear of all. You never knew when it might explode into full-blown terror.

One unusually warm winter morning, after a call to the admissions depart-ment at Georgetown Law, Laurel walked to the bank, baby Annie nestled in a wrap against her chest. She may not have been at Berkeley anymore, but she knew where to find all the good hippies, and therefore the best baby carriers.

Once at the bank, Laurel withdrew the sum of five hundred dollars and then chatted with the teller while another employee summoned the manager. He needed to speak with her, they said. Laurel braced herself as Annie wiggled against her chest.

"Is something wrong, Mr. Green?" she asked, heart thumping.

"I have a telegram for you, ma'am. Just came in this morning."

"Oh, thank you," Laurel said and took the paper.

She breathed in and started to read.

WESTERN UNION
TELEGRAM

1/7/1980
MRS LAUREL HALEY
C/O BANC OF BOSTON
10 BOYLSTON ST
BOSTON MA 02115

TO MRS HALEY
PLEASE COME RETRIEVE YOUR PAINTINGS FROM MY HOME
AT QUAI DE BETHUNE PARIS. I AM WITH CHILD AND
NEED SPACE. MUCH APPRECIATED YOURS TRULY MRS
JAMES SETON.

Mrs. Seton. Mrs. *James* Seton. Is this who Laurel had heard on the line? The wife of Jamie, not of Win?

Maybe, she thought. Just maybe . . .

Giddy with a prospect she didn't understand, Laurel took out two thousand more dollars and rushed home to pack. They were on winter break and classes would not resume for another few weeks.

The next morning she taxied to Logan Airport and bought a one-way ticket to Paris. As dusk draped across Boston, that so-called City of Notions, Laurel boarded a plane with only a backpack, a baby, and a head full of hope.

Eighty-five

"So you did go backpacking in college," Annie said when her mother stopped to catch her breath. "In a sense."

She noticed then how narrow the space between Laurel and Gus as they sat on the couch. What had they talked about in the ninety minutes Jamie and Annie were sipping wine downstairs? What had they decided?

"Except you told me that you went to Banbury," Annie said. "Not Paris."

"Oh, we went to Banbury. As soon as I realized that's where Win was."

Laurel stood and began pacing, hands planted firmly in the back pockets of her jeans. From across the room, Gus watched, eyes shining. At once Annie thought of a quote from Edith Wharton: "Each time you happen to me all over again."

Was that what Laurel was doing? Happening all over again? It'd been so long. Her mother was—Annie had to say it—middle-aged, clinging to the last vestiges of her forties. Then again, there was a lot of time left in the game.

Maybe . . . Annie thought just as her mother had so long ago. *Just maybe* . . .

"So then what?" Annie asked. "You took me to Banbury. You were single. Gus was if not single, at least unmarried. But nothing happened, given you ended up back where you started. In Boston. Finishing up at Wellesley."

"He refused to see me," Laurel said. "Had some intermediary tell me to 'bugger off.'"

"That was my sister-in-law," Gus said. "Though I put her up to it."

"Why would you put her up to it?" Annie asked.

"Fear. Nothing more. The reports of Pru's return were widespread. Everyone in the village remembered the young girl who lived at the Grange so they were all atwitter when she came back to inspect her land, toting a scrummy baby and sporting a diamond ring on her finger."

A diamond, as it turned out, that wasn't nearly as large as the first. It was a diamond Laurel purchased for herself, so no one would hassle her. Unwed mothers were still a stigma, pretty girls forever hit on, particularly when traveling alone.

"After I heard this," Gus said. "And saw for myself, from afar, I found I was spent. I couldn't go through it again."

"You refused to see her," Annie said to Gus. Then to her mother: "And you went back to Boston. For a second time."

Laurel nodded, her lips pressed tightly together. She tried to blink away the tears forming on her lashes.

"So when did Charlie die?" Annie asked. "How?"

"Can't we just . . ." her mom said. "Can't we just say he died? That there was an accident and leave it at that?"

"Tell her," Gus said, his voice like gravel. "Now. She deserves to know the truth."

"I know. God, I know." Laurel pushed her hands against her eyes and let out a small, strangled breath. "It's so damned hard."

She looked at the ceiling, for a minute, and then to Annie.

"If I'd stayed in Banbury," Laurel said. "If I'd stayed in Paris. If I hadn't stayed with Charlie. If I never went back to Boston. If I'd never met Edith Gray at all. What would've prevented that?" She pointed toward the door. "What would've ensured this?"

She pointed to Annie, and then to Gus.

"That's a lot of ifs," Annie said. "And they explain nothing. What happened?"

Laurel paused and opened her mouth. With this gesture she also opened every last part of her that had previously been closed. To Annie, to others, and even to herself.

Finally, Laurel began to speak. This time she wouldn't hold anything back.

Eighty-six

Laurel and baby Annie returned to Boston. Win refused to see her so Laurel gave up on him for good.

They took a cab from Logan, but two blocks from Laurel's building the roads were closed, as if a movie were being filmed, or a politician were caravanning through town. The street and sidewalks were littered with people, hundreds of people. Police. Reporters. News vans. Spectators socked together in packs.

Laurel didn't think much of it, at first. She lived in Boston, along with the well-known and well-to-do but not always well behaved. Scandals happened with some frequency, as did less posh crimes—shootings, larcenies. It was a city. Mostly Laurel was irritated that she'd have to walk the extra distance in the sleet with a newborn baby cocooned beneath her coat.

"Not sure I can get much closer, ma'am," the driver said. "Is that your building? Number fifty-five?"

"Yes," Laurel replied, peering through the glass and thinking the melee seemed greater than was typical for a dishonored politician or bad-acting ballplayer. "Do you know what's going on?"

"It's the Kellogg boy."

"The Kellogg boy?"

Laurel's heart thundered. His last name was Haley but Charlie was foremost a Kellogg boy.

There were lots of them though, she told herself. It was a big family, expanding by the day. Hell, Charlie had four siblings, two of them male, as well as buckets of cousins. There were plenty of Kellogg boys to go around.

"Yeah," the driver said. "You know. The one who . . . you been under a rock or something?"

"Out of the country," she whispered, her mouth dry.

Annie's eyes flickered open. She started to squirm.

"Right." He tapped his forehead. "The airport. International arrivals. Well, anyway, you know the Kellogg family?"

She nodded, her mind whirling.

"It was the tall kid. Good-looking, but lost a leg in Nam? You know who I'm talking about?"

This time Laurel couldn't even muster a nod. It was all she could do to keep breathing.

"Apparently his wife left him," the driver said. "She lived in your building. Had a baby, same as you. Well, he got some maid to let him into the apartment."

"He was in the apartment?"

"Yup. Shot the maid—"

"Blanka!" she cried.

The driver looked at her, confused. Blanka's name was probably nowhere in the story. She was merely the help.

"The boy shot the maid," the man went on, "then hung himself in the bathroom."

"Oh my God . . ."

Annie was full-on writhing now, struggling to break free of her mother's hold. Laurel squeezed her tighter into her chest.

"Oh my God," Laurel said again. "Is the maid okay? Is he?"

"Hell no. Gruesome scene between the shooting and the hanging." The driver shook his head. "Someone found him two days later. Crazy thing is, they don't know where the wife and baby are. I hope like hell that they're alive. Count yourself lucky, ma'am, that you've been out of town. Some people. You just never know, do ya? You never flippin' know."

Eighty-seven

ÎLE SAINT-LOUIS
PARIS
NOVEMBER 2001

Despite expectations to the contrary, Gladys Deacon Spencer-Churchill, Her Grace the Duchess of Marlborough, never made it to the century mark. She passed at ninety-seven in St. Andrew's Hospital, one step-grandson, one Pole, and one writer by her side.

Her lovers were many, her exploits vast, the storied lives that ran against hers already fill a thousand other books. And while it might seem sad, that all her passion resulted in but one very dry and bleak union, on her deathbed Gladys Deacon viewed it otherwise.

All she ever wanted was to be remembered. And she understood that memories happened in the mind but also in the heart. In the end, the love Lady Marlborough sought she gave instead. And that was enough for her.

—J. Casper Augustine Seton, final paragraph from
The Missing Duchess: A Biography

"He killed himself," Annie said. "While you were gone."

"Yes."

Laurel did not try to stop the tears now running down her face

"Why didn't you tell me?" Annie asked. "It's a horrible story, but why?"

"It was the violence. The manner in which he died, taking poor Blanka with him. I didn't want that to be your legacy. I was terrified of letting that shadow fall across our little family."

"Wow," was all Annie could say.

She wanted to tell her mom it would've been fine to confess the truth, that it wouldn't have affected what was indeed a pretty life. But Annie understood about the shadow. Already she felt it cool against her skin.

"I never stepped into that apartment again," Laurel said. "And so, as I had so many times before, I set off to a new home, with only the clothes in my pack." She smiled. "Of course, this time I had you. That's how I knew I'd be okay."

"That and Gladys Deacon."

"Absolutely," she said. "Thank God for Mrs. Spencer. It was a lot easier to move on by then because of her gifts. And I don't only mean the monetary ones. I ended up giving more than half of the inheritance to Blanka's family, not that it could bring her back. But I had to do something."

"So you finished school," Annie said, still dazed and picturing a one-legged man swinging from a shower rod, a poor maid with the unluckiest job in the world. "Despite everything that happened."

"I did, somehow. Afterward I went to Georgetown Law and later took a job in D.C. We lived in a bitty, wonderful apartment in Arlington for a few years before I bought Goose Creek Hill. And that's been our life ever since. You and me, kid. I'd like to think we've done okay."

"More than okay," Annie said and gave her mom a hug. After pulling back she asked, "But what about Charlie's family? Did you ever keep in touch with them?"

"God no. They blamed me absolutely. Not that I didn't blame myself, too. But they preferred to imagine I'd died along with their son and I was happy to let them."

"How come you never went back?" Annie asked and looked toward Gus. "To England or to Paris? You must've thought about him given you owned the Grange together."

"It didn't take the Grange to make me think of him."

"And I didn't own it for long," Gus said, his voice froggy. "I ended up trans-ferring my share to my niece, Jamie's daughter. She's about your age, finishing up at university. When she's not wrangling over property rights with phantoms from the past, that is."

"That's who you've been battling with?" Annie asked. "Gus's niece?"

"When Gus himself wasn't trying to get historical permits to slow the process down," Jamie added with a smirk.

"And thank you for that extra aggravation," Laurel said. "I knew the other party to the transaction was Clementine Seton, but I didn't know if it was his daughter or wife or what. Gus did get involved, eventually. He heard I was being difficult."

"It was like a siren's song," Gus joked.

No one said anything for several minutes. Annie closed her eyes, trying to put it all together.

Laurel had finally explained where she came from. She gave Annie what she'd wanted for so many years. And while Annie was grateful for the truth, what Laurel said those weeks ago was true. The past didn't make her. Charlie Haley was not who Annie was.

"Now you know everything," Laurel said, her shoulders relaxing for the first time that day, or even that decade. "Every last piece."

"Actually," Annie said. "That's not true. I know the past, all the background stuff, but as far as I can tell we're in the middle of the story. You have to tell me, Mom. Pru. What happens next?"

Eighty-eight

Subject: **Chapter One**
From: anniehaley79@aol.com
Date: December 6, 2001 09:15
To: eric.sawyer@usmc.mil

While you were arriving in Afghanistan, I was going home. Alone.

I couldn't get a direct flight, which meant I flew into Reagan instead of Dulles. We passed over the Pentagon and its gaping hole. A small reminder of the larger damage, a reminder of why you're not here.

You take care of business over there and then hurry back home. We have so much to talk about. "You will tell me everything. In the aftermath we will come home bringing to your comfortable armchairs that slight weariness exquisite at twilight and it will be a year before dinner is served." Those are the word of Gladys Deacon, Duchess of Marlborough, as said to Bernard Berenson, the man she loved.

I've been to England and to Paris. I've seen Boston, if only in my mind. I met a writer and a duchess. I saw my mother in love and found out about my dad. Yep. That old topic. It's nothing I can go into over e-mail. But wait until you hear the rest.

I've seen these places and feel like I've traveled a million miles. Now, after looking back, I'm trying my hand at moving forward. Yesterday I mailed an application to Harvard University. It's not what you think.

I applied for a six-month research fellowship, with the Berenson library, the very same Berenson I "met" on my trip. I didn't have the easiest time describing my qualifications and, oddly, "fake researcher" doesn't look all that impressive on paper. But years ago my mom applied for a job with nothing to back her up. Turned out for the best, in the (very long) end.

And what of the formidable Laurel Haley? Well, she stayed with Gus. That's right, the man from the pub you were so worried about. See how I could never fit these things in an e-mail? For now, let's leave it at this. My mom and Gus went to Paris once. And in Paris they remain.

You're doing your job—safely, I hope—but I wish you were here. At age twenty-two I'm an unexpected empty nester and this old farm is too quiet by myself. Don't worry. I do have some company, in the form of some very sick little girls who want to find some freedom on a horse.

Six months, seven months, whatever it takes. I might not be in Virginia, but that doesn't mean I won't be here for your return. When you arrive, we'll celebrate. Then we'll sit in our armchairs, in the weary twilight. You'll talk about the fight. As for me, I'll have a magnificent story to tell.

AUTHOR'S NOTE

I came across Gladys Deacon when researching my first book, *A Paris Apartment*, a novel based on the real-life discovery of an abandoned apartment in Paris. Inside this home, among hundreds of other magnificent relics, was a previously unknown Giovanni Boldini portrait, which eventually sold for more than €2 million at auction.

While digging into Boldini's life, I studied every luminary he brought to canvas. Amid renderings of such notables as Sarah Bernhardt, Consuelo Vanderbilt, Edgar Degas, and Henri de Toulouse-Lautrec, one woman outshone them all, her background every bit as colorful as the painting itself. This woman was Gladys Deacon, the Duchess of Marlborough.

Born to a wealthy Newport family, the dazzling Miss Deacon considered herself continental through and through. Though privileged, no one would accuse her of being sheltered. By age twelve, Gladys Deacon found herself in the middle of a worldwide murder scandal. At fourteen, she declared her love for the Duke of Marlborough, her future husband. She was living independently in Paris at twenty, finally married at forty, and turned up in a dilapidated Oxfordshire manse at almost a century old.

Here was a woman who carried a handgun, went temporarily blind due to excessive reading, and declared herself "a miracle": "Differential calculus was too low for me!" Her political savvy was no less impressive. "Of course I'm well-informed! I've slept with eleven Prime Ministers and most Kings!" She used this extensively gathered information to heckle her chief nemesis, Winston Churchill: "[Hitler] had the whole world up in arms. He was larger than Winston. Winston could've have done that!" All that, and they say she could've prevented World War I.

Because of these and many other details, when it came time to write, I immediately honed in on Gladys Deacon as the story's heart. Hugo Vickers's captivating biography *Gladys: Duchess of Marlborough* helped ignite the spark. The book contains a seemingly endless collection of duchess quirks and quotes and also inspired the character of Win Seton, but he is in no way meant to represent Vickers.

While my book is a work of fiction, I've used many of Gladys Deacon's actual mannerisms and adventures. She did tour the world with Coon. Proust did try to detain her in Rome by having her arrested. The kidnapped POWs, passion for firearms, and proliferate spaniels are all historically accurate as well.

Many of Gladys's direct statements are also included. She did indeed think "education smooths a life" and most of the barbs directed at Churchill are taken verbatim. Several of her letters are quoted throughout this novel, as are comments and opinions made by others. In the words of Virginia Woolf: "One does fall in love with the Duchess of Marlborough. I did at once." I know exactly what she means.

I tried to stick closely to another character in the book—Gladys Deacon's final home. As depicted, the Grange was in fact a run-down monstrosity and Gladys every bit as welcoming as her fictional likeness. The real woman treated visitors to reams of chicken wire, hails of bullets, and at least one "fuck you" sprayed in the lawn with weed killer. The contents of Tom's barn and Tom himself are also taken from fact.

Alas, this is a work of fiction so I did fudge dates and other elements for the sake of the plot. In Banbury, Gladys called herself "Mrs. Stuart," not "Mrs. Spencer." And while she had a difficult relationship with her stepsons, the true Marlborough family is no doubt far more delightful than what is portrayed in these pages. All other inaccuracies and fabrications are mine alone.

If you're intrigued by the woman who inspired this novel, I encourage you to read Vickers's biography. For a look at Gladys Deacon through the eyes of a probable "frenemy," check out *The Face on the Sphinx* by Daphne Fielding. All that plus a little Googling will show exactly why Gladys Deacon was once considered the most beautiful—and tempestuous—woman to ever exist. There's even a selfie or two to prove it.

One of my characters says "I always had the sense she was more legend than woman." While that could well be true, I personally found the craziest stories the most believable. Of course, the duchess would try to persuade us otherwise. When Hugo Vickers tracked "Mrs. Stuart" down in 1975 to inquire about her life: "she looked at me with a twinkle in her eye and said slowly: 'Gladys Deacon? . . . She never existed.'"

It is exactly the comment one would expect from a woman who insisted: "I was not born. I happened."

ACKNOWLEDGMENTS

The best part about finishing a book is getting to write the acknowledgments. I'm so grateful to all of the people who've helped along the way.

I have to begin with a gigantic thank-you to my fantastic and shrewd editor, Laurie Chittenden, for taking my extremely vague idea ("this duchess is crazy!") and helping me shape it into a bona fide story.

Always a tremendous thank-you to my agent, Barbara Poelle, for being smart, tenacious, hilarious, and a good friend. Thank you for always fighting for me, sticking with me, and telling me when I'm doing it wrong. And, speaking of agents, a shout out to Heather Baror-Shapiro for her hard work on foreign rights.

Thanks to the hardworking, savvy team at St. Martin's Press, including Melanie Fried, Laura Clark, Whitney Jacoby, and the amazing Katie Bassel, the best publicist in the business. The entire St. Martin's team has been so incredibly kind and gracious and cool, not to mention they grace me with the world's most fantastic covers. The pressure's really on now!

Thank you to Leslie Rossman, Emily Miles Terry, Sara Beigle, and the rest of the team at Open Book Publicity for doing so much to market my work.

A special thanks goes to my cousin Drew Thompson and his wife Amy for providing a little "artwork" for this book. Thank you also to Scott and Lisa Hourin for their insight into what the Marines were doing post-9/11. Scott, I hope I've used your intel believably and I apologize for any civilian mistakes!

To my funny, kind, and scary talented fellow San Diego writers: Sue Meissner, Tammy Greenwood, Margaret Dilloway, Jennifer Coburn, Jan Moran, Juliette Sobanet, and especially the wonderful Liz Fenton, for being such great friends and always having my back. You guys are all so inspiring, not to mention fun to hang out with. And thank you also to my wonderful local bookstore, Warwick's in La Jolla, Julie Slavinsky in particular, for the tremendous encouragement and support.

A thousand thanks to two great organizations, the Women's Fiction Writer's Association (WFWA) and Barbara Bos's Women Writers, Women's Books for not only supporting me but other writers worldwide.

And to two old (but not *old*) friends, fellow Tri Delts Elaine Turville Kropp and Anna Dinwiddie Hatfield for your support and getting people to attend my signings. Always huge thanks to Karen Freeman Landers, the best friend and greatest co-Chargers-season-ticket-holder a gal could ask for. Thank you also to Wendy Merry who not only sends people to my appearances but also Hollywood producers to my door.

Thank you to the people at Ellie Mae, especially Ed Luce and his wife Ann, for supporting this second career.

None of this would be any fun without my family alongside, including my hilarious, witty, and brilliant sister, Lisa Gable Wheatley, and my smart, fun, Chargers-loving brother, Brian Gable. Thank you to my dad, Tom Gable, for always inspiring me and cheering me on, and of course my mother, Laura Gable, to whom this book is dedicated. How do you thank one person for . . . everything? Thanks also go to Bill and Suzy Gable for hawking my books to patients and friends alike.

To my husband, Dennis Bilski, who keeps everything running. I always joke that if you made the slightest change to your schedule or availability, the entire system would shut down. Thanks for all you do for me, for our girls, and for making me the luckiest girl in the world.

To my spunky, smart, sporty daughters, Paige and Georgia. Thanks for being the easiest kids to raise. Sweet, independent, and responsible. That's why I get so much done.

I learned many things when my first book came out, my favorite was seeing firsthand just how awesome other people are. Thank you not only to my friends but also readers nationwide who showed up at my signings. I'll never be able to express what it means to meet you all in person. I'm also extraordinarily grateful for every reader's note sent my way. I've saved each one. I hope you all love the second book as much as the first.

And, finally, I want to close these thanks in memory of my beloved grandmother, Carol Gable, a woman so interesting that even in her final days she still had new stories to tell.

Michelle Gable
Cardiff-by-the-Sea, California